TOWA

"Hold on!"

The engine revved up, the sound drowning even Max's voice. The plane shuddered from the vibration, and then they were off down the runway, lifting from the ground like a graceful bird in flight.

Occupied with his controls and the instrument gages, Max was oblivious of her interested gaze. He was in his element, she thought, a man who wouldn't let obstacles deter him from his dream. She glanced away to the landscape below that lay in shadow patterns of charcoal and gray, struggling with sudden doubts that flooded her mind all at once. Had she been foolhardy to fly to Alaska with Max when she was so intensely attracted to him?

At that moment, the sunlight suddenly streamed through the window as the new sun peeked over the horizon. The morning sun, Katie thought, somehow it told her that she was where she was supposed to be—in the cockpit beside Max, watching the spectacle of a new beginning, the birth of a day. She glanced at Max and wondered if her future might include him.

Other books by Donna Anders:

NORTH TO DESTINY

SUN
OF THE
MORNING

DONNA ANDERS

LEISURE BOOKS ▟ NEW YORK CITY

For My Daughter, Lisa Pearce,
who was there at its birth.
And
For My Friend Ann Rule,
who loved it too.

A LEISURE BOOK ®

April 1991

Published by

Dorchester Publishing Co., Inc.
276 Fifth Avenue
New York, NY 10001

PART ONE

June 1938–February 1942

CHAPTER 1

WITH THE FIRST BLUSH OF DAWN, KATIE AALAND FINALLY felt at peace, her mind set free of her fears. Her limbs were numb from her long vigil throughout the night, but like the samurai women of old, she had tried to handle her grief with honor, going deep into herself, seeking the meaning of her loss. Now, as the garden came alive with the twittering birds in the willow branches, Katie stirred, the rush of the little waterfall suddenly loud in her ears. She stood, carefully, allowing the sensation of life to prickle back into her body. The morning sun was about to rise over Tokyo, awakening its mass of people. And she must face the day ... and the changes it would bring. Freda and Peter, her parents, were gone forever, victims of the deadly flu.

She pulled her kimono closer; the touch of dew

clung to her skin as she followed the rock path between the flowering azalea bushes and over the narrow arched bridge to the bathhouse at the bottom of the garden. Katie, an American like her parents, had conformed to the Japanese way of bathing right from her first week in Japan over fifteen years ago. She'd been three then, and she had no memory of America, or ways and traditions other than those of her life in Tokyo as the daughter of the English School principal and his adoring wife, a woman beloved by everyone for her eternal optimism. Although the Aalands had been Christian missionaries, her own beliefs were a mixture of her parents' training, the Buddhist influence, and even some Shinto. She, like the Japanese people, saw no conflict in the casual combining of all three religions.

The sun stood above the horizon when Katie left the bathhouse, sprigs of her long blonde hair curling around her face from the dampness. She felt renewed, stronger somehow, but her earlier peace was slipping away with each step closer to the house.

"God grant me understanding," she chanted, trying to hang on to her serenity. "Why did they get sick when the epidemic was almost over? And I didn't? Why did You let them die?" Her gaze fell on a scarlet rose in perfect bloom, droplets of dew sparkling on its velvet petals; by tomorrow it too would be dying.

As the tears came unbidden, she remembered her friend Michiko Kono's gentle words of only yesterday, words interspersed with deep bows of respect and sympathy. "Katie-san, my dearest friend, so sorry, please excuse me—but remember that the beauty of all living things today is even more beautiful when they are gone tomorrow. Having known that beauty is your treasure forever."

Pausing to regain her composure, Katie wished for some of Michiko's strength. She believed that the

Japanese people must be the strongest in the world when faced with death. Their belief in *karma* had not been obliterated by Western influence, and for all that the unbelievers—Christians—might scoff, it made coping with dying more bearable.

If only I could put my sorrow in a compartment, she thought. *If only I were not so—so impulsive, so quick to feel emotion, and act upon it.* She quelled her thoughts, knowing she was feeding her grief and destroying the peace that had taken her all night to summon up.

The house was still and she couldn't help thinking how quickly the life went out of a place. She glanced around her mother's sitting room, appreciating the austere beauty that was so Japanese, the simple furniture, and the *tatami* matting that was kind to bare feet. Freda's piano stood in the corner, as though waiting for the fingers that caressed its keys so lovingly, its tone in perfect pitch with Freda's soprano voice. For a moment Katie smiled, remembering the smoke wafting from her father's pipe as he put down his book to listen, and her mother singing their favorite songs, her eyes filled with a promise meant only for him. Sometimes Katie had looked away, respectful of the powerful love between them.

It was right that one should not live without the other, she reflected. But her next thought brought back the agony of her loss and she stumbled into the nearest chair. She had cabled her older brother, Edward, in San Francisco about both deaths and had not heard back from him as yet. What would she do now? she wondered, knowing she must stay in Japan even though she was alone. It was where she belonged, all she knew. She couldn't bear the thought of leaving Michiko and Tak, Michiko's older brother. She was almost nineteen and she would work, she decided. In her father's school.

For the first time since her father died eight days

ago, and her mother five days later, she felt a glimmer of direction. She must make plans now, and that meant seeing Mr. Kono. As board director of the English School, he'd once hired her father, and she knew he looked upon her fondly, she being his daughter Michiko's closest friend since childhood. Their house was only a mile away; she would go at once and ask him for a permanent job.

Pedaling her bicycle through the streets a short time later, Katie was oblivious to the "oohs" and "ahhas" of peddlers and businessmen on their way to work. She was used to the attention, knowing it was because she looked so different—a tall, slender, green-eyed blonde among small, dark people. As a child she remembered being touched and stroked and called a fairy child, all preceded with bows and a flow of Japanese. Freda had always smiled and nodded approval. Everyone had loved Freda, while Peter's Sunday sermons and tireless work for the school had held his flock in awe. He'd charmed rich and poor alike, and Katie had recognized her father's charisma at an early age. She loved them both; she'd never thought of life without them. But now they were really gone, and she must find work to support herself. Although her parents had left her a legacy of self-confidence and independence, there was little money in their estate. Katie couldn't afford to indulge her grief, even though her loss was beyond measure.

The sun was warmer and Katie pedaled faster. She must not miss Kenkichii Kono, Michiko's father. Now that she'd made up her mind about her future, she wanted it settled at once. She smiled wryly, knowing impulsiveness was one of her bad traits. According to the ancient teaching, one could only obtain inner peace by practicing patience and understanding.

She braked sharply to avoid a traffic jam of automobiles, bicycles and an ancient *jinrickisha*, all clustered near the arch to a Shinto shrine. Over the din, an errant thought struck her: if she'd insisted Freda stay in bed rather than attend Peter's funeral, would her mother still be alive? A tremor went through her as she remembered her mother's funeral of only yesterday. She should have known Freda was sicker than she admitted—and that nothing would keep her from saying good-bye to her beloved husband of thirty-two years, not even the certainty of her own death.

Freda had married Peter when she was twenty, and accompanied him wherever his Mission had sent him, bearing their three children in strange countries far from home, ending up in Tokyo right after the great earthquake of 1923. Katie's sister and brother, ten and eleven years older than she, had never known a permanent home until Japan, and by then they were bored and dissatisfied with their lot in life, unlike their parents. Even now, Katie clearly remembered the day they left on the ship to live with their grandparents in San Francisco. Freda's parents had offered a home and college to their grandchildren, faintly disapproving of Peter's lack of preparation for their future.

Both Johanna, the oldest, and Edward had laughed away Katie's tears. Although she was only eight then, Katie realized how happy they were to go—"to finally have roots," her brother had stated firmly. At first, they'd written regularly, but as the years passed, the letters became infrequent, a situation that grieved both her parents. Freda had nevertheless been faithful with her weekly letters to them, optimistic that the family would be together again when Peter retired and they returned to America.

But that was never meant to be. First Katie's grandparents died and left Edward their house, then

Johanna married and moved to Alaska, and now Peter and Freda would remain in Japan forever. As Katie was again pedaling furiously, she realized that Johanna and Edward were strangers to her. The thought never occurred to her that she might seek a home with them.

It was still early when Katie propped her bicycle against a willow tree in front of the Kono home, but she knew the Konos had been up since dawn. Mr. Kono and his son Takumi—Tak—often practiced the martial arts, Zen, and meditation before most people were awake.

She hesitated, breathing deeply of the wisteria-scented air and gathering her argument, for she knew Mr. Kono would have his own opinion of what was proper for the daughter of his valued friend, Peter Aaland. Maybe he'd insist that she move in with his family, at least until she heard from her brother Edward or her sister Johanna. He had respected her need for grieving alone, although Michiko had come each afternoon since her father died to spend some time with Katie.

Even Tak, Michiko's older brother, had made an appearance two days after her father died, his dark eyes carefully oblique, although Katie sensed deeper feelings in him. They'd sat in the garden, the maid had brought tea, and the next half hour had reminded her of how, in the ancient tea ceremony, lovers communicated in silence and without touching, the very pouring and drinking symbolic of unspoken emotions. It had been bittersweet for Katie; she'd adored Tak since he'd returned from California two years ago, freshly graduated from Stanford University after four years of living with his American uncle in San Francisco. But her feelings for Tak had remained unspoken, as had his; both respected the tradition and beliefs of the Kono family. It was unacceptable for Tak to marry anyone other than a daughter of a samurai family of equal status to the wealthy Konos.

"Katie-san," a man's voice said in almost perfect English. "You're out early. Is everything all right?"

Startled, her gaze flew to the tall, lean man who stepped from the garden, as though she had conjured him up from her thoughts. Katie hadn't seen Tak standing beyond the curtain of willow branches; the brown of his kimono blended into the shadowy foliage. For a moment disconcerted, she was suddenly glad she'd taken the time to change into a crisp cotton dress, one of her favorites. It was a pale green print rather than black, but she knew her parents would not want her to wear mourning clothes.

"Good morning, Takumi-san," Katie replied, aware that she had disturbed his meditation. "Please excuse my intrusion so early in the morning. I wish to speak to your father—if he can spare the time," she added, always aware that manners were so important. She also knew that she would miss seeing Kenkichii Kono at any other time of day. He was a busy man who headed a huge family business of factories and textile mills in both Tokyo and Hiroshima, where they had another house. The thought warmed her; if she couldn't work at the school, there must be a job within the vast Kono empire.

"My father is still meditating," Tak said. "Perhaps I can be of help to you instead, Katie-san." He bowed, and when his eyes again met hers, she saw a flicker of emotion, and was surprised. Tak was well-schooled in concealing his feelings behind his samurai training.

"I've been waiting the opportunity to speak with you," he went on. "After you were feeling stronger."

His words were formal, but Katie wasn't put off. She remembered Tak as the boy, the one she'd confided her loneliness to after Edward and Johanna were gone, the boy who'd patiently taught her and

Michiko about flying kites, and later the young man who'd learned to fly an airplane and, under his father's supervision, had taken both her and Michiko on a short flight, to their squealing delight. He'd explained the teachings of Buddha and Shinto and the value of meditation. But all of that happened before Tak went to America and returned to take his place in the Konos' Tokyo office. The tall, darkly handsome Tak, whose very presence made her aware that she had become a woman, would one day be the head of an old and honored samurai family. But oh, how Katie missed the Tak of her girlhood!

She nodded, thinking it might be a good idea to explain to him first; it wouldn't hurt to have him on her side. She knew Michiko would support her decision, even though Michiko had often said that her father would never allow her to have a job in one of their mills or factories. To do so would bring a loss of face to the family.

Tak ushered her through the double doors of the *genkan* where Katie automatically stepped out of her wooden *getas* and into soft cloth slippers; then they moved into the sparsely furnished, but elegant main room. The *tatami* mats muffled their footsteps and Katie was aware of the quietness that permeated the spacious, one-story house. Michiko and her mother would be in the bathhouse, the staff in the kitchen, preparing for the day.

Bowing, Tak motioned her to a satin cushion and took the seat opposite, a highly polished teak table between them. A maid in a brilliant red kimono appeared and Tak ordered tea, after asking Katie if she would join him. As the maid bowed and scurried away, Katie was silent, knowing Tak would only begin speaking after the tea had been served and the proprieties observed.

Aware that he watched her, Katie kept her gaze

elsewhere, not trusting what he might see in her eyes. He was so handsome it took all of her concentration to keep her outward veneer of calm. She cared for him and wondered—as she had many times—if she loved him. She'd secretly cherished a hope of marriage to him, even though she was well aware of the cultural taboos. The son of a samurai family did not marry a woman of another race—a blond American of Norwegian descent—even if she was Japanese in her heart.

Her thoughts spun in her head as her gaze wandered into the garden beyond the far windows, over the flowering shrubs and trees and large symmetrically perfect rocks, all placed to create a setting of peace and serenity. Long arms of sunshine filtered through the branches to create a leaf pattern on the floor around them. For a brief time, the room held Katie suspended in its serenity. Finally the tea was brought and poured and Tak broke the silence.

"You must go home, Katie-san," he told her softly. "Now that your parents are gone, there is no place for you in Japan."

Her eyes widened, more green than he'd ever seen them. He knew his words had shocked her profoundly, but he was powerless to take them back, even though he loved her—had loved her since that first day when his father brought the Aaland family to stay until their own house was ready for occupancy. He hadn't been able to take his eyes off the three-year-old Katie, never having seen anyone like her—white-blonde hair, large trusting green eyes, and a quick smile that bonded her to him forever. She had sat on his father's lap, unafraid that the Konos looked different. Even then, her courage was as much a part of her character as her looks, unlike her older brother and sister. Edward's darker blond looks and Johanna's reddish hair and light eyes were

pale comparisons to the delicate flower and the
steely will that was Katherine—little Katie-san, as
the Konos, following the Aalands' lead, called her.

Katie put down her cup, bringing Tak's thoughts
back to the present. "I have no home but here," she
told him. "I intend to work at the school. I don't
expect the school to go on supporting me." Her tone
firmed with resolve. "I'll stay in Japan; it *is* my
home."

She broke off as he held up a flat, silencing hand.
"There are new teachers coming to the school,
Japanese teachers." He watched her master control
and felt proud of her despite his other feelings. He
glanced away, allowing her time to gather her
thoughts. He felt awful, as though he'd committed
seppuku and his insides were all torn up. He'd give
his life for her—but the tradition and honor that was
his inherited responsibility precluded giving her the
only position that would allow her to stay—as his
wife.

He met her eyes again, his love for her carefully
concealed behind his facade of duty. To behave
otherwise would be to flout family honor, which was
unacceptable, and led only to the ultimate
atonement—*seppuku*, his death by his own hand.

"Times are changing, Katie-san," Tak said, delib-
erately formal. "Japan is fighting in China, has been
since invading Manchuria in 1931. Although my
father and I—and many enlightened men in Japan
—don't agree with policies aimed at full-scale war,
war is coming—"

"But I'm no threat." Manners or no manners, she
couldn't help but interrupt him. "I'm American
and—"

Again he silenced her. "If—when—Japan aligns
with Germany and that little man Hitler, it will
mean a world war, with America aligning with the
enemy. If that happens, you, as an American, would

be in danger living in Japan. The military machine in Japan will have no mercy." Tak's face was emotionless, his tone flat, but his eyes altered somehow, intensifying his words. "We . . . care for you." Despite his control, his voice faltered. "But you are not one of us, Katie-san. Therefore you must go home to America."

"My son speaks the truth, Katie-san," Kenkichii Kono said from the doorway. When she started to rise, he waved her back, taking one of the cushions instead. Katie wondered how long he'd been listening. Surely Michiko's father, the old man she'd listened to, believed in, and loved for most of her life, wouldn't send her away—to strangers in an alien land?

Kenkichii nodded to his son who was immediately on his feet, bowing to Katie. Before she could speak, Tak was gone. She realized that Mr. Kono wished to speak with her alone.

Again there was a proper silence while the maid brought fresh tea. He sipped loudly, as was the Japanese way when enjoying a drink. Then he put down his cup, his dark eyes suddenly direct. "Now Katie-san, before I explain my intentions, I would like to hear yours."

He adjusted his kimono and settled into a more comfortable position, patiently waiting for her to begin. She knew he would normally be in his suit by now and on his way to the Kono offices. What he would tell her must be important, she decided with a flash of dread. Instantly she controlled her fears, knowing this slight man's respect was vital. He was a *sensei*—a master of *kendo*, an ancient form of the martial arts which taught control and patience and a lifelong search for inner peace. He would not be impressed if she lost face, even if she was in mourning.

She looked him in the eyes, willed her hands to

stillness in her lap, and then she began. In as calm a manner as she could manage, Katie told him she meant to stay in Japan, that it was the only country she knew, and that she was willing to work and support herself. When she mentioned the school, he only shook his head gently. When she suggested a Kono mill or factory, saying that she'd even move to Hiroshima if he'd give her a job in their textile mill and reminding him of her love for the silk industry, he listened politely, although a flicker of emotion— pain?—touched his expression. Then he pressed his lips together and abruptly stopped her flow of words.

"No, small Katie-san"—How ridiculous, she thought, she was taller than he by six inches—"you must go home. Takumi was right—he spoke for me. War will come, if not this year or the year after, then the next. The focus of the *Diet* is toward war. Even if many people disagree with the course of our government, ultimately we will all do our duty and stand with our country."

He reached across the table and covered her hand in a rare outward display of caring. "I am so sorry," he said. "I also wish you to stay; your spirit is as much Japanese as Michiko's." Then he straightened with resolve. "*Hai*, you must go soon. I am sending Michiko with you—for a visit with her American uncle. You will not be alone."

In her desperation, Katie forgot her resolve to remain calm. "I *will* be alone!" she cried. "I don't remember my brother. I don't even know where my sister is!"

For a moment his mask slipped, and she saw that their conversation was as painful to him as to her. It was true that she hadn't heard from Johanna since her sister moved to Alaska with her husband, Dion Stefanini. Katie tried to remember more about Dion but could only recall that he was a pilot for a small airline that flew the most treacherous terrain in the world. Where was that? Katie had no idea.

"It would be your father's wish for you," Kenkichii said, disregarding her outburst. "He would want you safe in America. He shared my belief that Japan will escalate the China war." He hesitated. "I can do no less for my old friend Peter Aaland than concede to his wishes. So sorry, Katie-san, but you will go to America."

Then Kenkichii Kono stood up, ending their meeting. He told her that she would not leave for several weeks yet, to enjoy the days left to her. Several minutes later she was back on her bicycle, pedaling home—home for only three more weeks.

Katie was oblivious to the stares this time, unaware that her long blond hair flowed behind her like shimmering silk, that her slim body was poised forward over the handlebars as though she were trying to flee her demons, that her eyes were glistening emeralds in her pale face. She had never looked more startlingly beautiful to the street people—or so unhappy.

"So sorry, the Katie-san is so sad," an old man said to no one in particular.

"*Karma* is *karma, neh*?" a voice answered as Katie disappeared into the street traffic.

She'd been contemplating the rock that jutted from the center of the pool, trying to imagine it growing. This was a meditation tool that often worked for her, but she had no luck this time; her shattered thoughts wouldn't come together. Her mind kept going back to the letter from Edward, offering his condolences, revealing that he'd been unsuccessful in contacting Johanna in Alaska, that he trusted Katie to attend to their parents' affairs as he was unable to travel to Japan, and it was too late

anyway. He hadn't offered her a home and she'd felt
no emotion in his words, only duty. She'd sent him
another letter informing him of her arrival date, and
wondered how he'd react to that.

The Aaland family was no more, she thought.
Johanna didn't even know her parents were dead.
How sad and how odd that a child would not know
her parents were gone forever. She leaned back to
rest her head against the willow trunk and watched
wisps of clouds puff and scatter across the sky,
pushed by a fickle wind. Once, when days were
golden and whole, she would have taken her kite to
the highest hill to enjoy the friendly competition
with other kiters for supremacy of the sky. She'd
chosen her kites with care and often outflew the
experts, to applause and bows. Now her kites had
been given to her cook's grandson, along with her
bicycle.

How will I bear it? Katie asked herself. Her things,
together with the few family valuables, were crated,
ready for the ship in two days. Everything else had
been given away. Soon Japan would be nothing but a
cherished memory.

Too restless to sit, Katie jumped up and went back
into the house. But the main room no longer offered
her solace; the Aaland presence was gone. She had to
face it. She was really leaving.

But she hadn't given up easily, not even after her
meeting with the Konos. She'd gone to other family
friends to seek help in obtaining a job. No one had a
solution for her; all agreed that she must return to
her own people in America. Gradually, her hope of
staying had died. Without a way to support herself,
she had no option but to go.

"Katie-san?" a familiar voice said from the doorway to the garden.

Her gaze lifted at once to meet Tak's. Suddenly

disconcerted, she could only stare, unable to think beyond a faint *ohayo gozaimasu*—good morning.

Slowly he came to her, his face inscrutable, his eyes never leaving hers. His whole bearing was tense, as though he wrestled with a strong emotion, as though he were about to embrace her—a thought she dismissed at once. Tak would never lose control and dishonor himself in any way. The silence deepened, and Katie knew Tak was trying to say something he found difficult, something important. He had never looked more handsome—or more open to her. Her spirits soared. Was he offering her a way to stay in Japan?

"You're leaving soon, and once you're gone, we will never meet again," he began, hesitated, and glanced away. He couldn't bear the expectancy on Katie's face. She waited for his words, her eyes trusting, her cheeks reflecting the pink of her silk kimono, her loose hair framing the perfection of her features and flawless skin. Maybe he'd made a mistake—maybe he should have just accepted his *karma*. Or maybe what he was about to do was his *karma*, he reminded himself. She was so lovely, so desirable. He loved her—it was as simple as that, for all that it was unacceptable. Knowing he'd never see her again tormented him; it had impelled him to her side . . . with his offer.

"I wish you to stay in Japan, Katie-san," he said, suddenly direct.

"Oh Tak, that's what I wish too," she replied, hardly daring to hope. "Did your father reconsider?"

"My father does not know I'm here." Before she could digest his words, he'd closed the space between them, but stopped himself from taking her in his arms. "You would stay in a house in the mountains not too distant from Tokyo and—it would be maintained for you."

"You aren't offering a job?"

Other than a flicker of his lashes, he didn't reply, awaiting her comprehension, and her answer. She felt confused, then gradually his proposal took on a new significance. He was samurai, and at one time it was perfectly acceptable for a samurai to have a consort. Even now, she suspected, many Japanese men maintained a mistress on the side. *Is that what Tak is offering?* she wondered and stepped backward, her thoughts in turmoil. As she stared at him, unflinching before the intensity of his gaze, he suddenly looked away—and she knew.

Anger filled her; she could hardly contain it. He cherished his honor—but what about hers? She knew the Konos would never approve, and Tak's proposal was a dishonor to the memory of her parents and all they'd stood for. She loved him, had dreamed of being his wife—bearing his children—and he could only offer her a—a twilight world? Her thoughts carried the projection of such a life even further. She knew family responsibility would influence Tak to marry a proper Japanese woman who would be the mother of his children. She, on the other hand, would only have physical intimacy and secret visits. And she'd never again be free to enjoy the life she'd had as the daughter of Peter and Freda Aaland. She would be a woman of the *Floating World.* And she would grow old dishonored.

But you love him, she argued mentally. *And you want to stay in Japan.* Her emotions swung, emptying her of anger. Katie knew Tak cared or he would never have placed himself in such a precarious position; her refusal would cost him a loss of face. But he had not gone so far as to say he loved her. Had he said that, she could never have denied his wishes, never refused him. Slowly, she shook her head, not trusting herself to speak.

He stood for long seconds, inscrutable, unaware that even an expression of love would have changed Katie's mind. Then he bowed deeply—a bow of deepest respect—and turned back to the door. Katie didn't watch him go, but she flinched as his footsteps faded away. Her anger was gone; the man she loved was leaving her forever. She merely felt shame—and a deep sadness.

Now she'd lost *everyone* she loved.

The Kono ship was moving away from the dock when Katie glanced back to the waving crowd. She felt hollow inside and knew that if she looked at Michiko, who stood beside her at the rail, she'd shame herself with tears. Instead, she stared at the widening wake behind them, the diminishing figures of the Konos on the wharf, the shore sounds of workers and vendors and scurrying crowds that were fading into the past as well. She didn't bother to look for Tak. He hadn't come to say goodbye.

The morning sun was bright with promise by the time the ship left the shelter of Tokyo Bay and headed out to sea. A brisk wind tore at Katie's hair and clothing and churned the water into a foaming turbulence that mirrored her feelings. Mt. Fuji soared above the receding shoreline, a majestic last farewell to the mountainous island that Katie loved so much.

Sadly, Katie remembered how her mother always said that the sun of the morning represented hope for each new day. She grabbed Michiko's hand and tried hard to believe her mother's words. Would she find roots and happiness in San Francisco? And would Edward be glad to see her? She envied Michiko, who would return to Japan after a six-month visit with her aunt and uncle. Gradually, the land Katie was leaving took on an unfamiliar feeling as the ship left it behind, and she had a sudden premonition that she'd never see its beloved shoreline again.

Michiko squeezed Katie's hand, her long lashes sparkling with tears. "So sorry, Katie-san. I wish everything was different. I wish you were really my sister and we were both only going for a visit."

Katie smiled, and tried not to look as sad as she felt. *Yes, it is too bad, my dear friend,* Katie thought. *I wouldn't mind resembling you, being only five feet tall with long black hair and skin like fine porcelain. I too wish things were different. Then neither of us would be on this ship today.*

As though Michiko understood, she bowed slightly, then handed Katie a piece of rolled-up parchment. "It's from Takumi, Katie-san. He said it would explain everything." Then she turned away and disappeared below, knowing Katie would want to be alone to read Tak's final note.

Carefully Katie unfolded the paper. The words were printed in English, but nevertheless the calligraphy was as artistic as the poem, the ultimate tribute to a woman from a Japanese man of samurai lineage.

Long after she'd read it, she stared at the page, oblivious to the sea birds riding the air currents above the ship, or the spray that pricked her flesh with the cold touch of the ocean. Even after the words blurred into each other from the intensity of her gaze, she saw them in her mind—and knew she'd never forget them.

"In a lonely life
The silence screams
Unspoken words."

He loved her. Katie's throat tightened. But it had been hopeless from the very beginning. The poem was his good-bye, rather than a stiff bow and stilted words on the public dock.

The tears came then, brimming from her eyes and flowing unchecked down her face. She stood for a long time, watching the land slide behind the horizon, unaware that she was now alone on the deck.

"Good-bye, my mother and father," she said, her voice a broken whisper. "And good-bye, Tak. You are my treasures of Japan. Your love will go with me forever."

Then she turned and strode purposefully to the cabin she shared with Michiko. The hope of tomorrow beckoned. She would meet it head-on—as always.

CHAPTER 2

THE WINCHES CLANKED AND GROANED AS THEY PULLED the ship close to the pier. Katie and Michiko watched the gangplank being lowered, waiting with the other passengers to disembark. The trip had passed quickly, but Katie's heart sank when she saw the California coast grow on the horizon, an alien land. She hadn't confided her feelings to Michiko, not wanting to upset her friend, who was already unhappy about the changes in Katie's life. They planned to enjoy the six months of Michiko's visit; Katie realized that Kenkichii Kono had arranged it so that she would have Michiko for that time of adjustment. She would not allow herself to think about Tak, and what might have been. She knew that he would always hold a special place in her heart; she would remember him as the boy she adored, the first man she loved.

Katie looked down at the wharf and the people who'd come to meet the ship, and tried to decide which one was Edward. None of the men resembled the photographs of her brother. Maybe he wouldn't be there, she thought suddenly. She'd never received a return letter after informing him she was coming to San Francisco.

"Katie?" Michiko said, having fallen into the abbreviated version of Katie's name during the trip. "Do you see Edward?"

Katie shook her head. She tried to calm her sudden apprehension. Maybe Edward hadn't gotten her second letter—maybe he wasn't pleased by her announcement that she was coming to live with him. Michiko's hand on her arm helped steady her nerves. She shot her friend a grin, and remembered that if all else failed, she could go to the Kono home with Michiko until she found a room and a job.

"Okay, Katie?" Michiko looked concerned, anticipating Katie's fears. "Edward-san is here somewhere. We just don't recognize him."

The gulls circled, their cries a poignant reminder of Katie's own sadness, their bodies a flash of white against the backdrop of blue sky. Behind them the Golden Gate Bridge stood as the sentinel to the Pacific Ocean. The harbor was beautiful, a vast amphitheater in the shelter of the surrounding hills. The bay water was capping from a brisk wind that constantly changed the surface pattern of wakes and swell lines and tidal currents into elaborate, ever-moving designs. The port was alive with sea traffic and sail boats and ships flying the colors of countries she'd never heard of, and it was—oh, so different from the smells and commotion of her beloved Japan.

Katie swallowed hard. It would be all right, she told herself. She'd make it somehow—even if she must be totally on her own. She wasn't her father's daughter for nothing—or her mother's for that matter.

The gangplank swayed as they went down to the wharf. Men were already removing luggage, and Katie was aware of their admiring glances as she and Michiko followed the other passengers to the Customs and Immigration area pointed out to them by the captain.

"Katie?" a male voice called behind her. "Katie?"

Both Katie and Michiko turned at the same time to see a tall, husky man of around twenty-eight approaching them. Then Katie saw the resemblance to her father—the same dark blond hair, the same blue eyes and tall, broad-shouldered frame.

"Oh Edward!" she cried. "I'm so glad you're here. I was afraid you hadn't received my letter." She ran to him, her relief immense.

"My God!" Edward held her at arm's length, his gaze incredulous. "I hardly recognized you—little Katie all grown up."

His words were robbed of a full welcome by their lack of enthusiasm. Even his brief hug seemed only a courtesy. Then he stepped back and Katie was able to observe him more closely. His brown suit was rumpled and a bad fit, he needed a shave, and his body lacked the muscle tone of a man like Tak, who practiced the martial arts. Edward was definitely not as she'd pictured him. She remembered the boy who'd looked forward to a wonderful life in America. She wondered what had happened to him; was the man he'd become really as sullen and stuffy as her first impression suggested?

"You inherited the best features of both our parents," Edward said, his eyes narrowed to study her. "You've become the beauty of the family," he added dryly, almost as though he begrudged his words. His gaze took in the light brown skirt and jacket that fit her slim body with the perfection only a Japanese tailor could achieve, the long blond hair that she'd coiled into a prim roll that was somehow incongruous with the high color in her cheeks and the sparkle in her green eyes.

"Thank you, Edward."

Katie felt at a loss and knew her tone was stilted. He looked like their father, but his bearing was completely different. Edward was a stranger and she didn't know how to read him yet. But she vowed to keep an open mind. He was her only brother, after all; they shared the same background, the same blood.

"I hope you don't mind that I've arrived on your doorstep," she said lightly, to hide her own disappointment. Everything felt so strange—not at all as she'd hoped—and so far away from what should have been her life.

He shrugged off her words. "What else could you do? You had no other choice—did you?"

She shook her head and tried not to be discouraged by a suspicion that he did mind.

Then he shifted his gaze to Michiko, who had watched the meeting with great trepidation for Katie. Yet she sensed that Edward had his own fears. He seemed a sad and lonely man, one to whom life had not been kind. He was obviously not married, as no wife would allow her husband out the door with clothes that needed pressing, Michiko thought suddenly, and felt pleased, to her surprise. The realization of his continued regard brought a flush to her cheeks, and she glanced down at the board floor, disconcerted by her instant understanding of him.

"I wouldn't have known you either, Michiko," he said, and his warmer tone of voice pulled Michiko's gaze back to his.

The serious set to his features was softened by a slight upward curve to his mouth and a gleam of interest in his eyes, as though he liked what he saw. A rush of pleasure went through her; she was glad she'd worn the new suit—American style—that Katie had insisted she buy in Tokyo, pointing out, when Michiko demurred, that the off-white linen was a striking contrast to her shiny black hair and eyes. Michiko suddenly wanted to appear attractive to Katie's brother.

"We are very happy you are here, Edward-san," Michiko said with the correct blend of formality and shyness, her English accented by the inevitable slurring of the r's and l's. She paused to place her arm around Katie, encouraged by Edward's sudden show of friendliness. "It has been a very sad time for my good friend Katie-san. She needs the support of her family now. I am so happy she has you." Then, forgetting she was no longer in Japan, she bowed the deep bow of high respect.

Edward couldn't hide his pleasure as he helped them through the long procedure of clearing Immigration and Customs. Then he made arrangements to have their trunks delivered later. His solicitousness did not go unnoticed by Katie, who realized the reason for it—Michiko typified all the gentle femininity of a high-born Japanese woman. But as they stepped outside and onto the street, Michiko paused to glance around, a puzzled expression on her face.

"So sorry, Edward-san, but my uncle has not yet arrived for me."

Edward grinned down at her. "He's not coming. I offered to take you to him, as I was picking up Katie anyway. Your uncle agreed that I'd escort you home."

"You spoke to Mr. Kono?" Katie asked, realizing that Edward was full of surprises.

He nodded. "I work for Kono Imports, and as I

see Isami Kono every day, it was only fitting that I offer."

He seemed pleased with himself, but Katie was again surprised. She hadn't known her brother worked for the San Francisco branch of the Kono empire. All she knew about Michiko's uncle Isami Kono was that he'd migrated to California as a young man to set up an American office for the family business, had married a Japanese/American woman, and his property was in the name of his wife's family. The situation had puzzled Katie until Michiko explained that American law prohibited ownership of property to Japanese not born in the United States.

Edward led them to an older model Ford parked at the curb, opened the doors with a flourish Katie suspected was not typical of him, and indicated where they would sit, Katie in front and Michiko in back. Then he climbed behind the wheel, and in seconds they were headed up one of the steepest hills Katie had ever seen.

Both Katie and Michiko were intrigued by the scenery, the flowers and trees, the wider streets and square buildings, and the architecture that was more ornate, even gaudy by the Japanese standard of simplicity of line. The journey passed in a flurry of Katie's questions and Edward's answers, punctuated by an occasional low "ooh" or "ahh" from Michiko. Gradually, the business area changed to residential, then to an exclusive part of the city where elaborate mansions were set back from the street behind trimmed shrubbery, high walls, or a wide expanse of grass. Discreetly opulent was the description that came to Katie's mind. Only the very rich could live in such splendor, with a spectacular view of San Francisco Bay and the Golden Gate Bridge.

Edward turned the Ford into a driveway that curved to the front doors of a low, two-story house

surrounded by an exquisite garden—a Japanese
garden, Katie realized, and felt pleased, somehow
less anxious. The house had a Japanese feeling to it
as well, mainly because of the roof lines and shutters
and simplicity of design. The car came to a stop and
Edward got out to open the back door for Michiko.

"Welcome to Pacific Heights, the best real estate in
San Francisco," he said, still the perfect escort.

But his words had a strange edge to them; Katie
wondered why and made a mental note to ask him
later. Then the diminutive, but impeccably dressed
Isami Kono rushed out to greet them, bowing and
speaking in both English and Japanese, his wife right
behind him. Although the Konos were gracious
during introductions and polite in their thanks to
Edward, who was all smiles and compliments, Katie
sensed that they did not completely approve of him,
an employee, being the one to escort Michiko from
the ship—that it was probably the extenuating circumstances of their niece arriving with Katie that
allowed the breach of propriety. Kenkichii Kono
must have requested his brother to be understanding, Katie suddenly realized, even if it meant bend-
ing tradition a little.

Within minutes, she and Michiko had said their
good-byes, arranged to meet soon, and Katie was
again riding over the hills with Edward, down one
only to start up another, the engine missing and
backfiring as he shifted gears at each intersection.
Behind them at the bottom of the street, the bay
glistened in the sun, while everywhere the city
bustled with weekday activity. Edward was silent, no
longer the cheerful guide. He concentrated on his
driving, and she wondered if he was subject to mood
swings, or if his friendliness to Mr. Kono and his
solicitousness to Michiko had been contrived—but
to what purpose? Quelling her misgivings, she asked
instead about Pacific Heights.

"Huh!" he retorted instantly. "Only the rich big shots live there—as you can see."

He downshifted yet again and glanced at her, his expression a mixture of—what? she wondered. Jealousy? Awe? As he went on, she realized that his motives were more complicated than that.

"The Konos aren't welcome there because it's an exclusively white neighborhood. But so far they haven't been kicked out." He gave a sharp laugh. "Old man Kono's a sly fox—the deed is registered in the name of a business associate who's also white."

"You mean, they aren't wanted because they're Japanese?" Katie was shocked, as much by the discrimination as by Edward's attitude. He sounded spiteful, as though he secretly hoped they would have to leave their home.

"That's right. Everything in life isn't fair, even in America, little sister Katie." His features took on a hard cast. "The Kono Import Company is big and successful, mostly because Isami is a genius and knows the business better than anyone else on the West Coast. I was damn lucky to get a job with them—they only hire the best people, and they pay good wages to get them," he added with a hint of pride.

"How did you manage to get hired?" she asked, her thoughts jumping to her own need for work.

"I did what people have to do nowadays," he replied. "I used my influence. I told old Kono that my folks were close friends of his family in Tokyo and gave him Kenkichii's name as a reference. I figured he checked it all out, and eventually I was hired."

He made some quick turns to avoid a speeding cable car on its way down the hill, while Katie digested his words, feeling somehow ashamed of what he'd done. It was one thing to ask for work, another to manipulate friendships to get it, in

Katie's opinion. She didn't know how to reply without compromising her honesty, and she was relieved when he suddenly turned into a narrow, one-car garage facing the street, and switched off the motor.

"And this is my house," he told her, stepping from the car. "It isn't the Kono mansion, but the view here on Russian Hill is just as good as theirs. Our grandparents had the good sense to buy a choice location before the prices went up."

He took her bags but didn't bother to open her door as he had for Michiko. She followed him out of the garage, which had lost its doors long ago, and wondered if he always thought so much about money and choice locations and rich people. Edward opened a gate in the board fence that paralleled the sidewalk, and Katie stepped into a delightful, if overgrown, garden, then mounted wide stone steps to a small courtyard beside a narrow, two-story house. The same stone had been used in the wall that separated the yard from a steep drop to a street far below. And beyond that was the city and the bay. Katie stood transfixed. The setting was unexpected, and she loved it on sight.

"Did you have any luck today?" Edward asked Katie one evening several weeks later.

She looked up from her plate and shook her head. "I don't seem to have the right credentials for any particular job. They all say come back when you have experience."

She pretended not to notice his frown. She knew he was beginning to begrudge her being in the house, and in a way she didn't blame him. She had nothing to contribute to her support and the house itself was inadequate for the two of them, being much smaller than it had first appeared. The kitchen was tiny and lacked cupboard space, all the plumbing leaked, and the one bathroom was hardly more than a closet. The saving grace of her bedroom was the window with a sweeping view of the bay. The house had served her grandparents for many years, but then, they'd been a married couple who'd kept everything in good repair, an ability Edward obviously didn't possess.

"I do have one prospect," Katie added, although she secretly expected another rejection. "A job as a teacher's aide in a Catholic school down in the Mission district."

"Catholic?" He raised his brows. "You're not Catholic."

Annoyance flashed through her; he wanted her to find a job and then didn't approve of the only good possibility she'd had. "I'm not prejudiced, Edward," she retorted. "Children are children whatever their religious belief . . . or color, for that matter."

"True," he agreed, disregarding her curt tone. He went on eating and she wondered if he appreciated all the things she did to make his life easier— cooking all the meals, restoring the courtyard to an orderly haven of blooming flowers, weekly cleaning of the house. He'd commented on the yard but never thanked Katie for her other efforts, always acting the benevolent benefactor—so long as he wasn't asked to pay for anything. His attitude was becoming intolerable to her. How had he, the son of her parents, become so humorless and penny-pinching?

She picked at her food. "Michiko suggested I ask her uncle for a job," she began and paused. "As I know a little about silk and have been all through the Kono textile mills in Hiroshima, she thought—"

Edward slammed his fork down on the table, and stopped her before she could finish. "I won't have it! You'll jeopardize my job—uh, my credibility with the firm."

His reaction was so unexpected that Katie

jumped. Her anger was instantaneous, and it took all of her control not to tell him off. He really was a self-seeking weakling. There was no outward sign of compassion toward anyone, let alone her—his own sister!

She should have known from the first day, when he'd shrugged off all her questions about their sister Johanna. All he'd said was that she'd married a loser and was even more stupid to follow him all over a frozen frontier like Alaska, and that it was impossible to keep up with their moves and he still didn't know if she'd gotten his letters about the death of their parents. Katie was appalled by his apparent lack of feeling. She didn't know her sister, but she'd written a long letter updating Johanna on what had happened, then she'd addressed it to the last address, marking the envelope, 'Important—Please Forward.'

She stood up now, outwardly calm but inwardly shaking with anger, trying to remember all her early training on how to handle ignorance with patience. She knew losing her temper would only result in an argument with him. But he was pushing her toward a confrontation, and she knew it was only a matter of time before she'd have to have her say, even if he kicked her out.

"Well Edward, I'll try to remember that—and the other things you've made clear to me, like wanting me to move once I've found a job and can pay rent." His face flushed with anger, and she knew her eyes flashed right back at him. "But should I not get the job at the Catholic school, then you may as well know that I intend to apply at Kono Imports."

She gathered up the dirty dishes and strode to the kitchen, knowing he could ask her to leave at any time—that he wouldn't only because of what the Konos might think and how it would affect his job.

"*Karma* is *karma,*" she muttered, plunging her

hands into the dishwater. "What will be will be . . . and I'll deal with it when it happens."

Three days later, Katie answered the telephone to learn she'd gotten the job of teacher's aide. The sudden jolt of pleasure almost made her weak, but she restrained herself while the nun in charge of hiring explained the duties, the salary being offered, and that she was expected to begin the following Monday.

"Although you're not Catholic, your prior experience in your father's school fits our needs," the nun said. "And as your job is only helping, the religious aspect should not be a problem."

After thanking her, Katie hung up, then let out a yelp of delight and heard it echo up the empty staircase. She danced out into the courtyard, singing a favorite Japanese song of her childhood. She had a job!

"Katie-san, please excuse me, so sorry to interrupt, but—are you all right?" Michiko stood watching from the gate at the bottom of the stone steps, looking like a Japanese doll in her yellow silk floral *kimono* with a deeper hued *obi* outlining her tiny waist.

"Nothing's wrong, Michiko-san!" Katie exclaimed, dancing down to her friend to pull her into the delicate steps of their childhood game. "Everything's right—I'm now employed! I'll soon be making money!"

Katie knew the Kono sedan would be at the curb, the driver patiently waiting while Michiko visited. Michiko was a cherished, overly protected young woman who belonged to a family richer than Katie could imagine. But she didn't resent her friend's privileged life; she was about to make a new life for herself, and she was looking forward to it. Although she'd miss Edward's garden, she wouldn't miss

Edward, and her next project would be finding a
place to live—as soon as she'd saved the first
month's rent.

After she'd settled down, Katie made tea and they
sat in the garden to drink it, giggling together as
they'd done so many times in the past, toasting—
American style—Katie's future job with a clink of
their cups.

Katie sat back, for a moment wistful, and wished
that time didn't pass so quickly. The summer had
been lovely, but now fall was in the air; she could see
that the leaves had begun to fade, and the air was
cooler. Since arriving shortly before Katie's nine-
teenth birthday at the end of July, she and Michiko
had taken in the sights, from Golden Gate Park to
Chinatown and the Japanese section where Kono
Imports was located, to the local beaches and the
giant redwood forest north of the Golden Gate.
Isami Kono's Japanese chauffeur had put hundreds
of miles on the sedan to allow the two sightseers a
look at northern California. Several times Edward
had joined them, to Michiko's delight and Katie's
annoyance; her brother's interest seemed contrived
to Katie. But having Michiko's company had eased
Katie's searing nostalgia and homesickness for Japan and her dead parents, and for that she'd always
be grateful to Michiko's father.

"Now all I need is a little apartment," Katie said,
breaking the spell of companionable silence.

Michiko's smile disappeared. "But you are not
leaving Edward's house? Edward would be upset. It
is his place, as head of the family, to care for you."

Katie glanced out over the city to the bay that
sparkled like a carpet of gems under the late afternoon sun. She watched a ship steam toward the
Golden Gate, bound for the open sea, and she was
pricked with loneliness. Michiko would never understand Edward, no matter how much Katie tried to

explain, and that caused Katie anxiety. Edward's presence had a strange effect on Michiko; she would suddenly seem even more gentle and feminine, almost adoring of him. And Katie realized that Edward was not oblivious to Michiko; he too was different in her presence, his selfishness hidden. When it occurred to Katie that Michiko might be falling in love with Edward, she'd discounted it. Then, as she'd remembered her own feelings for Tak, Katie had become alarmed.

Sensing that now might be a good time to broach the subject, Katie gathered her wits and was about to speak to Michiko about Edward, when he strode in through the garden gate. His dour expression was instantly replaced with a pleasant smile when he saw Michiko. Demurely, Michiko lowered her lashes, but not before Katie saw the warm light in her eyes. Michiko *was* in love with Edward.

Damn! Katie thought, using Edward's favorite expression. *Damn him for coming home right at this moment!*

"Can a thirsty, tired man join the party?" he asked, and then sat down before Katie could plead "girl talk." He ignored his sister's brief frown and looked at Michiko instead. *Jesus, but she's exquisite,* he thought, *even if she is Japanese.* He'd never been attracted to a woman of another race before, but Michiko was different; aside from her beauty, she'd been trained in the art of knowing how to treat a man. That she was also rich and a Kono added to her attraction. Edward had decided, almost from their first meeting, that an alliance with her would benefit him both personally and professionally. Whatever the cost—the prejudice he might encounter—he meant to marry her; she was not returning to Japan if he could help it.

Watching his changing expressions, Katie read his thoughts and knew that Edward's motives went right over Michiko's head. She was determined to confront her brother and could hardly contain herself until Michiko finally stood up to go a half hour later. Edward walked her out to the waiting sedan as Katie once more gathered her wits. She knew she was facing a fight. She'd learned that Edward was relentless when he went after what he wanted—and he wanted Michiko for all the wrong reasons.

"I intend to marry Michiko—and that's that!" Edward stood in the narrow living room, his hand on the mantle of the fireplace that was no longer safe for a fire—another repair Edward hadn't seen to.

His words rang through the quiet house, shaking Katie to the core. As much as she'd miss her, Katie would rather Michiko returned early to Japan than be trapped in Edward's small house and life. But maybe Michiko wouldn't want to marry Edward, maybe she was making assumptions about her friend that weren't true. She immediately dismissed the thought. Michiko was in love with Edward, and her naiveté made her vulnerable to whatever he might demand.

She faced him from across the room, holding her ground. "Have you declared your intentions?" When he looked away rather than answer, she knew he hadn't and was relieved. "Michiko comes from an old and honored samurai family. A marriage between you is unacceptable." But even while she said what needed to be said, she felt sorry for him, remembering how she once felt to know she could never marry Tak.

"Are you saying I'm not good enough?" Angrily he straightened, every muscle tensing.

"No, Edward. I'm only saying you'll never have family approval from the Konos, and Michiko will never marry you without it. You're asking for trouble."

The clock gonged the hour of six, while Edward seethed at her meddling, her words that tore the scab off his own insecurities. All his life he'd been second best, and he resented Katie's interference, which once again pointed up his not-quite-good-enough status. He'd never made the college baseball team; then he'd flunked out of college; and he'd been denied the jobs he'd wanted, which was why he'd wangled the position at Kono Imports. Michiko was his chance to finally make good, and he was damned if anyone—including Katie—would stand in his way.

But he wished she'd stop staring, as though she read his thoughts. Katie was so oriental in some ways that it disconcerted him. Even now, under her calm facade, he could see her exercising the self-discipline of her Zen Buddhist training, and wondered how his parents had allowed her to be exposed to such pagan teachings. Only her clenched hands and flashing eyes gave her away, and he realized that the headlong child he remembered—the little girl who fearlessly dove into the pond before she could swim and climbed to the top of the willow tree to rescue Johanna's kite—was still present in the woman Katie. But all that was beside the point, and he would not discuss the matter of Michiko any further.

"It would destroy Michiko to be disowned," Katie went on, her tone softer, pleading for his under- standing. "Please remember that she would never have been allowed in your house but for visiting me." Although she wanted to scream at him, de- mand he be a gentleman with honor, she still held her tongue. Michiko's whole future might be at stake.

He didn't even bother to reply. Instead, he turned on his heel and strode out the door, banging it shut after him. Katie's anger overwhelmed her. She yanked a pillow from the chair and threw it across the room after him, more frustrated than she'd ever been in her life.

The living room smelled of furniture polish, and the fragrance of roses that wafted in through the open French doors from the garden. It was a beautiful autumn afternoon, but to Michiko, who leaned back against the highback chair opposite Edward's in a conscious effort to relax, the day's beauty went unnoticed. In the last half hour, her emotions had swung from joy to guilt, and then to a combination of both. She'd never felt so confused in her life, even though she knew one thing for sure—she loved Edward.

Since Katie started work, she and Edward had spent more time alone; he often adjusted his work schedule so that they had afternoons together. She hadn't meant to deceive anyone, but she'd allowed her aunt and uncle to believe her outings were with Katie, knowing instinctively that they wouldn't approve otherwise. Michiko hadn't confided in Katie either, as she suspected Katie's opinion would be similar to her uncle's. Katie would be influenced by her knowledge of Japanese proprieties and her own unhappy experience with Tak. Michiko realized that Katie and Edward were not close—that for some reason Katie did not understand Edward, or see the goodness in him. So sorry—too bad, she thought. Maybe Katie was still sad about Japan and Tak and the deaths of her parents.

"Katie has no right to interfere," Edward said, bringing Michiko's thoughts back to her predicament. "We love each other and it's only normal for us to want marriage."

Oh, how Michiko agreed, how she longed to be his wife. But she could not ignore her family. She must have their blessing even though she knew it wouldn't be easy to get. She lowered her lashes and tried to think of a solution that would make them all happy. Her mind went over the conversation with Katie, who'd been home when she arrived, school having been dismissed early. Surprised, Katie had realized at once that Michiko was there to see Edward, not her. She'd been more concerned than shocked by Michiko's confession of other meetings, but when Michiko shyly revealed that she was in love with Edward and they wanted to marry, Katie had been struck dumb. When she'd found her voice, words of advice and caution poured out. But Michiko wasn't swayed by Katie's warnings about Edward's faults and possible motives. For the first time in their friendship, they'd had a serious rift, and she'd warned Katie not to speak badly about Edward. Then Edward had come in and demanded Katie leave them alone, saying she was meddling where she wasn't wanted. Michiko hadn't contradicted Edward, so Katie had gone without another word, looking sadder than Michiko ever remembered seeing her.

"Don't look so unhappy, my darling," Edward said, going to her now and pulling her into his arms. "I love you—I'll take care of everything, you'll see." Then he was kissing her, his passion rising, his mouth murmuring love words against her lips. And Michiko knew she could never lose him—not ever.

"Say you'll marry me," he whispered. "And I'll go to your uncle and ask—even beg if necessary—for his blessing."

Michiko lifted eyes that brimmed with love for him—and more, infinite trust. Her Edward-san—her *husband.* The depth of her emotion rocked her. He would cherish her as her father cherished her mother. And this *was* America, as Edward had reminded her. Marriage between them was possible in America. Her uncle, who would speak for the family, might not like it, but ultimately he would

agree. Edward would conform to family tradition
and the Kono honor would not allow a refusal.
Slowly she nodded, and her spirit soared at the
expression of triumph on his face.

Holding her against him, Edward couldn't believe
he'd won. Speaking to Michiko's uncle was a hurdle
he didn't want to face. He knew there would be
strong opposition. *But I'll marry her with or without
family consent,* he decided. Once their marriage was
consummated, the Kono honor would force his
acceptance into the family. A feeling of power took
hold of him. He was on his way to success beyond
imagining—all because of Michiko. *And I am fond
of her,* he reminded himself. His sudden upswing of
fortune was a potent incentive for love.

Katie felt awful. She hadn't seen Michiko since the
afternoon she'd stumbled into her friend's secret
meeting with Edward. She believed Michiko was
avoiding her and knew it was Edward's influence. He
obviously didn't realize that he'd soon come up
against the Kono honor, just as she'd done in Japan,
if he pursued his intention of marrying Michiko. She
was ashamed of his actions; he'd shamed their
parents, who'd always been honorable, trusted
friends of the Konos. She knew Michiko's feelings
were genuine, but she doubted Edward's. He was too
selfish, and he had his eye on the Kono fortune, a
fact Michiko couldn't see because she loved him.
Katie meant to have another talk with her, but this
time she'd use more tact.

Feeling vaguely unsettled, Katie paced the room,
watching the sun set over the city, and then the lights
twinkle on below her—a constellation of diamonds
that reflected shimmering pathways across the great
black expanse that was the bay at night. She wondered why Edward was so late from work. She hadn't

seen him since early morning, when he'd hardly spoken to her. The ring of the telephone startled her.

"Katie-san, I have bad news," Isami Kono said after she'd picked up the receiver. His tone was guarded and barely masked his anger. "Michiko and Edward have sent a telegram from Nevada."

Katie dropped into the nearest chair and tried to brace herself for what she suddenly knew was coming.

"They have married."

CHAPTER 3

THE NEXT FEW DAYS WERE EVEN MORE UPSETTING FOR Katie. She met with Isami, who was cool toward her until he realized that Katie had also been deceived; then he told her that Edward had requested a meeting the week before and had alluded to his feelings for Michiko.

"I explained to Edward that an alliance between them was impossible, and he seemed to understand," Isami said. "I trusted his integrity, and then he betrayed all of us."

Shamed, she apologized on behalf of the Aaland family and tried to explain that it was Edward's fault, not Michiko's—that Michiko's decision to elope had been influenced by her love for Edward and her desire to please him.

"So sorry, Katie-san," Isami said with great dignity. "I cannot excuse Michiko's deceit. She has dishonored her family and placed me in an unforgivable position with her father, who trusted me with her welfare."

Katie left his office, fearful for Michiko. The family honor had received a terrible blow; the Konos had lost face. In earlier times such a breach of honor could only be pacified by the drastic measure of *seppuku* by the one in disgrace. But these were modern times, Katie reassured herself. She wouldn't dwell on other possibilities—such as Michiko being disowned.

Edward and Michiko returned the next day, Edward all puffed up by his coup, Michiko scared but radiant. Edward went directly to the office where he anticipated a scene with Isami Kono. But he also fully expected to be accepted after he'd been duly contrite and explained that it was his love for Michiko that had prompted his impulsive action. Isami listened in silence without a flicker of emotion on his face, and Edward began to babble as his confidence slipped away.

"I do not find your decision to marry my niece impulsive," Isami said coldly when Edward had finished. "On the contrary, it is obvious that you have been contemplating this treachery for weeks."

Edward flushed, telegraphing the truth. *God-damn Jap bastard!* he thought angrily. Still he tried to bluff it out, suddenly realizing the stakes. "I love Michiko," he said, but his voice was stilted and lacked conviction. "I'll make her a good husband and—" He was stopped in mid-sentence by Isami's hand lifted for silence.

"So glad, Edward-san. She will need your support now." He inclined his head to his secretary, who'd come quietly into the room and was now holding the door open for Edward's departure.

"What do you mean?" Edward blustered, not liking Isami's tone of dismissal.

Isami looked him straight in the eyes, allowing his disgust and lack of respect for Edward to show briefly on his face. "You've been fired, Edward-san," he said coldly. "And Michiko is no longer a Kono. Her belongings will be sent to your house."

A moment later the door closed behind him, and in seconds Edward was on the sidewalk. His stomach heaved, his body trembled, and he felt tears sting his eyes. He couldn't believe it. His plan had backfired in a way he hadn't anticipated.

He brushed a sleeve over his face. "The bastard— the God-damn bastard!"

But the words didn't help. He felt defeated again, just as he had all those other times in his life.

Living in Edward's house became unbearable for Katie. Edward blamed Isami for everything, and Michiko, although patient and loving to Edward, was suffering great emotional pain. Michiko's attempts to make amends to her aunt and uncle had met with failure. Isami had reminded her that she'd made the choice to disregard honor—that although he loved her, he must now conform to the family code and tradition. A wire from Kenkichii Kono in Japan substantiated Isami's words: Michiko had disgraced the family and must now live with her decision. In the face of their suffering, Katie held her tongue; it was too late for recriminations.

Edward's small savings account dwindled over the next several weeks, going to pay bills and buy food. As he collected job rejections, his mood became even more sullen. Katie was glad she had the possibility of sharing an apartment with another teacher's aide from the school to fall back on. She felt awkward being in Edward's house now that he was married, even though she contributed board and room from her wages. But she was concerned about leaving Michiko; Edward was cold to his wife's suffering, being too preoccupied with his own predicament.

"I want to talk to you about Michiko," Katie said one evening after Michiko had gone upstairs to bed. "Being estranged from her family is terribly hard on her, and she's losing too much weight. I think you—"

He glanced up from the newspaper as she spoke and his interruption was sudden and angry. "Shut the hell up and mind your own business, Katie!"

She sucked in her breath. It was hard to hold on to her temper. Michiko needed loving reassurance from her husband—and Katie meant for her to have it.

"I only want to remind you what losing her family means to her," Katie went on, careful to keep the edge from her tone. "She needs your encouragement to help her adjust. She feels awful—guilty even— and blames herself for everyone's unhappiness. Just treat her kindly, Edward, so she can get over all her hurt."

"And what about me?" he retorted. "How I've been treated? Don't I count?" He jumped up, crumpling the paper into a ball, his voice rising. "That's the trouble—you're more Japanese than American, Katie Aaland-san!" he shouted sarcastically. "You care more about them than me. You're a traitor to your own family."

The words tumbled out of her mouth before she stopped to think of the consequences. "And you're a selfish, self-centered bastard who's shamed our dead parents in the eyes of their dearest friends!" she shouted back, finally losing the control she'd been holding on to by a thin thread. "I'm ashamed of what you did—to all of us."

She stepped closer, her tone lowered from the intensity of her anger. "Do you know why I'm so

ashamed, Edward?" She didn't wait for his reply.
"Because I think you planned it all, right from the
beginning—without consideration for anyone but
yourself." She choked on the last word and knew she
was about to burst into tears. Whirling around, she
ran for the door.

"I want you out of my house, Katie!" he shouted
after her. "You've got until tomorrow night!"

His words stopped her cold. Katie faced him, once
more mastering her emotions. "Very well. I'll leave
as you ask—with pleasure!" Then, head high, she
went to her room.

For a long time, Edward stared at the empty
doorway. In a begrudging way, he admired Katie.
But he didn't understand her any more than she
understood him. She was so different from both him
and Johanna. Unable to sleep, he sat up most of the
night brooding, unaware that Katie was also sleep-
less, feeling more alone than ever before.

The next morning was Saturday, and Katie was up
early, packing. She waited until mid-morning, then
called Grace Adams, the teacher's aide who needed a
roommate. After arranging to move in that afternoon, she returned to her packing. Later, as she left
the house, Michiko hugged her, tears streaming
down her cheeks.

"I'll see you soon, Katie," Michiko whispered, her
words not meant for Edward who stood several steps
behind her, his expression grim. When Katie said a
cool good-bye, he merely nodded curtly. The taxi
driver finished loading her things, and Katie turned
once more to Michiko, who now stood next to
Edward, meekly deferring to his wishes.

"Good-bye, Michiko," Katie said and wondered
what would happen to her old friend now. She knew
Edward's main reason for marrying her was for her
money and to further his career. The thought revived

her anger, and without another word, she stepped into the cab and banged the door shut behind her. Edward was a mean man.

Upon arriving at her new home, Katie quickly settled in, but wished the apartment was not so cramped for space. As the weeks passed, she wondered how she'd ever afford something better. Although Grace was a considerate roommate, she was also dull and unimaginative and ultimately added to Katie's growing sense of hopelessness. Her job at the school was limited, and she knew she must get some training for a better position.

Her visits with Michiko were the high points of her week. Edward, still furious with the Konos and with Katie, didn't approve of Michiko and Katie's seeing each other, so the visits were never mentioned to him.

"Soon things will be better, Katie," Michiko said one day. "My husband has new job, with another import firm. He'll feel better now."

But after Katie questioned Michiko further, she realized that Edward's job had no status; it was only a flunky position with a small company. As she walked Michiko to the bus stop, Katie was thoughtful. Edward's meanness was easy to explain, even if she couldn't like it. She'd come to see that he was terribly insecure and inadequate, raised in the shadow of their father whose strong traits had probably been hard for Edward to live up to as he was dragged around the world throughout his childhood. And he had to know that the only reason he'd been hired at Kono Imports in the first place was because of family ties, another blow to his fragile ego. Now that he'd ruined his one chance for position and wealth, she suspected he felt saddled with Michiko, a Japanese wife who adored him nevertheless.

No, Michiko, my old friend, I don't think anything

will be better very soon, she thought, as Michiko waved from the bus. But Katie hoped she was wrong.

By Christmas Edward had declared an uneasy truce, and the three of them spent Christmas Day together. It was the first time that Katie had set foot in the house since she left, but she didn't fool herself that the rift was forgotten. Michiko was proud of her turkey dinner and served it with her announcement, "See Katie, I'm becoming American now."

In the New Year Katie signed up for business and typing classes, anticipating a better job once school was out for the summer. But by April she still felt discouraged, hardly believing it was already well into 1939. The blustery wind that blew the sea fragrance off the bay was a poignant reminder of kite-flying and visits to the Konos' Hiroshima home. She welcomed Michiko's visit that afternoon and their shared reminiscences of earlier times. Even though Michiko had confessed, in halting sentences, that she rarely went out in public with Edward—he was too conscious of disapproving stares—she didn't seem unhappy.

"People don't approve of Edward's marrying me," Michiko confided, as though her cloistered life wasn't Edward's fault. "Life is strange—Japanese don't approve either."

Katie was at a loss. Prejudice was so useless and stupid. Not wanting to shatter their pleasant afternoon, she was about to change the subject when Michiko did it instead.

She put down her tea cup, her expression suddenly radiant. "Oh Katie, I am—oh, so happy." She lowered her lashes shyly. "Edward and I are expecting a child—that is, I'm going to have a baby."

She looked so happy that Katie immediately concealed her first shocked response. Instead she hugged

Michiko, while her fears whirled unspoken in her mind. Oh, dear God! What will happen to Michiko now? Will a child make a difference in how Edward treats her?

Bubbling with plans for her baby, Michiko talked non-stop while Katie listened, feigning enthusiasm when she felt foreboding. "Don't you think it's time to write home now, Michiko?" Katie suggested gently. "Surely this will make a difference to your parents—their first grandchild?" Katie was also thinking of the world situation; remembered words of Kenkichii Kono often surfaced in her mind. War was closer, as he'd predicted; it was hovering on the very horizon. She worried that Michiko might be no safer in America than Katie would have been in Japan, if war were declared.

"No, Katie." Her long hair fell forward as she inclined her head in a slight bow. "My baby will only symbolize my lack of honor."

Michiko's pain was so obvious that Katie wished she'd kept her mouth shut. She wasn't sure Michiko was right, but she knew Michiko was too deeply hurt, and guilt-ridden, to be the first to write.

Later that night, after Katie had written yet another letter to Johanna, she made a snap decision and wrote to Tak herself. She reminded him that Michiko's position in America was similar to what hers had been in Japan. "You know Michiko," Katie wrote. "She'd never intentionally hurt anyone." She went on to give Michiko's side of the story, ending with the news of the baby and an apology for Edward's part in the affair. She signed her name, then stared at the letter for a long time, remembering. But she mailed it before she changed her mind.

Sleep didn't come easily to Katie that night. She worried about ever finding Johanna, and about Michiko's unborn child, a baby who would be half

Kono and half Aaland. Tears came unbidden. The baby would have the same blood as the child she would never have—hers and Tak's.

Dawn was a faint glow on the horizon when sleep finally overtook her. Her last thought was of that long-ago day when Edward and Johanna left for America. Once the future had held great promise for the Aalands. Now her family, her life itself, had shattered into many pieces. As feisty as she was, Katie felt adrift in a world seemingly never meant for her.

Then she slept.

It's nonsense to feel depressed, she told herself sternly. Katie clung to the side of the packed cable car as it hurtled down the hills, braking and sounding its warning bell at each cross-street. The wind whipped her hair and tore at her slacks and jacket, exhilarating her with the wonder of being alive. She noticed more than one admiring male glance, and her confidence lifted higher. She was young and healthy and *did* have a future. Once she'd made the decision to buy an authentic Japanese kite in the shop by the bay, her spirits had risen considerably. Now she was on her way to a waterfront park where she'd fly it, let it lift into the sky and soar out over the water, and she would pretend she was back in Japan.

She walked the last few blocks, and with each step her anticipation grew. Once at the park she noticed other kites, many of them diving and soaring inconsistantly from the inexperience of the person holding the string. In only a few minutes, she was ready, galloping along the bank, her face to the sky. For a moment she felt fourteen again, and nothing was dangerous or sad, and love was all around her. She could almost smell the chrysanthemums and tiny oranges and the soft scent of senwood. So enthralled was she, with her eyes on the tumbling kite that was already higher than the others, that Katie ran full-tilt into something solid.

She was knocked backward, and the stick with the wound string flew out of her hand. As she fought for balance, a strong arm grabbed her and set her roughly on her feet. She glimpsed a tall man with dark hair and eyes, his expression concerned. Disconcerted by the accident—and his closeness—she didn't know whether to yell at him for almost knocking her down, or thank him. For a long moment her gaze was held by his, and she noticed surprise—and admiration?—on his face.

As she was about to speak, a child's voice cried out for help behind them. She glanced at the water. A boy of six or seven had fallen into the bay, flailing and struggling to keep his face above the ripples breaking over his head. His young mother jumped up and down on the bank, screaming for help, unable to reach him.

"I can't swim! Oh God! Someone save my boy!"

In a flash Katie knew the child would drown. Her kite and the dark man forgotten, she was across the green in seconds, kicking off her shoes and throwing her jacket aside as she went. She could hear the man right behind her as she plunged into the icy water. For a second the cold took her breath away. She disregarded it, her fear for the child uppermost in her mind. The current was strong, fighting her. As she reached the boy, he grabbed her around the neck, terror-stricken, and they both went down. Katie struggled with him, but she couldn't make him loosen his grip. Sudden panic filled her. Her lungs burned for air. *We're both going to drown!* she thought. She couldn't control the child and fight the pull of the tide too.

Then strong hands grabbed them both, and they were yanked to the surface, Katie and the boy coughing and choking for breath.

"Take it easy. I've got you. It's all right."

The man's voice calmed, even while it demanded obedience. Katie suddenly knew they'd make it. Even the boy responded and stopped struggling. The man guided their way back to shore, where the mother claimed her child, sobbing hysterically.

"Jonathan! Oh, Jonathan! You're a naughty boy— but—" She broke off, hugging and kissing him, unmindful of the saltwater staining her dress.

"He would have drowned but for both of you," she told Katie and the man beside her.

Katie glanced at her rescuer. His clothes clung wetly, just like hers. He was a big man, bigger even than she'd realized when she'd run into him. He was the one who'd saved their lives, and she said so.

"Thanks." She pushed her dripping hair from her eyes. "For a few minutes there I thought the boy and I were finished."

"You saved the boy," he said, meeting her gaze. "If you hadn't gotten to him when you did, I'd have been too late. The undertow would have sucked him under."

"But you saved us both," she insisted, her sense of right not allowing herself full credit. Her teeth began to chatter, taking some of her dignity from her words. She suddenly felt cold—and shaky.

Their brief exchange was interrupted when another man came running from the parking lot and introduced himself as Fenton Stone, the boy's father. In the ensuing confusion, Katie and her rescuer were thanked again and again by the grateful parents. Then Fenton Stone pressed a business card into Katie's hand.

"I'll never forget what you did," he said, still shaken. "If you ever need anything, anything at all, let me know."

He and his wife bundled the trembling, subdued boy into a blanket and hurried him off to their waiting Buick. Katie glanced at the card, not recognizing the name. But she did recognize the firm he worked for. They'd just rescued the son of the president of the largest brokerage house in San Francisco.

"Well. That's that," the man said, a note of humor in his voice. Katie turned to him and was surprised to see he was grinning at her.

"What's so funny?" she managed, aware of how she must look to him.

He cocked a dark brow and his grin widened. She noticed that his teeth were slightly crooked, and very white against his dark skin, that although he wasn't typically handsome, he had a presence—a very male presence—that was attractive.

"Some might say you're impetuous, Ma'am . . . Miss?" he said. His brown eyes took in her clothes that clung wetly to her body, her long hair that molded her head, and her green eyes that flashed hotly under long, half-lowered lashes. He saw he'd annoyed her and was intrigued even further. She was lovely, exciting . . . and unpredictable. He couldn't hide his amusement.

"Some might even say you leap before you look. Some—not me—might say you're dangerous as hell without a horn blaring ahead to announce you."

For a brief second she got mad. "And some might say you don't know enough to get out of the way!"

"*Touché.*"

For another second she was at a loss. The man didn't respond in a manner she was used to. He was more open—more able to express his feelings. And he looked so darned funny—a six-foot, four-inch man who was at least two hundred pounds of lean muscle and bone, all soggy—that it was hard to feel mad at him. Besides, he'd saved her life.

He watched, fascinated by her honest scrutiny. But he had no way of knowing that all her feelings were not expressed on her face—that for the first time since Tak Kono, Katie felt her heart thump out of its normal rhythm.

"I'm Katie Aaland." She put out her hand.

"Max. Massimiliano Stefanini," he said and waited, as though he expected a reaction from her.

The name had a familiar sound, but it took a few seconds for it to register. Her eyes widened as he flashed another grin. Stefanini was her sister Johanna's last name. Was this Max her husband?

He anticipated her questions. "Johanna is my sister-in-law, Katie, not my wife."

She nodded, still shifting mental gears. Hearing about Johanna at that moment was the last thing she'd expected.

"How—?"

"Your roommate—a Grace Adams—described you and said you'd be at this park flying a Japanese kite."

She could only stare, too many questions clamoring in her mind to give one precedence. But one thing stood out above everything—she'd found her sister!

"I've brought a message from Johanna," Max went on gently, realizing that his words had gone deep. He hesitated, his eyes drinking in her blond beauty; she was so different from Johanna! "She wants you to come to Alaska."

Katie suddenly realized that her kite was gone with the wind, soaring freely over the city. But her conversation with Max Stefanini was just beginning. With one of her flashes of intuition, she knew her life was about to change yet again.

CHAPTER 4

THE WIND STILLED, ALLOWING THE AFTERNOON SUN TO warm the day. As Katie listened to the deep, calm voice of the man who'd rescued her, hearing news of her sister in Alaska, her teeth stopped chattering.

"And, as I said, Johanna hopes you will accept her invitation," Max finished, his words trailing off into a sudden silence.

Katie had been watching his expression, fascinated by the dominant thrust of his chin, the farseeing look in his dark eyes. He was a man of action. Even his deep voice denoted authority—a take-command tone. He was a force to reckon with, she decided, and then realized he watched her as well, his gaze discerning—and interested.

But in the second before she could react to his look, he took her arm and led her across the grass to

a park bench, grabbing her jacket and shoes from the
ground as they went.

"Are you okay? Warm enough to talk a while?"

She nodded. The chill had gone from her body.
Her dripping clothes no longer clung to her skin and
were already beginning to dry under the unseasona-
ble heat of the sun.

"Hey! Would you like to borrow a blanket?" a
voice called.

A young man had risen off his own blanket that
was spread on the grass a short distance away. He
held out an extra one to Katie as he approached their
bench. "I saw what happened. You were some picture, lady. A real flying machine—saved the kid's
life."

Smiling, Katie shook her head. "Not without
some help. But thanks—and for the blanket." She
took it, knowing it would be a shield against a
sudden return of the wind. And a glance at Max told
her that he might be chilled, too, although he seemed
unaffected by his wet state.

The man inclined his head, then went back to his
pretty companion. Katie draped half the blanket
around her, then offered the other half to Max. But
as soon as he took it, she knew it was a mistake. Both
using the same wrap brought them so close that their
shoulders and thighs touched. Katie was suddenly so
aware of Max that, for a moment, she felt disconcerted, even flustered.

Absurd, she thought. And silly to feel such a
reaction to a man she'd only laid eyes on within the
past hour. She willed her heart to slow, her hands to
still on her lap. *Have I forgotten* kendo *so soon and
lost all control of self?* she asked herself. Remembering the teaching of the *sensei* calmed her, and she
could again face Max with only thoughts of her sister
reflected on her face.

Direct sunlight struck her features as she met his

gaze, and Max forgot what he was about to say. Her
skin shone with the purity of fine silk, flawless over
delicate bone structure. But it was her eyes that
caught him and held his breath deep in his chest for a
long, heart-stopping moment. They sparkled more
brilliantly than any green he'd ever seen, trapping
pinpoints of light in their depths—expressive eyes,
and at the same time mysterious. She's controlled,
he thought, and wondered again about how different
she was from Johanna. This Katie was a self-
possessed young woman, but something about the
full curve of her lips, the upward tilt, suggested a
passionate nature as well. He was intrigued. He
wanted to know more about Katie Aaland.

A fickle ripple of wind brought the salty fragrance
of the sea, and then receded again. Behind Max,
Katie could see the other kiters giving up and putting
their gear away. The wind was no longer conducive
to flying. But kites and wind were not uppermost in
Katie's thoughts. She wanted to know more about
Johanna—and Alaska.

"Where in Alaska does Johanna live? I understand
that it's a huge territory."

Her voice was low and sounded slightly exotic in
both cadence and accent, although she spoke perfect
English. But it also reflected a sincere need to know,
and that eased the awkwardness between them.

He nodded. "Its coastline is longer than the whole
American coastline. It's vast, much of it unexplored,
some of it unchartered. Johanna and Dion live in the
interior—Fairbanks."

"Is that where you live too?"

He nodded again. "It's the base for our flying
service."

"You're also a pilot—like your brother Dion?"

"Uh-huh."

Katie digested the information. She assumed that
Dion was older, as it was obvious that Max, despite

his mature bearing, was twenty-six or seven at most, and therefore must be the younger of the two brothers. "Our flying service?" she repeated, and jumped to a conclusion. "So you work for Dion?"

Something flickered in his eyes and was gone. He reached into his shirt pocket for a cigarette, then crumpled the wet package before lobbing it into a nearby garbage can. "I'm the owner of the company, responsible for all its growing pains and not so occasional dips into the red ink on the ledger," he replied finally with a wry laugh. "Dion works for me. We have two planes, and we mostly fly the route between Anchorage and Fairbanks, although we take anything else we get as well."

While she wondered what 'anything else' meant, he went on to explain that the route was several hundred miles over mountain ranges, and few people lived between the two towns. "Alaska is different from anywhere else. It's a frontier—and a challenge. It's a place where a man can build his empire, if he's got the guts to do it."

His last words almost throbbed with ambition and determination. The longer he talked, the more Katie realized that Max was not an easy man to know, for all his appearance of openness. The little she'd seen and heard told her there was a great deal more to him. And she suddenly wanted to hear all about his life, and Johanna's and Dion's.

They talked for a long time, and Katie gave him a brief account of her life in Japan and what had happened to her parents; she told him that she'd wanted to stay and couldn't.

"Jesus!" he said, his expression compassionate. "It must have been tough. My parents died relatively young too, so I understand how you must have felt." He hesitated, and glanced out over the harbor. "It's hell—until you get over it."

When he didn't elaborate, she was curious about

the circumstances, but refrained from questioning him, as she sensed his reluctance—and a deep hurt.

Instead, he changed the subject to explain that both he and Dion had flown planes in South America after their parents were gone. "I wasn't much more than a kid, but Dion took me along, and that's where I really learned how to fly." He went on to say that they'd returned to San Francisco after two years because it was where they'd been born, the place they called home. He shrugged, and a smile touched his lips briefly. "I didn't stay long; I headed north to Alaska where flying opportunities were opening up to pilots. And I've been there ever since."

"When did Dion meet Johanna?" His overview of the past few years, although interesting, was vague, and Katie didn't understand how Johanna fit into the picture. Or how Max had come to own the flying service while his older brother only worked for him. His narration had gone from *we* to *I*.

"Almost seven years ago, when we came back to Frisco. They fell in love and married, then followed me north a year later, after I'd bought my first plane and settled in Fairbanks." He shifted on the bench, allowing some of the blanket to fall from him. "They lived in Anchorage and several other places before ending up in Fairbanks too." Max's gaze followed the distant ships slicing across the bay, his lids lowered against the glint of sun on the water. "After they arrived, I went into hock for a second plane— and Dion went to work for me."

"Not into partnership with you?" Her curiosity got the best of her and Katie had to ask.

He glanced at her sharply, his eyes suddenly unreadable. "I used my South American savings to start a business. Dion used his to get married."

Although she didn't mind directness, there was a note in his tone that was meant to rebuff her. She wondered if it was because of her question, or because he disapproved of his brother's marriage. She suddenly realized how little she knew of Johanna and her life. Was she happily married? Was she a good wife, Dion a good husband? Annoyance pricked her. Whatever the answer was, she'd picked up on something amiss with Max, and she wanted him to explain.

"I sense something—a resentment?—behind your words, Max. Didn't you approve of Johanna's marrying your brother?" She was equally direct, and it took him by surprise.

"I like your sister very much," he retorted, looking vaguely annoyed himself. He hadn't realized that he'd given away his feelings, but he had no intention of telling her that his brother often jumped into situations before he thought about ramifications— and often it was those around him who suffered. If Katie had been anyone else, he'd t$ll her to mind her own damn business.

"But I detect disapproval," she insisted with a determined set of her chin, not satisfied. Although she hardly remembered Johanna, Katie wasn't about to tolerate even a suggestion of criticism concerning her sister.

His sudden grin disarmed her, and his eyes, crinkling at the corners, were warm with humor. He put up his hands in mock surrender. "I don't disapprove of your sister, Miss Katie Aaland. I promise and cross my heart—and hope to die if I'm lying," he added with a chuckle, but the childhood litany rang with conviction. "So don't get your dander up. The truth is that I'm very fond of Johanna."

"Then—"

But he went on, more serious again, cutting her off. "I just have a different opinion about when a man should marry, and that concerns Dion, not Johanna."

"And when is that?"

"When he can afford to support a wife. I believe he should be financially solid before taking that long walk down the aisle."

Katie lowered her lashes. Max had just explained why his older brother worked for him. Obviously the two had opposite views on at least one subject. And it was equally obvious that Max had never loved a woman enough to give up something important for her. She wondered what financially secure meant to him. Yes, he was an enigma in some ways. And he'd raised yet another question—couldn't Dion support his wife without Max?

Abruptly he glanced at his watch. "Would you believe it's already four? Jesus! We've been sitting here for hours."

The blanket dropped from them as Max stood and took Katie's hand to pull her up beside him. "It's time I took you home so you can get out of those clothes."

Somehow they'd cleared the air. She laughed back at him and pushed her long hair away from her face as she spoke. "It's too late for that Max. I've already dried out." She folded the blanket as she talked, darting him a glance when she finished. "How about you?"

His deep baritone laugh pleased her somehow. "You're quite right," he agreed, equally pleasant, as though he too wanted to put any disagreements behind him. "I'm dry, if a little wrinkled." His dark eyes swept over her as she put on her jacket which gave her white shirt and black slacks a semblance of neatness.

Then he took her arm, leading her across the park toward the street that bordered the bay, pausing only once to return the blanket to the young couple. Upon reaching the sidewalk they continued in silence toward the cable car stop. They'd gone only half a block when Max stopped again, at the doorway of a waterfront restaurant.

"I've been in Alaska too long," he drawled. "Forgot my manners. How about a cup of coffee to warm up whatever is still cold from our dip in the bay?"

For only a moment Katie hesitated. Then she shot him another grin. "Why not? So long as they'll serve two bedraggled swimmers."

"As it's not the Ritz, I'm sure they will."

He again took her arm, and they went inside. No one seemed to notice their appearance, and they were immediately seated at a window overlooking the bay. Katie hid a smile; Max's self-confident manner precluded criticism. He insisted they have sandwiches with their coffee, and after the waitress brought the food they continued their earlier conversation.

"You never told me why you're in California," Katie said, sipping her coffee.

He'd bought a dry pack of cigarettes, and he lit one and blew smoke before answering. "I flew down with a friend because I'd heard about a good deal on a plane—a used one that's being overhauled. Once I looked it over, I grabbed it. The only hitch is that the work won't be completed for another couple of weeks, and I'll have to wait until it is so I can fly it back to Alaska."

"So you're adding to your fleet of airplanes." Katie hesitated, recognizing a passion in him—a passion for success. Katie wondered if he was as passionate about other things. "You're ambitious, Max," she mused aloud.

Without warning, her eyes were caught by his. Something passed between them, something powerful and silent and completely unnerving. Katie was the first to look away.

"I guess you could say that," he said, as though nothing had happened.

Another silence fell over their table, and Katie, anxious to stay composed, went on to the next subject. "So Johanna sent a message with you, rather than write a letter to give to me." She gave a short laugh. "Seems kind of odd."

"There wasn't time." Max ground out the cigarette, but he watched her, not the ashtray. "She received your letter on the same plane that took me to Anchorage. It was a turnaround flight. And the envelope had been forwarded three times by the time she received it."

It was suddenly clear why Johanna hadn't written over the past months; she hadn't gotten Katie's earlier letters, or Edward's either.

"She wanted you to know that she was writing immediately." Max hesitated. "She was quite upset to hear about her parents. Both Dion and I were worried about her, she being in such a fragile condition right now."

Katie put down her cup so fast it rattled on the saucer. "Johanna isn't well? What's wrong with her? Why didn't you tell me at once!"

"Oh, Christ!" His words were expelled on a quick sigh. "I'm sorry, Katie. I honestly didn't mean to scare you. Johanna doesn't have a terminal illness. She's pregnant, and has a history of miscarriages. She just has to take things easy, get lots of rest, that's all."

Her lashes fluttered with relief, and she averted her gaze to the hills across the bay, purpling now with the approach of evening. "I'm sorry too, Max, for jumping down your throat. It's just that I've hoped for so long to find Johanna—and then to think she was sick—" She broke off, struggling for a way to explain.

"Please, don't explain," Max said gently. "I understand."

Choked up suddenly, she managed a weak smile. Her reaction had surprised even her. She just hoped that the news of their parents' dying wouldn't cause Johanna to miscarry.

"Johanna will be fine," he said, and placed his hand over hers. Somehow the gesture calmed her. While she composed herself, he discreetly turned away to ask the waitress for more coffee. When he looked back, Katie had herself under control enough to ask more questions.

"How—how are medical facilities in Fairbanks? Are they adequate for pregnancy complications, Max?"

"We have doctors," he began carefully. "But Dion and Johanna have decided that she will go to Anchorage in a few months so she'll be close to a good hospital."

Lowering her lashes, Katie only nodded with a brief, "I see." But she wondered if Max, seeing her upset, was not telling her everything. And not knowing her sister, she had no way of knowing how serious the condition was for Johanna. All she knew was that she couldn't bear losing another family member.

"It would be good if you could manage a visit," Max said softly. "Do Johanna a world of good." He took his wallet out of his hip pocket and fingered through the soggy contents, extracting a twenty-dollar bill which he put down on the table. He didn't even glance at her when he added, "You're welcome to fly up with me when I go."

She was saved from an answer when the waiter came with Max's change. Later, he took her home on the cable car that clanked up the hills through the brightly lit city, and the chill of the night lowering around them seeped through Katie's clothes. They weren't completely dry after all, and suddenly they felt cold against her skin. The subject of going to Alaska didn't come up again until she was at her door.

"Just think about going, Katie," Max said, his tone hardly above a whisper. "Flying up the west coast would be the experience of a lifetime for you."

He stood so close that she could feel the warmth of his breath on her cheek, but she couldn't read his expression on the dimly lit porch. His face was all lines and angles and shadows. Yet something in his tone made her hesitate, not because she'd lost her tongue, but because her breath was trapped in her chest. Max had a strange and unpredictable effect on her, and she was at a loss to know how to react to it.

So she only nodded, and after he said he'd be in touch, he left her, his long strides taking him quickly into the night. She went inside with a sense of relief and a longing for her bed that quickly became a top priority. Katie was suddenly exhausted. Tomorrow was soon enough to think about all that had happened—when her head was clear.

But sleep eluded her. Her mind whirled in a kaleidoscope of changing scenes—her kite soaring, the boy in the water, and Max. After a while she got up and went to her desk. Her sister was on her mind and she felt compelled to write another letter. She now had Johanna's correct address from Max. When it was finished, Katie was finally able to sleep.

The apartment was quiet when she awoke late the next morning. She was glad that Grace had gone to Sunday service and she was free to have a long, undisturbed soak in the tub. By the time she was dressed, she'd decided to take Johanna's address to Edward, rather than simply call him on the phone. She quickly pulled on a sweater, grabbed her purse, and headed for the cable car to Russian Hill.

Michiko answered her knock, and her instant

smile welcomed Katie. They went into the living
room where Edward, still in his robe, sat reading the
Sunday paper.

"Good morning, Edward," Katie said, and as he
lowered the paper she saw by his expression that he
wasn't particularly happy to see her. She gave an
inward sigh; Edward was Edward. She doubted he'd
ever change.

"Tea, Katie?" Michiko asked, her eyes on her
husband, as though she asked for his approval.

He gave a curt nod, and Michiko scurried away to
the kitchen. Katie bit her lip and silently vowed to
keep the peace, for the sake of everyone. But she
hated to see Michiko being so subservient.

"I've heard from Johanna," she began. "And I
thought you'd want her address."

He put the paper aside. "Of course I want it," he
said curtly. "I haven't heard from her in months.
Where in that God-forsaken hole is she now?"

"Fairbanks, and it seems she's pregnant."

"Again?" Edward straightened in the overstuffed
chair. "Doesn't that damnable Dion ever learn that
it's dangerous for Johanna to be pregnant?" His tone
was quarrelsome, and Katie wondered if it stemmed
from his own discontent or a sincere regard for their
sister.

"So you know about her other miscarriages?"

"Yeah, but probably not the half of it. Come on,
Katie. Was there any good news from her?"

"I didn't have a letter, Edward. Only word through
Max, Dion's brother." Then she went on to tell him
about her meeting with Max, but she omitted the
incident of rescuing the boy, somehow knowing he
would find fault with her action. She handed him a
slip of paper with Johanna's address.

"Well, at least we know how to contact her now,"
Edward commented, his eyes scanning the sheet, his

tone softer. "Thanks, Katie," he added, surprising her. "I was worried."

Katie glanced away so that he couldn't see how his reaction affected her. Edward *was* sincere for once, and she was aware that the bond between him and Johanna didn't include her. She was on the outside looking in, and she wondered if they'd ever really accept her, a virtual stranger, as family. The insight hurt, and she felt the old loneliness move closer again. It was a relief when Michiko brought the tea, and for the next half hour she listened to talk of babies and layettes. When Edward, bored by the subject, went back to his paper, Katie took her leave. She was thoughtful all the way home, and sad, and again wondered about the course of her life. She felt depressed.

The phone was ringing when she opened the door, and she ran to answer it.

"It's Max," his deep voice said in her ear. "I'm glad I finally got you. Been ringing for the past hour."

"I was out," she began.

"Obviously." She heard a laugh in his tone. "But never mind," he went on without a pause. "I want to show you the sights—by plane."

"What do you mean?" Katie felt her old enthusiasm reassert itself.

"I've borrowed a friend's two-seater. I'm taking you for a spin up the coast—to see California from a bird's point of view." His voice was suddenly filled with that humor she'd glimpsed in his eyes—and liked.

"I'd love to. When?"

"Now. I'm right around the corner. Pick you up in ten minutes."

Before she could say another word, the line went dead. For a moment she stood with the receiver in her hand, her thoughts whirling. Then she ran to her bedroom, thinking about her hair and makeup and what she'd put on. She wanted to look better than the drowned rat of yesterday.

Excitement filled her; she bubbled with it. She remembered her first ride in an airplane. That had been with Tak—when she'd first realized how much she loved to fly. But it wasn't Tak who was on her mind when she examined herself in the mirror. It was Max.

CHAPTER 5

THE KNOCK ON THE FRONT DOOR SOUNDED EXACTLY TEN minutes later. Katie jumped up from her dressing table stool, went to her bed where she'd left her purse, and then ran to answer. In the small entry she hesitated, taking a final glance at herself in the hall mirror.

Her long hair shimmered from a touch of sunlight streaming through the narrow windows beside the door, and her cheeks were unusually pink—from rushing so fast, she told herself. A quick assessment of her green corduroy pants suit told her it fit to perfection and was a perfect match to her eyes. She smiled wryly, catching only a glimpse of white teeth and pink lipstick before moving to the door. She'd do. At least she looked quite different from the girl of yesterday.

She swung the door wide just as Max was about to knock again. For long seconds he didn't speak, his dark eyes caught by the girl who stood framed in the doorway. Although it was the same Katie of yesterday, it was a different Katie too. Her blonde hair shone like silver, framing a face that was tilted upward to meet his gaze. Even her lashes seemed to catch the sunlight, giving her eyes an even more mysterious look. As he continued to stare, her brows elevated in a question.

"Is something wrong?" she queried pertly as the silence stretched into awkwardness.

He gave himself a mental shake. "Uh—course not." He managed a grin and a normal tone. "Everything's great—including the weather."

It wasn't what he'd meant to say, but her directness again put him off balance, making him aware of how he was staring. He'd known she was beautiful, but the Katie before him was so breathtaking that it was hard for him to tear his eyes off her.

"Yes it is," she replied politely, but her expression had become guarded.

Was it possible she didn't realize how lovely she was? The thought was unexpected and Max explored it further as he stepped inside. Had her upbringing in Japan been so sheltered that she was unaware of how she appeared to others? He'd heard that vanity was not considered a strength of character in some Eastern cultures. And he didn't know Katie well enough to determine what her influences had been. But he knew one thing. It was amazing that she was unattached. And he also knew that he was glad she didn't belong to another man.

They'd become too aware of each other, both at a loss for words. Katie groped for something to say that would break the unexpected tension between them. Max spoke first.

"I was just admiring you," he said honestly. "Can't blame a man for staring when he sees a gorgeous woman. Am I forgiven?"

For a second Katie was even more flustered, until she heard the rich note of humor in his tone. She inclined her head, managed a shy smile, and then preceded him outside. As they walked to the Ford coupe at the curb, Max was already talking about the day's outing. Their awkward meeting was soon forgotten.

"You're in for a treat," he told her, glancing sideways as he maneuvered into traffic, a lock of black hair blowing rakishly in the wind from the open window. The car was borrowed from a friend, the same one who'd lent him a single-engine, open-cockpit plane for their flight up the coast. He drove with an ease that told her he would be an equally good pilot.

"I'm looking forward to it," she replied sincerely.

"The plane is old, but reliable—and it's so open it may feel like you're riding on its wings." Again he shot her a glance, and his dark eyes challenged her. "You're not scared of heights, are you?"

Her return grin was spontaneous. "I guess we'll soon find out," she replied and didn't explain how much she'd loved the one time she'd flown, or that she'd often wished she could learn to fly herself. She didn't think the open cockpit would scare her. She hoped not.

"What happens if I get scared—or sick?" she asked instead.

His response was a flash of white teeth. "Then I'll take care of you," he said with a matter-of-fact voice and swung the car onto the road that led to the airport.

A few minutes later Max had parked the coupe, led her to the plane, and given her a leather jacket and a pair of goggles to put on. He gave her instructions as he helped her strap into the seat behind his. Satisfied, he took his own place, revved up the engine, and then glanced back at her.

"All set?" he shouted over the din, his eyes hidden behind the goggles.

She nodded, and hoped she was. The airplane looked far more fragile and dangerous than she'd expected, and the roar of its engine was deafening, as if it would explode at any moment. But it was too late to change her mind; Max already had it taxiing down the runway. A few seconds later they left the ground and climbed into the blue afternoon sky. For a moment, the bottom dropped out of her stomach, but as the plane leveled out, Katie relaxed and began to enjoy herself. It was the ultimate sense of freedom to soar over the earth, her hair streaming behind her, secure in her seat but open to the elements. It was heady and invigorating, and Katie laughed aloud from the joy of it.

Max turned once, saw her pleasure and gave her a thumbs-up sign. He waved and gestured at the sights below—the redwood forest she and Michiko had visited, tiny towns and winding roads, vineyards and farms, the terrain more sparsely populated as they followed the coastline north. Katie was sorry when he finally turned the plane in a wide swoop over the ocean and headed back toward the airport. The landing was so smooth that Katie was hardly aware when the wheels touched down.

"So—how'd you like it?" Max pulled off his gloves and goggles and climbed onto the wing to help her.

"I loved it!" Her eyes were bright with the thrill of flying, her cheeks flushed and her smile of pleasure so genuine that Max felt his breath catch once again.

He was pleased. He'd expected—what? Certainly

not the joy he saw expressed on Katie's face, a love of flying he'd only seen in men who were addicted to being pilots because once they'd flown they could never be earthbound again. He smiled at his introspection as he helped her to the ground.

So excited was she about the outing that Katie talked all the way to the small office where Max returned the key to the airplane. A short man stood up from his desk as they entered and asked about their flight. Max introduced the man as Al Barnes, the friend who owned the Ford and the plane.

"It was such fun!" Katie told him. "Far more so than my first plane ride in Japan—the open cockpit made it a thrilling experience."

For some reason, Katie's revelation surprised Max. How would she have flown in Japan? Her parents had been teachers in an English school and, according to Johanna, were very proper people. The information only added to her air of mystery. He wondered if the pilot had been young and male.

"Japan, eh?" Al replied, his expression curious. "Bet you're glad you're not there now. The newspapers say that the damn Japanese are about to join up with Hitler—the bastard! He just marched into Prague and took over the whole Czechoslovak republic."

The joy of the day suddenly drained out of Katie. But before she could respond, Max said their goodbyes and led Katie back outside.

"Al didn't know he was saying something that would upset you," Max said as they walked. "He was simply expressing the opinion of most Americans. And he was talking about governments, not the people."

"I know that, Max," she replied. "I'm not a child!" But her harsh retort belied her words.

"Hey!" He brought her to an abrupt stop. "Let's

not spoil the day with war talk. I know you love
Japan, and I respect that." He hesitated. "Truce?"

For a moment longer, she hesitated. She thought
he was angry until she saw the little lights glowing
deep in his eyes. But she wouldn't have thought he
was struggling with a grin had she not seen the
quirking at the sides of his mouth.

Laughing—at her?

And then she saw the funny side too. She was like a
protective mother hen when it came to the country
she had loved so much. And where was her Eastern
training now—especially the part that taught patience with another person's opinion? She allowed a
little smile. She was becoming Americanized faster
than she'd thought possible, falling into the habit of
letting her feelings show.

He watched her face, noted the expressions, and
was relieved. Without a word, he dropped an arm
around her shoulders, and they continued on to the
Ford.

"How about grabbing a bite to eat and then taking
in a movie?" he asked, changing the subject completely. "There's a new Western in town—
Stagecoach, with John Wayne." He hesitated. "How
about it?"

They were sitting on the front seat, their shoulders
touching, Max's hand on the key in the ignition.
He'd turned to her, his eyes squinting against the
bright sunlight. But Katie saw something else in their
depths that sent her heart into a flutter. He seemed
poised for some action, and she sensed his hesitation, as though that action was not the norm to him.

Was he about to take her in his arms? she wondered
suddenly. Fear and anticipation and something else
—desire?—filled her with instant turmoil. She lowered her lashes, uncertain of how she'd handle things
if he did.

"I'd—I'd love seeing the movie, Max," she managed in a normal tone.

Another moment of silence passed before he replied and restored their earlier rapport. "Good," he said cheerfully, and then started the car. "And I know a terrific little cafe down on the bay—nothing fancy, but great food and a great view."

The Ford took off in a sputter and a cloud of dust. But Katie hardly noticed. *Coward*, she told herself. *What in God's name are you afraid of?*

But she knew.

The day after their plane ride, the blustery weather returned. Even when the sun shone, the wind continued to blow, bringing a salty fragrance that reminded Katie of her ocean voyage from Japan. Although she spoke to Michiko on the phone, her days were so busy that she had no time to visit with her old friend. But Michiko sounded content and looked forward to fall, when her baby would be born. Still, Katie couldn't help her own qualms about Edward and his self-serving ways. She just prayed Michiko would always be content with her life in America.

Her work at the school intensified as summer vacation approached, adding hours to her weekly schedule, but Katie still saw Max almost every day. Even her roommate commented on his attentiveness. They went for walks, saw movies, and had dinners together. And they talked. Katie found herself telling him about Edward and Michiko, and how the Konos had reacted to their marriage. For all she told him of her childhood, he was strangely silent about his, although he talked in great length about his life in Alaska. Katie was more and more drawn to him. She began to dread the day when he would fly north. And she realized that he was becoming impatient about the delays on his plane, even though she was secretly glad that its delivery date kept being postponed. She would miss Max after he was gone, more than she cared to admit.

But on the weekend when Max took her sailing on the bay, his leaving was the last thing on her mind. She'd decided to enjoy the time with him and let the future take care of itself.

"I used to sail every chance I got when I was a kid," he told her.

They worked together to ready the fourteen-foot sailboat. Katie followed his instructions eagerly and disregarded a sudden impression that he was sometimes amused by her attempts to help. *He's different today*, she thought as he saw to the sails and rigging. Clad in white trousers and a butter-yellow cotton shirt, he looked as muscular and fit as any sailor—and oh, so handsome!

Katie wore white cotton pants as well, topped by a sailor blouse, its large collar trimmed with blue braiding, its neckline plunging to a deep vee between her full breasts. She'd wondered if it was too daring, but Grace had reassured her, so Katie had worn it. She had no idea how attractive she appeared to Max with her hair tied back with a ribbon and her figure molded by her clothing.

"That's it!" he cried from the bow. "We're all set to go." He showed her where to sit out of the way of the rigging, careful to keep his feelings hidden behind his friendliness, because for all her daring and headlong ways, he realized that she was inexperienced with men. The last thing he wanted to do was scare her away.

The sails billowed in the wind as they left the dock behind, skimmed over the bay that was dotted with other sails, and headed toward the Golden Gate Bridge. Very soon Katie's hair loosened from the ribbon to fly behind her, and Max took advantage of being able to watch her without her being aware of his gaze. The fluid lines of her body, the occasional glimpse he had of her profile—the perfection of her—stirred him with desire. He knew he was falling in love with her—that he wanted her and couldn't bear the thought of leaving her behind when he left California.

The wind had taken them under the Golden Gate and then back when it suddenly died, leaving the sails deflated, their boat stilled on the water between the shore and Alcatraz Island. Sea gulls swooped above them, their poignant cries reminding Katie that they too were affected by the lack of wind currents.

Katie turned suddenly and caught Max's eyes. She grinned. "Does this mean we start rowing?"

His baritone laugh rang out over the water. "No, my sweet. It means it's time to eat."

As he spoke, Max pulled a basket from under a seat and then moved to the middle of the boat so that they could sit facing each other. He placed the basket between them, then uncorked a wine bottle and poured the rich Burgundy into glasses he'd packed with the food. Their eyes met again as he handed one to Katie.

"You're a man of surprises," she told him, conscious of keeping her tone normal. She hadn't noticed the picnic basket before, as she'd met him at the pier and he'd already loaded the boat.

His brows quirked, and a slow smile softened the lines of his face. Katie's breath caught, her lashes fluttered nervously, and she was suddenly aware of their closeness. Even though thousands of people lived in the city a short distance away, she suddenly felt as if they were cut off from the world.

"True. I *am* a man of surprises," he agreed, and as she wondered if there were another meaning to his words, he sliced French bread and piled white cheese and roast beef on each piece.

"How's that?" he asked, handing her one and looking amused as she contemplated the thickness of the sandwich.

"Wonderful," Katie said after taking a bite. "Makes me realize how ravenous I am."

"Salt water does it every time," he said.

They ate in companionable silence as the boat drifted. Occasionally the wind caught at the sails and Max adjusted their course. The sandwiches were followed with refills of wine, and Katie found herself feeling more relaxed, less fearful of meeting the dark eyes that admired her openly now.

"You're a good sailor, Max," she told him at one point. "Did your father teach you to sail?"

"No, my father was already dead by then." The hesitancy she'd sensed before was back in the briefness of his response. "A fisherman, another Italian immigrant who'd known my father, was the one who taught both Dion and me the power of the wind." He'd been looking beyond her, remembering, and now he glanced back to light a cigarette. "But Dion and I both became flyers, not sailors," he added with a wry laugh.

Katie nodded. She understood what he meant by the wind. She'd often felt its power while flying kites. Sailing, flying or kiting, the wind made all the difference. You either had the knack to gage it, or you didn't.

The water lapped gently against the side of the boat, and for a while neither spoke. "It must have been hard for your mother after your father died," she said finally. "I gather he died first."

"God-damned hard," he agreed, giving his head a vigorous shake, as though to banish the memory. "After he was gone, she worked herself to death so the three of us could eat." His gaze held hers through another long pause. "Unlike you, Katie, I grew up poor—dirt poor." He tossed his cigarette into the bay. "And I never mean to be poor again."

She felt at a loss. She wished she hadn't been so nosy. Now anything she might say would sound superficial. But she couldn't just sit there as though he hadn't shared something important.

"I'm sorry, Max. Your mother must have been a fine woman. And that has to be a good memory."

"It is, to a point. My regret is that she didn't live long enough for me to give her a better life." He poured the last of the wine into their glasses. "It helps that our old neighborhood is gone now—it's a junkyard, or a dump or something." He shrugged. "I never go back. It's the future that counts now, and making a success of my flying service."

"I'm sure you will, Max," she said, and understood why he seemed so motivated to succeed. But the realization also deflated her somehow. He would never commit himself to a woman until he felt financially secure. His past sorrows would never allow it.

The wind picked up as they finished the wine, and evening brought them back to the dock, tired and wind-blown and ready to call it a day. He drove her home through the quiet, dark streets, then walked her to the door.

"Thanks for a glorious day, Max."

She'd turned back to him and found him right behind her, so close that his face was only inches above hers. And she couldn't step away because she was already against the front door.

"Come with me to Alaska, Katie," Max whispered, passing over her thanks with his more important words.

"I haven't decided yet, Max." She managed to get the words out, but they sounded pinched from her sudden lack of breath.

"Johanna needs you. I get my plane next week—
and then I have to go."

"I have my job," Katie hedged, uncertain. "School
isn't out for two more weeks, and I couldn't go
before that. I can't let them down."

"I'll wait for you." His voice had dropped even
lower, seducing, coaxing.

Her lashes fluttered nervously under his persist-
ence. She wanted to go—there was Johanna. But
then, there was Michiko too. She ran her tongue over
her lips. And if Max left without her, he would take
the joy of her days with him. Despite her feelings for
him, the uncertainty remained. She was torn in two
directions.

And then she was in his arms, his mouth closed
over hers. His kiss was slow, gentle, but it jolted her
with a sensation she'd never experienced before. At
that moment she wanted to stay in his arms forever,
held with tenderness against his body, cherished and
protected like his most treasured possession.

Gradually, as his kiss deepened, Katie's thoughts
narrowed to only one—a powerful urge to submit,
because it felt so right. She was unaware when her
body moved slightly, arching to meet his, or when
she began to kiss him back. His response was instantaneous. His arms tightened, and his mouth demanded more, until her lips parted for him. One
gentle kiss wasn't enough—for either of them.

But it was Max who finally stepped back. His
breath was ragged, and when he spoke he sounded
hoarse with the passion he tried to master. "It's time
you went inside, Katie."

Still shaken by the sensations so new to her, Katie
could only stare at him. Strangely, she didn't feel
rejected, only relieved because he'd had the good
sense to stop. Her feelings were in tatters, because
she knew if he took her back in his arms, she'd be
lost again. It was unsettling. Katie knew something

had been awakened in her that would never sleep
again. She'd just glimpsed what it meant to be a
woman desired by a man.

She nodded and lowered her eyes, abruptly shy in
her new awareness. He took hold of her again, and
for several minutes they just stood holding each
other loosely, her head against his chest. Finally, she
knew she must go inside. They couldn't just stand
there, in view of anyone who passed on the street, as
if they were frozen in a strange mating dance.

As though she communicated her thoughts, he
gently set her aside, but the passion was still in his
eyes, and it fed her own cooling need again. But she
managed to control it this time.

"I'll need your decision—about Alaska—soon,
sweetheart."

"I know," she whispered, because her throat muscles didn't want to work.

"Goodnight, Katie."

She gave a slight nod, and it felt as if she were
leaving something vital when she went inside. Then
she heard the Ford sputter away from the curb.

"Oh, God," she prayed while she lay in the darkness of her room a few minutes later. "Show me what
I must do."

After a while a peace settled over her, and somehow she knew the answer would come. So she went
to sleep, a smile on her lips, and the dark, lean face of
Max pictured in her mind.

"Oh Lord!"

She sat up with a start. A glance at the clock told
her she'd overslept. Quickly she showered and
dressed, skipped breakfast, and ran out the door,
afraid of missing her bus and being late for work. As
she turned the key in the lock, her gaze fell on the
mailbox, and the line of white showing through the
slot. She'd forgotten to check the mail over the

weekend, and now, as she grabbed the envelope, she saw that it was addressed to her. But she didn't have time to do more than glance at it; the bus could already be approaching her stop.

The driver waited as she ran to catch the bus, and once she was seated and had caught her breath, she looked at the letter more carefully. It was stamped Fairbanks, Alaska. And the name on the return address was Johanna's. Her heart racing, Katie tore it open and scanned the page. Then she sat back, thoughtful.

But as the bus wound its way through the streets, stopping at every other corner, she read the letter again. Johanna's sadness for her dead parents was apparent in every sentence.

"I always believed I'd see them again," she wrote. "It seems so terrible that they've been dead all these months and I didn't know. Oh, dear little sister Katie, let's not let the time go by and not know each other. I so wish you'd come to Alaska for a visit."

She mentioned her pregnancy, that she had had "a few problems," and ended with another request to visit—reminding that by flying north with Max, Katie would even save transportation costs.

"Miss? Isn't this your stop?" The driver, who was a regular on her route, had twisted around in his seat to call to her.

With a start, she saw that he was right. Quickly she gathered her things, thanked him, and stepped off the bus. All the way to school several blocks away, and then during a busy morning, Katie's thoughts returned to Johanna's letter, and the message she read between the lines. Her sister needed her.

But it was during her lunch break that she suddenly made up her mind. She had prayed for an answer; Johanna's letter was it. Still, Katie hesitated; there was Michiko. But her next thought reminded her that she was out of a job when school dismissed for the summer. And Max, having anticipated her need to work, had offered her a part-time job in his office, enabling her to pay her own way in Alaska. Her decision was almost made, but she decided to talk with Edward and Michiko before it was final.

She phoned Michiko to say she was coming by after school and was invited for supper. After she'd hung up, Katie realized that Michiko had invited her without first asking Edward, and she wondered how he'd react to that. So later, on her way to their house, she stopped and bought a loaf of her brother's favorite bread and some freshly baked lemon tarts for dessert.

For once, the visit was congenial, to Katie's relief. It was only later, in the living room when they were having coffee, that she brought out Johanna's letter and handed it to Edward. She and Michiko, who already knew about it, waited as he read.

"Of course you're not going, Katie," he said, throwing down the letter. "Johanna is a damn fool to live in such a God-forsaken hole. To go would look as if we approved of their stupid move."

His harshness took Katie aback. She had expected his response to be concern for Johanna. But she should have known. Edward never did the right thing.

"Johanna doesn't sound like a fool to me," Katie replied tartly. "She sounds genuinely sad about our parents, and I believe she needs family support. I get the feeling that she's not at all well."

"She and that husband of hers should have thought of that before they left California. And come to that, Dion could move her back now—but he's too damned selfish."

Katie set her cup down so hard her coffee spilled into the saucer. "That's all beside the point, isn't it,

Edward? They do live in Fairbanks, and I suspect
Johanna has no more say about where she lives
than—than—" She broke off, then blurted the rest.
"Than Michiko has about where you decide to live."

An angry flush stained Edward's face. He didn't
like being contradicted by a woman. "Don't tell me
you're actually considering being as stupid as your
sister?" His voice was heavy with anger.

"I am." She tilted her chin, defying him. He was a
pompous ass to assume he always knew best. That
she'd expected a normal discussion of a family
problem was the stupidity. Edward was incapable of
being objective—or sensitive to another's plight.

"Oh, for Christ's sake!" he retorted. "You're a
foolhardy, impetuous young woman, Katie. Didn't
our parents teach you anything while you were
growing up? Like being responsible for your actions?"

"How dare you speak against our parents!" She
jumped up, facing him, and if she'd even thought of
kendo at that moment, she'd have ignored it. "And
I've always been responsible for my actions!" She
didn't know how she managed to bite back her final
words—*unlike you*!

He stood too, and from the corner of her eye,
Katie sensed Michiko's distress. But Edward had
gone too far. Michiko wouldn't stand up to him—
but she could.

"You're hell-bent for trouble with your damnable
quick decisions, Katie." Edward's voice shook.
"Don't think I didn't hear about you jumping into
the bay after that kid. What are you, an exhibitionist? Trying to get on the good side of Fenton Stone by
rescuing his son before he could?"

Her eyes widened. She couldn't believe her ears.
But his words had a strange effect on her; they
calmed her. He was so close-minded that the issue

wasn't worth clarification. He was beyond her words —and her anger. She picked up her purse and jacket and headed for the front door, where she turned briefly to face him.

"Unlike you, Edward, I didn't think of anything but the child," she told him with deadly calm. "You see, his father would have been too late. The little boy would have drowned."

"Please don't go, Katie," Michiko whispered, having followed her to the door. "Please. Have more coffee. You and Edward can make peace."

Katie dropped a kiss on her friend's cheek. "I must go anyway, Michiko. I have to work tomorrow." She glanced at Edward again. "I've definitely decided to go to Johanna," she told him coolly. "I'll phone before I leave."

He only nodded curtly. But an odd expression touched his features momentarily. "You could never resist a challenge, not even as a child. I trust you don't have cause for regret, as I expect your decision was influenced by that—that Massimiliano Stefanini," he added nastily.

For another few seconds, Katie held his eyes and had a fleeting impression that he envied her ability to meet a challenge, a thing he was incapable of doing. Then she dismissed the thought that he would envy anything about her.

"Good-bye, Edward."

After another good-bye to Michiko, Katie went to catch the bus. Her decision was made. She'd go to Alaska, see Johanna through the birth of her baby, then come back to her job in the fall, in time for Michiko's baby. Her modest savings would cover the return boat trip.

The ramifications whirled in her mind on the ride down the hill. Edward was right about one thing; she did make quick decisions, and they often changed

the course of her life. She wondered if her entire
world was about to tilt once more.

Michiko watched from the window until Katie
stepped on the bus and it drove out of sight. Still she
stood, already feeling her loss—Katie leaving San
Francisco! A sudden urge to cry caused her to blink
quickly and she swallowed hard. She mustn't break
down. Edward might see. Her husband had no
patience with tears.

She lifted her gaze beyond the city to the bay,
where the deepening purple-and-blue sky laid its
reflection across the water. Lights were blinking on
all over the city, like thousands of fireflies, to light
the approaching night. Oh, how different it all was
from her home in Japan! And from all those years
when she and Katie were so happy, so secure within
their families.

"Katie-san," she whispered, and the sound was
nothing more than a ripple against the lace curtain.
"Oh Katie-san. So sorry for the way things turned
out—for both of us. We lost those families. The past
is no more."

"Did you say something? Speak up. I can't hear
you when you talk so low." Edward had come up
behind her, his newspaper flung to the floor beside
his chair for her to pick up in the morning.

Slowly she turned from the window, relieved that
she'd been able to control her feelings of loss. But all
the same, it was well that her lashes were lowered, as
was proper for a wife.

"No, my husband." She bowed to him, as she'd
once watched her own mother bow to her father. "I
didn't speak to you. I was watching the lights come
on below." She lifted her eyes to his and hoped she'd
see something more than annoyance on his face.
"For a minute, I was thinking of Tokyo."

She needn't have worried that he would see her

distress. He never seemed to take note of her feelings, but she understood. He was not a man who
expressed himself easily. And neither was her father,
she reminded herself. And yet, somehow, she had
always known that her father's strength lay with her
mother. Their bond—though subtle—was strong
and undeniable.

"Time for bed." Edward's statement was her
notice that she was expected to follow him upstairs
after she'd switched off the lights and checked the
door locks.

Sighing, Michiko went to her tasks obediently. She
had been taught that it was her duty to obey her
husband. She loved him, despite his chronic dissatis-
faction with life, and accepted his expectations of
her. She had resolved shortly after their marriage
that she would be patient with Edward. She'd seen
how insecure he was about love, and that he needed
to know someone loved him unconditionally. Soon
he would be better, Michiko told herself. More
understanding. First she would demonstrate her
love, and then, one day, he would be able to do the
same.

But as she climbed the stairs, Michiko felt drained.
She worried about Katie. She knew Katie had once
loved Tak, and now she was involved with Johanna's
brother-in-law. She just hoped Katie was not going
to be disappointed in love again. She hoped Max—
as Katie called him—would take care of Katie's
feelings, not hurt her again.

Once in the bedroom, she began to undress, aware
that Edward watched from the bed. She went to him
slowly, willing her fatigue away. She would not be
allowed to sleep for hours yet. It would be her loving
chore to soothe his body, to caress away his tense-
ness, and then stroke his genitals until he was asleep.
It was doubtful that he would make love to her, and
she was too proud to tell him how her own body

desired his. And even when he did take her, it was over quickly, and afterwards he would turn his back, leaving her more alone than ever. She wondered if this was the way of all American men.

When she was finally able to rest, she lay awake and watched the light patterns of the city flicker across the ceiling. Beneath her belly she thought she could feel her baby move, even though it was early for her to feel life. Her mood lightened. The child was her real bond to Edward. It would make them the loving family she longed for. Then her husband would be proud of her, would take her out socially, and she would make new friends.

She cuddled to his sleeping form, her face and breasts against his back, soothed by his even breathing. She wouldn't let fears for her future take away her joy of loving Edward and having his baby.

And Katie will have returned by the time I give birth, she reminded herself. For the first time since hearing Katie's news, she felt better. She pressed closer to Edward and heard him moan. Then he turned and she felt his arousal.

"Jesus Christ," he groaned. "I'm going to explode."

He spread her legs, then plunged inside her.

"My husband—my husband," she chanted, and forgot all her fears, giving them up to the ecstasy of the moment. "I love you."

But it was over in seconds, and she was left with his semen—and nothing else.

CHAPTER 6

"HOLD ON!"

The engine revved up, the sound drowning even Max's voice. The plane shuddered from the vibration, and then they were off down the runway, lifting from the ground like a graceful bird in flight. Sitting in the cockpit next to Max, Katie took mental notes as he checked his instruments and adjusted the air speed to make the turn north. The morning sun was still minutes below the distant ridge of hills, and the Pacific Ocean lay like a dark carpet all the way to the western horizon.

The higher they climbed, the more she could see, and the more breathtaking it all became. She was higher than she'd ever been before, and still Max had the nose up to gain altitude. Occupied with his controls and the instrument gages, Max was oblivious of her interested gaze. He was in his element, she thought, a man who wouldn't let obstacles deter him from his dream. She glanced away to the landscape below that lay in shadow patterns of charcoal and gray, struggling with sudden doubts that flooded her mind all at once. Had she been foolhardy to fly to Alaska with Max when she was so intensely attracted to him?

Oh Lord, she hoped she was doing the right thing. She knew the trip would take over a week, maybe two if there were mechanical problems with the plane, or if they encountered bad weather. Once she'd told Max she was going, he'd instructed her on the proper clothes to bring—"just in case we have to set down somewhere and it's cold." So she'd spent some of her savings on boots, a heavy jacket, and some hats and gloves. She'd even bought long underwear in the men's department of a downtown store.

She hadn't seen Edward again, but she had managed to have tea with Michiko several days ago. She could tell that Michiko hated her to go, even if she was emphatic that Katie was doing the right thing. "Johanna's baby comes first. She needs you and then you can come home to us," Michiko had said.

Katie had smiled agreement, but had secretly wondered about the "come home" part. Where was her home? Certainly not with Edward. As she glanced out over the western ocean where the sun was beginning to lighten the dark expanse, her throat constricted from a sudden sense of aloneness. She didn't have a place where she belonged, or a person who loved her more than anyone else. Edward was not one who felt bound by family ties, and he had been cold to her last call, when she'd told him good-bye. His final words had been another warning. "You're flying into trouble, Katie," he'd said. "It's a hellhole up there—a frozen frontier where the sun disappears in the winter and shines all night in the summer. And the people are uncivilized!" He'd said nothing about when she returned.

She was well aware that Alaska wasn't her home either. She scarcely remembered her sister, and maybe she'd been wrong about the warm tone of Johanna's letter. Maybe Johanna would turn out to be just like Edward. She gave herself a mental shake and tried to quell her misgivings. She'd looked forward to going, she reminded herself. She'd been so excited she'd found it hard to sleep the last few nights.

At that moment, the sunlight suddenly streamed through the window as the new sun peeked over the horizon and sent its first rays of light streaking across the sky. The morning sun, Katie thought, and her mother's words flowed out of her store of memories to touch her with peace. The feeling was unexpected, and somehow told her that she was where she was supposed to be—in the cockpit beside Max, watching the spectacle of a new beginning, the birth of a day. She glanced at Max and wondered if her future might include him.

As though she'd somehow communicated her feelings, he turned to her and grinned. He'd just put on his goggles, and the new sun glinted on them so Katie couldn't see his eyes. But even so, his look gave her a shivery sensation. He was so attractive to her, in every way. She smiled back, a calm smile that didn't give away her awareness that something intense lay between them. She wondered where their attraction to each other would lead, because she hadn't known the cockpit would seem so intimate, that it would feel as if she and Max were the only two people in the world.

And so they were, she thought suddenly. Alone in

the heavens, high above everything else, on their way to another world.

They stopped to refuel at designated airfields along Max's route, overnighting at small hotels, taking off at dawn each day. Max was circumspect in his treatment of Katie, making sure she had her own room and bathroom. "But be warned," he told her with a half-serious grin. "Conditions will be different once we leave civilization behind."

Which conditions? she wondered as she nodded acknowledgment. Did he mean having hotel accommodations? Or his treatment of her? Since leaving San Francisco, he'd been a perfect gentleman. Maybe he wasn't as conscious of her being in the cockpit as she was of him. Maybe his new plane interested him more. It was a paradox to Katie; she wanted him to make love to her, yet she was glad when he didn't.

They landed in Seattle early in the day, and the plane was serviced during the afternoon. "Seattle is our jump-off point," he told her that night. "So have a long bath; it might be your last for a while."

They'd dined near the airport and Max had seen Katie to her room. Their conversation over supper had centered on the plane, which he'd assured her had checked out perfectly. She'd asked a few questions concerning the workings of the engine, and how it could be capable of lifting a plane into the sky and keeping it there. She was so fascinated by his explanation of the delicate balance of propeller against the drag of the machine in the air, and wing lift against gravity pull, that she forgot about her attraction to him. There was so much to know about flying, and she was interested in every aspect of it. But it was the twinkle of humor she saw in Max's eyes that had finally brought an end to her questions.

"Time for bed," he said now and, taking her room

key, unlocked the door and swung it open behind her.

Katie hesitated, then met his gaze, her own serious. "Thanks Max—for your patience in answering all my questions."

He held her eyes, as though he considered her words, and she wondered what he was thinking behind his still expression. Then he stepped forward and gently took hold of her upper arms. Time slowed, and Katie's breath hesitated, in anticipation of what he was about to do—what she wanted him to do.

His head lowered and her eyes closed—and his kiss on her cheek was an anticlimax. "Sleep well, Katie," he whispered, and as she backed into the room, he pulled the door closed, leaving her feeling suddenly alone. But she went to bed, determined to sleep. Max would not resist her forever, she told herself. But the thought was also disturbing. What would happen when he gave in? Was she ready for that?

In the next room, Max tossed and turned in his own bed. They had a long way to go, and he mustn't forget that, as he almost had a short time ago. Both he and Katie had sent wires to Johanna, who trusted him. Although he wouldn't have had reservations about making love to other girls he'd known, he couldn't compromise Johanna's sister. Not that he didn't want Katie. Christ Almighty! He wanted her—more than he'd ever wanted a woman. But he also wanted a future with her, so he had to wait. Making love to a girl like Katie meant committment, a pledge of marriage. And he wasn't ready for that yet. His financial picture was too precarious, too unstable to support a wife. His jaw tightened. And the one thing he wouldn't tolerate was his woman being forced to live in poverty.

The night crawled on. He couldn't stop thinking of

Katie in the adjoining room. The sexual tension had
been building in him for weeks now, since first laying
eyes on her, and it took sheer willpower to keep from
making love to her, regardless of the cost. But
tonight his need was a physical agony, and it
wouldn't go away.

Abruptly he kicked back the sheet and headed for
the shower. A few minutes later he strode back to the
bed, wishing he had something—anything—to read.
It was a relief when the alarm rang at five o'clock and
he could get up. When he met a bright-eyed Katie a
half hour later, she was unable to detect anything
amiss. After a quick breakfast, they headed to the
field and took off in the pre-dawn light, through air
so pure that the snow-capped Mount Rainier to the
south stood etched with startling clarity against the
sky. Max circled, then headed north up Puget
Sound.

Katie never tired of the view of mountains and
water dotted with lush islands of dense evergreen
trees. The farther north they flew—over the Strait of
Juan de Fuca to follow the rugged Canadian coastline of Vancouver Island, then on toward the Queen
Charlotte Islands—the more breathtaking and awesome the terrain became. Night accommodations
became more primitive, and Katie realized that Max
had been right about Seattle being a jump-off place.

Prince Rupert was their last touchdown in Canada, Ketchikan the first in Alaska. It was there that
Max again checked out the plane, and when Katie
asked if something was wrong, he glanced up from
changing the oil.

"No, everything's fine," he replied seriously.
"Alaskan pilots check over things themselves,
Katie." He straightened, the job finished. "She's a
great little plane, and I'm just making sure she stays
that way. Can't have her acting up—out there." He

gestured at the rugged mountains they had yet to cross.

His words came back to haunt Katie the next morning as they were gaining altitude after the takeoff. The throttle stuck, and Max couldn't correct the problem no matter what he tried, short of killing the engine.

"We have to go back!" he cried.

Katie barely inclined her head. She licked her lips and willed herself to not panic. How could he land when he couldn't control airspeed and lift?

Fortunately the plane was high enough for a wide turn, as Max feared they'd go into a spin if he banked too sharply. Once he had it on a direct course back to the airport, he cut the engine, knowing he couldn't go in hot with a revved-up engine.

"Oh my God!" Katie cried, then realized he'd done it on purpose. It was the last thing she'd expected. And the absolute silence was even more terrifying than the overworked engine.

"We'll coast in." Max reached to pat her clasped hands. "Don't worry, Katie. I've landed with no power dozens of times—and not on a runway."

He sounded confident, and she believed he could do it if anyone could. But she also saw it would take nerves of steel and all the flying skill he knew to bring them down safely.

"I'll buy you a drink when we get down," he told her without breaking his concentration.

She was about to answer when the plane hit a down current, and without power, dropped suddenly, taking the bottom of her stomach with it. They were at the mercy of the wind, and the one thing in their favor was fair weather. Had it been bad, they wouldn't have stood a chance. As it was, Katie had her doubts.

The field loomed ahead, and she saw men scurrying on the runway, obviously aware that a crippled

plane was trying to land. The wind stilled, and they
went in like a butterfly fluttering onto a flower, Katie
thought inanely, as the plane touched, bounced, and
then touched and held the ground. In seconds Max
brought it to a gentle stop. Katie expelled her breath
and just sat there, for a moment unable to move.

"Jesus Christ! What in hell happened?" a man
hollered as Max helped her out, because she shook
from reaction. "We figured you for a crash. You sure
did one sweet job in landing that baby!"

Katie silently agreed as Max pulled her close,
calming her fears. "You've got what it takes, sweetheart," he whispered in her ear, and his words
worked magic. Her heart palpitations lessened, and
gradually she regained her composure. As Max and
the men fixed the stuck throttle, Katie watched, and
it helped to make her feel better.

"It's a minor problem," he told her a short time
later, as they readied for their second takeoff of the
day. "So long as the plane is on the ground," he
added with a wry grin.

The plane responded perfectly as they left the
airfield behind them again. Aside from short bursts
of conversation, they flew in silence for the next
couple of hours. Katie drank in the changing scenery
below them as they followed a jagged, mountainous
coastline dotted with remote islands. The engine
hummed with a steadiness that dispelled Katie's
earlier fear that the throttle would stick again.

The change in sound was sudden. One second
everything was fine, the next brought a vibration that
shook the whole plane.

"Shit!" Max ground out between clenched teeth.

"What is it?" All her earlier fear came flooding
back. So much for his wonderful plane.

"Feels like a stuck cylinder!" he shouted above the
rising noise.

"Is it serious?" A feeling of helplessness—and panic—pressed down on her.

He didn't bother to answer, intent on his flying. "Here we go again. Hang on, Katie! I've gotta find a place to land!"

Although the plane had lost altitude, it continued its course. Katie knew the situation was serious; the vibration was getting worse. But where could they land this time? She scanned the coastline below her. In many places the waves crashed right up against the cliffs.

"This is it!" he cried, and for a fleeting second he glanced at her, and behind his goggles she saw his concern for her in his eyes. Then he concentrated on the controls, and she was forgotten as he fought the plane. The lower they descended, the faster they seemed to go. Katie clutched her seat, bit her lip, and tried to control her absolute terror. The patch of beach Max was headed for looked too short, even with the tide out, and she just knew they wouldn't make it this time.

They came in low over the waves, following the island's rocky coastline toward the strip of sandy beach. Katie glanced at Max. His jaw was set, and his hands gripped the controls so hard that the muscles in his arms bulged under his jacket.

Katie braced herself for the crash. She'd realized that they'd flip like a top if the sand caught their wheels, or they'd hit a cliff if Max didn't get them stopped in time. At the last moment her eyes squeezed shut of their own volition.

But again Max gauged it right. The wheels hit perfectly for an easy landing, and the plane coasted to a shuddering stop. Somehow he'd put it down at exactly the right place between the soft and hard sand, for the wheels had sunk only a few inches. Katie couldn't get out of the plane fast enough. And once on the ground she saw that the danger wasn't over. The tide was coming in.

Reaction hit her. She began to shake uncontrollably.

One glance and Max was at her side, his goggles tossed back into the cockpit. "Sweetheart, oh sweetheart. It's all right. We're safe," he murmured, and took her in his arms to hold her against him. "I'm so sorry."

"I'm sorry too—for being such a baby. Oh Max—I was so scared."

"I know," he crooned. "I was too—but these things happen up here and it's usually okay. Especially near the coast where there are beaches."

He pulled off her cap and her hair tumbled around her face. Her eyes were dilated from fear, her skin felt clammy, and she leaned against him as though her legs wouldn't hold her.

She couldn't stop shaking. Katie tried to remember the mental steps of mind control, but it all escaped her now. For the moment it was enough to feel the safety of being in Max's arms. That they might be stranded hadn't occurred to her yet.

She's too pale, Max thought, and another fear rippled through him. She'd been in two near-crashes in one day, and her body was reacting. He knew she was on the verge of going into shock.

"I'll be fine in a minute," she managed, but her voice sounded strangely hollow. "I'm—"

"Shhh," he whispered, but his thoughts were already on what needed to be done. She must be kept warm.

She tilted her head so that she could look at him. He looked so concerned—and worried—that she felt silly all at once. After all, they hadn't crashed, and she knew he should see to the plane. Even in the scant minutes she'd been in his arms, the tide had inched upward.

"I'm okay, really I am, Max," she said. "I know you need to take care of the plane." She smiled into his eyes, and her expression was so trusting and filled with gratitude that it moved him deeply. "I'll just sit on a rock and watch," she added with a return of normalcy.

Something altered in his expression, and she wasn't sure what. But his arms tightened as his face lowered to hers. His kiss did for her what nothing else could have done at that precise moment. It sent the warmth back into her limbs, fire coursing through her veins.

It seemed to go on forever, as they clung together feeling the power of life, stronger now that they'd faced the possibility of death. When Max finally lifted his head, Katie pulled him back. She wanted his mouth on her, his kiss that silently told her all the things he'd never said aloud.

But again he pulled free, because he had to. "Will you be all right for a little while?" he asked softly.

"Of course," she replied, stronger. She was still shaky, but she no longer felt chilled. And fear no longer controlled her—it was desire that filled her thoughts now.

He climbed into the plane and brought out a blanket which he wrapped around her. "I'll build a fire shortly," he promised, his eyes tender as he made sure she was still tucked in when she sat down on a dry rock.

She nodded, and for the first time her thoughts shifted to the condition of the plane—and if Max could fix it. Again she watched as he tossed his leather jacket aside, rolled up his sleeves and began work on the engine. He looked so competent, so sure of himself, that her admiration for him grew. His black hair had fallen over his forehead, and occasionally he would elbow it away, only to have it fall again. He was so handsome, so much the bush pilot in his dark pants and laced-up boots. He exuded confidence. She could almost believe he was invincible.

Finally he glanced up. "It's what I suspected, all right—a sticky valve. It's fixed now," he added.

The blanket slipped a little as she stood. "So we can take off?"

He squinted past her, gaging the tide and how much it had risen. "Too late. Not enough beach left," he said, his gaze returning to hers. "We're here for the night, Katie."

The sun hung low in the sky, but she knew it would be a while before it was dark. The farther north they'd flown, the later the sun set. This was Alaska, land of the midnight sun, she reminded herself. But even if it had been dark, she wouldn't have worried. She was with Max, and she felt safe.

Within the next half hour, Max had started the plane and taxied it up the beach beyond the tide-mark. Then he'd covered the engine with a canvas as protection against the salt spray.

"She'll be safe here for the night," he told Katie as he finished.

"Unless the tide is high," Katie suggested, voicing her concern.

"It shouldn't be. The weather is fairly calm, and there's no wind to push the current." He glanced at her, relieved to see color back in her face. "Come to think of it, we've had good weather all along."

"I know," Katie replied, realizing what he'd left unsaid. Had the weather been bad, the ending to their mishaps would have been very different. She gazed at the dense evergreen forest that rimmed the beach, away from Max who wiped his hands on a rag. She was suddenly too aware of spending the night with him, further from civilization than she'd ever been.

"C'mon." A rakish grin lit his face, and his tone

was light, as though he sensed her apprehension and wanted to put her mind at rest. "We'll make camp."

"Camp?" she repeated. "I assumed we'd spend the night in the plane."

He shook his head. "Be too cold, for one thing, and uncomfortable."

He was already pulling gear from the plane—sleeping bags, food rations, a five-gallon container of water, an ax, shovel and a 30-30 rifle. "Bush pilots come equipped," he remarked. And when she stared at the rifle with a question on her face he explained, "This is an untamed land, Katie. A man has to be prepared for anything."

"Like a brown bear? Edward said they're huge."

He only nodded, not wanting to scare her again.

"Are they vicious?"

"Usually not, but they're unpredictable."

Swallowing hard, Katie tasted another worry. But she'd try not to think about what lurked in the forest, animals who might already be aware of their presence. Instead, she watched Max set up their camp.

He wouldn't let her help, and in a short time Max had a big fire going, a pot heating canned soup, and places cleared for them to sit. He'd cut down some brush and made a little lean-to against a boulder at the very top of the beach, one side open to the fire a few feet away. Then he'd spread the sleeping bags under it. Katie averted her thoughts. *They would be sleeping together.*

Then he surprised her again by producing a bottle of wine from his food bundle. "Remember I promised you a drink when the throttle stuck?"

She nodded, suddenly unsure.

His brows arched in a question. "I think we've earned it, don't you? Even if it is a little past the crisis."

It was unlike her to be so nervous and uncertain. But she knew why. She was stranded with the only man in the world who was a threat to her virginity—not because he'd tried to seduce her, but because if he did, she didn't know if she could resist him.

The day had passed into a strange twilight, and although Katie knew it was getting late, it still wasn't dark. The firelight threw pale shadows across Max's face as he uncorked the bottle, but its light was caught dramatically in his dark eyes as he handed her one of the cups he'd filled with wine.

She thanked him, and sipped, and time slowed. Gradually the wine relaxed her. They talked for minutes at a time, and then let more minutes go by in silence, each listening to the fire and the surf and their own inner thoughts. When Max handed her a mug of soup and some crackers, she ate them obediently, grateful that he was so prepared for emergencies. She was hungry.

As he ate his own soup, Max watched Katie. He knew her energy was spent, and she needed sleep, just as he did. Her long hair shone like silver satin in the firelight, and her eyes were dark and mysterious under half-lowered lashes. She was so God-damned beautiful that he could hardly keep his hands away from her, and he knew sleeping next to her would be a form of torture. But the temperature could drop below freezing later, and sleeping together in the shelter would keep them warm. So he banked down the fire and put the food back into the plane, where there'd be less possibility of attracting a wild animal. When he returned to Katie, he hoped the next few minutes wouldn't be awkward.

"I feel like a rag doll all of a sudden," she said, and realized it was as much from the wine as the day's events. "I think I need to sleep."

Her large eyes were filled with trust, and he thought his heart would turn over in his chest. Without a word, he helped her up, holding her against him for a second longer than was necessary. Then she tilted her face to look up at him.

"Thank you, Max," she whispered. "Thanks for everything you've done today." And standing on her tiptoes, she kissed him on the mouth.

Her gesture was unexpected, but he responded instantly. His arms tightened around her and she was suddenly crushed against his chest. He felt her soft breasts through the fabric of their clothing, and he wondered if she felt how hard he was against her. His return kiss was a passionate demand for more.

As their mouths separated, and her lashes fluttered open, he again saw the trust reflected in her eyes. It was like a dash of cold water, cooling his intent if not his passion. She didn't yet understand her feminine power, how her softness, her body speaking its own need, could affect a red-blooded man. She'd only thanked him, and had no idea that he was a breath away from making love to her until she forgot what planet she was on, until her passionate nature blossomed into ecstasy.

So he helped her to her sleeping bag and marveled at his own willpower. Later, as he listened to her quiet breathing, he was even more incredulous that he'd been able to resist the powerful urge to possess her. Time and again he propped himself on his elbow to stare at her sleeping face, her long lashes that lay in half-moons on her delicate cheeks.

And much later he dozed, only to be awakened by Katie's scream. She sat straight up in her bag, her long hair tumbling around her face, her eyes wide with a terror only she could see. In an instant he was wide awake, realized that she was having a bad dream, and pulled her trembling body to him. He held her close, and whispered soothing words to calm her fears. Gradually, reason asserted itself, and Katie realized what had happened.

"Oh, Max," she whispered, lifting her head from his chest. "I'm so sorry. I—I guess I had a nightmare. I thought we were crashing and—" She broke off, unable to stop the tears welling in her eyes or the tremors that had taken hold of her limbs.

"It's all right, sweetheart. You're safe. Nothing will harm you now." He spoke with calmness, repeating the words over and over against her hair as she instinctively cuddled into his arms. Where her face rested on his chest, she could hear the steady beat of his heart. Propriety didn't even cross her mind. The world seemed so far away; it was as if it didn't exist at all. She gave herself to the seduction of his voice, the shelter of his body, and the tension within her began to slip away.

Beyond their camp, faintly lit by the dying coals of last night's fire, it was finally dark. The rhythm of the waves was hypnotic, but the thick blackness of the forest behind them, with all its strange little sounds, brought a new apprehension to her. This was the wilds of Alaska. Anything could happen.

As though Max felt her fears returning, he wordlessly pulled her free of her sleeping bag and settled her into his. Then he lay down beside her. A second later he'd pulled the zipper closed. Instead of feeling trapped in such tight confines, Katie only snuggled against him, her head on his arm, her legs entwined with his and her back pressed against his chest. For the first time in the past twenty-four hours, she felt truly safe.

His hand smoothed her hair, lightly brushed her cheek and neck, caressing, lulling her. The darkness no longer reached from the forest, no longer haunted her imagination. But as her fears receded, she became aware of new sensations—the heat of their two bodies so close together, the way his touch seemed to possess her, as though his fingers communicated through her flesh to that part of her untouched by a man. He was so quiet, his breath only a steady ripple over her hair, that she wondered what he was thinking. Did he wish he could go to sleep? Did he think she was behaving like a baby?

Then she felt his mouth on her hair, heard his breath catch. He gently tilted her head, ever so slightly, so he could look into her face. "Are you better, Katie?" he whispered.

Because his lips were so close, or because his eyes looked so black and mysterious in the light from the dying coals—so filled with awareness of her?—she found it hard to reply. She ran her tongue over suddenly dry lips, and managed a nod.

Their eyes locked, and everything stilled around them as the night receded. Only the waves, in and out, sounded in Katie's ears, as if the very pattern of the earth waited for what would happen next.

His eyes seemed even darker as he lowered his mouth to brush a light kiss over her forehead. It was unexpected in that she had braced herself for more —had expected more. A faint moan escaped her, followed by a sound deep in Max's throat.

"Katie . . . Katie," he said, and his voice was low, affected by the same emotion she saw in his eyes. "I'm going to make love to you, darling. You know that, don't you?"

Her lashes lowered, and then closed. When she opened them again, he still waited for her answer. But he'd begun to fumble with the buttons of her blouse.

"Yes," she murmured. She couldn't say no—or think of even one of the many objections a nice girl was suppose to have. That she might be experiencing a form of madness, of separation from the civilized world, didn't faze her. She wanted him— unconditionally and at any cost to herself. The long-ago control she'd once worked so hard to master was gone, and she realized it had been going since her first meeting with Max. But if they crashed tomorrow, she needed to know they'd had this moment.

I love him. The impact of her revelation shook her to the core. And it calmed her. She knew very little about the act of making love, but she trusted Max to help her.

And then she concerned herself no more. Max claimed her mouth, his tongue probing, electrifying her into a passionate response of her own. She needn't have worried about her inexperience after all. Her body seemed to know all the proper responses.

He'd unzipped the bag and removed their clothing, so that she lay naked under him. He was the master now, kissing her, nibbling and trailing his mouth over her flesh, as though he couldn't get enough of her and was prolonging the foreplay. And all the while he murmured love words.

She moaned, her desire mounting until she couldn't stand it. She saw that he was ready for her, as she felt his hardness. But still he tasted her, and explored the soft mounds of her breasts.

"Max—Max, please," she whispered, the words wrenched from her throat. "Now—now!"

His body stilled. He lifted his head to see her face, taking in her slumberous eyes, her mouth swollen from his kisses. She moved slightly, arching to him.

"I want you, Max," she said simply.

His eyelids lowered, but she saw how deeply her words affected him. Then his body lowered over hers, and she thought no more. Sensation after sensation rocked her after the first sharp pain of his penetration. She began to move with him, soar with him until he groaned and shuddered and spilled himself into her. Even after it was over, and they lay side by side, spent, she continued to feel a throbbing sensation that only gradually subsided.

Max pulled her close and covered them with the spare sleeping bag. "You're some woman, my darling," he whispered, his arm tightening possessively. "And now you belong to me."

"Mmm," she murmured, suddenly too spent to question him. She already knew she belonged to him. She pressed closer, and his hand moved to cup a breast. Katie had never felt more sated, more contented.

She fell into a deep sleep almost at once, but it was a long time before Max slept. He savored the feel of her softness in his arms. Even though he'd made love to her, he wanted her again, felt the beginning of his arousal. He couldn't get enough of her, and with a sudden flash of intuition, he knew that would always be so. From this night on, no other woman would ever satisfy him like Katie. She'd staked a claim on his heart—and it was forever.

CHAPTER 7

BY THE TIME KATIE AWOKE IN THE MORNING, MAX HAD already loaded the plane and removed the canvas covering from the engine.

"Morning, sweetheart," he called from the cockpit where he was checking his instruments. "Be with you in a few minutes."

His voice sounded normal, as though nothing had happened between them. But it had, and her life would never be the same. She'd given herself to him. He'd made passionate love to her!

Katie took a deep breath as she waved and made an effort to compose herself. What did she expect of Max? That he would sit over her until she woke up so that he could ease any remorse she might experience the next morning? Childish—that's how she was acting. After all, he hadn't ignored her, had in fact been pleasant.

Quickly, Katie managed to struggle into her clothes while under the sleeping bag. The process was awkward, and she kept darting glances at Max, whose back was to her. Despite his having explored every inch of her last night, the morning had brought back her modesty. She didn't have the courage to stand before him nude. Not because she was embarrassed or felt guilt—she didn't. She was only unsure. And vulnerable.

Taking her cue from Max, she decided to ignore last night, at least for the time being, and went about her morning ablutions, washing herself in the privacy behind their shelter. She found clean pants and a blouse in her suitcase, and a pale green sweater to ward off the morning chill. Once she'd powdered her face and applied lipstick, she brushed her hair and clipped it back, so that it fell in soft waves down her back. As she finished, Max handed her a mug of coffee and leftover crackers.

"Something for the wrinkles in your stomach," he said casually, but his carefully controlled expression told her everything. Last night was on his mind too.

"Thanks." Acutely aware of him, Katie was unable to sustain her gaze and sat down near the dying fire. The air was crisp, and a mist still hung over the breakers, but the day promised good flying weather. The tide was low, but she didn't think there was enough beach for a takeoff yet.

"You're looking terribly serious this morning." Max squatted near the fire to pour himself more coffee.

She glanced up, met his eyes briefly, and quickly lowered her lashes. She was jumpy, and his proximity did little to calm her state of nerves.

"Just tired, I guess," she managed.

"I thought you slept like a baby. Once you finally went to sleep," he added with such nonchalance that he might have been talking about the weather.

She stiffened. Was that a hint of humor in his voice? Surely what happened to them wasn't funny. They'd crash-landed, camped in the wilds, and she'd had too much wine. *And she'd ended up sleeping with Max!* Even the thought brought a flush to her cheeks.

"I don't regret last night, Katie," he said suddenly.

Her head jerked up and she met his gaze. "I didn't say you did!" She sounded defensive, a dead give-away that he'd guessed her fear. Katie felt even more awkward, and she tried to make sense of her feelings. Was she really upset because he'd made love to her? Or was she only uncertain about his feelings and how last night would affect their future? She admitted to herself that being loved by Max had been sheer ecstasy, and even now, as she sat prim and proper, little sensations were making themselves known to her. He'd awakened her sexuality, and her body ached for more of him.

Watching her, Max too was uncertain. Katie seemed so distant, yet so vulnerable and—guilty? Jesus Christ! She probably hated him now—blamed him. He put his mug down and went to her, pulling her onto her feet so that she had to face him. He resisted a sudden urge to hold her, kiss away her guilt, make passionate love to her so that she had no doubt about his feelings. But now was not the time, he reminded himself. He had to put some perspective into the situation or risk a misunderstanding that could affect their future—not to mention the hundreds of miles they had yet to fly.

"You can see how different it is in Alaska— primitive even compared to the States or Japan— can't you Katie?"

Katie didn't like the way his features had tightened, the way his eyelids hooded his eyes. The humor was gone from his tone. Had she only imagined it earlier? And what was he trying to tell her—that making love to her was acceptable in Alaska? She went hot all over. Maybe she'd misread last night and his feelings for her. Oh God! she thought. She'd made a fool of herself.

"Can't you, Katie?" he prompted.

"Yes—of course I can," she retorted, pride coming to her rescue. She'd be damned before she let him see how shaken she felt—about everything.

"And you noticed my survival gear?"

Waiting for him to come to the point, she only inclined her head.

"It's common practice to carry emergency supplies, just as it's common to do whatever it takes to survive if a plane goes down." He paused to light a cigarette, and his eyes were even more unreadable behind the smoke. "And that means sleeping together if necessary—to prevent shock, or to keep from freezing to death."

"I understand," she managed in a normal tone, but it took all of her willpower to not look away. Was he implying that his lovemaking was an accident? She wanted to confront him, and again her pride wouldn't allow it.

"Good." He contemplated the cigarette in his hand. "Then you realize that I didn't set out to—seduce you." His pause dropped between them, suspending the moment. "It just happened."

She wanted to scream that it didn't just happen—that it was meant to be because she loved him. But she couldn't. He hadn't once mentioned love, not now or during the hours in his arms—even though he'd told her she belonged to him. Instead, she met his damnable logic with stiff politeness.

"Thanks for explaining, Max. I appreciate honesty, especially under the circumstances." She turned away. "And thanks for being concerned about me last night—for taking care of me." She dumped her coffee grounds onto the embers, and concentrated on the sudden burst of steam—and on mastering her emotions—until she could cry in private.

He came up behind her and gently took hold of her. His breath was a warm ripple on her hair as he spoke. "I'll always take care of you, Katie."

There was a huskiness to his voice, a suggestion of unspoken thoughts. She suddenly wondered if he was as calm and objective as he seemed. He gave her mixed messages, and she was more confused than ever.

She twisted to see his face so she could read his expression. But he'd already released her and was striding off toward the plane, his booted feet digging deep into the sand. Katie was left with an impression that he hadn't wanted her to see his face.

"We need to get going!" he called over his shoulder. "The tide's already coming back in."

A glance told Katie he was right. It hadn't gone out as far as they'd hoped. She grabbed her things. Her questions could wait. They had to go now, or maybe spend another night on the beach. As she followed him to the plane, a knot of fear formed in the pit of her stomach; she hoped the sticky valve was really fixed. Once the gear was stowed and she was strapped into her seat beside Max, her apprehension grew. He taxied into the best position on the beach and revved the engine.

Bracing herself, Katie tried to ignore the fact that Max was tense about the situation. And she soon saw why. The length of beach was hardly adequate for takeoff, even smaller than what they'd landed on the night before.

"It's okay! We'll make it!" Max shouted above the engine. His gloved hand reached to tilt her chin in his direction. "Didn't I just tell you that I'd always take care of you, sweetheart?"

For a second their eyes met, his warm with a promise, hers startled by what she saw—love? And then they were hurtling over the sand, headed for the outcropping of rock that meant the end of the beach. At the last second, Katie couldn't look and braced for the crash. But miraculously, the plane lifted, skimmed the rocks, and soared out over the Pacific.

Max shot her a jubilant grin, his eyes alight from the challenge. "What'd I tell you? Nothing to it!"

Shakily, Katie smiled back, her admiration for his daring obvious from her expression, as were her deeper feelings of love.

A ray of sunshine suddenly glinted on his goggles, and she had no way of knowing how affected he was by her look. It was a good thing that making love was impossible while flying, she told herself firmly.

The trip was without further incident and the scheduled stops went as planned. Katie and Max settled into an easy relationship. Strangely, the night on the island had cemented something unspoken between them, and although Katie was no closer to understanding Max, she stopped trying—for the time being. Instead, she enjoyed the sights of the wild and rugged country. Once Max, in a daring maneuver, circled a huge glacier, so she could "ooh" and "ahh" over the unexpected brilliance of the blue ice. The crossing of Prince William Sound was spectacular, its fjords and glaciers and densely forested islands beyond description. But once over the Chugach Mountains, it was a relief to know they were on the final approach over Cook Inlet to the Anchorage airport. The weather had finally turned stormy, and the air turbulence and low ceiling made their landing the worst one of the trip.

It was mid-morning of the next day before the clouds lifted enough to take off for Fairbanks. They flew in heavy weather all the way. But it wasn't the

bumpy ride that gave Katie butterflies in her stomach as they came in for the landing. It was meeting
Johanna.

They taxied to a stop and Max switched off. As the
engines died, he faced her, pulling off his goggles.
Without a word, he dropped a kiss on the end of her
nose.

"I'm going to miss having a copilot." His smile
was regretful.

"I'll miss you too, Max." She swallowed hard, and
found herself thinking how dark his skin had become from all the sunny days of flying. But their trip
was over. Their lives would change now.

The propeller wound down, and a quiet settled
over the cockpit, as though neither one wanted to
end their time together, fearful of what the change
would mean to them.

"Remember what I told you on the island, sweetheart?" he said finally.

Then he pulled her into his arms and his mouth
gently closed over hers. Time fell away, and it was as
if they were back on the beach, and he was making
love to her.

"My darling," he murmured against her mouth.

She moaned softly, and pressed closer to him. Her
lips opened for his tongue to explore, then she kissed
him back. In only seconds their passion exploded
into uncontrollable need. But the next minute
brought them back to earth—before they'd had a
chance to talk about their future relationship.

"Hey there, Max! You nesting on the field or
something?" The voice came from behind the plane,
and a second later a bearded man popped around the
wing.

They were already unstrapped and climbing out of
their seats by the time he saw them, much to Katie's
relief. She didn't want to start off her visit with

gossip. Before they jumped from the plane, Max brought his hand down on Katie's arm, stopping her.

"One more thing," he said in a low tone meant only for her. "Now that the trip's over, we're going to take up where we left off on our island."

Passion still glowed deep in his eyes, banked now by the iron control she'd witnessed in him time and again during their trip. She didn't question what he meant. She knew. And she suddenly realized why he'd restrained himself since that night, even though the sexual tension had been building between them ever since. He didn't want things to go wrong. They needed time—in the real world—to allow their feelings to develop naturally. After all, there was so much they didn't know about each other.

But there were other considerations, too, she reminded herself as she was helped to the ground. Making love meant commitment to her—a commitment of love. Hadn't she once turned down Tak because he'd never expressed his love? As much as she desired Max—had fallen in love with him— he'd never come right out and told her how he felt. She knew he wanted to make love to her—but did he love her? No matter how much she wanted his touch, his kiss, she vowed to go slow. For all she knew, he make love to all the women he was attracted to.

"She's quite a number!" the bearded man was saying. "You did yourself proud with this baby!"

Katie's eyes widened, glinting green fire. Max, seeing her startled expression, dropped an arm around her shoulders, his lips quirking at the corners.

"Katie, I'd like you to meet Fred Hagstrom— known as Fickle Fred in these parts. Fred's the best engine man in Alaska."

Fred pulled off his fur hat. With the realization that Max's passenger was a woman, an awkwardness settled over him and his personality slid behind a veneer of shyness.

"Pleased to meet ya, ma'am."

"Fred here was just admiring my new airplane," Max told her, barely suppressing his grin. "He always calls planes *numbers* and *baby*."

"You didn't—uh, you didn't think—uh, I was talking about you—did ya, ma'am?"

"No," she replied quickly. "Of course not." And then trying to recover her poise under Max's amused gaze, she rushed on. "Why are you called Fickle Fred?"

His instant grin revealed tobacco-stained teeth. "'Cause I changed my mind too many times 'bout where I'd land," he explained, and Katie sensed an innate niceness in him. "Used to fly up on them danged glaciers—and damned if it wasn't necessary to change my mind just as fast as the weather changed."

As he finished, Katie saw a man and woman come out of a square clapboard building some distance away. The man was tall and lean and handsome in a rakish kind of way. He walked with a swagger, as though he knew women found him attractive. Her gaze shifted to the woman, who at first glance seemed older than the man. She walked with the awkwardness of pregnancy, and Katie knew it was Johanna.

"Little Katie!" Johanna cried, and tried to run the last few steps. Tears sparkled in her eyes, and her smile was wide and welcoming, dispelling Katie's earlier apprehension about their meeting. Then Johanna was hugging her.

Little Katie, indeed! Katie thought, pleased. Her sister was at least a couple of inches shorter. Hardly able to say more than her sister's name, Katie hugged her back, feeling the frailness of Johanna's body, aside from her swollen stomach. As they finally looked at each other, Katie tried to hide her shock. The pale, tired woman before her resembled their mother, but Katie couldn't remember Freda appearing so gaunt, not even when she was almost sixty and dying. And Johanna was barely thirty-one.

"My goodness, Katie. You're so grown up." Johanna stepped back to hold her at arm's length. "And you've become the beauty of the family." There was a note of pride—and admiration—in Johanna's voice.

"Oh, Johanna," Katie cried, feeling a little self-conscious in front of the men. "That's exactly what Edward said when I stepped off the boat. You're both exaggerating."

"The hell they are," Dion said, cutting his wife off as she was about to reply. His words were drawn out and his eyes narrowed on her in an appraising once-over. "Kid—you're a knockout!"

An awkwardness dropped over the group, and Katie tried to hide her distaste. Before she could think of a response, he'd stepped forward and kissed her on the mouth, taking her completely by surprise.

"Welcome to Alaska," he drawled, and because he had dropped his arm around Johanna, and she beamed too, Katie was left undecided about how to handle his bold gesture. She hadn't liked it one bit.

"Dion," Max said coolly, not bothering to hide his irritation. "You could have waited to welcome Katie after you'd been introduced."

Aware that Johanna's smile wavered, Katie suspected that Dion gushed over any woman. He was certainly different from Max—thank God, she thought.

Dion, undaunted, cocked an eyebrow. "Guess I got carried away," he said, "because Johanna has been so excited by Katie coming to visit."

Suddenly conscious of Johanna's watchful eye on her husband, Katie wanted to end his stream of conversation. He seemed insensitive to her feelings, and she didn't want to be a party to her sister's distress—if that's what it was. Edward's disdain of Dion surfaced momentarily in her thoughts. She hoped to God that Edward hadn't been right for once.

She needn't have worried that Dion would continue to gush over her, for his attention was soon drawn away to the plane. Very soon Katie saw that the brothers shared one great passion—flying airplanes. The men hardly noticed when she and Johanna, walking arm and arm, started toward the square building.

"It's wonderful to be here, Johanna," Katie said sincerely. "I wrote and wrote and was beginning to think I'd never find you."

"It was my fault," Johanna replied softly. "We've moved so much that letters got lost, and I didn't write to let anyone know each new address."

The men lingered at the plane, examining it while Max unloaded their luggage. Katie was glad of the opportunity to be alone with Johanna, who opened the door to an office cluttered with papers and stacked cargo.

"This is Max's office—such as it is," Johanna added with a laugh and a sweep of her arm at the overflowing desk and chairs. "You'll soon find out that Alaska lacks all the orderliness of your life in Tokyo." She faced Katie, her expression going serious, bringing back all the worry lines. "You won't mind our lack of amenities, will you, Katie?"

"Of course not," Katie replied at once. But in truth, she was appalled and wondered how anyone could conduct a business in such chaos. But she helped Johanna clear two chairs by the window, careful to hide her disdain, glancing instead beyond the glass where she could watch the progress of the men on the airfield.

"Katie," Johanna began, and then hesitated. "I can't tell you how devastated I was to learn that Mama and Papa were gone."

Her voice broke, and suddenly they were both crying, leaning together, their arms entwined. All of Katie's carefully maintained control of the past year was gone as if it had never been. For the first time since the funerals, someone else felt the loss of her parents as deeply as herself.

When they could finally talk, Katie explained what had happened, how they had died. As Johanna listened, Katie went on to tell her how much both parents had loved them and had talked daily about Edward and Johanna—so that Katie would remember and know her brother and sister when they all returned to America one day.

Johanna blinked away a fresh flow of tears. "And I didn't write to them as I should have," she whispered, stricken with guilt.

Katie took her hands, feeling her sister's pain. "It's all right. They understood." She hesitated, aware of Johanna's frailness. "You know how Mother was," she went on, contriving a lighter tone. "She always thought the best. But I won't lie. Both of them would have liked to hear from you and Edward more often. But they loved you very much—and certainly wouldn't want you to agonize over it and make yourself ill."

"I know, Katie. I know. It's just that I lost my perspective for a few years." She lowered her lashes, and took a deep, ragged breath. "I had two miscarriages—and a baby who died five days after birth. I just gave up for a long time." Her words trailed off into a broken whisper.

Holding Johanna close, Katie was so glad she'd come. The death of their parents must have brought

all of Johanna's agony back. She saw how important
the new baby was to her. And she had a niggling
suspicion that there might be more behind Johanna's
loss of confidence. She wondered how supportive
Dion had been. But those things could wait, she
decided. For now, Katie wanted to calm her sister's
guilt.

"Do you remember what Mama used to say?" she
began softly.

Johanna lifted her gaze.

"About the sun of the morning?"

"Bringing hope," Johanna broke in. "I'd forgotten. She used to say it all the time, didn't she?"

Katie nodded.

"Oh, Katie. I'm afraid I've forgotten so much."

"I'll remind you," Katie said gently. "We have a
lot of years to catch up on."

And as Johanna wiped her eyes, Katie saw Max
and Dion approaching. She quickly composed herself. What had transpired between her and Johanna
was private.

The men came inside with a gust of wind that
ruffled the papers on the desk. "Jesus Christ!" Max
cried, stopping short to glance around. "I see the
work has stacked up while I've been gone."

"Well, there wasn't time for everything!" Dion's
instant retort was defensive and faintly sarcastic,
and it drew the attention of everyone.

It was obvious to Katie that Dion didn't like
criticism, and equally apparent that Max was upset.
He felt her gaze and glanced at her, and for a second
she saw more than annoyance in his expression. A
moment later it was gone, and she was unaware that
he'd picked up on her tearful reunion with Johanna
and had no intention of subjecting the sisters to
another emotional scene. It could wait, Max decided, and bit back a frustration with Dion that went

back to childhood. He hoped to hell that Dion hadn't cost him valuable contracts by neglecting important paperwork. If Dion hadn't been his brother, he wouldn't employ him at all. But he knew why he did . . . Johanna.

"Quite a mess, uh?" He was embarrassed too. This wasn't a favorable first impression for Katie.

"It sure is," she replied honestly. "I wouldn't know where to begin."

"That so?" He pulled out his cigarettes, giving himself time to shift mental gears as he lit up. "And here I was hoping that you hadn't changed your mind about working for me—after you and Johanna have a few days to visit, of course."

Her sister and Dion were already moving to the door, and she and Max followed them out to the Model-T Ford parked beside the building, Katie's luggage strapped on top.

"I don't know if I could make head or tail of it," she began, evasive because the state of his office boggled her mind.

"You'll manage fine," he replied, heading off a refusal. "Let me know when you can start." His sudden grin disarmed her, and she quickly climbed into the back seat. "Besides," he went on in a low tone as he bent closer, "think how much you'll miss not seeing me every day, sweetheart." He paused, and even though he kept a straight face, she sensed his smile. "And think about how much you'd enjoy organizing my life."

She licked her lips, even more disconcerted when she realized his eyes were on her mouth. She knew what he was thinking . . . and remembering.

"I'll give it serious thought," she managed.

He inclined his head, his eyes filled with her, and then closed the door and stepped back. The car jolted forward, but it wasn't the wheels bouncing

over the potholes that caused the swimming sensation in her stomach. It was sudden desire, an all-
consuming need to feel his arms around her again,
his lips on hers.

Her last glimpse was of him striding toward his log
house behind the office. She *was* going to miss him.
Dreadfully.

CHAPTER 8

"I DON'T GIVE A DAMN IF SHE DOES HEAR!"

Katie sat up in bed. Dion's raised voice had startled her. Beyond her drawn shades the sun had already risen, even though it was still too soon to be up. It was the time of year when the days were long. Then she remembered that Dion was flying out early, taking mail to a mining camp in the mountains. From the kitchen she could hear Dion and Johanna talking, but she couldn't distinguish their words. But it was obvious that Dion was upset and Johanna was trying to calm him.

Not wanting to eavesdrop, Katie lay back down, but she was no longer sleepy. She hoped Dion would leave soon, so she could get up. She wouldn't join them now, as whatever they were arguing about was

private. Annoyance pricked her. She disliked some
of Dion's ways and had come to see that he wasn't
the man her sister thought he was. Her first impression had been right.

Sighing, she turned so that the pillow muffled the
sounds from the kitchen. She'd been in Fairbanks for
a week now and had already seen all the sights of the
town. Johanna's rented, two-bedroom cottage was
near the Chena River, and the airfield was within
walking distance. Accompanying Johanna on her
errands to the grocery store and other business
places, Katie had met many of the people as well.
Everyone seemed to know everyone, and everyone
was outspoken about everything from the weather to
when and if the United States would enter the war.
But they were also open and friendly, and Katie
found herself drawn to the "Alaskan type." Although
the weather had been decent and surprisingly warm
since her arrival, she heard tales of what to expect in
the winter when temperatures dropped to fifty or
sixty degrees below zero. It was hard to imagine.
Although the people lacked many of the modern
conveniences, and were used to coping with harsh
weather, and they seemed to take it all in their stride,
claiming they wouldn't live anywhere else.

Even as she thought about the weather, she was
suddenly aware of the evergreen branches scrapping
against the side of the house. The wind had come up;
did that mean a change from the nice days?

She pushed the shade aside and glanced out the
window. Clouds obscured the distant mountains,
and the sun, low on the horizon, was only minutes
away from being gobbled up by the dark mass of
cloud that churned across the sky. Immediately she
thought of Max, who was due back from Anchorage
today. Her stomach lurched. Surely he wouldn't fly if
the weather was bad, she reassured herself, trying

not to think about how fast the weather could change once a pilot was committed to the sky. She let the shade drop back over the window.

Swinging her legs out of bed, Katie got up. Maybe Dion didn't plan to leave early after all because the weather was socking in. She put on her kimono and slippers and was about to leave her room when the whole house shook from the front door being slammed. There was no mistaking how the argument had ended.

After waiting five minutes, Katie left her room. Johanna heard her coming and glanced up from where she sat at the table, staring at her coffee cup. Katie managed a smile, but it was hard to be cheerful when her sister looked so unhappy.

"I suppose you heard us arguing," Johanna said, sounding plugged up from her recent cry. She lowered her eyes, but not before Katie saw more tears.

"You shouldn't upset yourself, Johanna." Katie spoke gently as she poured coffee for herself, then took the opposite chair.

"I know." Johanna's words were muffled behind the napkin she dabbed at her eyes.

A wood fire burned in the iron stove, and its crackling was loud in the sudden quiet between them. Katie tried to think of a way to calm Johanna and still remain neutral about Dion, so that she didn't make matters worse. Her gaze wandered over the room, from the water tank that was connected to the stove by pipes to heat the water, to the old-fashioned sink that hung on the wall. The linoleum was highly polished but worn down to the wood in places; cupboards were sparse, but then, so was Johanna's supply of dishes and utensils. Her glance fell on the empty whiskey bottle on the drainboard. *Damn Dion!* she fumed silently. He had money for whiskey, but none for the necessities. She'd heard him flare up before when Johanna had asked for grocery money.

"Know what I'm thinking right now, Katie?"

Shrugging, Katie feigned good humor.

"I was thinking about the morning sun that just went behind the clouds. Do you suppose that means there's no hope for today?"

It took a second for Katie to get the meaning. Something like fear touched her spine. Johanna was terribly depressed. She wished she dared tell Dion a thing or two. What kind of a cold, unfeeling bastard would upset a pregnant wife?

"Of course not," she began, and then decided to be direct. "Johanna, can I help?"

She shook her head. "I'm sorry, Katie. Things really aren't as bad as I'm making them seem. Pregnancy just brings out my weepy side." She managed a wan smile. "Dion and I had a fight— that's all. And I got upset."

"What caused the fight?" Katie suddenly remembered Dion saying *I don't give a damn if she does hear.* Maybe he begrudged her staying with them. In any case, Johanna needed to talk about her feelings so she could get past them.

"Oh—just my nagging," Johanna evaded. "I shouldn't expect more than Dion feels we can afford."

"Like what?" Katie knew she was pressing, that Johanna wanted to avoid the real issue. But Katie also knew she couldn't stay in their house if it was a point of conflict between Johanna and Dion. She had no intention of leaving Alaska while her sister needed her, but she could live elsewhere.

Johanna's lashes fluttered and her cheeks flushed. "Just things married people get upset about."

"Was it because of me?"

"Oh no, Katie! Please don't think that."

"You wanted money?"

Slowly Johanna nodded, even more embarrassed. "To buy groceries. But I can make do," she added quickly. "Dion's right that we can't be extravagant."

It took a minute for Katie to control her anger. Johanna sounded like Michiko when she defended Edward. Surely all women didn't grovel to their husbands like that? It wasn't conducive to a happy marriage, in her opinion. She busied herself by pouring more coffee. When she finally spoke, she'd mastered her feelings. Adding more upset to Johanna wouldn't help matters.

"You have a right to expect food money," Katie stated flatly, but with kindness.

Johanna only smiled and looked resigned. "You always were feisty, Katie. In a similar situation you'd probably get what you wanted." She hesitated. "I guess I should be more like you."

Frustration pressed down on Katie. Over the past week, she'd seen how much Johanna was like their mother, with the same adoring manner toward the man she loved. But Freda had been married to a loving man who realized his good fortune in having her, whereas Johanna's husband was all talk and no real support during the hard times, undermining her confidence. Johanna couldn't even make a decision on how much food to buy. Katie suspected that Dion made sure he had enough money for liquor and for visits to the saloons in town. She didn't believe he stayed late at the airfield every night—not for one minute.

"You should just be you, Johanna," she replied finally. "Being feisty, as you put it, has gotten me in trouble in the past. We each have to cope with our own traits, and sometimes we have to examine our weaknesses, so we can gain strength to face our lives."

Without being offensive, Katie was trying to tell her to stand up to Dion, to take a little more control of her own life. But it was clear that Johanna, for all her niceness, was as insecure as Edward with all his meanness. And she might be incapable of defying the man she loved.

"But don't ever change," Johanna said, skipping over her sister's advice to redirect their conversation. "You have daring—and courage, Katie. I admit I was surprised that you flew thousands of miles alone with Max. We all expected he'd have one or two more passengers, since the plane seats four."

"As chaperons?"

"Oh, no. But I just thought that Max—"

"Speaking of Max," Katie interrupted. "I promised to start work at his office the first of the week."

"But you don't have to do that, Katie." Johanna was abruptly aware of the conversation drifting back into deep water.

"But I want to," Katie replied. "You know I paid room and board when I stayed with Edward, and I intend to do the same here. It's what I planned all along."

Johanna looked away. "It isn't because of my fight with Dion, is it, Katie?"

"You know better than that." Katie's gaze was steady. "Max and I had already discussed it—before I'd even decided to come. And besides, I'm looking forward to the challenge of organizing that messy office of his."

"You and Max—uh, like each other, don't you?"

"We get along just fine," Katie replied with a laugh, unwilling to discuss her feelings for Max, even to Johanna. She drained her cup and stood up. "I'm going to dress now, so we can go shopping before the storm hits."

"But I told you, Katie. I don't have any money."

"You do now," Katie said over her shoulder. "I'm paying weekly—and in advance."

As she went toward her bedroom, Johanna's words followed her.

"Thanks, Katie. I'll accept board and room, so long as you enjoy working with Max."

Katie heard the relief in her voice and was grateful that she could take at least one worry from her sister. And she did look forward to working again—with Max. Being with him was much better than just dreaming about him, she told herself firmly.

The rain settled the dust, but the dirt soon changed to mud. Surprisingly to Katie, the planes were able to keep their schedules, even though Max had been delayed for a day in Anchorage. Upon his return, Katie met with him in his office and they went over his bookkeeping procedures. She could see that the ledgers were sloppy, his freighting contracts needed separating, and his payroll showed money draws by Dion that sometimes left the company in a precarious financial situation. Even though Max allowed his brother to be paid in advance, Katie saw why they weren't partners. Dion's methods would bankrupt them quickly.

Although Katie saw Max daily when he was in Fairbanks, there were other times when she didn't see him for days. He was all business when it came to his company, and he accepted every charter that came his way, flying the more dangerous routes himself. He flew miners and trappers to remote camps and grabbed new mail routes not already taken by the Wien Brothers or other established fliers.

"Don't ya worry 'bout Max," Fred told her one day as they went over a freight invoice for an upcoming flight up the Yukon River. He'd come to know Katie and liked her. He sensed her concern for Max and wanted to reassure her. "The boss has the soul of an angel, but the luck of the devil," he said, his grin peeking out of his full beard. "No one else can fly into ice fog and manage to see through a white-out to land on a frozen river." He shook his head. "Now that's luck!"

"What's ice fog?" Katie's hands stilled on the ledger.

"Moisture in the air that freezes and covers everything with a glaze of ice." He cocked his head, not realizing how he'd startled her. "It's unearthly—can't see a damned thing when it happens."

"And if you're flying, how do you land?" Katie spoke quietly, but her tone was fearful. Max was still an enigma. Everyone knew Alaska flying was dangerous and accepted that, but taking chances was something else. Was Max so ambitious that he'd risk his life?

Fred busied himself with his stack of papers and pretended he hadn't heard the question. He'd suddenly realized that she was in love with Max—and he'd just scared the living Jesus out of her. It was a relief to hear Max at the door.

"Here's Max now," he said, and stood up.

Katie kept her eyes lowered on her work as he came in the door, too aware of her feelings at that moment. Max had flown in late last night, taking advantage of the long hours of daylight, as was his habit. She'd stopped both Fred and Dion from disturbing his sleep this morning, reminding them that Max was exhausted. And she'd kept an eye on Max's little log house behind the office, making sure that the new pilot Max had hired didn't wake him either.

Once Fred had gone back to the shop, Katie glanced up, aware of the sudden quiet in the room.

Her gaze was caught by his, and she realized that Max had been watching her work.

She pushed back her hair that had fallen forward and smiled. "You look rested."

He grinned suddenly and cocked a black brow. "And you look ravishing." His voice teased, but his eyes were steady and intense. "It isn't often that I see a woman in a pink blouse and pants that exactly matches her lipstick—not in this office anyway."

And pink cheeks, she thought, feeling the sudden heat in them. Then she noticed that he wore his laced boots and leather jacket—his flying garb. Although he wasn't scheduled for a flight, she wondered if he was leaving again.

"Are you flying today?" she asked, hiding her disappointment. They'd hardly had time alone, and she'd hoped they might today, the first time since she started her job that he wouldn't be gone. She was beginning to wonder if he avoided being alone with her because he didn't want to make a commitment.

"I brought provisions for a trapper down on the Tanana River, including medical supplies." He glanced through some papers as he spoke. "They arrived in Anchorage too late for the regular plane, so I brought them on my flight last night."

"So you are leaving." She tried to sound as if it didn't matter, matching his nonchalance.

"Later, after I catch up on my paperwork. It's only a half-hour hop each way." He glanced up abruptly, catching her gaze. "I thought you might like to go along."

For a second, his matter-of-fact question didn't register. Then her eyes widened with pleasure. "I'd love it! Oh Max, it would be such fun! I've never met a trapper before."

Something warm ignited in his eyes. His grin was wide, and devastingly male, and she suddenly knew he'd planned to ask her all along. "It's settled, then," he said. "We'll send a message with Dion to tell Johanna you'll be home late."

During the next few hours, Katie could hardly concentrate on her typing or the ledgers. She told herself it was because she would be flying again, not because of Max, who worked quietly at his desk, seemingly unaffected by her presence. It was a relief when they finally crossed the field to his old Fairchild.

"Get in, sweetheart," he said, and she did, happily.

"Want to take the controls?"

They were on their way back to Fairbanks, and although it was already eight in the evening, the sky was still bright and sunny. The trip had been smooth, landings and takeoffs perfect. Katie had enjoyed the trapper, "Swede," who'd insisted they have a bite with him. Now they'd reached altitude and were following the Tanana River, reversing the route.

"Are you serious?"

He nodded, and waited. His eyes crinkled at the corners, but he kept the smile from his lips. He knew she wanted to.

They exchanged seats, and somehow he managed to keep the plane level. Then, without hesitation, she took the controls. Her hair caught a shaft of sunlight through the side window, and momentarily Max was reminded of an angel's halo. But she was far from looking angelic; her face was too set with determination.

For once Katie forgot Max. The thrill of flying filled her, an awesome and wondrous accomplishment that verged on being miraculous. A contented smile touched her lips as her thoughts reverted to those long-ago days when she flew kites in Japan. But this was the ultimate in flying, beyond anything she'd ever done before.

"You're a natural, Katie!" he cried above the sound of the engine and the natural vibration of the aging plane.

She glanced at him, seeing his eyes bright with admiration. Her heart thumped out of sync; she'd been wrong. There was one experience that surpassed flying. It was being admired—loved—by Max.

"If you weren't a woman, I'd hire you"—he snapped his fingers—"that quick."

It was a compliment, but the woman part took the pleasure from his words. "What does being a woman have to do with it?" she retorted. At the very moment he'd made the comment, she'd been contemplating the possibility of her own pilot's license.

His smile didn't waver. "Like I said, you're good, Katie. But summer flying like today is child's play compared to the other ten months of the year. Alaska flying is risky business. It takes its toll of inexperienced pilots."

Their eyes met and locked.

"It's too dangerous, Katie, too dangerous for the woman I—"

He broke off, his gaze now on Fairbanks in the distance. Quickly they exchanged seats again so that Max could make the turns and altitude changes for the landing. Katie watched each move, each adjustment of the controls, but her mind was on the end of the sentence he'd left unfinished, the reason she hadn't argued her position on women pilots. Had he been about to say *the woman I love*?

Again the landing was smooth. But Katie's heart sank as they climbed out of the cockpit. The outing had ended too fast—and on a sour note, at least for her.

His hand dropped around her shoulders as they

crossed toward the office. Preoccupied with her own thoughts, she hardly noticed that everyone had gone home for the night, or that they'd altered course and were now headed for Max's little house.

Abruptly, she stopped and turned to him, a question in her eyes.

"I figured we could use something more to eat." His voice suddenly seemed too low, too husky.

The strange light of the lingering dusk was surrealistic. It suspended time, held them in its unearthly grip. She knew it wasn't food that was on his mind.

She went with him into the house.

CHAPTER 9

THE HOUSE WAS A SURPRISE. SHE EXPECTED CLUTTER AND disarray, and found order instead. Primitive native art hung on the log walls, and a brown bear fur lay on the floor in front of the stone fireplace. The living area was one large room, with the kitchen against the back wall, the bedroom in the loft. But Katie noted the charm of the house only in passing. She was too aware of Max, who took the leather jacket he'd lent her for the flight and hung it on a peg near the door with his own.

Then, without a word, he pulled her into his arms. She swayed to him, and he pressed her closer, so that they were molded to each other. Her eyes fluttered shut as his mouth closed over hers, gentle at first, then with rising passion. She moaned, a soft animal sound that she hardly recognized as belonging to her.

"My darling," he crooned between kisses. One hand was buried in her hair, the other stroked her back, gradually sliding around her body to cup a breast.

His touch was an electric shock that jolted exquisite sensations into the part of her that belonged only to him. Katie knew she was lost. At that moment there was nothing more important in the world than being fulfilled by the promise of his love.

"Max—oh, Max," she murmured, the control she'd always prided herself on—her pride itself—forgotten. She'd never felt so unencumbered by proprieties.

When he edged her to the couch, still holding her, still kissing her, she expected that he'd make love to her. But he hesitated, as though he'd suddenly had second thoughts.

"God-damnit!" He raised himself so he could look directly into her face, and what he saw only added to his resolve. "I can't, Katie," he whispered hoarsely. "I can't take advantage of you."

His words startled her, and she opened her mouth to speak, but she was suddenly without the ability to utter a sound. She'd come to him without question, and now he rejected her. Her humiliation was complete. She struggled to move out from under him.

He shook his head, as though to shake the confusion from his brain, holding her so she couldn't twist away. She didn't understand, and he needed to explain. The shadows of the room reached out and surrounded them in the gray aura of his rejection. While Max formed his thoughts, her luminous radiance faded, and her lashes swept down over the brilliant green eyes—but not before he saw the deep hurt he'd inflicted. *Good intentions be damned!* he thought, and his willpower snapped.

"I want you, Katie. I've always wanted you." His voice was gruff, and his need was greater than ever.

"Then why? Why—"

He stopped her questions with his mouth. "Because I want to be fair—I don't want to hurt you," he said between kisses.

"You hurt me now," she whispered and turned her head to the side. He had reservations about her, and now they stood in her way. He had to explain, or she couldn't allow his lovemaking. She did have her pride.

He dropped his arms and sat back, then reached for a cigarette in his shirt pocket. Lighting it gave him something to do while he decided how to broach the subject that had tortured him for weeks. Finally he knew there was no easy approach. He could only be honest.

"I want to make love to you again, Katie. I want it every waking minute of the day. I dream about it at night."

"Then what's wrong? You look so serious, Max. I don't understand." Katie's voice shook with uncertainty, and the random thought that struck her next hit with such force that she had to speak quickly, while she could. "Is there someone else? Another woman?"

"Jesus!" The word exploded through his lips, and his eyes, so black in the fading light, looked tortured. "Oh, my baby—my darling. After you, who could there be?"

"Then just tell me, Max." The cigarette smoke rose above him on lazy air currents. "I can take it—whatever it is."

But still he hesitated. Would she really understand why he couldn't make a permanent commitment to her yet? For a moment he remembered how his mother had struggled, because his father had died without providing for the future of his family. He had to be financially secure before he married, because death always rode the sky with an Alaskan

pilot, and because his wife would never be left as his
mother was, should something happen to him.

He tossed the cigarette into the fireplace, and his
eyes hardened with resolve. "I've never wanted a
woman as I want you. But I'm not in a position to do
anything about it right now."

"What do you mean?"

He edged closer, but he didn't touch her. "You
know my financial situation, Katie. I can't made a
permanent commitment to you."

"You mean, you won't."

"Yes, that's what I mean," he agreed, and before
she could express the distress he read on her face, he
rushed on. "I don't own this house, I owe on my
planes, and I'm only leasing my space at the airfield." He hesitated. "I'm only as solvent as my
weekly contracts dictate, and as long as my planes
stay in the air. At this point, my life is still a gamble,
and I won't allow anyone, especially you, to take the
risk with me."

"That's not fair, Max." She barely spoke in a
whisper.

"You're wrong, Katie. It's more than fair, if you
look at it objectively. How would a woman—my
wife, maybe with a couple kids—pay back all my
debts if something happened to me?" He shook
his head. "She couldn't. She'd be stuck with
them."

Her lashes had lowered as he spoke, but as his
words trailed off, she fixed him with a determined
green stare. "You aren't considering the woman in
all this Max. Maybe she'd want to take the risk—if
she loved the man."

He knew what she was saying. But then, he'd
always known she had courage. He also knew she'd
never been subjected to poverty as he'd known
it—or as his mother had. The thought of Katie being

reduced to an old woman before her time was beyond consideration. Dion had married without being solvent, and Johanna was another good example. Max knew he was right.

It was a stalemate, and Katie knew it. Max was a man driven to build his empire. Her intuition told her that now was not the time to push him. He'd been honest, and she'd have to be content with that. For now.

And take what he offered now? she asked herself. Lovemaking—sex—without a commitment? She'd once turned down Tak on those very grounds. But this was different, she argued mentally. She was already committed, and for the rest of her life.

"I accept your terms, Max," she said simply.

When he still hesitated, Katie didn't lower her gaze. She had the courage of her convictions, even if she didn't understand his—and even if he still rejected her.

His movement was sudden, and his arms possessive as she was brought back against him. "Are you sure, my darling?" he asked, so close to her that his breath was a tickle on her lips. "Very sure?"

Her answer was to claim his mouth, silence his words. And for a long time they didn't speak. As he undressed her, he hesitated again, giving her a last chance to stop him.

"It's all right," she whispered. "I want you too, Max."

It was her last rational thought. He made love to her on the bear fur, and the rhythmic movement of his body rocking in and out of her sent Katie soaring into the sensations of her own throbbing need, a need so exquisitely agonizing that she cried out again and again at the climax of their joining. When it was over, she lay in his arms and wished she could stay there always.

"This is forever," he promised softly, knowing how she felt.

"Forever," she repeated.

It was only later that Katie realized that, for all the wonderful things Max had promised, he hadn't said he loved her. *But he does*, she reminded herself often, and decided he equated expressing love with having to make a commitment of marriage.

Once more, they found time to be alone in his little house, and again he made love to her. She belonged to him now, her body and her thoughts, and she worried each time his plane disappeared into the sky. He was gone even more than before, trying to establish more contracts for his company so his profit margin could widen. She wondered what it would take to make him feel secure enough to include her in his life on a permanent basis.

By the end of June, the days were so long that the men were able to take on more flights. Max took the long ones that kept him away for days at a time, leaving the short hops for Dion because of Johanna's advancing pregnancy, and the third pilot took the overflow. The nights had been reduced to only a few hours of twilight, and Katie found it hard to sleep. She feared that Max was overdoing it, and she worried that he'd fall asleep at the controls.

Johanna was also finding it hard to rest, and Katie spent more time with her. Her sister, although not due until September, confided that she was showing blood and was concerned about miscarrying again.

Katie had a talk with Dion, who surprised her with his own display of genuine worry. He suggested that she and Johanna should go early to Anchorage to await the birth. Later, she learned that it was Max who'd made all the arrangements, having already rented a house for Johanna and Dion. She should have known, she thought. Max was the brother who took the responsibilities, Dion the one who only talked about them.

"I hadn't mentioned it before, Katie," he began, after she'd thanked him on Johanna's behalf. "But I'm bidding on a sizable contract to fly freight out on the Aleutian Chain, and if I get it, I'll move my whole operation to Anchorage by fall."

She was surprised. Max was certainly a man of few words when it came to some things. But the news reassured her. It meant a move up for Max's business—and that could be important to their future.

It was Max who flew them out when the departure date arrived in early July, after Katie had his office in order so that he could manage without her. Their leaving wasn't any too soon, Katie thought as she watched over Johanna during the flight. Her sister was definitely not doing well, and Katie had her doubts about the baby's survival. Once the whole thing was over, Katie had decided to have a talk with Johanna and advise her not to try again.

Max made a second trip to bring Johanna's household goods, which Katie unpacked. They were able to spend that evening together, but they weren't alone, as Johanna was in the other room sleeping. He took her into his arms as he was leaving.

"It looks good for the move," he said, meaning his relocation to Anchorage. "This could mean a great boost to my financial status," he added with a grin.

"And that means?" she prompted, tilting her chin to a better position for his kiss.

"We'll see," he replied, and disappointed her by being noncommittal. "In Alaska, it doesn't pay to count chickens before they're hatched. There are too many variables. And I don't have the contract yet."

"Isn't the weather out on the Chain unpredictable?" she asked, fearing it was one of the variables he meant. "I heard that clear days are rare out there and the wind blows constantly." She knew what storms meant—delays and soaring costs. And added risks.

"It does get heavy weather off the Pacific," he said, evading a direct answer.

He grinned suddenly, but his eyes were filled with feeling for her. "Don't worry, Katie," he went on in a lower tone, as he traced a thumb over her lips. "It's a great opportunity, and the hazards aren't as bad as you think." And then he kissed away her concerns. By the time he left, they were both frustrated. It had been impossible to make love with Johanna sleeping in the next room.

When he was gone again, Katie concentrated on Johanna. She tried not to dwell on Dion's lack of concern, and why he didn't take more of the Anchorage flights now that his wife was there. Katie had her suspicions. Being alone in Fairbanks meant he could gamble and drink to his heart's content. She just hoped he stopped short of cheating on Johanna with another woman. But Katie didn't put anything past Dion.

Katie wrote to Edward and Michiko and informed them of the address change. She explained Johanna's condition and the possibility of Anchorage becoming Max's permanent base of operations. As she walked to the post office to mail her letter, all her old concerns for Michiko surfaced in her thoughts. Michiko's baby was due in November, and she hoped everything was good for her friend.

A letter came back from Michiko in mid-August. "So sorry that Johanna is not well," she wrote. "I pray she is better and the baby will be healthy too." Michiko went on to talk about San Francisco, and how much better things were for Edward. He now looked forward to their baby as much as she did, she wrote.

Katie gave the letter to Johanna and was thought-

ful as her sister read it. For some reason, she had the
feeling that Michiko was too anxious to seem happy.
But it was her impression alone. Johanna felt everything was fine, that Edward and Michiko were growing in their relationship, and the baby would be their
unbreakable bond.

But the doubt lingered for Katie. She just hoped
Johanna wasn't being naive as usual. But when Max
and Dion turned up in Anchorage the following
week, Katie soon forgot all about her concern for
Michiko. Max had gotten his prized freight contract
and was already in the process of moving his equipment to Anchorage. That night, the four of them
celebrated in Johanna's small kitchen, eating the
special salmon dinner that Katie had prepared. She
was jubilant. Now she'd be working for Max again.

Her future had brightened once more.

"I'm not asking you, Dion." Max's tone was cold,
dangerous even. "I'm telling you. Have a little more
consideration for your wife."

Dion's handsome features tightened as his eyes
narrowed on his brother. "Always did tell me what
to do, didn't you, Max? Have you forgotten that I'm
the oldest brother here?"

"Than act like it!"

"Fuck you! And all your self-righteous preaching.
I'm taking care of things, but I have a right to relax.
Flying out there—never knowing if I'll get back—
takes its toll, and I need to unwind before I go home
to face a sick wife."

Max felt the old frustration come over him. He
could fight with Dion, as they'd done since Max was
old enough to know that Dion was a loser who even
lied to their mother, taking credit for Max's achieve-
ments. But their mother's high hopes for her oldest
son had stopped Max from telling her the truth, so
Dion had gotten away with his manipulations. Even

now, Max was stuck. He'd only hired Dion because his brother had a wife and couldn't hold a job anywhere else.

"I'll put it this way, Dion. Your wife is pregnant with your kid. If you don't start treating her right, then you're fired."

Dion jumped up from his chair. "You'd fire me? Your own brother? I'm the best God-damned pilot in Alaska."

Max snapped his fingers. "Just like that if things don't change."

Their eyes locked. Dion saw the stubbornness—hardness even—in Max's that he'd always hated. He knew Max wouldn't back down. He'd always been protective of their mother, and he expected Dion to be the same way with Johanna. And it had gotten worse since Katie's arrival. He wondered if she complained about him to Max.

"Shit, Kid," he said, reverting to his childhood nickname for Max. "Maybe I have been a little lax with Johanna. But it hasn't been a picnic for me either."

"So what is it? Change, or get out of Stefanini Air Service?"

Max was relentless. He'd had it with Dion's drinking and gambling and flirting with anything in a skirt. Katie hadn't said a word, but he'd seen her feelings on her face. She saw through Dion, but Johanna didn't. And because of Johanna's feelings, no one dared criticize her husband. So Max only had one club over Dion's head—his job.

"I guess it won't hurt to spend a little more time at home, see her through her pregnancy."

"Is that a promise?" Max hadn't softened his tone. He'd heard Dion's promises before.

"Yeah, it's a promise, Kid."

With a return of nonchalance, Dion shrugged.

Then he slipped into his leather jacket and opened the office door. "See you in the morning."

Max watched him go and wondered how long his good behavior would last this time. But when Max was in town later that evening, he was pleased to see that Dion had kept his word.

At least things were better than they had been, Max told himself after a couple of days passed and Dion stayed away from the bars. Maybe his brother was finally showing signs of growing up.

"Is Dion here?" Katie's question was directed at Fred, who'd moved with the company to Anchorage.

"Ain't seen him around. Thought he went home already."

"Well, he didn't!" Katie knew she sounded impatient, but she was so worried she could hardly sound civil at all. Johanna had been rushed to the hospital, and Dion was nowhere to be found. She supposed it was too much to hope that she'd find him at the airfield. It was only luck that Fred was still working on an engine at nine o'clock on a Sunday night.

Fred wiped his hands on a greasy rag. "What's wrong?" He knew something was, as he'd never seen Katie lose her patience. And for that matter, he'd never seen her without makeup, or with her hair so wild, as though she hadn't fixed herself up before leaving home. But it was her darting eyes that told him she was scared to death about something.

"It's Johanna," she managed. "She's gone into labor—and something's terribly wrong. The doctor hasn't left her side except to tell me to find Dion."

"Jesus Christ! I hope she's okay." His face drained of color, and Katie saw that her words had brought back his own painful memories. Max had told her that Fred's wife had died in childbirth fifteen years before, and he'd almost destroyed himself with the bottle as a result. Tossing the rag aside, Fred strode out of the workshop and locked the door behind him. "I'll find him," he said tersely, "but I'll need to use the car."

"Thanks, Fred," she said, so relieved she felt shaky. "You can drop me off at Providence Hospital —and bring Dion as soon as you find him."

They ran to the Ford and he took the wheel. Fred floorboarded it, and didn't let up on the gas until they reached the hospital. The car door was barely closed behind her when he accelerated again. Fred realized the seriousness of the situation, and her regard for him went up considerably. Fickle Fred was someone to count on in a pinch. No wonder Max thought so highly of him.

As she hurried inside, Katie couldn't help wishing that Max hadn't flown to Kodiak. She needed him to tell her Johanna wouldn't die. It was small consolation to her that the hospital was new, its up-to-date facilities making it the best in Alaska.

The next hour was the worst of her life, aside from when her parents died. Finally the doctor stepped into the waiting room, and Katie leaped out of her chair to face him.

"Your sister has delivered a healthy, six-pound girl," he told her, but Katie saw no pleasure on his round face, only a guarded expression in his eyes.

"And Johanna? Is my sister all right?"

"I need to speak to her husband," he evaded. "Is he here yet?"

Katie shook her head, damning Dion in her mind for not paying attention to Johanna's deteriorating health. "Please, tell me if Johanna is all right!" she cried.

The doctor was about to respond when Dion rushed through the doorway, every inch the concerned husband. "How's my wife, Doc? Has she had the baby yet?"

"You have a beautiful daughter, Mr. Stefanini."
The doctor looked relieved to see Dion. "But your
wife hemorrhaged—badly. The bleeding has slowed,
but we haven't gotten it stopped yet." He hesitated,
as though he hated what he had to say next. "I'm
afraid it's touch-and-go."

"You mean—" Dion's face went white. "You
don't mean—she could die?" His words dropped to
a whisper, but he grabbed the doctor's arm. "You've
got to save her, Doc. *You've got to!*"

Herself terrified by the doctor's words, Katie was
still surprised by Dion's reaction. He was a badly
frightened man. In his own way, he did love
Johanna. She was his anchor; without her, he had
nothing.

The doctor left them to return to his patient. Katie
and Dion waited together, bonded by their shared
fear for Johanna. Somehow knowing he loved
Johanna altered her feelings for Dion. When they
finally knew Johanna would live, neither spoke, their
relief was so profound.

But they both cried.

Elisabetta had been born on the tenth of September, but Johanna and her baby didn't come home
until the first part of October. Katie, who'd been
working for Max during those weeks, took the time
off to care for her sister.

"She's beautiful," Katie said the first morning
after bathing Elisabetta. The tiny girl had a full head
of black hair, a round, perfectly shaped head, and
large eyes so navy blue that Katie knew they'd surely
turn brown.

"And worth the suffering to have her," Johanna
said, her eyes shining with pride.

Katie left her sister to her breast feeding, and went
to the kitchen to clean up the mess she'd made
bathing Elisabetta. She loved the baby and felt a

longing for a child of her own. But she and Max were no closer to a commitment of marriage than before. Although she'd been in the office daily, she'd hardly seen him, the treacherous weather out on the Aleutian Chain often precluding his return. She feared that he took terrible chances, pitting his flying ability against violent storms. Their time together had dwindled to almost nothing.

I love him, but maybe he doesn't feel the same, she thought as she worked, blinking away tears of frustration and doubt. He'd still never told her he loved her, and until he did, she'd never know for sure.

She quickened her work, moving to the dishes in the sink. She wasn't about to slip into self-pity. But soon Johanna would be back on her feet, and Katie would need to make a decision about returning to San Francisco. Michiko had asked about it in her last letter, in which she'd sent her congratulations to Johanna. Katie knew she had to decide before the weather socked in for winter.

Her next letter from Michiko was written on the last day of October, the day after Michiko delivered a baby girl—Anna Su—a couple of weeks early. "So beautiful, Katie. She looks like Edward. I'm so very happy."

For a long time Katie stared at the letter. She had two nieces. But when would she ever have her own child?. And in that moment, she decided to stay in Alaska for the winter. Michiko had managed to have her daughter just fine without her. It even sounded as if Edward had changed.

But she knew her decision was really based on a whole other matter. She wanted to stay near Max. She couldn't bear to leave him.

CHAPTER 10

"SOMETHING'S IN THE WIND," DION SAID TO MAX one morning in the cramped office where Katie was bent over the ledgers. "I can smell it."

Max glanced up from the bid he was preparing for a government contract. "What was that, Dion?" he asked absently.

Dion was about to fly over to Fairbanks, and he paused at the door, pulling on his leather gloves. "It's obvious. America is gearing up for war."

His words caught Katie's attention, and she looked up too. All winter there had been talk of the war in Europe, and by mid-spring the first American troops had arrived in Anchorage to set up an Alaskan Defense Command. Now the newspaper was filled with stories about Italy having aligned with Germany against Great Britain and France.

"Mark my words," Dion went on. "It's June now, and I predict we'll be right in the middle of it by this time next year—if not sooner."

"But President Roosevelt claimed neutrality." Katie hated the thought of war—which would include Japan as well.

Dion's brows shot up. "Then why did he submit that huge defense budget to Congress?"

Pushing back his chair, Max stood up. "We don't know how this whole thing will end, Dion. All we can do is our part, and hope to hell it's over before next year."

"Christ Almighty! You know better than that." Dion gave a sharp laugh. "You've just signed a government contract to fly freight out to new airfield sites—sites you flew all over the Territory to help find. So what does that tell you? C'mon, Max. You don't have to protect Katie. She knows as well as anyone what construction of airfields in the middle of nowhere means. Protection from attack."

Chilled, Katie had to agree. A glance at Max told her that he, too, thought war loomed on the horizon. *He just doesn't want me to know what he's doing,* she thought suddenly. *Because I'd worry.*

For the rest of the morning Katie found it hard to concentrate on anything, and she was glad when she was finally alone in the office. Although Max wouldn't leave again until morning, she knew his next job would keep her away for weeks, and knowing that left her flat—rejected even. His freight pick-ups for the government were often somewhere other than Anchorage, and the delivery could be any one of the new airfield sites. It was total frustration for Katie. She was left to take care of the office work, while Dion and the other pilot took over the regular flying routes. Even Johanna suffered; Dion was never home either. Max's words, "The new government contracts will give me the financial boost I've been working for—the security for our future," spun in her head. Didn't he ever consider the possibility that she might give up on him? She was beginning to wonder if anything would be enough for Max.

"Hey! Why so serious?" Max's words preceded him into the office, startling her out of the discouraging contemplation of their relationship.

"Just thinking," she evaded.

"So you're not too busy to lock this place up for an hour or so?"

He leaned against the doorjamb, a shaft of afternoon sunlight touching his black hair with a silver sheen. His shirt sleeves were rolled up and exposed his muscled brown arms, while the Levis he wore fit his legs like a second skin. Katie's heart lurched. When he looked at her like that—his eyes hooded, a slow, knowing smile on his face—she couldn't resist him, and she forgot all her doubts until he left her again. Because of the long separations, their love-making was intense, the pleasure of their joining always more exciting than the time before. It was at those times that Katie knew all her agonizing about the future was in vain. In her most private moment, she'd admitted to herself that she could never leave him, even though she couldn't understand his desperate need to succeed, or how he could risk losing her to it.

About to ask him why he wanted her to lock up, she suddenly blushed. Surely he didn't expect her to go upstairs to his quarters in the middle of the day, with Fred in the shop?

He saw her mind make the jump, and his grin widened. "That too," he drawled. "But later. Right now I want to show you something."

Before she could do more than nod, he strode forward and grabbed her hand. A minute later she was beside him in the Ford, headed for town.

"Where are we going?" she cried over the sound of

the wind that streamed in through the open windows.

He flashed her his special grin, the one that always made her aware of how appealing slightly crooked teeth could be. "You'll see," was all he said.

They hurtled over the road, their hair blowing in all directions, and she knew something important was about to happen. They skirted the town and Max turned off onto a remote street that was little more than a track. He stopped on a rise, the car faced in the direction of the Knik Arm of Cook Inlet. He jumped out, ran around, and opened her door to take her hand as she stepped to the ground.

"What do you think?" Max's arm was around her, holding her close to his side. His voice was calm, but she sensed his excitement.

"It's—nothing short of spectacular." Katie's gaze took in the perfection of the location. The view of the water and distant mountains against a cloudless sky was breathtaking.

"I just bought it," Max said, and then turned her into his arms. "And I'm going to have a house built on it—when I can afford to."

His eyes burned into hers, as though they spoke the words he wasn't yet prepared to say aloud. And then his face lowered, hovering just inches above hers. The fragrance of salt water drifted around them on warm air currents, and the cry of sea birds pierced her with a longing so profound that her throat constricted. And she knew. This place would be their place. When Max was ready.

The first kiss was tender, a tribute to all that was soft and gentle between them. The second demanded more. And the third merged with the passion that burst between them into raw need. They fell to the grass, and in the shelter of virgin evergreens, he took her, unable to help himself.

"Oh, my darling," she murmured, over and over again. "I love you."

"Yes, yes," he groaned. "Oh my God—*yes!*"

A vortex of sensation took hold of Katie, and she went beyond rational thought, spinning into its eye of ecstasy.

He held her close to him after it was all over. They lay for a long time, her head against his chest, and she listened to his heartbeats gradually slow to normal. Overhead, the birds and wind sounds blended with the rhythmic cadence of distant waves.

For now, Katie was content, her mind washed of fear. She felt loved.

The days were suddenly so busy that Katie only had time to think about Max when she was finally in bed at night. Stefanini Air Service had more requests for flying freight than they could handle. As the government hired more pilots away from private companies, their business grew until Dion often flew two trips a day, taking advantage of the "midnight sun." When their third pilot was hired away from them, Fred took over some of the short hops, but his air hours were limited because of the importance of keeping their planes in good running condition.

Little Elisabetta took her first steps, and Katie worried that Dion hardly knew his little girl, as he often slept in Max's quarters, too tired to drive home. Johanna was upset about his work load, and Katie often wondered how to ease it. Dion had never been a good husband, and the present situation made matters worse. When a solution hit her, Katie knew it was the answer for all of them. So she presented it to Dion.

"Why not?" she demanded, sensing Dion's interest despite his first incredulous refusal. "It would solve some of our manpower problems, and give you more time with your family."

His handsome face was creased in thought. She didn't push further, but let him think it out. Katie knew Dion would first consider the effect of her suggestion on him directly—such as his salary, which Max had increased dramatically since leaving the Aleutian flights to him.

"Jesus!" he said finally. "Max'd have my hide. He'd kill me if I taught you to fly."

"He wouldn't know until after the fact, when I was already flying the short hops, the little trips that just about do you in."

He nodded. It was true that the half-hour flights down the Arm, or up into the Matanuska Valley, on top of twelve or fourteen hours of flying, had proven dangerous because he'd had a hard time staying awake.

"And if I eventually did the short trips while you're gone, it wouldn't affect your salary at all."

"True." He dragged the word out, still considering.

"You could take me up whenever you had spare time, and I could practice out over Cook Inlet." She saw that he was weakening, that he saw the validity of her argument. And Dion, being an excellent pilot, would be a good teacher, even though he was a failure in many other areas of his life.

"Okay," he said, but his eyes narrowed. "I'll give it a try. If you show talent, we'll continue. If not, I won't be a party to your death."

"That's blunt."

"No. That's the way it is. We'll go up tomorrow. That's all I'll need to make my decision."

He went out of the office, on his way home for once. And for the first time Katie saw a resemblance between Max and Dion. She smiled wryly. Since the night Johanna almost died, she and Dion had gained a strange understanding of each other. She still didn't approve of his ways, and he considered her too independent for a woman, but they tolerated each other, even liked each other sometimes. Despite their differences, Katie knew she was about to become a pilot.

By Elizabetta's first birthday in September, Dion pronounced her experienced enough to fly alone.

"You really caught on fast," he told her one morning as she landed the single-engine Fairchild. "I think you can manage a couple of short flights a week, don't you?"

Excitement bubbled up within her, and she could hardly get the words out fast enough. "You bet I can manage!" Katie knew the places she would service, and the landmarks along the way, as she'd flown to them many times with Max. It would be simple compared to the routes Max blazed over unchartered territory, following a river, or counting the mountain ranges, and then marking everything on a virgin map. She didn't worry about trying for a pilot license, as no woman had one in Alaska.

At first she only flew once or twice a week, but then, as they were delivering winter supplies before the weather turned vicious, Katie found herself in the air on a daily basis. Somehow Max never found out, and she suspected that even Fred was careful not to mention it.

One afternoon in early October, her luck ran out. Although the weather had been stormy off and on, it had also been sunny between the storms. Katie chose the between times for her short flights, knowing there were usually at least a few hours between fronts. She was coming in low over Cook Inlet, trying to stay below the mass of clouds that had gathered so fast she could hardly credit their movement. First she'd tried to outrun the storm, but when it overtook her, she dropped altitude to fly under it. She saw Anchorage in the distance, but her relief was

only momentary. In seconds, she was engulfed in a
fog so dense it seemed to press a weight against the
windows. She was blind.

Panic hit her hard. For a second, she lost her
bearings, felt confused as to which direction was
ground and which was sky. Forcing herself to stay
calm, Katie remembered her *kendo* training to master control of fear. She talked aloud to keep herself
from falling apart.

"The nose was down for landing. I'm on course.
Even if the ceiling is fifty feet, so long as I'm over
water I should be able to drop below the clouds." She
kept up the chatter, holding her nerves by iron
control.

All of a sudden she burst free of the clouds and
almost reacted instinctively to pull up. Again she
managed to control her first impulse. But she was
scarcely thirty feet above the tidelands and almost
on top of the airfield. If the fog hadn't cleared when
it did, she would have crashed.

Wisps of fog flew past like angry ghosts as she
touched down and taxied to a stop. For a second she
just sat in her seat, shaking as the propeller wound
down, unable to believe she was really safe. Then she
popped the cockpit and climbed out—straight into
Max's arms.

Without a word he yanked her into his arms,
holding her so tight she could hardly breathe. His
breath came in ragged gasps, and it was a few
seconds before he could speak.

"You almost died, Katie!" There was a high keen-
ing note to his voice, like the cry of a wounded
animal. "I think I'm dreaming now. How in Christ's
name did you bring that plane down? God himself
couldn't have seen through that cover."

She could only shake her head. She didn't know.
As scared as she'd been—still was—he was even
more upset. He must have flown in right after she left

and found out what she was doing. Katie lifted her face, and was shocked to see how deeply moved he was. He was grim—as if he'd just faced her death and she'd been saved at the last moment—which was basically what had happened.

"I'm sorry, Max," she whispered. "I'll explain everything later—when I stop shaking."

His grip tightened. "You can explain later, Katie, and I'll listen. But I'm giving an order right now. No more impulsive decisions. Damn it all, anyway! I forgot how hell-bent you can be to help, even if you kill yourself trying." A new inflection edged his tone, one that said his word was law. "*No more flying.*"

She leaned against him, because her legs still felt rubbery. "I agree, Max. But only until next spring when the weather is good again," she added meekly.

"We'll see—after you've filled me in on what's going on," he replied, still too shocked to ever agree to her flying without him present.

That was good enough for now. Katie nodded.

"We have other things to discuss as well," he said as it started to rain and they headed for his quarters, his steadying arm guiding her way.

"Other things? Like what?" She wondered if there was something else she'd done to upset him.

He shot her a sidelong glance, one that reminded her of what a good lover he was. "I've decided it's time to put first things first."

"Like what?" she repeated.

"Like us getting married.

As was the pattern, time precluded setting a definite date, although two local carpenters began construction on a small, two-story house on Max's property. But as the weather socked in, even that work was suspended until spring. Max was away most of the time, and Dion was often grounded somewhere between Dutch Harbor, Nome, and Anchorage because of sudden and violent storms. Remembering her own experience in the fog, Katie shuddered to think what they were up against when the wind blew over a hundred miles an hour, or they were caught in a white-out of snow or ice fog.

By December, the days were so short and dreary that Katie had to have a light on to work in the office. She came to work in the dark, and left in the dark, and was reminded that winter was the extreme opposite of summer with its midnight sun. But each day she took advantage of the couple of hours of light to drive to the site of the house. Even though the cold wind off the Arm whistled through its framed-up studs and beams, a lonely, forlorn sound that spoke of glaciers and desolation and a vast frozen land, she somehow felt closer to Max there. Those minutes alone reinforced her belief that he was safe.

Christmas was spent with Johanna and the baby, as neither Max nor Dion was able to make it back. They celebrated on New Year's Eve instead. Katie wore the new emerald-green velvet dress she'd had Michiko send from San Francisco, together with matching high-heeled pumps. She'd taken pains with her make-up but let her hair fall in its natural waves, as she knew it was the way Max liked it. Katie stood by the fireplace as Dion opened the front door for Max. He came in with a rush of cold air that smelled of fresh snow. He shrugged out of a heavy overcoat, and her heart was suddenly beating too fast to speak. He was incredibly handsome in his casual tweed suit, and his gaze was immediately on Katie.

He came to her side as soon as he'd spoken to Johanna and little Elisabetta, who was on her way to bed. Dion went along to tuck in his daughter, leaving Katie and Max alone.

The next second she was in his arms, his lips claiming hers. "You're so beautiful, my darling," he whispered. "And you're mine—you know that, don't you?"

Her lashes lifted so that he saw the answer in eyes as green as her gown. Her cheeks had deepened under the powdering of rouge, and her full pink mouth was parted, inviting more kisses.

"I only belong to you, Max, if—" She hesitated, but knew she had to say it, the one question that had haunted her thoughts far too long. "If you love me as I love you."

First she saw surprise, then puzzlement on his face. "You've never said you love me, Max," she managed, her words low but distinct.

A soft animal sound tore out of his throat. "I love you—I love you. Oh, my God, Katie—how can you doubt it? *I love you!* You've become my reason for being—for building my empire—*for living.*"

He shook his head, then ran his hands through his hair, mussing the black waves, desperate to convince her. She was right. He had failed to say the words because they meant everything to him, including marriage. At a loss, he only held her and willed her to understand. And then he kissed her again, passionately, and Katie's last concern was gone.

It was only awareness of the others in the house that kept him from undressing her and taking her right there. She excited him as no woman ever had, and he suspected he would still want her when they were both in their rocking chairs. It wasn't Katie's beauty alone that compelled him to possess her; it was the essence of her, an elusive quality he'd never quite been able to grasp. Just when he thought he'd found the bottom layer of her personality, he'd been brought up short by the realization that it went even deeper. It was a mystique rooted in her oriental background, he'd decided. She was equally at ease in an office, flying a plane, or making love to him. She

was so much a lady, so fiercely independent and
loyal, yet she was a wanton temptress in his bedroom.

Aware that Johanna and Dion would return at any
moment, Max led her to the davenport that faced the
fire, and they sat down. "I want to give you your
Christmas present," he said, his eyes on her face as
he reached inside his jacket and pulled out a tiny box
tied up with a red ribbon. He handed it to her.

Swallowing, she calmed herself and forced her
fingers to move without fumbling. She wanted to
prolong the moment, one she knew would go into her
bank of memories, to be taken out time and again for
all the years to come. When she sprang open the lid,
she could only stare at the beautiful ring, her eyes
blurred by tears.

"Don't you like it?" he asked finally.

She glanced up then and he saw her expression.
Their eyes locked, and a commitment more profound than any word passed between them. He
slipped the ring on her finger, but the brilliant
emerald that was set in a cluster of diamonds didn't
sparkle half as much as Katie's eyes.

"I'll treasure it always," she whispered. "I love it,
Max. And I love you."

"Is the first Sunday in May okay for the wedding?"

Too choked up to answer, she put her arms around
him—her beloved bush pilot—and kissed him.

Later, after they'd eaten supper and opened their
presents, Katie gave Max his—a gold pocket watch.
He turned it over and silently read the inscription on
the back.

"Thank you, Katie," he said solemnly, and the
firelight reflected in his eyes told her everything.
Forever My Love, Throughout Eternity, he silently
pledged back to her.

* * *

The package came one month after Katie's letter to Michiko about her wedding in May. Johanna helped her cut the strings and unwrap it. A letter, between the outer brown paper and tissue paper that still covered the contents, slipped out first. It was from Michiko, and Katie read it aloud to Johanna before they progressed further.

"So happy for you, dear friend Katie. Remember when we were children and you always said you would be married one day in the fine silks of Japan? That is our wedding gift to you. Japanese silk for your wedding gown." She went on to wish her best.

Katie put down the letter to stare at the tissue paper, remembering the glorious days when she and Michiko played their childhood games and pledged to be at the other's wedding. The kitchen fire crackled, the snow fell beyond the lacy curtains, and for a moment Katie felt sad. It was cozy in Johanna's little house—but oh so different from the life she'd once shared with Michiko in Japan, and all the dreams that had never come true.

"She's a wonderful friend," Johanna said softly. "Edward is a lucky man."

The spell was broken and Katie opened the tissue to see Michiko's gift. Not only was there white silk that shimmered even in the dreary winter light, but white satin and lace and ribbons as well.

"I'm a good seamstress," Johanna began after they'd admired the high-quality materials. "If you'd trust me, I'd be happy to make your gown."

"Oh, Johanna," Katie cried. "What could be more perfect? The material of my wedding gown given to me by my sister-in-law and brother, and its being made by my sister."

They immediately began their plans for the gown, and the search for the right pattern took weeks. In the end, they combined several to make their own

creation. There was even material left over for a
dress for Elisabetta, who was to be the flower girl.
The wedding plans took Katie's mind off Max, who
was still away doing his government flying. Even
their house was coming along slowly as weather
permitted. Katie tried not to think about the war, or
that a Japanese submarine had been sighted on
Prince William Sound. She just prayed nothing
would stand in the way of her becoming Max's wife.

"I do," Katie whispered as she stood next to Max
in Johanna's small living room. The minister, a
solemn man who read from the Bible, faced them,
his back to the bouquets of flowers Johanna had
placed on the mantle.

She was gowned in Johanna's exquisite creation of
silk and satin trimmed in old lace that matched her
train and long gloves. Johanna, standing next to her,
wore pale blue, and little Elisabetta was adorable in
her dress that was made from both the white and
blue silks. Max wore a formal black suit and a white
shirt and dark bow tie. Dion was the best man and,
as Katie glanced around, she saw him hand Max the
gold wedding band that matched her engagement
ring.

"I pronounce you man and wife," the minister
said several minutes later. "You may kiss your
bride."

Max gently turned her to him. He lifted her veil,
and she waited expectantly, her eyes wide, her lips
parted. To one side, the photographer, hired for the
afternoon, positioned himself for the picture.

But Max wasn't in a hurry. It was a moment to
hold, to remember—the face of the woman he loved,
her expression of total commitment—her giving
over of self.

His breath caught. Did he deserve such a gift? he

wondered suddenly. She was a woman apart from any other, and he must never let her down—not ever.

Sensing his hesitation, but not for a second doubting him, she smiled sweetly. He was her man now, and all the world would know it. She would stand beside him, no matter what, for all the days of their lives.

"Forever," he whispered, repeating the words she'd once inscribed for him. "Throughout eternity."

"Throughout eternity," she repeated.

He kissed her then, lifted his mouth, and kissed her again. Then, taking her hand, he ran with her out to his car in the driveway. Under a hail of rice, they took off for their honeymoon—their new little house on the bluff overlooking the Arm and the cozy rooms that Katie had so lovingly decorated before the wedding. For them, the seclusion of their own home was a far enough distance to go. It was paradise to know they would have four days and nights alone, and no one would disturb them.

She snuggled close to Max as he drove. When they reached their house, he carried her across the threshold, then closed the door on the world.

When Max flew off again the following week, Katie was left with the promises of their whole future. She sat by her window and watched a storm gather over the distant mountains beyond the Arm. Her letter to Michiko, with a wedding photograph of her and Max, was already in the envelope, ready to send. It was a long letter with all the details, a letter warm with Katie's happiness. She'd even drawn a map of Anchorage and the harbor, showing Michiko the location of her new house by circling it in red.

"I love you, Max," she said aloud, her eyes on the

sky. He hadn't been gone long, and already she missed him. But he'd be back soon, she reminded herself. She got up and went outside to the car. She'd mail Michiko's letter on her way to work.

CHAPTER 11

"MAMA! MAMA!"

Michiko had started up the gangplank when Anna Su began to cry. Michiko ran back to the wharf where her small daughter stood beside Edward. Stooping, she pulled the girl into her arms, soothing her with gentle words and a promise of a Japanese doll when she returned from Japan.

"You'd better go, Michiko," Edward told her impatiently. He hated long good-byes. "They're about ready to lift the gangplank."

Still Michiko lingered, hugging Anna Su. Edward was suddenly stricken with qualms. Maybe she shouldn't go after all. The political situation with Japan didn't look good, even if America was still using the Pacific shipping lanes. Although Michiko had been allowed to return to Japan because she was still a Japanese citizen, Anna Su, who was American, was a different matter. The red tape would have taken too long, and Michiko had to go immediately, as her mother was dying.

A grimace twisted his lips. It had taken her mother's dying wish to influence Michiko's father and brother to finally break their silence. Tak's letter had been brief. "Come at once if you hope to see our mother alive. Uncle Isami will arrange your passage."

"Good-bye again, my husband." Michiko had straightened up, and he saw the pain in her eyes. She couldn't bear to leave her small child, and yet she'd never forgive herself if she ignored the summons to her mother's deathbed. It had been a terrible decision for her, and even Edward had wished Anna Su could go. He wasn't used to the responsibility of a child.

"Almost forgot," she said, and opening her purse, she pulled out an envelope. "Please send to Katie." She handed it to him, suddenly too shy to tell him how much she loved him and would miss him in the weeks they'd be apart.

He gave her another quick hug, and a peck on the mouth, and then watched her go, her innate dignity obvious in the determined set of her small head, the graceful movement of her body. She didn't look back.

"Shit!" he muttered under his breath. He'd miss her. But as he turned to go, he glimpsed a couple up the wharf who were looking at him and talking. Edward quickened his step, and Anna Su, who hung on his hand, had to run to keep up.

Edward knew what the couple had been saying. *Interracial marriage.* The bastards! And in his heart he was suddenly relieved that Michiko was leaving. It was too bad that Anna Su couldn't have gone too.

He could have used a break from the constant sidelong glances because his wife and child were Japanese.

On the way home, he dropped Michiko's letter in the mailbox.

Katie scanned the letter, then plopped down on the chair. "Oh my God!" she said to the empty room. Michiko had gone to Japan. The letter explained the circumstances, but what about the war? She just hoped Michiko was right in what she'd written—that America and Japan would never be at war, and she'd return to California before August anyway.

By September, Katie worried about not having further word from Michiko. Her letters to Edward went unanswered, but that was nothing new. Edward had left the writing to his wife. Did that mean Michiko was still in Japan? she wondered. By late October, Katie was becoming alarmed. The newspaper reported that Premier Konoye had resigned in Tokyo, and Emperor Hirohito had designated Tojo as War Minister—a man whose policies were threatening to the United States.

"Christ Almighty!" Fred ran into the office on the seventh of December, having just heard the news on his shop radio. "The Japs bombed Pearl Harbor this morning! It's war!"

"Dear God!" Katie, who'd been filing ledgers, staggered backward into her chair. "It's really happened."

Then she went with the others to sit by the radio and listened in horror as the description of burning ships in a burning harbor thousands of miles away was broadcast over the airwaves. The death toll continued to mount. There was no mistake; it was really war.

The news brought panic to Alaska. Would they be

bombed next? Invaded? War also brought more
American troops, intense acceleration of defense,
and even more work for Max. "The Allies will never
stop the combined forces of Germany, Italy, and
Japan," Dion exclaimed as he readied to fly out his
regular route, a route that could be dangerous now
for his unarmed plane. "They're so prepared—and
we're not."

Katie wished he'd never said his fears aloud—
because they were her fears, too. At any time, one of
their own little planes could be shot down by the
Japanese. But it still shattered her to know the
Japanese people were now enemies of America.

There were other fears that haunted Katie's lonely
nights—about Max's safety because she knew he
flew to the places the Japanese would attack—if they
attacked—and about Michiko. Had she gotten back
to California before Pearl Harbor? Why didn't
Edward write, so that she and Johanna would know
what happened?

Expecting a letter, his wire to Katie came as a
shock. "Come at once. Stop. Anna Su in danger.
Stop. Needs home."

All the way over to Johanna's house, she felt
frustrated about the communication system in Alaska. If she lived in Juneau, she could at least call
Edward on the radio telephone and find out what his
wire meant. She suspected it had something to do
with America and Japan being at war—and Anna Su
being half Japanese. There had been immediate
reaction to the bombing of Hawaii—by congress-
men, journalists, and private citizens—to "round up
every Jap and put them in concentration camps."
Fear reigned over Alaska as well as the Lower
Forty-Eight. The West Coast had gone to full war
alert. Nevertheless, Katie knew she could never
abandon her dearest friend's child, who was also her
niece.

Did the telegram mean that Michiko was still in Japan? she asked herself as she pulled up by Johanna's front door. Once inside the house, she simply handed Johanna the telegram.

"What are you going to do?" Johanna asked as Dion came out of the kitchen. Having heard their brief interchange, he looked puzzled, and without a word read the telegram over his wife's shoulder.

"Christ! You aren't flying to San Francisco, are you?" Dion asked, his eyes narrowed on her as he guessed her intent. "And bringing her back up here?"

"You can't!" Johanna cried before Katie could answer. "Edward shouldn't expect such a thing! I know you love Michiko, but this is war now. And you know how absolutely terrified everyone is about anything Japanese."

"But Anna Su is our blood—and she must be in danger," Katie said, surprised by their reaction, especially Johanna's. "Edward has many faults, but exaggeration isn't one of them."

"Katie," Dion said, for once serious. "If you brought a Japanese child up here it would draw attention to all of us. It would reveal that you'd lived most of your life in Japan. It would jeopardize our government contracts!"

"I think you should wire Edward back and—"

"And refuse!" Dion interrupted, his tone emphatic.

"I'll talk it over with Max when he gets back this afternoon," Katie said, seeing that they would never understand how she felt—that Anna Su was a person first—a small girl, not just a war casualty.

She left them and was completely unsettled until Max returned and she could talk with him. At first he was as incredulous as Johanna and Dion that Edward should expect Katie to assume the responsibility for his daughter.

"Forget all the other ramifications," he began, trying to be supportive of her feelings even while he had to be firm. "I can't have you flying south now, and Anna Su would never be allowed to fly up here, even if this wasn't a Japanese issue. Flying is too dangerous. We don't know where the enemy is located. They could be right off our coast."

"But all the air routes haven't been closed." Katie's fear for Michiko and her little girl was growing. She had no idea what had happened, but somehow she knew it wasn't good. The more she thought about Edward's terse telegram, the more she knew that he wouldn't have done such a thing lightly. They'd hardly been speaking when she left San Francisco.

He shook his head. "They can't be—at least not yet. They're our only connection to the Lower Forty-Eight."

"Then I'm going, Max," she said, her tone low, but vibrant with determination. "Nothing must happen to Anna Su."

He grabbed her then, pulling her roughly into his arms. "I can't let you, darling, even though I know your motives are pure and loving. If anything happened to you—" His voice broke with emotion. "I'd die myself."

"I have no intention of leaving you—ever," she replied huskily. "I love you more than anyone on earth. But I can't abandon Anna Su. I could be her only hope—in whatever has happened."

He claimed her mouth then, so she would stop trying to convince him, and his kisses were demanding, possessive. He wanted her to forget her sense of responsibility toward her brother's family, because it was dangerous. And for a long time, the conflict between them was forgotten. Later, as she lay in his arms, content and sated from his lovemaking, she brought up the subject again.

"We haven't been invaded yet," she began. "So maybe the Japanese will never attack the West Coast as everyone fears." She hesitated, sensing a sudden tensing of his body. "I'm going, Max. I have to."

She went on to express all her feelings, the reasons she couldn't ignore Edward's request for help. Finally, seeing that she wouldn't be dissuaded, Max reluctantly agreed, although he had grave reservations. His Katie, so fearless when faced with danger, wouldn't forgive herself if she turned her back on a loved one. She never placed herself ahead of others, and he suspected the trait grew out of the combined backgrounds of loving, religious parents, and her understanding of ancient Eastern beliefs.

But having her go will be hell, he thought, and pulled her to him once more.

Since he knew he couldn't stop her, Max arranged her travel plan himself, flights down and back. He managed to get her on a cargo plane that flew an interior route, away from the coast and a possible enemy scout. Although it was hundreds of miles longer, Katie was thankful to have the seat and grateful to Max who understood why she had to go. She packed immediately, knowing she must get down to San Francisco and bring Anna Su back on the return flight. The air routes could be closed to civilians without notice.

"Take care, sweetheart," Max told her just before she boarded the plane. "And come back safe. I love you."

"I love you, Max." She hated to see him looking so tense, the lines on his rugged face so pronounced. "And I'll be back, I promise." Katie went up the steps into the plane without looking back. She couldn't.

The morning sun was shrouded by storm clouds, the ragged mountain peaks and wooded islands hidden beneath a billowing froth of gray fog, as the plane circled Cook Inlet and headed southwest. Turbulance rocked and tossed the plane, and it only became worse as they flew inland, above the mountains to avoid the coastline.

It's not an omen, Katie reminded herself over and over again. But her fear of crashing was real.

PART TWO

Winter 1942–Summer 1945

CHAPTER 12

THE HOUSE ON RUSSIAN HILL REFLECTED MICHIKO'S absence. It was cluttered, dusty, and in need of a good cleaning. Edward had met Katie at the door with a hug, and for once his bearing was humble, as though he had suffered. When Katie heard about the drastic measures being taken by the government toward Japanese people living in America, she realized that Edward's desperation about Anna Su was valid.

"Can you take Anna Su to Alaska?" Edward asked bluntly.

They were sitting in the living room that reminded Katie of her pre-Alaska days. But it was Anna Su, sitting next to her father on the davenport, who commanded Katie's attention. The little girl was dainty in her pink pinafore and white ruffled blouse.

Although her hair was black and silky, and her eyes brown, she looked more Caucasian than Japanese. Katie had an urge to hold her close, but the child's innate shyness held her back. She kept her distance, but smiled often at Anna Su and was pleased when her smile was finally returned. She resembled the Aalands, but her mannerisms were Michiko's.

"It's been terrible," he went on when she didn't reply at once, and the whine she detected in his tone pricked her with annoyance, which she suppressed. "Who would have thought being married to a Japanese woman could cause such trouble. Anna Su should have gone with her mother. She'd be better off in Hiroshima than discriminated against in California."

At his words, Anna Su's lashes lowered, and Katie suddenly realized that the child had often heard her father speak in such a manner. If Katie hadn't already decided upon taking her niece, she would have at that moment.

He leaned forward, his expression tight. "And it's getting worse. Isami Kono and his family are being taken to an internment camp, and their home and business and other assets have been confiscated—to be sold at a fraction of their value."

"Oh, my God! Those poor people. They might lose a fortune."

Edward shrugged. What happened to the Konos wasn't his problem, and he didn't feel much sympathy for them anyway, not after what they'd done to him. But his daughter was a different matter.

He took Anna Su's hand, and Katie saw that in Edward's own way, he loved the child. "I can't have her going to an internment camp, Katie."

"Surely they couldn't take an innocent child—whose father is American?"

"The world has gone crazy. Anything can happen.

That's why I wired you. You can take Anna Su, can't you?"

"Of course," she said simply. "Michiko is like my own sister. I'd do anything for her, as she would for me."

His relief was obvious as he sank back on the cushions. She smiled wryly. He didn't care about her reasons; he only needed her to say yes. He's still the self-serving Edward he's always been, she decided, with a return of annoyance.

"And there's also the possibility you'll be drafted," she said, her eyes on the child. "Most men your age are going into the service."

He lowered his gaze, embarrassed. "I won't be."

"Why not?"

"It seems I have a heart murmur."

Later, when Katie was alone in her room, she wondered about Michiko. Even Edward didn't know what had happened, why she hadn't returned, and it angered Katie to think he hadn't tried to find out until it was too late. She knew Michiko would never have left her beloved child behind on purpose. She must be frantic, Katie thought. In hearing the whole story from Edward, she realized that Mrs. Kono's illness was probably a ploy to get Michiko back to Japan before a war broke out. Katie sighed, staring at the light patterns on the ceiling. They hadn't anticipated the red tape involved for Anna Su to accompany her mother, and that Michiko would go without her child, believing her mother's death was imminent.

For the next two days, while they awaited the plane's departure, Katie spent her time getting to know Anna Su. They went on outings together, and Katie realized again how much she loved San Francisco with its moderate climate and steep hills and beautiful harbor. But life is a tradeoff, she reminded herself. To live in the Bay Area meant not having

Max, and she'd live at the North Pole to be with him.
So she contented herself by telling Anna Su about
Alaska, and her little niece listened politely, as
though she understood every word.

But Katie gained her trust, and the sweet expression on the little face told Katie that her love would
soon follow. The next morning they flew north.
Katie felt relieved; the West Coast was on a complete
blackout, with no lights allowed after dark. She was
also apprehensive. She must get back to Anchorage
before the situation worsened, or she could be stuck
in the Lower Forty-Eight for the duration of the war.

Johanna met the plane, much to Katie's disappointment. Worn out from the long flight, she felt as
if she'd been away from Max for months, not ten
days. Even the sky was low and gray, obscuring the
mountains. Her arrival was not the welcoming one
she'd hoped it would be.

"Max is at Dutch Harbor, and Dion's in Nome,"
Johanna said as they climbed into the car, and Anna
Su was placed on the back seat next to Elisabetta.

The difference in the two little girls was not so
great: both had dark hair and eyes. It was Anna Su's
bearing that was different. She was shy, with the
innate dignity of an old and honorable Japanese
family, while Elisabetta was all American in her
out-going, expressive personality.

Once Katie was back in her house, she realized
how much she'd missed it—and Max. Despite her
fatigue, she put on coffee, and as the little girls played
in the next room, she and Johanna talked.

"Katie," Johanna began, her expression worried.
"I'm really concerned about your bringing Anna Su
to Alaska, and I need to be honest with you about my
feelings. I think it was a mistake."

"I disagree." Katie was equally direct. "And in
any case, it was the only thing to do. Too many

people knew about Edward's marriage to a Japanese woman, and it's possible that Anna Su would have been sent to an internment camp, for her own safety if nothing else. Hatred for the Japanese is incredible in California."

"Here too," Johanna said softly. "Things have gotten much worse while you've been gone. The whole Territory is gearing up for an invasion. Japanese families in Alaska will also be taken to internment camps."

"Oh, Lord! I didn't think things would go that far up here."

"And it'll probably get even worse," Johanna added.

"At least no one knows Anna Su is Japanese. She doesn't look it, unless you know her background."

"That's true, Katie." Johanna glanced at the two little girls just beyond the doorway. "But if it ever got out, and that you—even I—grew up in Japan, Dion believes we'd all become suspect. And Stefanini Air Service would lose the government contracts, which is our mainstay now that we're at war."

So it's Dion again, Katie thought as Johanna gathered up Elisabetta and went out to her car. It was hard to believe that people could hate an innocent child, no matter what their parents or country had done. She tried to put it all out of her mind, and concentrated instead on settling Anna Su into her new home. But her mind kept reverting to the internment camps, and Katie wondered if she'd be in one if she'd stayed in Japan. One thing she'd realized over the past weeks—as much as she loved the Japan of her childhood, the Japanese were wrong to bomb Pearl Harbor. She was loyal to America.

That night, after Anna Su was asleep in the bedroom upstairs, Katie lay in bed listening to the wind howl around the eaves. Did Max share Dion's feelings? Because of the fears and panic, maybe he'd changed his mind about Anna Su's living with them. She hoped not, because she couldn't send the little girl back to California now. Anna Su was the sweetest child she'd even known, and Katie already loved her as her own.

But her body ached for Max. She loved him with all her heart too, in a whole different way than her feelings for Anna Su. She wouldn't rest easy until they talked—and she was reassured by his love.

"Hi, sweetheart! Miss me?"

Katie whirled around from the kitchen sink. Before she could worry about how she looked with her hair tied back and dishwater splashed against her middle, or that he wasn't due in until tomorrow morning, she was in his arms with his lips on hers in a kiss that took her breath away.

When he finally lifted his head, Max glanced around the room that was lit by only a small light over the sink. "Where's Anna Su?"

"She's already tucked in for the night. You'll meet her in the morning."

The light was suddenly caught in his eyes, accentuating their blackness. But there were dark circles beneath them as well and deeper lines and sharper curves to his features. He looked tired. And as Katie stepped back, she saw that he'd also lost weight, even though he was still the muscular pilot in his leather flying jacket and laced-up boots. She wanted nothing more than to have him make mad, passionate love to her. But first he must eat, and have a bath.

"Putting me off?" he asked when she suggested that he bathe while she fixed him something to eat. He said it jokingly, but Katie sensed something else in his tone—hurt, perhaps.

Putting her arms around his neck, she stood on tiptoes and kissed him squarely on the mouth, a long, passionate kiss. She wanted to reassure him, so that he didn't harbor thoughts that she might have put Anna Su ahead of his feelings.

"I love you Max—and I missed you desperately." His arms tightened to press her close. "Each night while I was away I dreamed of your making love to me—and I could hardly stand it." She took a quick, shuddering breath, her senses swimming as she saw his eyelids lower in the way they did when he was about to swoop her off to bed.

Again she managed to step back, a hopeful smile on her lips. "So a bath and some food will restore your energy for—for later."

He stood there with contrived nonchalance, a glint of humor in his eyes. "Think you can handle it—all that's going to happen later?"

Beyond the window, the night had come down over the mountains and water. A moon drifted in and out of clouds that trailed like kite tails across the sky. The wind fingered the house, whispered against the eaves, and rustled the spruce boughs over the wood siding. And Katie trembled, the rich timbre of his voice telling her more than his questions.

She nodded.

"Then I'll take the bath, and eat."

His knowing smile did nothing for her state—her complete awareness of him, and her own need.

"It won't take long, sweetheart." He shot her a masterful grin. "I'm inspired. Can't wait for the dessert."

Then he disappeared into the bathroom.

They didn't talk, aside from short periods between their lovemaking. They couldn't get enough of each other. The war and all its problems were forgotten, and Katie wished she could hold on to the precious hours forever. When there is love, she thought many times during the night, sex only gets better, more intense in its exquisite ecstasy.

Dawn crept into the room around the edges of the shades, and they finally talked. She lay on his arm, her head in the curve of his neck, contented. The afterglow of lovemaking was as special to Katie as the act itself. Lying so close afterward was a benediction.

"How is Anna Su adjusting?" Max asked softly.

"Fine, I think." Katie was thoughtful for a minute. "She's a gentle child, and I suspect that life with Edward after Michiko was gone wasn't nurturing to her. I sense she's bewildered about what's happened."

Katie went on to tell him about San Francisco and that Edward hadn't heard from Michiko and assumed the situation in Japan had precluded her return. "I think the family tried to get her and Anna Su back to Japan before war broke out, and hadn't counted on Michiko going alone."

Max shook his head. "War does terrible things to people, motivates them to do things they wouldn't normally do. I just hope it all turns out all right for Anna Su in the end."

A chill touched Katie, and she pulled up the blankets. He'd expressed her fear for Anna Su. But Katie pushed it aside, determined to be optimistic. "You'll love her, Max. She's like a little China doll."

"Then she looks Japanese?"

"Not in her features, only her femininity—which is uniquely oriental."

He propped himself on an elbow to look down at her flushed face. Even though the light was dim, the brilliance of her green eyes still reflected their passionate night. Her blond hair lay in long tangles around her face, but she'd never looked more desirable—or beautiful. She, too, possessed the oriental mystique, he thought. He knew her intimately now, knew she loved him unconditionally, but still she continued to surprise him with hidden depths.

Her love was based on trust, and because he could never abuse that trust, he had to be honest now.

"I have to admit I'm glad she doesn't look Japanese," he began slowly. "The people up here have panicked, worried that the war will be on our doorstep any day now. And that might very well happen; the threat is real." He hesitated. "Right or wrong, Katie, anything connected to Japan would raise questions."

"I know." She glanced away. "Johanna told me that we would be under suspicion if our background in Japan was known."

"I'm sorry, sweetheart. We have to keep Anna Su's race a secret for now." He chucked her under the chin, so that she met his gaze. "But we'll love her so much that she won't miss her parents, and one day she'll be back where she belongs." He bushed her lips with a kiss. "Okay, Katie?"

"Okay," she whispered, and then his kiss, demanding once more, took all her thoughts save one. Loving her husband.

Some time later Katie slipped out of bed, careful not to disturb Max, who'd finally fallen into a needed sleep. Grabbing her robe, she went to the kitchen and placed kindling on the embers in the kitchen stove. Once the fire was going, she put on the coffee pot, and then went to check on Anna Su.

The little girl was awake, sitting quietly on her bed, her flannel nightgown splayed over her legs, looking at a picture book she'd brought from California. Her constant companion, her Raggedy Ann doll, sat on her lap. Katie went to her, speaking softly, and hugged the tiny body. It brought a lump to her throat when Anna Su's arms encircled her back. She was so good—too good, Katie thought. Anna Su needed to be a child who played and laughed, not the solemn, heartbroken child before her.

Katie took her hand and they went to the kitchen

where it was warmer. Anna Su sat at the table, watching, as Katie started breakfast.

"So this is Anna Su?"

By the time Katie turned around, Max was already pulling up a chair next to Anna Su, talking to the child about her doll. Within minutes he had her in a conversation, and a short time later she was on his lap, showing him the pictures in her book.

A slow smile touched Katie's lips. Among all his other abilities, Max was a natural with children. Max would be a good father.

A new longing took hold of her. She wanted Max's child.

"Is that all, Mrs. Stefanini?"

"That's it," Katie told the butcher and handed him the money for her meat. She had Anna Su hold one side of her shopping bag as she placed the wrapped roast on top of the groceries. Turning from the counter, Katie paused to let two women go around her. The elder one stopped, her gaze darting between Katie and Anna Su.

"Stefanini? No one would guess that you're Italian from your looks," she told Katie. "But there's no doubt about your daughter."

"Italian!" the other woman sniffed disdainfully. "They should be shipped off like the Japanese!"

Taken aback, Katie could only gape at their rudeness. Then a wave of anger swept through her so fast that she began to shake.

"How dare you talk to me like that!" she cried. "My nationality is none of your damn business!"

"Hmph! Indeed it is! In case you haven't heard, we're at war with Italy. And—"

"See here!" the butcher interrupted sharply, directing his words to the two women. "I won't have this in my store. Mrs. Stefanini's husband is a flyer, doing important work for the military."

"Hmph!" the woman said again. "The military? And he's Italian? Something's wrong here."

After a nod to her companion, the woman turned and headed out of the store, the other woman right behind her. "We'll get our meat elsewhere," she snapped over her shoulder.

The door swung shut behind them, leaving the butcher and Katie looking at each other. Katie was shaken, and Anna Su clung to her skirt. She managed to thank the butcher, who'd lost his customers sticking up for her. Then she took Anna Su and left him. All she wanted was to get home.

Outside she slowed her steps, conscious of Anna Su trying to keep up. Oh my God! Katie thought. Johanna and Dion and Max had been right. Fear was a madness that afflicted everyone. She glanced again at Anna Su. They'd thought she was Italian!

What would have happened if they'd known the truth? She quickened her step, suddenly longing for the safety of her own house. Crazy—crazy—crazy! she chanted under her breath. But the war was real. And she knew the madness wouldn't end until it was over.

CHAPTER 13

"FOR CHRIST'S SAKE, MAX! YOU KNOW DAMN GOOD AND well what'll happen if it leaks out!"

Dion's face was flushed with anger, and although Max agreed it wouldn't be good if it were known that Anna Su was Japanese, he also thought his brother was inordinately upset. Dion was more affected by the war sentiment than he should be, Max thought.

"Look, the kid isn't hurting anyone. And no one will think to question her nationality." Max returned to his invoices and wished Katie was still able to work in the office. Her time was limited now with Anna Su to look after, but he knew she'd been looking for a reliable woman to baby-sit.

"Don't bury your head in the sand, Max."

Glancing up again, Max was annoyed. "Will you just shut up about it? She's here and she stays!"

"You know, Max—you're still the same fuckin' do-gooder as when you were a kid!" Dion slammed down his log book. "It doesn't seem to register in that pea-brain of yours that the local radicals have already singled us out as Italians who shouldn't be doing government work. Just think about what's important—a Jap kid, or Stefanini Air Service?"

Max jumped up so fast that his chair thudded over on its back. "*The Jap kid*—as you put it—happens to be Johanna's niece too."

"And Stefanini Air Service is our living!"

He slammed out of the office, and Max was left shaking with anger. Dion always took the easy way out. He could never be counted on in a pinch.

"Shit!" Max threw down his pen. If Dion wasn't such a good pilot, he wouldn't put up with him. And no other air service would hire him, even with the shortage of pilots, he reminded himself. His drinking and undependable ways were legend. Max headed toward the shop to tell Dion just that. It was time to put the matter to rest once and for all.

During the days that followed, Katie sensed the tension between Max and Dion. When she asked Max about it, he told her what had happened, and that Dion wouldn't give an inch on the issue. Even Johanna seemed distant. Although regretful about the estrangement, Katie had no time to indulge their pettiness, as Max would soon leave again for several weeks. She was sure they'd never reveal Anna Su's background—if only for their own sakes.

It was almost a relief when Max left for Dutch Harbor out in the Aleutians, as Dion had to take over other flights and was gone more as well. Katie's only regret was that military restrictions forbade her to accompany Max to destinations that were "off limits." Although Max had never come right out and said so, she suspected that secret airfields were under construction out in the Aleutians.

She worried constantly, but at least it was spring and there was more daylight for flying, even if the weather stayed stormy out on the Chain. Again she spent more time with her sister, and Johanna confided that she was pregnant again.

"Oh, Johanna!" Katie cried, shocked. "You know the doctor told you another pregnancy could kill you!"

Johanna glanced down, looking so tired and miserable that Katie immediately regretted her outburst. "It just happened. I didn't want it either.

Katie lowered her lashes, hiding her anger. Damn Dion! she fumed. All he cared about was himself—and his selfish urges!

The next week, Katie managed to hire an Aleut woman to baby-sit and went back to her job in the office. The work had stacked up, and she was astounded by how much of it had to do with the military. It took several more weeks to catch up with everything. Several times, when Max was in Anchorage, she was able to make a short, round-trip flight with him, so they could spend a few more hours together. Even Dion and other Alaskan pilots were flying supplies for the military, as signs pointed to a surprise enemy attack. The rumors didn't help Katie's constant worry, nor did the bad weather reports from the Aleutians. She'd heard that many reconnaissance planes had gone down because of the weather—the inexperienced pilots from the Lower Forty-Eight didn't know how to cope with ice build-up and white-outs and sudden gale-force winds.

"Katie," Max said one night as they lay in bed. "I shouldn't repeat this, but I want you to take extra precautions. Army Intelligence believes an attack is imminent."

"How do you know?" she whispered. The house

was dark, as was the whole city under the strict blackout order of General Buckner.

"I know that the North Pacific Fleet of nine ships is preparing for battle. That's all I can say, Katie. But be careful, and keep your eyes open. Our house is out here by itself near the Arm." He paused, as though he considered whether or not to go on. "And there have been sightings of Japanese submarines off the coast of Alaska."

"You think they might land troops?"

"Anything's possible." He turned her to him, his arm on her back, so that her breasts were against his chest, their legs intertwined. "Just be careful, sweetheart, that's all. It worries me to think of you here by yourself."

"I'll be fine, Max. It's you who has to be careful." She snuggled closer so that their lips touched. "Don't take chances, Max."

They kissed, and she moaned softly, anticipating his touch. As their passion took hold of them, Katie was transported to another time and place, where there was no war, only love. For a long time they didn't talk at all.

But the next morning, his words of warning came back to her. About to leave for the airfield with Max, Katie hesitated, her gaze on Martha, the grandmotherly woman she'd hired to care for Anna Su. Martha and Anna Su had immediately liked each other, and Katie felt fortunate to have found the woman. Martha had come to Anchorage from one of the far Aleutian Islands to live near her married children. Now Katie wondered if she should leave them alone during the day—in the light of what Max had said.

"Maybe they shouldn't stay here alone if—"

Max interrupted, understanding her fears. "They're better off here than at the airfield," he said gravely. "Although it isn't Elmendorf Air Base, it would still be one of the main targets."

She only nodded, but she felt scared. She was quiet all the way to the airfield, even when Max pulled her next to him as he drove. They went into the office to find Dion talking to Fred.

"Hell," Dion was saying. "I think it's another false alarm, like all the other rumors. The Japs haven't attacked yet, and I don't think they will."

"You're wrong, man!" Fred retorted. "The government ain't goin' to all this fuss and bother for nothin'."

Dion only shook his head. "I fly out to the Aleutians, down the Arm, across Prince William Sound to Cordova—and I've never seen one enemy scout plane, or a submarine."

"But others have," Max interrupted as they went inside and closed the door. "Many times."

"Christ!" Dion pulled on his gloves and zipped his leather jacket. "For all the brass says, I have my doubts that Japan is stupid enough to face the hardships of a war in Alaska."

"Even if it put them within striking distance of the Bremerton Naval Yard, and the Boeing bomber plant down in Washington?" Fred asked. "What in hell changed your tune about the war?"

Dion shrugged, tossed off a jaunty grin, and went out to warm up his plane.

"I'll be out in the shop," Fred said, and followed Dion out the door. Max and Katie were left staring at each other, both wondering how Dion's mind worked. He always thought differently from everyone else. If they'd been the ones saying there would be no attack, he'd surely disagree.

By the first of June, several weeks later, there had been no attack, and it began to seem that Dion was right. If the Japanese intended to invade Alaska, they certainly would have done it by now, Katie thought as she got ready for bed. She'd just bathed, and as she dried herself, anticipating her bed, something occurred to her.

Jolted, she dropped the towel and stood examining herself in the full-length mirror. The midnight sun cast its strange light through the window behind her as her gaze lingered on breasts that seemed fuller, nipples more pronounced. Her tummy was as flat as ever, but as she thought back, she realized that she'd missed last month's period, and her next one was overdue.

She was pregnant!

Her joy was instant. Thank you, God! she thought as she danced naked around the room. If only Max were there. She couldn't wait to tell him.

Abruptly, she stopped. She didn't know that she was pregnant for sure. Women could miss periods. She'd make an appointment with Johanna's doctor, she decided, make certain before she told Max. Besides, he was flying in tomorrow, and he'd promised to take her on his flight out on the Chain because it was a shorter one that didn't go all the way out to Dutch Harbor. She suddenly knew he wouldn't take her if he thought she was pregnant.

For once, Max was on schedule. They were able to enjoy a leisurely supper with Anna Su, and later, after they'd made love, Max shared some of his concerns about the war situation.

"I've thought about this for a long time," he began. "Even though General Buckner has finally gotten more planes and pilots, our defense is still inadequate. The B-26 Marauders need extra-long runways for takeoff, and most of the Alaskan airfields can't accommodate them—not to mention that their round-trip range is less than a thousand miles. We only have a few of the LB-30 Liberators with the couple-thousand-mile range and the capability of landing on the shorter fields."

He paused, his eyes troubled. "If it comes to

all-out war, Alaska might not have the defense to
ward off an invasion."

Katie swallowed hard, bracing herself. She knew
what was coming next. The general had already
evacuated military families, and she feared that's
where Max was leading the conversation. But she
wouldn't go. She couldn't leave him. And besides,
there was Anna Su who shouldn't go back to San
Francisco now.

She kissed him and in seconds diverted the conversation. "Tomorrow is the third of June already,
darling. It's months since Pearl Harbor. Dion might
be right. The Japanese have probably decided that
the cost is too high to buck the weather conditions up
here."

And then they were too occupied for the next few
hours to even remember their earlier conversation.

The passing twilight of the night brought the day
early. Katie had arranged for Martha to come at four
a.m., and she and Max were already airborne an
hour later. As they flew southwest, down Cook Inlet,
the weather worsened, but Max managed to fly
under the cloud cover over the water. Alone in the
cockpit with Max, Katie was reminded of their trip
from San Francisco. The war seemed far away as
they soared through the sky.

Then the radio crackled to life. "Japanese bombing Dutch Harbor! Alter course, Max!"

"The bastards!" Max cried over the engine
sounds. Without hesitation, he made the adjust-
ments to the controls, and tipped the plane onto its
side to change course. In seconds, they were headed
into the cloud cover.

Max talked briefly to the radio dispatcher, setting
his new coordinates. Their peace was shattered, and
somehow Katie knew it was gone for a long time to
come. For a second their eyes met.

"I love you, sweetheart," he said. "Don't ever forget that."

"And I love you, more than anything in the world."

By the time they landed on a tiny field in the middle of nowhere, one of the "secret ones" she hadn't known existed, they learned that the Japanese bombers had returned for a second run on Dutch Harbor. The information was sketchy, but one thing was certain. She wouldn't continue the flight with Max, once he had the clearance to go. Instead, they kissed good-bye on the windy, desolate field, painfully aware of the men around them who averted their eyes. She watched him fly into the clouds and wondered if she'd ever see him again.

She was put on a cargo plane back to Anchorage the next day and learned upon landing that the Japanese had bombed again for the second day. All airfields had tightened security.

"Jesus! I'm glad you got back okay," a shaken Fred told her. "Them damn Japs are liable to hit us next."

"I know," Katie replied. "Has there been any word from Max?"

He shook his head. "Or Dion. There're both out there where they can't radio us."

She'd been afraid of that. Now all she could do was wait.

"But I did hear that the base at Dutch Harbor wasn't destroyed, even though the American fighters from Cold Bay arrived too late to help." He shrugged in a gesture of frustration. "Not because those bastards didn't try, but because of the low cloud cover. For once the weather was on our side."

He went back into the shop, and Katie knew he'd be working around the clock overhauling the engine on their third plane. Alaska needed every aircraft ready to fly.

Knowing that Johanna and Martha would be worried, she went first to check on her sister, then home. She spent the next few days between the house and the office, hardly sleeping at night. A brief visit to the doctor's office, between her other duties, confirmed her pregnancy. It was her one bright light in a world suddenly dark with foreboding.

Max returned unexpectedly. She heard his plane circle the field and was outside to meet him before the wheels had even stopped on the runway. He jumped out and she was in his arms.

"Thank God—thank God!" was all she could say between kisses. Fred ran out to greet him as well, and Katie and Max walked with him into the office.

"What's happened, Boss?" Fred asked as they closed the door.

Max tossed his gloves and jacket onto the chair. He was pale and strained, and his eyes were red-rimmed with fatigue. Katie knew he hadn't slept for days. She tried not to think of what that kind of exhaustion could mean flying in terrible weather.

"While the Japanese were bombing us, the Americans gained their first war victory at Midway in the South Pacific. The brass think the Alaskan attack might have been a diversionary tactic so we'd strengthen our forces up here, and they'd win in the South Pacific."

"And it didn't work?" Katie didn't quite understand.

Max shook his head. "I heard a rumor that Army Intelligence in Hawaii had broken a Japanese code prior to all this, and realized what might be happening, so they were ready for them down there. It seems the Japanese had divided their naval power by having part of their fleet up here—enough to fool us into thinking this would be their primary invasion point—and then they'd take Midway, which they assumed would be relatively undefended."

"So that means they won't invade us?" Katie's question was hopeful.

He spread his hands, his dark brows drawn together in a frown. "No one knows," he evaded.

"And don't forget," Fred began drily. "They have a whole fuckin' fleet up here now, and they sure as hell ain't gonna waste it."

Max shot him a warning glance, which Katie intercepted. "Fred's right. Don't try to shield me, Max. I need to know, so I can be prepared too."

Fred went back to work, and Max went over some paperwork that needed immediate attention. Later, when he and Katie finally went home so he could sleep for a few hours, they talked again.

"You know that this means you can't be in the air at all until it's over, don't you Katie?"

She hated being a woman at times like these. But she nodded. "I understand."

"So no flying, Katie. Even if you think it's an emergency."

"I won't fly," she agreed, and lowered her lashes to screen her eyes. But she couldn't promise not to fly if there was an emergency. In these times, an emergency could mean anything, including a threat to the lives of her loved ones.

They'd been undressing for bed, and when he saw her step out of her last garment, all other thoughts went out of his head. He even forgot how tired he was. He took her quickly, out of passion and desperation and fear for their future. Later, as she lay on the curve of his arm, her favorite position, she spoke softly, and for a second her words didn't register.

"I'm pregnant, Max. I'm going to have our child."

Then her announcement hit him. He propped himself to look into her face. "A baby? When?"

A sweet smile touched her lips. He sounded so tender—so humble—God, how she loved him at that moment! "Sometime close to Christmas."

"Why didn't you tell me, Katie? We have to be careful now." He touched her bare stomach, gently trailing his fingers over her flesh. "Maybe—uh, that is, did I hurt you—before, when I make love to you?"

She moved closer, one hand caressing him, arousing him again. "You can't hurt me, darling, no matter how passionate your lovemaking. And I don't want you to stop either." She paused to let her words sink in. "Woman are made to be loved—and to have babies. Sex only contributes to their well-being."

With a low groan, he took her words as gospel, but this time he didn't rush things. He would never get enough of her, not even when he was too old to only dream of nights like this.

But much later, Katie allowed their passion to cool. He had to sleep. But she lay awake throughout the long twilight night, content for those hours, unwilling to sleep away the short time they had together.

Too soon he was gone again, and all her worries and fears returned stronger than ever. It didn't help matters to learn that the Japanese had occupied Kiska and Attu Islands at the tip of the Chain. Although Dion had never flown out that far, Katie knew Max had, and when she asked him about it the next time he was home, he only evaded answering.

"The visability is so poor out there that planes could pass and never see each other," he joked, trying to lighten her worry. She didn't tell him that he only made it worse. She knew weather conditions took more planes than the war.

"By the way, Katie," Max said one day before leaving yet again. Although his tone was light, she sensed he was about to say something important. "My Italian background was investigated recently, before I got higher military clearance."

"Why did they do that?" she cried, alarmed.

"Just procedure," he answered, and decided not to elaborate. "We—Dion and all of us—just have to be above reproach," he said instead.

Minutes later, he waved from the wing of his plane, then climbed into the cockpit and roared off down the runway. Katie watched him out of sight, and knew what he'd really meant. It must never get out that Anna Su was Japanese.

It began to rain, depressing weather to match her mood. *Please don't let Max take terrible chances,* she prayed, *just because he's Italian and needs to prove his loyalty.*

If only people could be compassionate about their fellow Americans—who happened to have the wrong ancestry. God, keep him safe. She couldn't live if he didn't live too.

CHAPTER 14

THE SUMMER PASSED IN A BLUR OF WORRY AND IMPENDING attack by the Japanese. In September, Johanna delivered her baby, a boy they named Oliver. Dion was present for the birth, and surprisingly, Johanna got through the whole thing without the severe problems she'd experienced before. Katie took care of her for several weeks once she'd been released from the hospital.

It was a relief to Katie as the days shortened, and fall brought back longer nights. But as November drew to a close, and the daylight hours shrank to only a few, she began to dread the sub-freezing temperatures and the snow and ice of winter. It meant Max would be gone even more.

Her own pregnancy had progressed normally, but the day the pains started caught her unprepared, as it was two weeks ahead of her due date. A month earlier, she'd hired a retired railroad man to take over the office work and used her extra time to prepare a nursery in the room next to Anna Su. Because Max was in Nome, Katie got herself ready for the hospital, then drove over to Johanna's house where she was to leave Anna Su.

"What?" Johanna cried when she heard Katie was in labor. "Katie! Why do you do such impulsive things? You can't drive with labor pains!"

Katie had no time to argue. She'd taken too long to get ready, and now she wondered if she'd make it. Quickly, she handed Anna Su's overnight bag to Johanna, and then climbed back under the wheel, knowing she had to hurry. Her pains were closer and more intense.

"I have no choice," she said, biting her lip as another one tightened her stomach. "There's no one else to take me." She let out the clutch and the Ford jerked forward. Her hair fell out of its pins, but she merely pushed it behind her ears and stepped harder on the gas pedal.

The nurse at the admitting desk was equally incredulous to see her drive up to the emergency entrance, but she didn't linger with questions. Katie was immediately taken to the maternity ward. The doctor was summoned and arrived just in time to assist the birth.

"She's a beautiful little girl," he told her, smiling. "And I might add that your delivery went faster than any I've assisted. You could probably have a dozen kids with no trouble at all."

They took her to a private room and later brought her baby wrapped in a pink flannel blanket. Humbled by the miracle of the birth, Katie lovingly examined the perfectly formed infant. Her features were delicate, her round head capped by blonde fuzz. Even as she unwrapped the blanket to see the tiny feet, the little fists began waving and the mouth puckered. She was only minutes old and already hungry.

As the baby nursed at her breast, tears welled in Katie's eyes. Max had missed his daughter's arrival into the world. She watched the tiny face, the eyelids closed over deep blue eyes that would turn brown like Max's, and realized how much her new daughter resembled her father. Although the hair was light, and the features delicate, she was a picture of Max.

"My sweet baby," Katie whispered, and felt a new kind of love, so deep that it choked her up. "Oh, Max," she murmured. "Our baby is so special, so beautiful. If only you could have been here."

But she knew he was grounded in Nome, as he'd radioed being socked in by fog. She sighed, and was glad that they'd at least chosen names together, for either boy or girl.

"Little Christina," she told the sleeping baby in her arms. "Your papa will be so proud." And she gently kissed the soft cheek.

And later still, as she drifted into an exhaused sleep, she thought of something else. Christina had been born on December 6th, one day before the first anniversary of the bombing of Pearl Harbor. Groggily, she wondered if the war would go on forever.

The news of his daughter's birth was radioed to Max. He waited impatiently for the weather to lift, then flew out of Nome during a lull between storms. It was risky, but he had to get to Katie. It was hell not knowing how she'd come through the delivery. His mind kept returning to Johanna, who'd almost died when Elisabetta was born.

Max was thrilled with Christina, and Katie hid a smile when he held her for the first time, gingerly and as though he feared he'd drop her. When he looked up, Katie was rocked to the core by his expression.

His eyes were filled with wonderment—and love. She'd never seen him look so humbled.

"She's so beautiful—so tiny." He placed Christina back in Katie's arms. "Thank you, my darling. I love you so much—" He broke off, shaking his head. "There aren't words to express how much." Then he pulled her to him, gently so as not to disturb the baby. "I don't know how I existed before you were in my life, Katie." His voice lowered to a whisper. "I've been blessed."

By the time Katie left the hospital and was back on her feet again, Max had already been gone for a week. Knowing Anna Su was an added burden for Johanna, and not very welcome in Dion's house, Katie took her home early.

After the first of the year, Katie looked forward to longer days; winter was depressing with its limited daylight hours. But mid-winter brought even more disturbing news when Max accidentally mentioned Kiska Island one night as they lay in bed.

Katie stiffened. "The Japanese occupy Kiska Island. You aren't flying out that far on the Chain, are you, Max?"

"Listen, Katie," he began, his tone abruptly serious. "You know I can't discuss this. But I'll admit I have flown supplies out on the Chain."

"Oh, Max. Don't do it. You're not in the Army."

"But only because I'm a civilian pilot working for the military," he reminded her gently. "And it's kept me from being drafted and sent to fight in Europe." He hesitated. "Flying out there isn't as dangerous as you think, because of the cloud cover."

"Have you ever seen a Japanese plane?"

"C'mon," he said, reverting to his earlier mood of playful lovemaking. "Let's not spoil our last night before I leave again."

As he feathered her face with kisses, she suppressed her fears. He was right about the Japanese being a lesser threat than the weather out in the Aleutian Islands; it was the worst in the world, so bad that trees couldn't grow because the wind kept them from taking root. Maybe it's better that she and Johanna don't know where Max and Dion were most of the time, she told herself.

After Max made love to her, he fell into an exhausted sleep. She stared into the blackness of the room and remembered her other life in Japan. Strange how the world changes, she thought. Now she feared the very people she once loved and respected. She wondered how Michiko was surviving the war—without her beloved child. Oh, how she must worry and grieve, Katie thought. Often Katie talked to Anna Su about her mother, and although she never mentioned "Japanese," she made sure her niece would never forget Michiko.

She turned so that she snuggled closer to Max, curling against his back. For now, she'd just enjoy being with her husband. She'd leave her worries for tomorrow.

The winter days dragged toward March, and Katie found herself living for Max's next visit. The days and weeks between, she concentrated on Christina and Anna Su, who loved her new little cousin. The advent of the baby had been healthy for Anna Su, who'd quietly assigned herself as the adoring and protective "big sister."

Expecting Max to fly in any day, Katie was disappointed when light snow began to fall late one afternoon. She just knew the storm would preclude his getting home. After the children were in bed, Katie took a leisurely bath in the faint light of one candle, always aware of the blackout. Then, on impulse, she took her green satin kimono from a hanger and slipped it over her nightgown. Since being in Alaska, she often wore a more practical robe of heavy flannel, but tonight she felt in the mood for something more glamorous.

The crackle from the fireplace was the only sound in the living room, and Katie decided against putting on another log, conscious of light showing beyond the shaded windows. She sat down in a comfortable, overstuffed chair and stretched her legs toward the warmth of the hearth. When the chill became too great, she'd go to bed.

For once the wind was still, suspended by the infinite peace of the falling snow. The fire had cast the room into shadowy humps and vague shapes, and as she stared into the flames, her thoughts drifted. The wall cabinet clock in the hall struck the half hour, but it wasn't that sound that disturbed her reverie; it was the click of the front doorknob being turned.

It's Max! Katie thought, and reacting instantly, ran to the front hall. The fact that Max had a key didn't occur to her at that moment, and she quickly slipped the bolt and flung open the door, a smile of anticipation on her face.

Her welcoming smile froze, and her eyes widened. Fear was sudden and paralyzing. The man in white, from his storm boots to his hooded fur parka, wasn't Max. Before she could react, he was in the hall, the door shut behind him.

"Don't cry out," he whispered urgently, as though he sensed the scream that was straining for release in Katie's throat. His voice was vaguely familiar, even though the dark hall obscured his features. "Or I'll have to gag you." He grabbed her arm as he spoke, and his hood slipped off his head.

"Tak!" she gasped. But it was impossible! She couldn't believe it was him.

He gave a curt nod, as his gaze darted over the hall

and up the stairway, making sure they were alone. Then he led her into the living room where the firelight gave more illumination to his face.

Her limbs shook, reacting from fear and shock, but when his eyes fastened on her again, she was hit by another emotion. For a moment she was back in Japan, feeling the desolation when he left her. Her voice was unsteady and whispery when she finally spoke.

"What are you doing here? How did you know where I was?"

The intensity between them mesmerized her; his gaze locked hers to him. He was lean to the point of gauntness, and the flickering light cast his features into sharp angles and odd shadows, and his black eyes were penetrating and cold. *He looked dangerous!*

She stepped back, and his hand dropped from her arm, but she saw, by the alert stance of his body, that he would spring forward and grab her the second she tried to run. This was not the same Tak she once knew, Katie realized, and a shiver of fear touched her spine. He'd removed his gloves, and his holstered gun was only inches from his hand. She knew that he would be as proficient with handling it as he'd been with everything else in his life.

"How—?"

His raised hand, flat and silencing, was a gesture she remembered from those long-ago, hazy days in Japan. When she subsided, he pulled a crumpled paper from an inside pocket, and with a snap of his wrist, it unfurled to its full letter-size. Astonished, Katie recognized the Anchorage city map she'd once sent to Michiko, with the circle of red ink to show the location of her new house. She lifted her eyes to him in a question.

Although his expression was remote, Tak's feelings were far from cold. He hadn't reckoned on his old love for Katie to surface when he saw her—or that he'd be affected by all the feelings he read on her face—shock, fear and remembering. *Oh, little Katie-san, my lost love, have you forgotten my kendo teachings so soon?* he thought. But he expressed nothing, knowing he couldn't, not then and not now—or ever. It took every ounce of his own *kendo* to keep him from taking her into his arms; she was even more lovely than he remembered. She was still a golden fairy child, and a woman more desirable than all others to him.

"I'm here because of Michiko, Katie-san," he said finally, his tone flat under his iron control.

"Michiko? Is she all right? Oh Tak—I've worried so about Michiko."

Her rush of words gave him pause, and again it took effort to maintain his facade. He shook his head. "She's living in Hiroshima with our parents, who moved from Tokyo at the start of the war. But she's been sick with worry over her baby." His tone hardened as he remembered how emotionally fragile Michiko had become since they'd brought her back to Japan—how frantic when she couldn't return to her husband and child. "I know Anna Su is with you."

"But how did you know? There was no communication after—" She broke off as she remembered what Japan had done at Pearl Harbor, to Dutch Harbor. And Max's danger because the Japanese occupied the far islands of the Chain.

"Pearl Harbor?"

He finished her sentence, and she saw a glint in his eyes she didn't like. Quickly she changed the subject, bringing it back to their niece.

"How did you know?" she repeated, her voice stronger now that her first fear was gone.

"Japanese Intelligence knows about the American internment camps, and my—someone got word to us that Anna Su had been taken to Alaska, by you, for her own safety."

She knew he'd been about to say his uncle—which meant that word did leak out of America to the Japanese. The thought sent new ripples of apprehension through her. *Tak was the enemy.*

At once she lowered her lashes, because she knew he read every thought that touched her mind. But that realization only added to her growing fears. He'd risked his life to find her. Did that mean he meant to kidnap Anna Su? She licked her lips, her mind in chaos.

"Katie, Katie." He closed the space between them, and with two fingers, tipped her chin so that she had to meet his eyes. "I volunteered for this reconnaissance mission only because I wanted to see Anna Su—to make sure she's really here. I'm not going to hurt you."

But his eyes still glinted with that expression she hadn't seen in the old Tak. Was he telling the truth? Why else would he have come?

"My own government would shoot me, Katie, if they knew I'd jeopardized the mission like this—as fast as yours would if they caught me."

"Then why—?"

Again he interrupted, as though his words had made him conscious of the time. "Because I don't trust Edward—who has already betrayed the Kono family," he retorted, and for the first time he revealed an emotion—anger.

"But I do trust you, Katie," he went on. "To care for Anna Su until she's reunited with her mother one day. And to keep my visit a secret, so I can send word to Michiko that her child is safe—and restore her sanity."

She considered his motives. She knew he was capable of taking the child, despite the consequences. A samurai valued honor above all, and if family honor meant going against military honor, he would make the choice, and then commit *seppuku* to restore his face in death. He must be telling the truth, she decided, as he was risking a mission by his action. To take Anna Su would be a last resort—if he decided she would report him. And if he did—was she in danger? His waiting expression told her nothing.

"Anna Su will always be safe with me," she told him, unable to disguise her hurt. "How could you think otherwise? The blood in her veins is the same as it would have been had she been our child," she reminded him softly.

Turning away, she didn't see the momentary pain in his eyes. "Come," she said. "I'll show you." She swept to the stairs, her long blonde hair shimmering against the green kimono.

Silently he followed her up to Anna Su's room, then stood in the doorway, his eyes on the sleeping child. Finally he nodded, and they started back to the steps. But at the open door to Christina's room he hesitated again, this time his eyes on the baby in the crib.

"She's mine," was all Katie could manage under his inscrutable gaze.

Once downstairs again, an awkward silence fell over them. Little night sounds, the crackling of the fire, even the ticking of the clock, grew in magnitude, and Katie's apprehension returned. She suddenly remembered Edward's recent letter—that Kono Imports had been on the market at a fraction of its worth and he'd managed to buy it. Katie had been astonished by his news, incredulous that he was in a position to buy such a large business. But most of all she'd been ashamed that he'd capitalized on the misfortune of the Konos. Had Tak's information source also revealed Edward's latest breach of honor?

But there was something even more important to consider at the moment, she reminded herself. Tak was a spy—*and she knew.*

"Katie, I—" He was interrupted by a sound at the front door, like someone kicking snow off his boots. Tak's hand went to his gun.

"No, Tak!" Katie jumped between him and the door. She knew it was Max this time.

It only took a fraction of a second for Tak to understand—and decide. He bolted toward the kitchen and the back door. For a brief moment their eyes met, and Katie glimpsed the Tak of those golden days in her memory. And she knew he could not have hurt her. Then he was gone in a swoosh of icy air, and she would never know what he'd been about to say.

Everything happened so fast that Katie was left disoriented. Somehow, she managed to pull her ragged emotions into a semblance of normalcy by the time she opened the door to Max a few seconds later. And her kiss of welcome was genuine. But he saw something was wrong.

He stepped back, throwing his hat and gloves into a chair as he spoke. "Aren't you glad to see me, Katie?" He grinned lopsidedly. "After I flew through a hellish storm to get home?"

"Oh, Max," she began, but her voice wobbled. "Of course I am."

He took her in his arms and kissed her mouth lightly. "So what's wrong, sweetheart?"

The mental images of the past half hour whirled in her mind while she tried to think. He waited, looking more concerned with each passing second. She loved him, and she couldn't lie; he trusted her. In the end Katie decided to tell the truth.

"Jesus Christ!"

She'd hardly finished when he'd bounded to the

back door and disappeared into the night. A short time later he was back, his hair glistening with snow.

"He's gone. But I saw his footprints." Max went to the hall closet and took a gun case from the top shelf. "In case he comes back."

"My God, Max! Tak won't be back."

He faced her, his face tight with concern—or anger. "Do you understand how serious this is, Katie?"

"Yes—I do," she said, subdued by the inflection in his voice. Now that Tak was gone, the magnitude of his having been there hit her hard. If they didn't report Tak, they might be letting him get away with valuable information. If they did, would the authorities understand the situation? And most important, would Max lose the government work that was so important to the future of his business and their country? Katie even wondered if they'd be arrested.

"What are we going to do?" Suddenly overwhelmed, Katie slumped into the overstuffed chair.

Taking a deep breath, Max took hold of himself, and sat on the davenport, his gun beside him. It was a hell of a mess. But he realized it wasn't Katie's fault. She must have been shocked to see Tak at her door.

"I'm not sure," he said finally. "In any other circumstances, I'd have already reported him. But we don't know that he had any other reason for being here, aside from what he said. As crazy as it seems to us, it could be legitimate for him to go to such lengths for Michiko, given his culture."

"He said he was on a reconnaissance mission." Again Katie couldn't lie, if only by omission.

"Jesus!" he retorted. "What a dilemma. Reporting him means everyone will know Anna Su is Japanese, and they'll know about the family connection to the Konos."

He ran his hands through his hair, and Katie saw how tired he was. Oh, dear God, she hated being responsible for a new worry. She felt terrible, even though it wasn't her fault.

"And worse, there would be suspicion," he went on. "Because we had contact with a Japanese spy. It would mean the end of everything for us. I doubt that anyone would believe our story." He hesitated for long seconds. "I certainly wouldn't be trusted with government secrets."

Abruptly he got up and checked the bolts on both front and back doors. Back in the living room again, he managed a brief grin.

"It's too big an issue to decide tonight," he told her. "Tak's long gone anyway, probably back to his sub by now. We may as well get some sleep and decide what to do in the morning.

As Katie went upstairs with him, sudden anger swept over her. How could Tak have put them in such a horrible position? War! It destroyed everything that should be sacred. And it changed lives forever.

"I've decided it's best to keep quiet about this," Max said the next morning. "There's nothing to gain by having our loyalty challenged. We'd only destroy ourselves, and Dion and Johanna too."

She nodded and glanced out the bedroom window where the new snow lay like a benediction over the land. All trace of Tak was gone. "I'm so sorry about this, Max. I feel responsible."

He came to her and folded her against him. "No, sweetheart, you're not. Even if Tak's real mission was spying, we wouldn't have known but for his coming here."

"But what about *our* honor? We have a responsibility to our country." As much as she hated the truth, she had to say it. "Tak is the enemy."

"I haven't forgotten," Max said, his voice hardened with resolve. "I intend to start a rumor of possible enemy infiltration—and see that it gets checked out."

His words raised goose flesh on her skin. If Tak were caught, he could be shot. The faces of his parents surfaced for an instant in her mind. Tak was their beloved son. It was too much for her to even think about.

"And I'll take precautions in case he ever tries to pay a return visit here." The inflection in his tone told Katie that Max wouldn't hesitate to use his gun either.

"Tak won't be back," she told him quietly.

"It's possible. The Japanese are known for suicide missions."

But as Katie went downstairs to start breakfast, she knew Tak wouldn't return. Tak trusted her. Their unspoken bond went too deep, far beyond the war. It was something she could never discuss, not even with Max. Although she loved Max more than anyone else, there was a part of her that would always love Tak. But karma was karma. And she might never see Tak again.

CHAPTER 15

"YOU REALIZE THE RAMIFICATIONS OF THIS, DON'T YOU, Mrs. Stefanini?"

"Of course I do," Katie retorted, unable to keep the irritation from her voice. "But it's as I explained, Major Laird. I was shocked to hear that Tak Kono had been caught by your people—to even hear he was in Alaska."

She sat in a hard-back chair facing the uniformed officer behind the desk, a round-faced, balding man in his forties whose steely eyes belied his otherwise benign appearance. Although no one had said so, she suspected he was with Army Intelligence. She'd been summoned to meet with him because they'd captured Tak, two weeks after his late-night visit. Tak had been searched and questioned, but had managed to escape, vanishing without a trace. Katie's map to

Michiko had been in his possession, and Katie discovered very soon after arriving that she'd already been investigated, and her relationship to Tak Kono had been uncovered. She tried to control her nervousness and her guilt about lying.

"And the seriousness of the situation?"

She nodded, and quelled an urge to fidget, keeping her hands folded on her lap. Katie knew she looked prim and proper in her navy suit and pumps, an unlikely spy. "Although I grew up in Japan, and knew the Konos, doesn't mean I'm not loyal to my country," she told him tartly.

"You more than just knew them, Mrs. Stefanini," he said drily, toying with a pencil. But his eyes behind the horn-rimmed glasses were penetrating, watchful for even a suggestion that she lied. "Your brother is married to Tak Kono's sister. His young niece lives with you."

"That's true," she agreed at once, her tone level. "I've already explained all of that to you. It all happened long before the war—long before any of us believed Japan would be our enemy." She hesitated. "Except for Anna Su living with us, and I've explained those circumstances as well."

"Then why did your sister-in-law return to Japan —shortly before Pearl Harbor?" He leaned forward, and she suspected that he was trying to trip her up by rewording the same questions.

Taking a deep breath, Katie drew upon her early teachings of patience and calm. "She believed her mother was dying," she repeated for the second time. "In the light of what we know now, it's possible that story was only a ploy to get her to Japan. But Michiko believed it, or she wouldn't have left Edward and Anna Su. She expected to return to them."

"So you took Anna Su rather than let her stay with her own father?"

Looking him straight in the eyes, Katie replied at once. "The reason I took Anna Su is exactly as I've stated." She tilted her chin, and again annoyance crept into her voice. "And I won't apologize about that action to anyone. Anna Su is my niece, and I love her. She's a harmless child, and I couldn't see her coming to harm because of her mother's nationality. Her father is an American citizen, after all."

She didn't add her feelings about Edward, or that Anna Su was an embarrassment to him. That part was none of the major's damn business! she fumed behind her calm facade.

But she was worried. It was within the major's power to send Anna Su away, discredit Max, even hold her for further questioning. Katie tried to avert her thoughts from what the major was thinking, that Tak had an accomplice—her. At all costs she must convince him of her innocence. He could never be told that Tak had actually been to her house.

"Your—uh, Michiko took your map to Japan, but not her daughter—is that correct?"

"I told you, she believed her mother was dying and left at once. She didn't wait for the necessary paperwork so Anna Su could go along. Michiko planned a short trip." Katie wondered if he'd ever be satisfied. "And I can only assume that she had my letter, with the map, in her purse so that she'd have my address to write."

"And did she write?"

"No, she didn't."

She wasn't about to elaborate on that either, that she'd often wondered why Michiko hadn't written in the weeks before Pearl Harbor.

A silence settled over the office, but the major's gaze didn't waver from her. Katie didn't look away either, determined that she wouldn't succumb to his intimidation. A typewriter clacked in the outer room, a car started up in the street beyond the dusty window, and the tapping of his pencil was in time with the ticking wall clock.

"Since he had your map it would indicate that he intended to look you up," the major said, breaking the heavy silence. "Perhaps he meant to take you, or the children, hostage."

"Hostage? Why?" Katie's surprise was genuine.

"For information."

"But I have none. I don't know anything that would be of interest to the Japanese." *But Max does*, she thought suddenly.

Braced to defend herself further, Katie was taken off balance when the major abruptly stood up, his wooden chair scraping loudly on the bare floor.

"I think we've covered it all for now," he said, but his tone was noncommittal as to his final determination of the incident.

Katie stood as well when he came around the desk. He took her elbow and walked with her to the door. "We'll be in touch," he added.

Only as Katie walked to the Ford did she begin to tremble. *Oh, God!* she thought. Was their whole world about to crumble around them? She started the motor, and even though she wanted to put space between her and the major, she drove away slowly. Once on the main road, she pushed the gas pedal to the floor. She needed to get home where she felt safe.

During the next couple of weeks, Katie felt suspended in a vacuum. She didn't hear from the major again, and as the days passed, her nervousness grew. She couldn't even discuss her feelings with Johanna, as both her sister and Dion were upset about being questioned themselves and blamed Katie for bringing Anna Su to Alaska in the first place. But one night when Max was home for supper, he put most of her fears to rest.

"I was questioned too," he said over coffee, after

Christina and Anna Su had been put to bed. "The Tak Kono issue is closed."

"Closed?"

They had moved from the kitchen to the living room and were sitting on the davenport in front of the fireplace. Although the days were lengthening with the advent of spring, the nights were still cold, and Katie had lit the fire.

"Major Laird—the officer who talked to you—called me in. Of course, they're still concerned about Tak Kono, but they've decided that you were telling the truth, Katie."

"Thank God!"

He pulled her next to him, his arm around her shoulders. "Just one thing, Katie." He hesitated. "We can never conceal information again. Tak is the enemy, and if he ever returns, he'll be shot."

"I know, Max," she said, and went on in a lower tone. "But I'd hate to think of you shooting him."

"That isn't likely," he replied. "I can almost guarantee that he'd never make it as far as this house."

What did that mean? she wondered. That their house was being watched? Katie questioned Max further, but found him unwilling to pursue the subject. As they went to bed, she couldn't get over a niggling suspicion that Max hadn't told her everything, although she believed the issue of Tak was closed. But was it forgotten? Even when Max made love to her, Katie couldn't completely forget her worries. She prayed that Max's work wasn't in jeopardy, that Anna Su wouldn't be sent back to California.

The next afternoon, Katie left the girls with Martha and drove over to Johanna's house, anxious to relieve the tension that had grown up between them over Tak. She confided what Max had said and was relieved when Johanna relaxed and invited her for coffee. It was a good omen, as Johanna and Dion had avoided family contact since the investigation.

"Maybe it's all behind us now," Johanna said hopefully as Katie was leaving.

After more reassurance, Katie drove off to do her grocery shopping. She hurried through her list once she was in the store, eager to complete her errands so she could surprise Max at the airfield and give him a ride home. Katie was looking for oatmeal when she overheard two women talking in the next aisle.

"All I heard was that the girl is half-Japanese, not Italian like everyone assumed. And that the authorities questioned the whole family."

Katie stopped in mid-stride. *They were talking about her!*

For a minute she didn't know how to react. Then anger propelled her to the end of the aisle so she could confront the gossipers. But they'd already purchased their groceries and were on their way out of the store. She took several deep breaths and reminded herself that creating a scene wouldn't help. It would only stir up more gossip.

Quickly, she went to the cashier and tried to be patient while the woman added up her purchases. It only added to Katie's upset that the clerk wasn't friendly either. She was glad to get outside and back into her car. She drove all the way to the airfield with the window down, to cool her hot cheeks.

By the time Katie pulled up in front of the office, she'd restored her calm. Max had been in Anchorage for several days and was scheduled to leave again in the morning. She wanted their evening together to be relaxed and pleasant.

"Hi, Katie!" Fred said, coming from the shop. "I'll tell Max you're here."

"That's all right. I can find him myself," she replied with a smile. "Is he in the office?"

"No, the shop."

About to alter her course, Katie was stopped by Fred's hand on her arm. "Er—'scuse me," he stammered, embarrassed. "But I'm 'fraid you can't go in there, Katie."

Her eyes widened in surprise. "Why not?"

"Orders," he said, and glanced away, grateful to see Max emerge through the shop door.

"Orders. Whose orders?" Katie demanded, her upset returning.

"I'll explain, sweetheart," Max said. "Let's get in the car. I'm calling it a day." But he gave her a smile instead of the explanation. He obviously didn't want to discuss it in front of Fred. "Hope you have something good for supper. I'm starved," he added as they walked to the car.

"What's going on, Max?" she asked once they were away from the airfield.

He saw her upset and decided to be honest. "You've been banned from the field. I didn't know you were coming out to pick me up, or I would have warned you."

"How long have you known about this?" Katie kept her voice level, but she felt betrayed somehow. Max should have explained before.

"Since yesterday."

"I see." Katie glanced out the window, realizing that this was the thing Max hadn't told her the night before.

The car suddenly veered off the road onto a shoulder and came to an abrupt stop. Then Max turned to her, and took hold of her upper arms to pull her to him.

"Let me explain before you get more upset."

His eyes seemed darker because of the deep shadows under them. Or was it because his face had drained of color? Her own hurt was suddenly second to her concern for him. He was the man she loved with such passion, and she saw that he was hurting even more than she was.

"I can guess," she said, her tone low with resignation. "It's the Tak thing, isn't it?"

"That's not been mentioned in connection with this. It's a security measure, that's all. You aren't the only person banned from the field."

He was bareheaded, and the wind had mussed his hair so that it tumbled in crisp black wings over his forehead. Absently, he pushed it back, and Katie was suddenly reminded of the first time she'd met him in the park. His hair had been mussed that day too. Silently she put her arms around him and hugged him close.

"I understand, Max," she murmured, realizing there was no point in getting angry. It wasn't his fault, and there was nothing she could do about it in any case. She suspected that he was under terrible pressure to stay above suspicion, and the security measure confirmed her fear. Katie knew it was because of her, even if Max would never admit it.

After a light kiss on her lips, Max put the car in gear and they headed for home. Although she snuggled against him, they rode in silence. *Now even our relationship is suffering*, she told herself. Her own husband must keep secrets to spare her feelings.

The tires bumped and bounced over the potholes, but Katie didn't even notice. She just wanted the damnable war to go away, and take their awful problems with it. She sensed that Max was thinking the same thing—even if he no longer felt he could share all of his feelings with her.

An American invasion force of eleven thousand men landed on the beach at Attu in early May, and by the end of the month they took the island from the Japanese. Katie heard that more than five hun-

dred Americans were killed in the battle, but the
Japanese lost most of their garrison, their casualties
numbering well over two thousand. Only eighteen
Japanese were taken prisoner, chosing instead to die
in suicide charges. Although Max wasn't involved in
the battle, Katie knew he was somewhere in the
Aleutians, and the worry kept her tossing and turning every night. Even Johanna commented that she
looked tired and thinner.

The children weren't sleeping well either, and
Katie decided that the lack of darkness had something to do with it. By the end of June, the sun shone
until midnight, followed by twilight until it rose
again several hours later. Katie longed to be working
in the office. She didn't even go into town unless she
needed something, as she couldn't stand knowing
that some people still gossiped about her. The
thought of another long summer without Max was
almost unbearable.

Katie came to know Martha quite well, as the
Aleut woman still came several times a week to do
housework and take care of the girls when Katie did
her errands. Their conversations about the Aleutian
Islands helped Katie understand the conditions Max
faced while flying the Chain. On the morning Katie
wanted to wash the outside windows, a storm threatened and she told Martha they'd have to wait.
Storms in summer could be as violent as in the
winter, even if they lacked ice and snow.

"We'll do them next time," Katie said, her eyes on
the ominous clouds. "I'll do my shopping instead."

Martha nodded. "Best to wait."

About to go change from her work slacks, Katie
saw a car approaching on the road. It pulled into her
yard and Johanna jumped out with both her children. Then she waved to the driver, who drove off,
back toward Anchorage. Katie recognized her sister's neighbor. Something was wrong.

"It's Dion!" Johanna cried as Katie ran to her. "He's crashed and radioed for help." A sob caught in her throat. "And there are no available pilots—not any close enough to get to him for a couple of hours."

Martha quietly took charge of the children as Katie pressed for more details. She saw that Johanna was on the verge of collapse and was holding herself together by only a thread of control. Her own heart felt as if it galloped in her chest; she had always feared the day when she'd hear that either Max or Dion had gone down. But she tried to stay calm so that she could get the details.

"He's down on the Kenai Peninsula—was on his way to Dutch Harbor. Oh Katie—if the weather socks in, no one will be able to reach him—and he's hurt!" Johanna broke into sobs.

"I'll go." Katie was already running to the house for her jacket. If Dion was hurt, he could die from exposure. She knew Max's old Fairchild wasn't being used because of the shortage of pilots, but Fred kept it gassed up and in good running condition.

In minutes, Katie had given Martha instructions concerning the children, had kissed them good-bye, and was on her way to the Ford, Johanna right behind her.

"But Katie!" Johanna cried over the sound of the Ford's engine starting up. "You can't fly. They won't even let you on the field!"

Katie only shook her head. She'd fly all right. A glance at the turbulent sky told her that she had to.

She drove right up to the shop, and Fred's helper tried to stop her when she jumped out of the Ford. Katie waved him aside and asked for Fred.

"That's another thing," Johanna said, still behind her. "Even Fred wasn't available. He's in Fairbanks and won't be back until tonight."

"You stay by the radio in the office," she told Johanna after writing down Dion's last coordinates.

Then, disregarding everyone, she climbed into the Fairchild, checked the instruments, and switched on the engine. As she taxied down the field, Katie closed her mind to the ramifications of her action. She was flaunting security, not to mention Army Intelligence. But Dion's life was at stake. She had no choice.

Lift-off was smooth, and as Katie soared into the sky and headed south over Cook Inlet, the plane gained altitude effortlessly. The storm was moving in fast, but the sky above her was blue and calm. She knew she had to find Dion before conditions changed, as they would quite suddenly.

She was glad that Max had installed a radio in the Fairchild, and as she was about to try for radio contact with Dion, another voice came over the air instead, calling her by name and asking her to respond.

"This is Katie Stefanini."

"You're ordered to turn back and land at once!" The static voice was not anyone at the airfield. The note of authority told her she was being contacted by the military airbase. Fear touched her with a moment of dread. She was in for it once she did land.

"Do you have another plane to pick up Dion?" Katie skipped the proper protocol of radio communication. There was no time for formalities.

"One has been diverted to his location."

"When will it reach him?"

There was a hesitation. "We're not sure."

"That's not good enough!" Katie cried. Already the Fairchild was into intermittent clouds, and she was picking up turbulence. "The weather will sock in before that."

"We order you to turn back!" The voice hardened. "You won't make it either!"

"I'm Dion's only chance!" She found herself almost yelling, as even in those seconds, the wind had strengthened. "I'm not turning back! Either give me radio bearings or get off my radio!"

There was no answer, and Katie concentrated on flying below the clouds, following the coastline down the Kenai Peninsula. There was no mistake that the weather was against her, and she kept a sharp lookout. An occasional Japanese scout plane had been sighted in the area.

Resolved to radio silence, she was startled by a return of the same voice. Without preamble, he gave her updated coordinates to where the plane was down. "And—good luck, Mrs. Stefanini."

The weather pushed down on her, cutting visibility and buffeting the plane with violent gusts of wind. *I could crash as well*, she thought, fighting panic. She was already flying in conditions beyond her experience, and she fell back on the instinct she'd once made use of in flying kites. *But this isn't a kite*, she reminded herself sharply as she adjusted airspeed and altitude, flying even lower, almost skimming the water. She prayed she'd find him before all visibility was gone.

When she spotted his plane, her first reaction of relief was quickly smothered by fear. He'd crashed on a short strip of beach—and the tide was coming in. She didn't even know if there was enough space to land. Katie bit her lip, and her hands tightened on the controls. It was now or never.

Lowering the nose, she headed straight in, struggling to keep the wings level, hoping a down draft wouldn't slam her into the ground. The wheels hit the beach hard, and the plane rocked dangerously before righting itself. The wet sand helped to slow the landing and she managed to stop next to Dion's Cessna. She could see him slumped in the cockpit.

With no time to lose, she scrambled out of her plane and ran to him. The door to the cockpit was jammed, and it took her a minute to force it open. It began to rain, and in seconds she was soaked, her hair plastered to her head.

"Katie." His voice was weak. "I didn't think anyone would make it in time. How—"

"Shhh. We can talk later." It was an effort for him to speak; she knew he was badly hurt. Blood oozed from a deep gash on his forehead. He needed immediate medical attention. Somehow she managed to pull him out of his plane and half drag him to the Fairchild, where he collapsed onto the seat.

Quickly, Katie prepared for takeoff. The tide was rising fast, and she wondered if Dion's plane would still be there when it receded. She'd realized at first glance that there wasn't enough beach to land an Army plane. If she'd turned back, Dion would have died.

Once she'd taxied to the far end of the beach, she revved the engine. They were airborne just in time, and as she circled out over the water to gain altitude, a plane suddenly swooped out of the clouds. Startled, Katie thought it was about to land on the beach she'd just left. But it banked, and it was then that Katie saw the painted sun on its tail—a Japanese scout!

"Jesus Christ!" Dion cried. "Head for cover!"

But Katie was already doing that. She braced for the worst, trying to maneuver the bucking Fairchild away from the scout, and expected to be strafed at any moment.

Again she was startled by an American voice on the radio. "Move your ass, Fairchild!"

Then she saw the P-40 fighter drop out of the clouds. For a moment both the American and the Japanese planes were in full view. Then she was in the clouds, flying blind, and Katie seriously doubted they'd make it. After several minutes of no visibility, she decided her chances were better under the clouds, even if she became a target.

The trip was a nightmare. Katie thought the plane would come apart at the seams from the battering it took. Through sheets of wind-driven rain, she managed to bring it down on the airfield. The wheels had hardly come to a stop when men ran out to help. In minutes, soaked and shaking, Katie was in Max's office facing the same Major Laird who'd interviewed her after the Tak incident, and Dion was on his way to the hospital with Johanna.

"That was some feat, Mrs. Stefanini," he said, finally breaking the silence. "Are you okay?"

She nodded. She was wrapped in a blanket, but her trembling limbs had nothing to do with being wet. It was delayed reaction. Katie still didn't know how she'd managed to do it—or how the plane had withstood the violent weather front. She also knew the major's concern would be brief. He had other things on his mind, or he wouldn't have been there to meet her.

"You do realize that you defied a military order, in a war zone?"

"I felt I had no choice, Major." Her voice didn't show how much he intimidated her. "You saw for yourself. Dion could have died. And I'm sure the other American pilot told you the beach would not have accommodated his plane."

Another silence dropped over the room while he regarded her intently, tried to disconcert her. She wished Max were there. He'd understand that—rules or not—she'd done the right thing.

"Why do you suppose the enemy plane didn't fire on you?" He lit a cigarette and blew smoke, waiting.

"I have no idea," she retorted, recognizing where he was leading. "But I'm glad he didn't. I was a sitting duck!"

Something flickered in his eyes behind the glasses and was gone. "Still, it is strange, don't you think?"

She'd had it. Army Intelligence be damned! She wasn't putting up with his insinuations. Katie jumped up, and the blanket fell from her shoulders.

"What are you saying Major Laird? That I flew out there—through a storm that almost tore my plane apart—just to meet an enemy scout? Are you suggesting I had an ulterior motive other than saving my brother-in-law's life?"

Throughout her tirade he merely puffed on his cigarette, listening with hooded eyes behind the smoke.

"Let me put it to you this way," she went on, too angry to stop. "Do you think I arranged for Dion to crash so that I could fly to his rescue and meet a Japanese scout?" She whirled away and flounced to the door where she faced him for one last retort. "Because if that's what you think, you can—you can go to hell!"

She was about to grab the knob when the door swung open and Max stood framed in the doorway, worry etched on his face, his dark eyes taking in the scene. For several seconds they all seemed frozen in place. The major was the first to react.

"I think that's all, Mrs. Stefanini," he said calmly, and stood up. "We'll be in touch concerning this matter. You're free to go."

Katie saw that he was dismissing her. She nodded, but she wondered what would happen to her now. The major was no fool, and she had no doubt that he'd already made up his mind about her latest run-in with him.

"One more thing," Major Laird said.

She met his eyes once more, aware of Max's intense interest in what was happening and that she was now sheltered by his arm, which had dropped around her waist as though to protect her.

"Off the record." The major lit another cigarette. "You're some woman, Mrs. Stefanini. Foolhardy, but courageous."

"Thank you," she managed.

"And one last thing."

She'd been about to leave again. Here it comes, she thought. He's probably having me arrested tomorrow. Once more he surprised her.

"I believe your story, Mrs. Stefanini—uh, Katie. Because it's as you pointed out—too incredible to be otherwise." He blew more smoke. "Good night."

After a brief conversation with Max, the major left. Then Katie and Max got in the Ford. On the way home she explained everything.

"I understand why the major needs to investigate," Max said. "They've had a few substantiated security leaks, and it's his job to check out anything that seems odd."

"Especially if the person involved has known connections to the Japanese?"

They had just pulled up in the yard, and Max faced her after switching off the motor. "That's true, Katie," he replied seriously. "But you heard him. He believes your story. He's a man who says exactly what he means."

He kissed her then, murmuring in her ear. "But you have to stop doing these things." He lifted his head, his eyes so close she could see herself reflected in them. "You were lucky to make it back. God only knows why you weren't shot out of the sky."

That was something she wondered too. The Japanese plane had been there ahead of the P-40—and it had been about to land. She hadn't told the major

that. But as she ran through the rain to the front door
with Max, she decided it would be best not to. He'd
only change his mind and decide she *had* been there
to meet the scout.

At the door, Max paused to kiss her again. "Hurry
and see to things," he said huskily. "I'll be waiting in
bed."

And she forgot about everything else.

CHAPTER 16

THE WIND WAS GENTLE AGAINST KATIE'S FACE, FRESH with the salty fragrance of seawater. She sat on the grass beneath the lone pine on the bluff, her favorite place to go when she needed to think. She'd left Christina and Anna Su with Martha and had walked the short distance from the house. Max would be home soon, and before they talked she needed to be clear about her feelings.

Beyond the arm of Cook Inlet, the mountains were clearly etched against the blue sky, a reminder of the wild, vast, uninhabited land that stretched for hundreds of miles to the north. It was a perfect day that allowed the majestic splendor of Alaska to be showcased in all its glory. Oh dear God, she thought. How could she leave? For all its hardships and violent weather, it was home to her now. She was married to

the man she loved, they had their own house, and her
child had been born here.

She pulled her knees up so that she could rest her
chin on them, allowing the wind to fan her long hair
around her face. Finally she permitted herself to
remember the conversation she'd had with Major
Laird only yesterday and the words that had frightened her far more than her flight down Kenai to
rescue Dion.

"We have no real evidence against you, Katie," he
said, and she'd been amused that he'd dropped the
Mrs. Stefanini. "But word has gotten out about this
latest—uh, escapade of yours, and the heat has come
down on us from the brass."

"I'm sorry about the security thing," she replied.
"But I explained—it was a life-or-death situation."

"And I believe that part, as I told you then. But
there are just too many questions concerning your
background. So when the Japanese plane turned up,
it raised even more questions—questions that have
no answers."

"Are you suggesting that I'm a spy?" Katie
jumped up.

She couldn't see his eyes behind the smoke, as he'd
lit another cigarette. But his retort was sharp and
instant. "Are you?"

"No, I'm not!" Katie cried, so frustrated she
feared she'd burst into tears. "But I guess I'll never
convince you of that!"

He got up and came around his desk, pausing only
to stub out his cigarette, and she knew the conversation was over. "I'd like you to think of going back to
California, Katie. Until the war is over."

"But I can't." She tried to read his expression; it
was futile. "My home is here."

"It would stop the gossip," he went on, as though
she hadn't spoken. "And that's what we're all trying

to achieve—you, Max, and us because of Max's
work for the military."

She lowered her lashes, screening her eyes while
her mind whirled. Was he telling her she had to leave
because it was a war zone?

"Just think about it, Katie."

He'd opened the door for her and she'd gone out
of his office, so upset that she had to sit in the car for
a few minutes until she felt calm enough to drive.
She'd come to know the major well enough to know
that everything he said was for a reason. He wanted
her to leave Alaska, and he was giving her a chance to
decide before she was told she had to go.

Now, as Katie stared out over the water, watching
a ripple of wind race over its surface, finally touching
her with the fragrance of places she'd never seen, or
ever would see, she felt shaken. Maybe she was
wrong about having to go, she thought. But she knew
she wasn't.

Damn the war! And damn Tak for putting her in
such a terrible position! Why hadn't he trusted her?
Now he'd only placed all of them in jeopardy.

"Katie?"

Scrambling to her feet, she faced Max. She hadn't
heard his approach and wondered how long he'd
been standing there. She went to him and laid her
head against his chest. That he looked so tired and
strained and thin wrenched her heart. She suspected
his worries were more concerned with her than with
his missions.

Gently, he caressed her hair, holding her. The sea
wind soughed in the pine branches above them,
adding a plaintive note to the beauty of the day. He
wished the moment could last forever, so that he
didn't have to bring up a subject almost too painful
to even consider, much less talk about. His loyal,
courageous Katie. Her headstrong ways had finally

placed her in a position that was beyond his ability to change. The major had made that very clear.

"What's wrong, sweetheart?" he asked after several minutes had passed. "Surely it isn't so bad." He tipped her chin so that their eyes met, and he was careful his own upset didn't show. She'd been sitting under the tree staring into space, looking so sad . . . and so beautiful.

She smiled, and an arm of sunlight streamed through the branches to illuminate the perfection of her face, the brilliance of her green eyes. "I was just waiting for you," she replied softly.

They sat under the tree, his arm draped loosely around her. For a long time neither spoke, and it was finally Max who broke the silence.

"I talked with Major Laird today."

Katie nodded, and glanced away. She didn't have to ask what was said. She knew. She also knew that Max was worried sick. If he lost his contracts, he couldn't meet his business expenses, and ultimately he would lose his company and his dream of an airplane empire after the war.

"He feels it would be best for you to be in California for the duration of the war. I guess you know that."

"He told me."

"Oh, my darling." Max tightened his hold, aware of how distraught she was. "You don't have to go. We'll work something else out—"

She interrupted him. "I'm quite sure that my going is our only choice, Max." She managed a smile. "As the major pointed out—this is war. And this Japanese thing has gone too far for anyone to trust me now." Her lashes fluttered nervously. "God, I wish I was wrong. But, in a strange way, I even understand the major's position."

Max stared out over the water and felt the chill of the wind. It was August, but fall was around the corner. Would he be alone by then, his Katie and Christina gone? For how long? Would he ever see them again?

It was agony watching his changing expression. She must use her *kendo* now. If she were gone, and the gossip died down, maybe Max would stop taking terrible chances to prove his loyalty. Even Dion worried about Max, because he flew when no one else would. For the next half hour, they discussed her going and what it would mean, weighing being separated for the duration of the war against what their business could mean for the rest of their lives. Katie was grateful that Max discussed it as if they had a choice. Maybe that would make her going easier for him, she thought. Or maybe he believed it would take some of the sorrow out of it for her.

"I'll stay with Edward," she said finally, a brave smile on her face. "But in the meantime, until I go, I intend to enjoy every minute we have together as a family."

He kissed her then, and neither one revealed how very devastated they felt. Hand and hand they walked back to the house.

The plane engines revved up, and the propellers created a wind tunnel that plastered Katie's dress against her legs. She stood beneath the steps to the transport plane, holding a squirming Christina, with Anna Su clinging to her hand. They were about to board—after final good-byes.

"Katie! Oh Katie, what will I do without you?" Johanna, tears streaming from her eyes, suddenly hugged her close. "I've gotten so used to having a little sister . . . ." Her words trailed off.

"Yeah. We'll miss you, Katie," Dion added. "Thanks for all you've done for us."

Although Katie knew both Dion and Johanna were grateful to her for flying that day, she also knew

they were relieved she was going—and taking Anna
Su with her. She forgave them their feelings, because
she'd come to realize how hard it was to live with
prejudice. She smiled at them, too choked up to talk.

Then it was Max's turn. He took her in his arms,
Christina between them, and kissed her long and
hard, as though it had to last for a long time. Johanna
and Dion turned away, leaving Max and Katie to
their final good-bye.

"Always remember how much I love you," he
whispered against her lips.

"And I love you, Max." She swallowed hard, but
tears still brimmed her eyes. "Please be safe—
promise?"

"I promise."

Then he kissed his daughter, her golden curls and
her chubby hands. Her dark eyes sparkled with glee;
she was oblivious that her life was changing.

"Bye-bye, Dada," she chirped as he kissed Anna
Su too.

It was time. Katie hurried up the steps where she
let a soldier take Anna Su inside so she could turn
back one last time. Max stood as though he were
carved from granite. Only his black hair moved,
caught by the wind. Even from that distance, Katie
saw the pain in his eyes.

She turned away, but his image went with her. And
as the heavy plane lifted awkwardly into the sky, she
couldn't get his beloved face out of her mind.

Keep him safe. Oh, dear God! Keep him safe.

By the time they reached San Francisco, Katie was
even more exhausted than the children. Their flight
had taken them first to Fairbanks, and then south
over Canada, and on down to the Lower Forty-Eight,
stopping many times at remote airfields to refuel.
The trip was long, as the plane flew an inland route.
She'd telephoned Edward from the first airport in

the States, and she didn't give him time to register his surprise, only told him when to expect her. He met the plane.

"What happened?" Edward asked once they were back at his house on Russian Hill and the tired little girls were finally asleep upstairs.

Katie wished she could join them, but she patiently explained, filling him in on Tak's visit and all that had happened afterward. "So I had no choice," she finished.

"What do you think they would've done, had you stayed?"

"I don't know," she replied slowly. "I've often wondered that. Arrest me, maybe?"

"That bastard Tak!" Edward's face contorted in a frown. "He ruined everything!"

Glancing away, Katie chose not to comment. It was apparent that Edward wasn't happy to have them. As she glanced around the living room, Katie was suddenly aware of how different the room was since she last saw it. The oriental rug on the floor was new, the furniture had been reupholstered, and there were nice paintings on the walls. And the house was so clean that she knew he must employ domestic help. Edward's financial situation had obviously improved considerably.

"And you, Edward? How are you doing, now that you're the head of a company?"

He couldn't help the smug grin. "Doing great. Best move I've ever made."

When he didn't elaborate, Katie didn't press for details of how he afforded it. It was enough for him to get used to her being there. She just hoped it lasted until the war was over, or she'd have to find a place to rent, and that would present other problems— such as who would keep Anna Su?

Over the following weeks, when he didn't lose his temper beyond his continuous complaints about not

allowing the children to make messes, Katie knew
that Edward too had his fears. He didn't want her to
leave him with Anna Su, which in turn would create
more questions about his marriage to a Japanese
woman. With his new social status, he wanted no
hint of scandal. So they coexisted with an unspoken
agreement—Katie could stay, so long as everyone
believed Anna Su belonged to her.

Anna Su was given her own room, while Christina
and Katie shared her old bedroom. They settled into
a routine, but Katie lived for Max's letters, writing
each night to him. But she didn't mention that a man
from American Intelligence paid her a visit, and
although he was pleasant and told her to call him if
"anything came up," she realized that she would be
watched until the war was over. It was a chilling
thought. Because she knew she would never do
anything out of line, she decided not to tell Edward
either about the man's visit.

Instead, she devoted herself to caring for the girls
until the war ended. She planned projects at Christmas and Easter and took them to church each
Sunday. In the spring, she bought a small kite and
taught Anna Su to fly it while Christina watched.
They swam in the summer, and when fall came
again, Katie decided against placing Anna Su in
kindergarten, as she didn't want to risk anyone's
asking questions about her mother. Edward was in
complete agreement. "You do what's best," he told
her. His attitude wasn't fatherly, but at least it
avoided friction. She hardly saw Edward, as he spent
many nights away from home because of social or
business obligations.

The war threat receded in Alaska, as the Japanese
had evacuated Kiska Island in the Aleutians a year
earlier. But still Katie was not allowed to go home,
because the war still raged in Europe and the South
Pacific, and Alaska, along with the West Coast,

stayed on war alert. She dreamed of Max often, longed for him, and sometimes even woke up believing he was beside her, only to go back to sleep with tears on her lashes.

She continued her pattern of activities into the second year, and by another spring, Anna Su was a proficient kite flyer. Katie always made reference to Michiko, so that her niece would know her mother by words, if not by sight.

In April, the country was stunned by President Roosevelt's sudden death from a cerebral hemorrhage. Harry Truman assumed the presidency, and in May, when Germany finally surrendered, Katie was so happy she could hardly contain herself. But still she couldn't make plans to go home; Japan was still fighting. The summer dragged into August, and Katie began to think the war would never end. But when Edward burst through the door unexpectedly one afternoon, she soon heard that it had.

"Katie! Katie, where are you?" he cried from the front hall. "Come quick!"

She ran down the steps, fear suddenly overwhelming her. It wasn't time for Edward to be home. *Something had happened to Max!*

"What? What's happened?"

"God save us!" he cried, his face stricken with shock. "We've bombed Hiroshima."

"Michiko's in Hiroshima! Oh, Edward, I hope she's not hurt—not—"

Something about his expression stopped her cold. Wordlessly, he handed her the newspaper in his hand. She scanned the front page, and her eyes widened in horror as she read about the atomic bomb.

"The whole city? All at once?" She grabbed the hall table to steady herself.

He nodded, more stricken than she'd ever seen him. For all his facade, his pompous attitude about where he belonged in society, the news had hit him hard.

Then he went to get two glasses of whiskey, and with shaky hands, Katie downed hers in one gulp.

Dazed, Michiko stood trembling, unable to credit her own eyes. *No. It cannot be*, she told herself. She must still be in the trance of meditation, struggling against the dark forces of her own thoughts. Her mind blocked the reality of what was before her. Instead, she closed her eyes and went over the morning again.

She'd bathed at dawn after meditating all night, a practice that helped her be patient until she could be with her beloved Edward and her own sweet Anna Su.

She smiled as she thought of Anna Su. Her baby was so precious, with such an old soul for one so tiny. Anna Su was her gift to Edward, a part of herself that was also part of him.

But she digressed. This morning. She was thinking about this morning. After she'd dressed, she'd gotten on her bicycle and ridden through the quiet streets, to the outskirts of town where she'd rested before the ride back. Exercise helped to clear the haze that sometimes edged her mind, that made her feel confused and uncertain—and afraid she'd never see her husband and child again.

The bright light had blinded her. Instant heat had consumed her and she'd been blown like a rag doll over the street, coming to rest against a curb. She couldn't remember how long she lay there, but when she finally got up, everything was on fire. She'd had but one thought—to get home to safety.

Unable to find her bicycle, she'd started to cry, and no one noticed. Several people had been tossed into crumpled heaps, like puppets suddenly cut loose of their strings. Others had run past screaming, and

others only shuffled along with vacant eyes. Not even
the special make-up used on actors to represent evil
in a *Kabuki* play had looked as frightening and
grotesque as the people she'd seen. Finally she'd
ignored them, decided they were make-believe too,
and started for home. But she hadn't found her
home. Instead, she'd been caught in a landscape of
death and destruction.

Still she hadn't believed—not even when she
came to where her house had once stood, nestled
among willows and wisteria, manicured lawns and
flowering shrubs, the most peaceful place on earth.
That's when she'd closed her eyes, willing it all away,
telling herself that the pain wracking her body and
the acrid smoke that burned her throat was only a
part of her meditation that had slipped into a
nightmare.

Now, as she opened her eyes again, Michiko's
mind had nowhere else to go. Certainly not to the
smoking rubble that surrounded her for miles in all
directions. Her whole world, and everyone in it, had
been turned to ashes.

It was then that she began to scream. The sound
went out of her head into the void. It circled the
devastation, searching and not finding, and finally
returned to make her one with the terrible gray world
where color no longer existed. Then the gray faded to
nothing at all.

"He's arriving today!" Katie was so excited she
couldn't think. The war was over, and Max was on
his way to her. "Daddy's coming!" she told Christina, who shrieked with glee, not quite understanding
but loving the game.

The telegram had lifted her spirits. She'd been
worried sick about Michiko, and now she couldn't
help but believe her old friend was safe. After all, the
Konos had a house in Tokyo too.

"Daddy hasn't seen his little girl for two years," she told the happy Christina.

And then Katie stopped short. Max hadn't seen her for two years either. She glanced at herself in the mirror. Would he still think she was beautiful—still want to make love to her?

Quickly she calmed herself and put Christina to bed for a nap. There was lots to do—her nails, her hair, deciding what to wear.

Oh God! She was so happy. Tonight she'd be in her husband's arms.

In a rare show of consideration, Edward took Anna Su to a movie, so that Katie was alone when the taxi drew up outside. She was suddenly overwhelmed with a case of nerves—like a schoolgirl, she thought, giving herself one last glance in the hall mirror. Her hair flowed over her shoulders in soft waves, as she'd decided to leave it casual in the way he'd always liked it. She'd darkened her long lashes with mascara and used a pale pink lipstick to match her silk dress. Her cheeks hadn't needed rouge, as they'd been flushed with anticipation for the past several hours.

Christina stood beside her, a storybook child in her blue organdy pinafore, a ribbon perched atop her blond curls, her dark eyes curious about the father her mother always talked about.

Then Katie flung open the door just as Max ran up the steps to the porch. They both hesitated, their eyes locked. A second later she was in his arms, his mouth on hers, her desire for him blocking out all other thoughts. It was Christina tugging at her skirt that finally brought Katie back to her surroundings.

Max lifted his face, so that he could look into hers. "You're even more beautiful than I remember," he said softly, his lids hooded over eyes that were alight with raw passion.

But Katie also saw that the lines beside his eyes were deeper, his cheekbones more sharply etched, and there were little wings of gray hair above his temples. The years they'd been apart had been hard ones for Max. Even though he was not dressed like her beloved bush pilot today, garbed instead in a tweed jacket and dark trousers, she could tell that he was still lean and fit.

"Oh, Max. I can't believe you're really here," she managed, her eyes unexpectedly brimming with tears.

"My daddy?" Christina's small voice piped from somewhere around their knees.

In an instant Max bent to swoop the child up in his arms. She giggled, glancing between her parents. Impulsively, she gave the tall man a hug, then glanced shyly from under lowered lashes to see his reaction.

A slow grin curved his lips. He shook his head slowly, his gaze on the sweet, delicate face of his daughter. "She's a seductive beauty—just like her mother," he told Katie over the curly head.

"But she's like you, Max," Katie replied softly, intimately. "Even with my blondness, Christina is her father's girl, in temperament as well as looks."

"She's ours." He nuzzled the curly head with his chin, while his eyes told Katie all the things she'd dreamed of during the long nights without him.

They moved into the living room, and as Christina played around their feet, they talked about their experiences during the time apart. Katie served a light dinner, and then they put Christina to bed in her crib, which had been moved into Anna Su's room. Finally they were alone in the bedroom.

Soft light glowed under the fringed shade of the bedside lamp, but it seemed caught in Max's eyes as he came to her. He didn't kiss her, didn't pull her hungrily into his arms. Instead he slowly undressed her, savoring each part of her, kissing her neck, her breasts, kneeling to remove her stockings, caressing the intimate place that belonged to him alone, as though the reality of his own dreams was too precious to hurry. When she stood before him naked and flushed, her head tipped back, her eyes closed, and her breath a shallow flutter, he could wait no longer.

He carried her to the bed, gently placing her on the turned-down blankets. Then he undressed, this time in haste, tossing his clothes to a nearby chair. Katie watched, and when he too was naked, a lean body of manhood in its prime, she saw that he was ready for her. For a second longer they were apart, savoring the exquisite torture of holding back the moment of their joining.

Thank you, God, Katie thought hours later. *Thank you for bringing Max back to me.*

"Still love me?" he asked sometime before dawn.

"Forever."

And he took her again.

PART THREE

Fall 1945–Spring 1954

CHAPTER 17

"EASTERN IMPORTS WAS GREAT COLLATERAL," EDWARD said one evening, a day after Max flew north. "The banker gave me the financing for the house without batting an eyelash."

Edward had just bought a huge house several blocks away, still on Russian Hill, with a sweeping view of the city and the bay. But it wasn't his new house that gave Katie pause; it was the name of his company.

"When did you change the name from Kono Imports?"

Both little girls were in bed for the night, and Katie and Edward were sitting in the living room discussing Anna Su's future. Edward had been explaining why the new house would benefit his daughter, help her adjust to Katie's leaving. It was because of Anna

Su's insecurities, and being unable to adjust to
school, that Katie had stayed behind when Max went
back to Anchorage. It had been a hard decision for
her, and she knew Max hadn't approved, although
he'd tried to understand. "I need you too, Katie,"
he'd said. "I need my family." She'd promised to
follow within the month.

"Uh—sometime back," Edward answered vaguely. "It was one of the stipulations made by Fenton
Stone when he lent me the money to buy it."

"*The* Fenton Stone?" Katie leaned forward on the
chair, her gaze wide and questioning.

A flush spread from Edward's neck into his face.
He was suddenly unable to meet her eyes.

"Surely not the father of the boy I rescued from
the bay in the very incident you chastised me for, as
being an exhibitionist—and foolhardy?"

"A man has to do what he can to get ahead," he
said, his voice raised defensively.

"So you reminded him that I was your sister?"
Katie was disgusted, and her words reflected it. Now
she knew why Edward hadn't clarified how he'd
managed to buy Kono Imports. He'd capitalized on
something that shouldn't have a price—saving a
child's life.

"These kinds of things are done all the time in
business," Edward argued. "It's called *calling in a
favor.* No one thinks anything of it."

"But it wasn't yours to call in, Edward. And I
mind—very much."

"For Christ's sake, Katie! You begrudge me own-
ing the company, don't you? You still haven't gotten
over all that Japanese bullshit about honor."

She sucked in her breath angrily. Then, remembering that she still had Anna Su to consider, she
controlled herself. "Honor, in any culture, isn't
bullshit, Edward," she managed in a calmer tone.
She wanted to add that it was something he'd never

understand, because he always put his own needs first. But again she thought of her niece and what she hoped to accomplish between father and daughter in the coming weeks.

"And did Mr. Stone also see to the financing of your new house?" she asked, altering the focus of their conflict.

"Of course not!" Edward retorted. "I have my own banker now."

"I see." She sat back. What was done was done. She couldn't change anything. All she could do was try to make things good for Anna Su before she left. And that meant convincing Edward that he must be a more loving father and forget the Japanese stigma that still prevailed, even though the war was over.

It was a relief when the conversation reverted back to Anna Su. As they discussed the child's insecurities and her fearfulness of the classroom, Katie suggested that the alternative would be to place her in another school that included Asians.

"No way!" Edward cried instantly. "My daughter goes to regular school. She has dark hair and eyes, but she doesn't necessarily look Japanese. I want this whole background mess to become a thing of the past!"

"Then you'll have to take an active interest in her life—let her know, show her, that you love her."

"Well I—uh, do love her, of course."

"You have everything to gain, Edward. Anna Su is a wonderful child." She wanted to tell him he was wrong to deny her heritage, but again she resisted. Edward could only deal with one thing at a time, and that was always in accordance with his own needs.

Suddenly tired, Katie stood up. She'd had enough of Edward for one night. Dealing with him fatigued her, and yet she realized that he was trying—in his own way. He hadn't suggested that she take Anna Su back to Alaska, and she suspected that he did like his daughter. He was just inadequate, she decided. But for all his failures in the past, he seemed to be a success as the head of his company. Maybe he'd come through as a father too, she thought hopefully as she went up to bed.

Two weeks later the American Red Cross contacted Katie with news that the Kono home in Hiroshima had been destroyed and the family presumed dead. Katie put down the phone and slumped onto a chair. She'd been trying every avenue she could think of to find out about Michiko, and now someone had finally confirmed her worst fear. She watched the girls play in the little garden beyond the French doors, the very garden where she and Michiko had visited over tea and shared their new impressions of California. Her eyes blurred, her lips trembled, and finally the tears ran unchecked down her cheeks.

"What's wrong, Katie?"

She hadn't heard Edward come in, and even though she glanced up at him, she was unable to speak. He dumped his hat and gloves on the table and strode to her, surprising her with concern.

"Michiko," she managed.

"Michiko? Did you hear from Michiko?"

She shook her head. "Someone from the Red Cross called. They said that—" She took a deep ragged breath and struggled for control. "The Kono family is presumed dead."

Edward glanced away abruptly, and she couldn't see his face. But her words had hit him like a physical blow, for he slumped suddenly, as though the wind was knocked out of him. Poor Edward, she thought. He was torn. Michiko had probably been the only woman in the world who could really love him, and he'd loved that devotion, and maybe even her. And she knew that he'd missed her after she'd gone. But he also hated being the underdog, being looked down upon because his wife belonged to another race. So when he finally met her eyes, Katie wasn't surprised to see relief on his face as well.

Wordlessly he went out on the terrace to be with his daughter, and Katie was heartened when he hugged her and sat patiently while Anna Su told him about her day in school. Christina, always congenial, merely watched happily.

It was strange how adversity brought people closer, she thought, seeing it happen right now with Edward and Anna Su. She should be able to leave by the first of November, she thought suddenly, and felt uplifted. It was up to father and child to establish their own relationship without her interference. Besides, Christina needed her father too.

But she'd never forget Michiko, or the Konos. They'd been dear people and hadn't deserved to die. It was so sad. Everyone she'd loved in Japan was gone now. But Tak? She wondered if Tak had survived the war. She'd probably never know.

The Alaska Airlines flight from Juneau swooped low out of the sky as it came in for a landing at Anchorage. Katie looked down at the city that sprawled beyond the boundaries she remembered from only two years before. She quickly powdered her face and tried to smooth some of the creases out of her navy pants suit, wanting to look attractive to Max. Beside her, Christina slept, her blond head against Katie's arm, her overalls and shirt soiled from food spills and dirt smudges. The child was exhausted; the flight had been long, with layovers in Seattle and Juneau. But Christina, like both of her parents, loved flying and was never sick, no matter how turbulent the flight.

Minutes later the wheels touched down, awakening Christina, who craned her neck to see outside,

excited to see her daddy again. By the time the plane
had taxied to a stop and they were in the aisle,
waiting to disembark, Christina was pulling at
Katie's hand, trying to hurry the process.

"Daddy! Daddy!" she cried when they'd descended the steps to the field, and Max hurried to
meet them. Christina twisted free and darted between the other travelers to hurtle herself into her
father's arms.

He swung her up against him, hugging her so close
that the pale hair blended with the black. Katie
paused, watching, so moved by the love between
them that a lump formed in her throat. Her Max,
every inch the romanticized version of a bush pilot,
was so rugged—so handsome—that she was momentarily stricken with shyness.

But there was no time for hesitation. Max set
Christina down and strode forward. In front of
everyone, he swept Katie off her feet and kissed her
so passionately that several people clapped when he
finally lifted his mouth from hers with a whispered,
"Welcome home, sweetheart."

"Oh Max," she murmured. "I've counted the
minutes."

She smiled—as sweetly as little Christina, he
thought suddenly, and was abruptly anxious to get
home where they could be alone. He scooped his
giggling daughter back into one arm, and with the
other around Katie, he walked them to where they'd
collect the luggage. The conversation centered
around a little girl's chatter, interspersed with meaningful glances at his wife. Finally they were on their
way, an airport worker following with the bags.

The same old Ford waited in the parking lot, and
as they drove away, Katie snuggled wordlessly
against Max, Christina on her lap. She hardly noticed the changes in Anchorage, anticipating the first
glimpse of home. The cloudy sky reflected its gray

onto the surface of the distant water, and the mountains were obscured by the low ceiling, but when her house came into view it had never looked more welcoming to Katie.

The wind hinted of the sea and of the snowy winter ahead, but her impressions were fleeting, a backdrop only to the joy of having returned, once Max had opened the car door and she really stood in her own yard. Katie glanced around, savoring the moment. Everything looked just as she'd left it, even down to the smoke coming out of the chimney.

"It's Martha," Max said, seeing her question about the smoke. He'd taken the suitcases from the trunk and now stood beside her. "Martha continued to clean once a week after you'd gone," he added softly. "And she's been as excited as I have about your coming home."

Feeling teary, Katie blinked hard. Then Christina diverted their attention by darting ahead to wrench the door open. As she disappeared into the house, Max suddenly dropped the cases, a big grin on his face. Before she could do more than wonder, he'd picked her up and carried her up the steps to the porch.

"Max—Max! What are you doing?" she squealed happily.

"What else?" he said with a meaningful glance. "Carrying you across the threshold."

"But that's for brides and honeymoons," she protested, although she liked his romantic gesture.

His eyes darkened, and in that instant the world receded; even their little daughter's chatter from the living room faded. "Believe me," Max began gruffly, "this house has never known a honeymoon night like the one about to happen." And while her heart thumped wildly, he strode with her on into the house, much to the delight of their watching child.

Much later, after Christina was in bed, Katie

bathed and then slipped on a flame-red silk kimono
she'd bought in San Francisco. She knew she'd never
looked more sexy as she went to join Max in the
living room. Yet she was nervous, and she tried to
understand why. Was it because their long separation had made them strangers in a certain way?

They needed to talk, to catch up on their lives. Yet
she knew that Max had never been one to discuss his
unhappy childhood, and she suspected he'd never
talk about what he'd faced after she was gone either.
In some ways he was an enigma, an unknown
quantity that only made him more attractive. But he
was a man's man for all his expertise in the bedroom, a man who dared to challenge an untamed
land that didn't give second chances. *What an odd
thought*, Katie chided herself as she hesitated by the
doorway. She was back where she belonged, and
nothing would ever separate them again.

He saw her then, his gaze grabbing hers so completely that all other thoughts fled her mind. Her
mouth parted, but no words came. He'd been sitting,
and now he stood, his feet firmly planted on the
grizzly hide that served as a rug, a bear he himself
had shot somewhere in the wilds. His lean form was
etched against the fire in the fireplace behind him,
standing so still he might have been carved from
stone. He too wore only a robe. A log suddenly
settled lower, sending a shower of sparks up the
chimney. The hall clock gonged the hour, and the
wind nudged the outside walls, tentatively, as though
it was uncertain too.

With a low cry, Katie ran to him. Within a
fraction of a second he was kissing her, his hands
cupping her breasts, pushing away her kimono so
that it shimmered from her body onto the floor. His
robe followed, and unlike the other times when he'd
made love to her, patiently building the tension to

unimaginable heights, he had no patience now—
only an urgency to reclaim his woman.

"Katie—Katie. Oh God, Katie!"

Slipping to the rug, the fur was soft on Katie's
back. His mouth closed over hers again, demanding,
almost savage. There was a desperation that came
from all the nights they'd been denied. Each strained
for the other, eager for the release that came from
their joining.

"Now, Max! Please!"

He entered her then, and everything ceased but
Max and the sensations he caused in her body. When
it was over, he didn't release her, and gradually it all
began again. Later still, they moved to the bedroom,
and it wasn't until morning that they finally slept.

"You don't know how I've missed you, Katie,"
Johanna said the next afternoon as Katie was leaving
her sister's house.

Having stopped in to visit, Katie hadn't stayed
long, as Christina had been reduced to tears several
times by Ollie, an unruly little boy who liked to
bully. Elisabetta was the opposite—a pretty girl with
the dark looks of her father, she tried to make Ollie
mind, a skill that completely escaped Johanna. Ollie
ruled the roost, and Katie wasn't about to allow her
own daughter to be victimized by the little tyrant.

"We'll get together soon," she promised Johanna
as she started up the Ford. But as she drove away,
Katie realized that their lives had grown apart.
Johanna had no interests aside from her children
and the new house she and Dion had bought a couple
of months ago. And Dion no longer worked for Max,
having started his own flying service. How he'd
managed to do it eluded both her and Max. "He
must have saved more money than I thought," Max
had commented only that morning. "And of course

there's a surplus of government planes now. I've even picked up a couple of them myself for little or nothing."

Christina sat beside her, still looking glum and tear-streaked from her visit with her cousins. Katie patted her knee, and the dark eyes glanced at her.

"How about a strawberry ice-cream cone?"

The little face brightened. "Can we stop at the soda fountain?"

Katie nodded, even as she drew up in front of the store. "We're already there."

It was the first time Katie had been to the shopping area of Anchorage in two and a half years, and she pushed back remembered scenes of the past. But she still had qualms when she walked into the store.

"Mrs. Stefanini!" the proprietor cried, coming around the counter to greet her. "Welcome home."

She smiled, but was taken aback.

"How can we be of service today?" he asked, smiling back and winking at Christina.

"I want a strawberry ice-cream," Christina announced.

The stout man beamed. "With pleasure, Miss."

As he scooped, he talked nonstop about Max's feats of bravery. "Yes sir, Mrs. Stefanini. Your husband is a hero here in Alaska. He helped win the war."

Driving home, Katie's spirits began to soar. She was really back where she belonged. The discrimination she'd suffered during the war was a thing of the past. She stepped on the gas pedal once they'd left the business area behind. She felt like preparing the best dinner Max had ever eaten. He was her hero too. But there was one difference between her and the people of Alaska—she was the woman who slept with him.

"Mommy's happy?"

She hadn't known she was smiling until Christina

spoke. She glanced at her, and her smile broadened.
The sweet little face was smeared pink with strawberry ice-cream.

"Mommy's very happy," she told her daughter.

The fall turned cold, and as the days shortened
into winter, Dion's little business fell on hard times.
When his plane was forced to land on a beach, he
was rescued, but they couldn't save the plane before
the tide came in. It was the last straw, and he went
back to work for Max.

Max's company was growing fast, and Katie
sensed that Dion resented Max's success. She also
knew he was jealous because Max was considered a
war hero. In a way, Katie felt sorry for him, but she
also realized that his failures were brought on by his
drinking and gambling. He didn't have the discipline
to be an empire builder like his brother.

Again Martha took care of Christina while Katie
went back to work in the office. Her time was
limited, so she no longer saw much of Johanna.
She'd become impatient with her sister, who
wouldn't stand up to Dion. "Have you ever thought
he might change if you gave him an ultimatum—if
you told him you aren't putting up with his drinking
any more?" Katie had asked when she couldn't stand
seeing Johanna's desperation.

But Johanna had become defensive, and Katie
decided to keep her mouth shut after that, except
when it came to Ollie's being mean to Christina. By
spring, both she and Max were so busy that all their
off hours were spent with their own daughter. Yet her
sadness for Johanna lingered, even if there was
nothing she could do to change things for her sister.
That was up to her.

Spring also brought a new worry to Katie. While
the business was growing, and she was grateful, she
wished that Max would slow down a little. It con-

cerned her to know he took on jobs that meant
dangerous flying conditions. When she broached the
subject, he raised his brows.

"But sweetheart," he began, his dark head tilted to
the side, as though he was really giving the issue deep
thought. Then she saw the twinkle in his eyes and
knew he was teasing.

"But Max," she countered. "I worry. We don't
need all of that work." She hesitated, anxious that he
consider her feelings. "I don't want you in danger.
And if you insist on taking those routes, then share
the flights with the other pilots."

He put down his pen and came around his desk to
take her into his arms, his expression serious now. "I
can't. Not yet, anyway," he said softly, and paused,
as though to form his thoughts so she'd understand.
"Nothing's changed, Katie. I'm still the guy you met
in the park, still with the same dream to build my
empire." His tone lowered. "And the only way I can
do that, in a land where other pilots share the same
dream, is to fly the routes no one else will fly."

He brushed a kiss over her lips, and she knew he
wanted her understanding and her approval. But
would he stop without it? she asked herself. What if
she gave him an ultimatum, as she'd once suggested
Johanna should do—that he curtail his flights or lose
her? Even as the thought hit her, Katie knew she
couldn't do it. His dream was older than their
relationship, and she didn't have the right to destroy
it.

"I understand," she replied finally, and then
kissed him back, a long, meaningful kiss that said, 'I
love you.'

His eyes were hooded when he lifted his head.
"We'll save the end of this conversation for tonight,"
he said meaningfully. "And maybe I'll give you
something else to occupy your time—like a little
brother for Christina."

They both went back to work, and Katie vowed to keep her fears to herself after that. After all, he was right; she'd known his occupation when she married him.

Katie had to remind herself of her pledge often over the following months. Each time the weather socked in, she told herself that the sun could be shining beyond the next mountain. But the elements only added to her worry. The April earthquake in the Aleutians was so huge that it generated tidal waves that swept all the way to Hawaii and Japan. If it wasn't snow and wind and rain, it was earthquakes and tidal waves. Alaska wasn't for the faint of heart, she told herself, and tried not to think that it still took its toll of pilots.

A letter from Anna Su always lifted her spirits. Katie read each one to Christina, so that she wouldn't forget her cousin. But as summer drew to a close and another school year loomed on the horizon, Anna Su's carefully printed letters couldn't hide her unhappiness. Katie figured Edward had fallen down on his fatherly duties. She wrote to him as well, and his reply seemed to confirm her suspicion.

Guilt pricked Katie; she hated to think of Anna Su being so sad and alone. She mulled the situation over for days, and finally the subject came up accidentally one morning at the office. Max had been signing checks as he waited for his plane to be serviced for a flight into the mountains north of the Yukon River. It was the kind of trip that scared Katie, especially in early fall when the weather could change in minutes.

"How's Anna Su?" he asked casually. "I saw we had another letter yesterday."

For all her worry about Anna Su, the child was the last thing on her mind at that moment. She didn't want Max to go, and she hadn't slept well the night before, her imagination conjuring up terrible pictures of white-outs and iced-up wings. The area was remote, no people for hundreds of miles, and if he had an emergency there might not be a place to land.

"Things aren't good, I'm afraid," she replied, but her mind was still on his trip.

"Oh?" He closed the check register and stood up to put his leather jacket on over his heavy wool sweater. "How's that?"

Quickly she explained her thoughts about Anna Su and Edward. But the knot in her stomach had nothing to do with them; she wanted to suggest he postpone his flight, remind him that the dark sky might mean snow, which could mean terrible weather where he was going.

Although she'd vowed not to interfere with decisions concerning the jobs he took, she was torn. She seemed to be getting more worried about the situation all the time. Katie wondered if she was overreacting because she loved him so much. But there were limits, she reminded herself, and Max was tempting fate when he went beyond them. Again she swallowed her fears, and concentrated instead on the situation in California.

"You know, Max," she began, "I was thinking. Maybe it wouldn't hurt to bring Anna Su back to Alaska for a while."

He'd been pulling on his gloves, and stopped, his gaze suddenly direct. "Your earlier decision was the right one, Katie. You can't assume the responsibility of your brother's child, just because he does things differently. Anna Su is his daughter, not yours."

His words were a gentle reminder, not an accusation, but Katie, her nerves already frayed with worry over him, felt a flash of anger.

"How can you say that, Max? The child is being abused!"

He looked surprised by her outburst. "Says who?" he asked, his tone so calm that she felt frustration on top of her anger.

"I do," she snapped, her voice sharper than she'd intended.

"And you could be wrong. You're too emotionally involved, Katie. You've completely lost your perspective on this."

She flushed. It was the first time Max had ever criticized her. How could he be so insensitive when she was worried sick about his safety?

"What if I sent for her anyway?" she blurted, now more hurt than angry.

Nothing changed in his expression, but she suddenly knew he was angry too.

"I wouldn't do that if I were you." His l tone held a warning.

She gulped a quick breath, and fe' defeated somehow. Katie knew she'd grabbed onto the Anna Su issue and blown it out of proportion, said things she hadn't meant because she was frustrated by not having a voice in things important to her—like his safety. In one long, disjointed sentence, she told him just that. "You don't consider my feelings! You only do what you want!"

Even as she accused him, Katie knew she was being unfair. But she was too upset to stop him when he strode out the door.

"We'll talk about this later," he said curtly over his shoulder. "When you've come to your senses."

She slumped into the chair and tried to calm herself. She'd behaved like a child having a tantrum, reacting to a surface situation to avoid the real one. Several planes took off during her contemplation, and a short time later she began to feel ashamed of herself. Grabbing her coat, she went out to the shop to apologize.

"Max has already left," Dion said, hardly glancing up from the motor he and Fred had taken apart. "Didn't you hear his plane take off?"

"Oh, yes," Katie stammered, and went back to the

office. She felt terrible. A hollowness settled into the pit of her stomach and only got worse as the day progressed. Max had gone without saying good-bye, and it was her fault. She'd made him mad. What had possessed her to be such a bitch—to let him fly off believing the awful things she'd said?

By evening, she was sick and couldn't sleep, haunted by her hateful words. The next morning she left home as soon as Martha arrived, horrified to see a skiff of snow and more threatening clouds lowering above her. She decided to radio her apologies to him, even if everyone on the airwaves heard her. She tried to shake a terrible premonition that Max was in trouble.

But static precluded direct radio contact. By early afternoon, word came relayed through Fairbanks. Dion brought the message, standing in the open doorway, his face as white as the little snowflakes that flurried behind him.

"Max crashed!"

CHAPTER 18

THE WEATHER WORSENED, AND TO KATIE IT WAS SYMBOLIC of her despair. The front pages of newspapers all over the Territory carried the story, and as the weeks passed with no sign of the wreckage, the story moved to the back pages. The search was finally called off.

"It's not off!" Katie cried when she heard the news. "The visibility was poor even when the search planes were out there. It's too soon to stop!"

Dion only shook his head. "Katie, you have to face it. Max went down—we all know it can happen." He hesitated, choosing his words carefully. Katie wouldn't accept that Max was dead, and wouldn't allow anyone to say it in her presence. She'd worn herself out with worry and had lost so much weight that her clothes hung on her. He didn't think she'd even cried yet, because crying would be a recognition of Max's death, an admission of defeat.

"I know he crashed," she replied, and concentrated on keeping the high-strung note from her voice. "But we don't know that he's dead. He could have survived—he could be waiting right this minute for a rescue plane."

"He couldn't have survived, Katie. The temperature drops to 50 below zero in the winter. Soon we won't even be able to fly up there. Right now we're risking men each time we do."

His own voice echoed his fatigue and grief. He'd been gone for days at a time, trying to retrace Max's route, to no avail. He'd found nothing. He also knew Max might never be found. The area was wild and mountainous, and aside from a few trappers and prospectors, uninhabited. Max had been on his way to a tiny settlement and had never arrived. He'd disappeared without a trace.

"Don't say that!" Katie cried. "I won't give up! Not ever!" She turned away, not allowing his words to penetrate. Her Max—her strong, fearless bush pilot—couldn't be dead. He could land anywhere— hadn't she seen him do it many times?

"Until the weather prevents it, our own pilots will take turns searching," she stated flatly.

He nodded and left the office. If Katie didn't cry soon she'd have a breakdown, he thought, and went to arrange the schedule according to her wishes.

But Dion had been wrong. Katie soaked the pillows every night. If Max didn't come back, her life was over. She couldn't live with her guilt; it haunted her. Would he still be alive if he hadn't left in anger? she asked herself endlessly. Or maybe he wouldn't have gone if she'd expressed her fears calmly, rather than hide them under a facade of anger.

In the back of her mind, she knew the search was futile, but she couldn't stop, not until the weather stopped it for her. It was Christina's sobbing one night that finally brought her to her senses, to a place where she could gradually accept the truth.

"Daddy's not coming home!" Christina cried, her words coming in shuddering gulps. "Ollie said my daddy's gone forever. You lied, Mommy. You said he would come back."

"My precious child," Katie said, holding her close. But Katie could no longer deceive either of them, and she told the truth—that Max had died.

"Daddy's in heaven now," she said, her voice shaking, her eyes swimming with tears. "But Daddy will always be with his little girl, even if you can't see him. Daddy loved you more than anyone in the world, Christina."

Christina sobbed, and when she couldn't stop, Katie took her back to bed with her. She whispered reassurances again and again, as much for herself as for her daughter, and finally the little girl drifted off into a fitful sleep.

The Territory mourned his passing, but to Katie and Christina, Max was still alive, if only in their hearts. Katie knew she'd never stop loving him— and never be completely free of guilt. But for Christina's sake, she must go on. Max would have wanted that.

With Dion's help, Katie kept the business going, although it meant longer hours to work up bids, order supplies, and schedule the flights, jobs Max had done. Dion and Fred were invaluable, but often Katie and Dion disagreed. It was clear that Dion didn't have any business sense and couldn't see that some decisions were based on future projections, not the here and now. Somehow, she got through the first winter, and by summer she realized that business had slowed considerably. A certain energy had died with Max, and she knew contracts that should have

been theirs were going to other companies. But
selling Stefanini Air Service wasn't an option, as
Max had not been ruled legally dead.

The second winter without Max was bitterly cold,
and often when Katie snuggled under her quilts in
her heated house, the wind howling outside, she
agonized over what had become of him. Oh God, she
hoped he hadn't suffered. But she knew he was dead.
She couldn't fool herself into believing otherwise.

A spring audit showed Katie that business profits
had slipped even more. She knew it wasn't her fault;
it was because Max wasn't there to fly the dangerous
routes, and the more desirable jobs were so competitive, she and Dion couldn't match the low bids.

The day the coroner's jury ruled on Max, Katie sat
in the courtroom feeling profoundly sad, but relieved. She would finally be free to consider other
options for the business, before it slipped into the
red.

"No one could live through two Artic winters
without provisions, even if we assumed he hadn't
been injured or killed in the crash itself. Massimiliano Stefanini is assumed dead," the judge said.

After hearing his death become a legal fact, Katie
went straight home to Christina. *I still have our
daughter*, Katie reminded herself. And at unexpected moments she would hug or kiss her.

The next morning Katie went to the office with
new resolve. She'd work out a plan to save Max's
empire. There just had to be a way, even if it meant
merging with one of the other airplane companies.
As early as she was, Dion was there before her,
awaiting her arrival.

"Now that Max is legally dead," he began, and
hesitated. "We have to settle his estate."

Katie was about to put her purse in the desk
drawer, but her hand stopped in mid-air as her gaze
flew to his, surprised that he'd mention something

that wasn't any of his business. She knew Max hadn't left a will, and there were legalities to attend to because of it. "I realize that, Dion," she replied coolly. "I have an appointment with a lawyer."

"Then you'd better have him take a look at this." He pulled a document from his jacket pocket and handed it to her. "Max drew this up before he went to San Francisco and met you."

Puzzled, Katie started to read, and felt a horrible sinking sensation as she scanned down the page. When she looked up, she saw by Dion's expression that he was completely serious.

"This is a will—naming you Max's sole heir."

He nodded, noncommittal.

"Why are you showing me this now? Surely you don't consider it valid? Not after Max had a wife and daughter."

"It's legal, Katie. Take it to your lawyer and get his opinion."

"What are you saying, Dion? That you're claiming Max's estate? You can't be serious!"

He glanced away, unable to meet her eyes. "Just see your lawyer—and then we'll talk," he said.

Abruptly, he turned and strode to the door, closing it behind him as Katie stared, incredulous. Then she was furious. How dare Dion expect to take over everything Max worked for while he was out drinking and neglecting his family. He'd see hell before she turned anything over to him!

She hurried out to the shop and asked Fred to watch the office, then she drove back to town. She couldn't wait for her appointment. She was seeing the lawyer immediately.

"It's legal." Mr. McBride glanced up, his narrow face concerned. He'd handled land purchases for Max in the past, and one or two small claims when freight had been damaged. He'd understood at once what was involved when Katie presented the document to him. Although he was careful not to show his feelings, he was furious with Dion. It was despicable to take what didn't belong to you—even if it was legal.

Stunned, Katie jumped up and went to the window to stare at the traffic on the street. Her head spun; what would she do? Dion could take her house and her livelihood. *He'll do it*, she thought. Didn't Dion always take the easy way out? She turned back to the lawyer.

"We have no recourse?"

He stood up too. It was situations like this that made him want to change professions. "We'll challenge the will, of course. But in the best of circumstances, and because you have Christina, all we can hope for is what Max acquired after he married you."

"He bought the property and had the house built before our marriage."

"I know. But we'll still go for it."

He walked Katie to the door, giving her encouragement he didn't believe. He just wished Max had taken the time after he was married to change his will—even if he was busy with the war. But like most people, he'd put it off.

As Katie drove back to the office, she was thinking the same thing. She was at fault too. Although she hadn't known about the earlier will, she'd avoided thinking about such topics. She'd been superstitious —fearful that discussing a will would be bad luck for Max, who'd defied death every day.

And he died anyway, she told herself, so dispirited that when she went back into the office, it was a minute before she saw that Dion again waited for her.

She went hot with anger and marched past him to her desk, where she sat down, too upset to trust her

legs to keep her upright. When she met his eyes,
Katie knew hers told him exactly how she felt, but
she had to say it anyway.

"You God-damn bastard!"

His gaze wavered, but he stuck to the decision he'd
made after he knew Max wasn't coming back. He
deserved the company after all the years he'd worked
for his brother. Max's success was equally his; he'd
help build the business from the start, not Katie. So
he straightened his shoulders and got on with what
he had to do.

"I only want Stefanini Air Service," he said curtly.
He tossed two more documents on her desk. "One is
my release of ownership to Max's personal bank
account. The other is for the house." He paused,
letting his words sink in. "They're legal too, Katie."

"You really planned this, didn't you?" Her words
dripped acid. She couldn't thank him for his generosity. He probably realized how everyone would
react if he stripped Max's widow and child of
everything. She had no doubt that he would have
kept the house otherwise. But he couldn't have bad
gossip when he planned to live and run a business in
Anchorage.

"Skip the recriminations until you've heard me
out!" Dion retorted, as though he was the injured
party. "I intend to eventually pay you for the company, once I'm making a good profit."

"Your promise doesn't change a damn thing!" she
cried, remembering how his own attempt at running
a business had failed. "Does Johanna know about
this?"

He ignored her question. "One day you'll thank
me. Once you—"

"I'll never thank you for taking advantage of your
own brother's tragic death," she interrupted. "Do
you honestly believe for one second that Max wanted
you to steal the inheritance he meant for his wife and

daughter?" She leaped up, suddenly wanting to sock him. "Get out! Get out, you bastard, you vulture!"

He glared back. But she didn't care. She suspected that her own sister was in on it too. Johanna would be too weak to go against Dion. Katie felt disgust for them both.

When the door slammed behind him, Katie tossed her personal things into a box and went home. There was no reason to stay. The business was no longer hers. Later, after she'd gained her perspective, she thought about it all. Maybe, if Dion kept his word and eventually paid for Max's company, the division of property would work out for the best in the end. Dion wasn't completely bad, she decided finally— only too weak to say no to the opportunity that dropped into his lap.

Later still, she made another decision. There was nothing left for her in Alaska. She'd move back to California—before fall when Christina started school.

She made moving a game, so that Christina wouldn't feel so bad about leaving her friends and cousins and Martha. After she'd packed and crated the things she couldn't leave behind, and after everything was settled between her and Dion, Katie put her house in the hands of Mr. McBride, to rent until she could bring herself to sell it. Somehow, the house represented Max and the love they'd shared. Katie regretted not giving him the son he'd wanted, but that too had probably worked out for the best. Supporting herself and Christina would be hard enough.

"This is getting to be a habit," she joked, as Edward met their plane.

"Sure as hell is," he agreed, but this time his welcome was friendlier than in the past. He picked up their few cases. "This all?"

"The rest comes down on a freighter. It'll take weeks."

They talked as they walked through the airport to the street where he'd left his Cadillac. While he put the bags in the trunk, Katie helped Christina into the car and marveled at its luxury. Edward appeared prosperous.

It was evening as they drove up the hills, and the sky over the bay was streaked with pinks and purples, bold banners of color and texture that were reflected on the smooth surface of the water. The Golden Gate Bridge, caught in the dying sunlight, was a magnificent arch of design etched against water and sky. Katie relaxed for the first time in months. She'd done the right thing in coming. She'd find a job and they'd make it fine.

They'd hardly stopped in the curve of Edward's driveway when the front door of his mansion opened and Anna Su flew down the steps.

"Auntie Katie! Auntie Katie! You're really here!"

Before Katie could do more than glimpse the child, she was in her arms, hugging her. Then Anna Su went to Christina, kissing the sleepy child on each cheek.

"You've really grown up," she told Christina, who only smiled, darting glances between everyone.

"And so have you, Anna Su," Katie said, and saw that the changes had been drastic. Although her features were the same, she was taller, with more poise and less fearfulness. "My goodness. I hardly recognized you."

As they walked into the house where they were greeted by a housekeeper, Katie tried not to think that Anna Su had been the topic of her argument with Max, the last words she'd ever have with the man she'd loved so passionately.

The house was far more elegant than Katie had expected, decorated with Louis XVI furniture,

Georgian-style paneling, and oriental carpets on highly polished floors. Ornately framed paintings hung on the walls and heavy drapes on the windows. She glanced at her brother, a wide grin on her face.

"This is lovely, Edward. You must be doing very well indeed."

The housekeeper had taken the bags, and Anna Su had taken Christina off to the kitchen for cookies and milk, leaving her alone with Edward in the wide hall from which a staircase stretched upward to a landing.

About to speak, Edward was interrupted by a tall, well-dressed woman in a trim white suit and high-heeled pumps. She stepped from the drawing room, surprising them both.

"Edward," she drawled, and went to him and pecked him on the cheek while Katie watched, trying to decide whether she was amused or astounded.

"I dropped by, hoping to meet this sister of yours from the wilds of Alaska."

Her eyes were small but appeared larger because of the mascara she wore and the penciled lines on her upper lids. Even her brows had been plucked into a narrow arch in an effort to enhance her eyes. She was stunning, dramatic, but not pretty, Katie decided. Her brown hair was swept up into a Betty Grable style, and her narrow mouth was painted into a red heart that matched the color of her long, tapering nails. Katie wondered who in the world she was— Edward had never mentioned her in a letter, and for that matter, neither had Anna Su.

"Katie, I'd like you to meet my—uh, a friend. This is Loretta Moore."

"Nice to meet you," Katie replied. "I hope you haven't been waiting long. Our plane was over an hour late."

"As a matter of fact, I was about to give up and go." She smiled, and Katie suddenly knew it was contrived. "Daddy expects me home for dinner. We're having guests."

"I'll drive you," Edward offered.

"Not necessary, darling. My car's parked in its place in the garage."

She flicked a glance at Katie as she spoke, and Katie realized that the woman—Loretta—was staking her territory and letting her know that. She hadn't come to meet Katie; she'd come to assess the situation. As Edward walked out with her, obviously wound around Loretta's little finger, Katie couldn't help but think it was ironic—Edward had selfishly manipulated everyone, including Michiko, and now he was being manipulated, and didn't even know it.

When he came back beaming, a side of Edward she'd never seen before, he called to the housekeeper and told her to bring fresh coffee. Then he escorted Katie into the drawing room where they sat down on twin sofas, a Louis XVI table between them.

"I hadn't said anything until now because of all the upsetting things in your life, Katie." He paused, unable to stop smiling. "I'm in love with Loretta, and we plan to marry when we can."

She digested his announcement. Her first impression of Loretta was not flattering. She suspected the woman was interested in Edward's obvious wealth and position—the same reason he had married Michiko. All she could do was nod and wait for him to go on.

"We have to wait until I finally get through all the damn crap concerning whether or not Michiko is legally dead, so I'm either free or can file for divorce." He didn't notice Katie's moment of absolute disgust, and continued talking, his tone sinking into the whine she remembered. "And Anna Su is a stumbling block too. I'm afraid Loretta isn't fond of the Japanese."

The housekeeper brought the coffee, her presence

stopping the retort that had sprung to Katie's lips. In the next minutes she was able to compose herself, having realized she'd gain nothing by fighting with Edward. And she didn't want to upset Anna Su either. It looked as if her niece wasn't as happy as she'd thought.

He handed her a cup, and they both sipped as a silence fell between them. When he spoke again, he'd changed the subject to ask what had happened between her and Johanna and Dion.

As much as she hated the topic, she grabbed onto it with relief and explained what had happened.

"That lousy bastard!" he cried.

"That's what I called him," Katie said drily.

"How Johanna puts up with him I'll never know. She should divorce him—show some backbone for once."

The pot calling the kettle black, Katie thought suddenly, and was again saved from further discussion by the girls' coming into the room, Christina drooping with fatigue. Katie thanked Edward, promised to continue their conversation tomorrow, and then followed the housekeeper upstairs to the rooms they'd been assigned. But Christina was fearful of sleeping alone, and Anna Su invited her to sleep in her room. In the end, both girls slept with Katie.

It's symbolic, she thought. She was the only security either of them had. Oh God, she couldn't fail. She had to make it. But her fear for the future kept her awake for hours. When sudden inspiration hit her—a course of action she could undertake the next day—she was asleep in minutes.

She watched the process of Edward's thoughts on his face. Once he would have turned her down flat. But now he had something to gain—Loretta.

"I don't know, Katie. It might not be a good idea

Both girls were in the Christmas program at school, and Katie coaxed Edward into attending, even though Loretta flatly refused, stating that "those little events are long and boring." It was a night Katie would remember forever. Anna Su did a reading, but Christina marched up on the stage with the choir, and sang a four-line solo in the middle of a song. Katie just sat there, astounded by the clear, pure voice of her little daughter. Why hadn't she known that Christina had a beautiful soprano voice?

After the first of the year, Katie requested a conference with Edward before he went off for another week with Loretta.

"I've got a fix on all the prices and tariffs," she began, careful not to upset him. "But we've lost some of our outlets in the past year."

He nodded curtly. "I already know that, Katie."

She ignored his impatience. "I want to show you something," she began, and then spread the facts and figures she'd been compiling for weeks in front of him. "Once you've gone over my accounting, then I want to show you a new plan of action I've come up with." Again she paused. "And I hope you'll approve it, because I know it'll work."

It took a long time for him to go over everything. Finally he glanced up, and his eyes were glazed with excitement. "Christ Almighty, Katie. You're a fuckin' genius!"

She grinned, disregarding his way of expressing enthusiasm. "So? What's the verdict?"

"Go with it! Get started!"

"You'll need to promote me," she suggested, her gaze direct. "So I can implement it—so your employees will take my orders."

"You've got it, Katie. And a raise to go with it."

By the time he returned from his trip, the project was already in the works. By spring it was reaping the results of new outlets for their imports. And by early summer, when Katie wanted to gear up even further with a big promotion campaign she'd come up with, a delighted Edward offered her another salary increase.

Shaking her head, Katie told him bluntly that she'd take some shares in Eastern Imports instead. Edward hesitated, but then realized it was small compensation when he still owned 80%, and agreed. As Katie watched the profits go up, she was rewarded with the knowledge of a job well done. *And it's only the beginning*, she thought. But then she remembered that the business had once been as profitable, probably more so, when it was run by the Kono family. It's only justice that Anna Su will one day inherit Eastern Imports, she told herself. And in the meantime, Anna Su's Aunt Katie would make it as successful as possible, earning a good living for all of them. She would honor her own commitments to Michiko's family, even if none of them were alive to know.

She celebrated her first anniversary back in San Francisco by taking the girls on a kite-flying outing down by the bay. The days were flying as fast as the kites, she thought later. The new school year was even more filled with activities; Katie's life felt full. One of the nuns began voice lessons for Christina, and Anna Su turned up with straight A's on her first report card. Edward spent less time with his daughter and less time at work, allowing Katie free rein with the work she loved. Katie had sent word to Mr. McBride that he could sell the house, and when the check came, Katie went overboard with Christmas presents for the girls and for poor children of the parish. She bought herself a Buick Roadmaster for the family. She even went to a show with a man she met at church, and found herself bored to death with him. Her one wish was that Johanna would answer her letters, even though Dion wasn't living up to his word.

"I'm blessed," Katie told herself as she glanced over the spring financial report. They were prospering on all fronts, and she was euphoric to know that the leap in profits had come about through her efforts. When the phone rang on her desk, she picked it up, expecting a business matter. With Edward in New York, she had twice the number of calls in a day.

"Katie? Is that you?" The voice belonged to a woman, but it was so shaky and faint that she couldn't place who it belonged to.

"Who is this?" she asked, still not alarmed.

"It's—Loretta."

"Who?" Katie thought the woman said Loretta, but that wasn't likely, as it didn't sound like Edward's fiancee—besides, she was with him on the East Coast.

"Loretta—Loretta—Loretta!" she cried hysterically. "Can't you hear? Edward's in the hospital— and you can't even hear me!"

"My God! What's happened?"

"He's in a coma!"

She heard the name of the hospital before the long distance connection went to static, and finally there was only a dial tone. Katie grabbed her purse, told her secretary to get her a flight on the next plane, and ran out of the office.

CHAPTER 19

"THIS WAY, PLEASE."

Katie followed the nurse down the quiet hall. It was almost midnight of the day after Loretta's call. Her flight had been late, but she'd talked to Edward's doctor right after she checked into the Plaza Hotel, and had learned that her brother had never been in a coma, but was in critical condition nevertheless. He and Loretta had been to a party, Edward had gotten drunk, and when they returned to their hotel, he'd insisted on going for a swim. Showing off, he'd made a running dive—into the wrong end of the pool. He was knocked unconscious, and some of the hotel staff had pulled him out and called an ambulance. The doctor had been very frank with Katie. "We fear Edward is permanently paralyzed, Mrs. Stefanini," he'd told her. "He may never walk again."

The nurse left her at the door to Edward's room after a final admonition—"only a few minutes, now." The room was in shadows, lit only by a night light. Although an intravenous tube was connected to his arm, Edward was so still that Katie wondered if he was breathing. As she stepped next to him, his eyes fluttered open, and she expelled her own breath, suddenly relieved.

"I can't move my legs, Katie," he whispered, his eyes frightened. "Oh God, I'm scared."

She took his hand, unsure of how to answer, uncertain of what the doctor had told him. "I know, Edward," she said soothingly. "But you mustn't worry. You've had a bad accident. You've got to give yourself time to recover."

"Do you—do you think I'll get over this numbness?" His face was stricken; she'd never seen him like this before, as vulnerable and frightened as a child.

"The doctor is doing all he can, Edward," she said, evading a direct answer, but still wanting to calm his fears. "I'm sure these things take time." She bent and kissed his forehead. "You must be patient."

He glanced away. "I know. But it's hard." He met her gaze again, his own tormented by regret. "I was a God-damned fool for jumping in that pool. When I think of what I've put Loretta through, I feel even worse."

Katie lowered her lashes. She'd expected Loretta to be at Edward's bedside. After all, she was engaged to marry him.

"Where is Loretta?" she managed casually.

"She had to fly back to San Francisco," he said. "Her father is sick—would you believe the timing?" He shook his head and then winced. "God, it was terrible for her—she was so torn. I told her she had to go, that I was being taken care of, and that you'd be here to see to things."

"So she went."

"She had to, Katie." He paused, and Katie suspected that his words were an attempt to convince himself as much as her. "Besides," he said in a lower tone, "she isn't used to coping with hospitals and sickness."

"Can I get you anything?" she asked, changing the subject because it had been on the tip of her tongue to remind him that she'd been called home to do just that—if her father was really sick. Somehow Katie doubted it. Loretta was a lightweight.

"In the closet," Edward said, his voice abruptly weaker, and Katie saw at once that his strength was gone. "Loretta brought my things from the hotel. Bring my briefcase."

Placing it on a chair next to his bed, she shook her head when he wanted to go into his papers. "Whatever needs to be done, I'll do it," she told him.

In a few halting sentences, he told her where to find his appointment book, and about some unfinished business in the city. "Mainly with David Feldman," he managed. "I've been negotiating to sell him fabrics from the Orient. He owns garment factories, and his business would mean a lot to us. Can you take over, Katie?" His voice trailed off, and his eyes closed.

"Of course I can," she reassured him, suddenly alarmed by how weak he looked.

"Good. Everything . . . is in . . . the briefcase."

Before she could answer the nurse had spoken from the door. "You have to go now. Mr. Aaland needs to rest."

After a final glance at his still form, Katie moved to the door. "I'll be back first thing in the morning," she told him, but there was no response.

She followed the nurse back to her station, and after leaving her phone number, Katie left the hospital and caught a cab back to the Plaza. Once in her room, she stood looking out over Central Park because she couldn't sleep. The doctor's words whirled in her mind—Edward might be in a wheelchair for the rest of his life. What would that mean to Loretta? And Anna Su? And Eastern Imports? And how would Edward ever cope with it? For all of his selfishness in the past, he didn't deserve that.

Oh God, she thought. When would the tragedies end? Once her life had been one golden day after another, and she'd believed that was how it would always be. And then she'd been orphaned, forced to leave her home . . . Max.

The tears came unbidden as his face surfaced in her mind, so handsome, his eyes filled with desire for her, his mouth—that had once kissed her so passionately—curved in the smile he'd reserved for her alone.

With a cry of pain, Katie squeezed her eyes shut, pushing away the memories. When she was calmer, she opened Edward's briefcase, determined to keep her sorrows where they belonged—in the past. It was almost dawn when she finished reading over the papers, and as she went to shower, she knew she was ready to tackle this David Feldman. She willed her fatigue into the wings of her mind; she meant to get the contract. It was the least she could do for Edward.

The outer room of the Feldman office was spacious and elegant, and the young woman at the desk, although friendly and pretty, spoke with a clipped New York accent. Everything, from the leather furniture and brass lamps to the obvious breeding of the secretary, spoke of success and good taste. It was a little intimidating, Katie thought as she sat waiting for her appointment.

But she was prepared. She had all the facts and figures down pat. Once she'd dressed for the day in a stylish black suit and pumps, her hair combed into an upsweep and her make-up accenting her eyes and mouth, she'd gone to the hospital. But her visit with Edward was short, as he was wheeled out for more tests on an upper floor. So she'd called home and was reassured by Mrs. Mendoza that the girls were fine. Katie talked to Anna Su, explained that her father was recovering, but didn't mention the after-effect of the accident because the doctor still wasn't certain that Edward wouldn't regain the use of his legs. "We'll know more in a few days," he'd told Katie.

Her call to Eastern Imports took much longer, as she went over her instructions to her secretary. After that, she'd even had time left to review the proposed Feldman account one more time. Then she taxied to his office, anxious to be on time.

"Mrs. Stefanini?"

Deep in her own thoughts, Katie hadn't heard the door to the inner office open, and now her gaze flew to the man in the pinstriped suit and crisp white shirt who waited for her to join him. Her heart gave an instant jolt as she met his dark eyes. At first glance he reminded her of Max. A more detailed look told her he was as tall, and as lean, but his features were not as rugged, and his black hair was curly and frosted with gray, whereas Max's had been thick and crisp and only white at the temples. And the man before her was older than Max would have been, at least fifteen years her senior, Katie guessed.

Having undergone her quick appraisal in patient silence, he smiled suddenly, and again Katie felt a fluttery sensation in her heart. "Please come in," he said coolly, his accent even more New Yorkish than his secretary.

"Thank you," she managed in her best business

tone, and went past him into his office. She was very aware of him watching her and resisted a glance at him, choosing instead to maintain her professional attitude. She sat down in the black leather chair he offered, then watched as he took his own place behind a huge desk that had unique patterns of inlaid wood on its surface, a piece of furniture she estimated to be priceless. Although she appeared composed and businesslike, her nervous system was on full alert. It hadn't occurred to her that she'd be conducting her negotiations with a man she found physically attractive.

He opened the file on his desk, giving himself time to shift back into a business mode. When he'd learned that Edward Aaland was in the hospital and that his sister, who also worked with him, would take over the appointment, he'd considered postponing it, expecting a female version of Edward. But he'd been floored when he saw her. Even in her sedate suit, he'd never seen anyone to compare in looks and figure. She was a knockout. And he saw intelligence in those brilliant green eyes. But it was her hair that was so astounding, and it only took a second glance to know the color was real and hadn't come out of a bottle.

Damn, he thought. He had no desire to do business with her. He wanted to take her to bed.

"I have Edward's work-up on your proposed account," Katie said, breaking the silence that was unnerving her. She needed to get started before she forgot everything she'd boned up on during the night.

He glanced up, his eyes hooded and unreadable. "Good. Let's begin then."

For the next half hour, she apprised him of how Eastern Imports would benefit his company. "If your orders are big enough, we can do even better on the silks," she ended, her voice fading into another silence as he studied her.

He's only considering the business ramifications, she told herself, bringing all of her old techniques for maintaining control into play. He doesn't even see me, even though he's staring. But despite her resolve, the dark eyes of the man before her brought a faint flush to her cheeks, and her long lashes blinked nervously. With determination, Katie kept her eyes steady and began to feel annoyed.

And then he smiled, so wide that she could see his perfect set of teeth all the way back to the molars. "I see no reason why we can't do business. Will it be possible to meet with your brother in the near future, so we can finalize our agreement?"

He watched her face, trying to read her, and found he couldn't. That was another thing that intrigued him. She didn't flutter around like a butterfly, trying to land on him with all her feminine wiles. She had a mystique, an aura of being different from other women. He wondered if she really was—or was simply playing a feminine game with a new twist. He meant to find out.

"I'm pleased, Mr. Feldman. I know my brother will be as well." She pulled on her gloves and stood up, wishing her tone didn't sound so damned stilted. "But I can't tell you exactly when you can see Edward." She went on to explain briefly. "However, I can assure you that I'll carry out his wishes to the letter. And of course you'll have time to go over everything in private, so you're comfortable with the terms before you sign our contract."

"I appreciate that," he replied, and for a moment she thought she saw a flash of humor in his eyes, as though he saw the real reason for her prim and proper tone of voice.

Again the room went flat between them, a pause that swelled into awkwardness for Katie. She started to turn toward the door and David came round his desk to shake her hand.

"Thank you for coming," he said warmly. "I've enjoyed doing business with you."

"And thank you." Katie smiled for the first time, unaware that the sunshine coming in through the long windows behind him had touched her eyes with green fire, her hair with silver.

"Oh, one more thing," he said, as they walked to the door.

She hesitated, waiting.

"Your brother can't have meetings, but can he have visitors?"

"On a limited basis," she replied, puzzled.

"Then I believe I'll stop by and give him my decision in person. After I've gone over the papers, as you suggested."

Taken aback, Katie was at a loss. Didn't he believe that she spoke for Eastern Imports? Maybe he was one of those men who considered women too stupid to conduct business. She bit back a retort; she wouldn't botch things with her annoyance. But she was unprepared to counter his next proposal.

"I should be finished by mid-afternoon." His regard was professional. "And you're at the Plaza. I'll pick you up there at—say, three."

She opened her mouth, then closed it. By the time an excuse presented itself, he'd already flashed another smile and closed his door. She went through the office and out to the elevator, wondering how he'd managed to turn the conversation so quickly.

It's the reason he's such a huge success, she decided in the cab. The man was like no other she'd ever met. Except Max. There was a similarity between them, aside from their both being tall and dark; it was an aggressiveness they shared in common. But Katie knew she'd better be careful with David Feldman. He was sophisticated, far beyond her experience with men. Yet, as she paid the driver and went into the hotel, Katie was already thinking she'd wear her new green silk dress with the matching jacket.

He came for her in a chauffeur-driven Cadillac, a car so elegant that it made Edward's Cadillac seem plain by comparison. David helped her into the back seat, then stepped in behind her. As they settled back onto the cushions, the driver eased into the Fifth Avenue traffic and headed toward the hospital. Katie smoothed the skirt of her dress, placed her purse between them on the seat, and folded her gloved hands on her lap.

"Lovely dress," David said, the first to speak after their greetings.

His tone was casual, but his awareness of her was acute. Sitting so close, he could see that she was even more beautiful than he had thought at their first meeting. Her skin was flawless, her lashes incredibly long, and her features a perfection of symmetry. She was probably one of the few women in the world who was too perfect to be a photographic model. He forced his eyes from her. He'd never been so affected by a woman, and he tried to analyze why she was so special, aside from her appearance.

"Thank you, Mr. Feldman," she said with a brief smile. "The material is from the Orient, the quality we import for our people."

He nodded and let his gaze move over her, appraising the garment, how it molded her high breasts and clung to the curve of her thighs. *She's controlled, as though unaware of her effect on a man*, he decided. She was almost oriental herself, in the way she was able to remove her emotions from a conversation or a business negotiation. He realized that he knew nothing about her aside from the fact that she worked with her brother.

The car made slow progress through the traffic.

Again Katie felt an awkwardness, because she was too aware of the man beside her. She cast about in her mind for a topic of conversation, and came up with the only thing between them—business.

"All our silks are the best quality available," she said. "We've been known to ship back flawed orders."

"Excellent," he replied, and paused. "Have you worked with your brother for a long time?"

She glanced at him and saw his sincere interest. "Close to two years," she replied. "Since my return from Alaska."

"Alaska! You lived in Alaska?"

He sounded surprised, as if it was the last thing he'd expected, and Katie couldn't help her grin. "That's right, Mr. Feldman. From before my marriage to the time of my—" She broke off, suddenly aware that she'd said too much.

"And your husband? Doesn't he mind his wife being in New York without him?"

Had she looked at him, Katie would have noticed his sudden disappointment, but she was too intent on her own feelings at that moment. "I'm a widow. My husband died in a plane crash, Mr. Feldman," she said finally. "Without him, I felt it would be best for both my daughter and I to live in California."

"I see." David glanced out the window at the passing scene. He was exhilarated all at once, and knew it was because of what she'd just said. In a matter of minutes, he'd gone from intense interest to disappointment and then relief. But his voice didn't reflect any of his emotions. "I'm sorry. It must have been hard," he said softly.

Their eyes met, and held. Although he was a worldly man, Katie sensed a niceness. "Yes, very," she agreed, and then changed the subject with a question for him.

"And your wife? Does she also work with you?"

His brows shot up. "I'm a confirmed bachlor," he said with a laugh. "I'm afraid I never met the right woman to make that kind of commitment. Too busy establishing my business—building my little empire."

For a second, Katie was again reminded of Max. He'd always talked about building an empire too. But this time, she put Max right out of her mind. It was time she stopped comparing every man to him.

"I'm surprised, Mr. Feldman."

"Oh? How so?"

"Well, I suppose I assumed a successful and attractive man such as yourself would be attached," she managed, suddenly uncomfortable by his amused eyes.

"Since we're both unattached," he began as the car drove up to the hospital, "I'd like to assume something else." He'd moved forward on the seat but hesitated in opening the door, his regard steady. "That you'd have dinner with me this evening."

"I don't know," she evaded, disconcerted again and unsure. "There's Edward and—"

"After you feel comfortable leaving Edward, of course. Remember, this is New York, and New Yorkers eat late."

She grinned then, unable to resist what she finally recognized as his charm. "I'd enjoy having dinner with you."

"Great! And call me David, please—Katie."

The chauffeur helped them out, then David took her arm and they walked to the entrance. As they went through the glass doors, Katie caught a glimpse of their reflected images—a distinguished dark man and a blond woman, prototypes of the perfect couple. For some reason the thought pleased Katie.

Over the next two weeks, Katie saw David every day, if not for lunch, then for dinner. One Saturday night he took her to the theater, on another to the opera. They went to Coney Island, drove out Long Island, and spent a day at the art museum. They had long conversations, and as Katie knew him better, she found herself telling him about Max, and how deeply she'd grieved when he hadn't come back.

"My dear, how very sad." David was sympathetic, and although he was falling in love with her himself, wanted her more than ever, he had compassion for what she'd lost. He knew he had to go slow if he were to win her. He'd altered his first urge to get her in bed because he didn't want a one-night-stand—a fling, as most of the other women in his life had been. He wanted Katie for his wife.

He'd confided his business plans for the future, how he intended to expand to the West Coast, even the fact that his Jewish family considered him a failure in the marriage department. "Of course, they expect me to marry a nice Jewish girl and have six kids," he joked.

He's not joking, Katie thought. David's being Jewish hadn't been a consideration to her, but it was to him. Later, she wondered what that would mean to their relationship; she found herself caring more and more for him. That he didn't attempt to make love to her, aside from a good-night kiss, only strengthened her respect for him—because the sexual tension was growing between them.

"You grew up in Japan? I can't believe it!"

She'd just explained about her childhood as they sat with after-dinner drinks one night. Startled by his response, she met his eyes and wondered if she'd just discovered his flaw—prejudice.

"Yes, I did," she said, abruptly cool, remembering her treatment during the war. She tilted her chin and went on to explain Michiko and Anna Su. *Let him disapprove right now*, she thought, *before I get any more involved*.

"My darling," he said softly, as her explanation faded into the soft music of the lounge. He put his hands over hers, his eyes warm with reflected candle-light. "I'm sorry about Michiko, and I can't wait to meet Anna Su, but my surprise about your back-ground stems from an entirely different reason."

A flush stained her cheeks. She felt foolish, and embarrassed.

"When I first met you, I had a fleeting impres-sion," he began, "that you seemed as oriental as the fabrics you were selling. And now I know why; you grew up in Japan."

"You aren't prejudiced?"

He tipped back his head and laughed. "Oh, Katie, you're precious. Have you forgotten I'm Jewish? I might be asking you that question."

They finished their drinks and he saw Katie up-stairs to her door and unlocked it. Then he took her in his arms for his typical good-night kiss.

"You know I want to spend the night with you, don't you, Katie?" he said as he lifted his mouth from hers, so close that she seemed to breathe his breath. "But I'm going to resist, because you're too important to me. I won't risk losing you." He didn't add that he wanted to be sure she was completely over Max, because he had to come first to the woman he married.

Then he kissed her again, a hard, passionate kiss that opened her mouth under his and filled her with a need she hadn't felt since Max.

"Good night, Katie," he whispered hoarsely. "I'll see you tomorrow."

He left her with a nonchalant salute, but his final burning look stayed with her until she went to sleep. And her first thought in the morning was of David.

For all the hours she spent with David, she didn't neglect Edward, and kept in close contact with his doctor, hoping for good news. But even after all the tests, the prognosis was still unclear, and Katie suspected the worst. The next day brought the verdict she feared.

"He's permanently paralyzed from the waist down," the doctor told her after taking her aside. "There's nothing more we can do for him. I'll give you the name of a doctor in San Francisco for when Edward goes home."

"Will that be soon?" Katie asked, shaken. They'd already discussed Edward's depression, and the fact that physical therapy wouldn't help the irreparable damage to his spine. She tried to be strong; tears wouldn't help her brother now.

"By next week. But he can't sit in a regular airplane seat. You'll have to make arrangements for a hospital bed."

She only nodded and thanked him, and later explained everything to David. "I'll see to it," he said, holding her in his arms. "It'll all work out. Just have faith, darling."

Edward was another matter. She was present when the doctor told him. It took a sedative injection to calm him when he heard the truth. Katie tried to encourage him, reminding him that the doctor could be wrong, and that he'd see a new doctor in San Francisco and maybe begin therapy. "And don't forget, you'll soon be with Loretta again."

That thought cheered him a little, as he'd spoken to her every night by phone, and she looked forward to his return. Katie blocked out thoughts of how Loretta would react to Edward in a wheelchair, and the fact that Edward had given false information about his recovery. She'd worry about that after they were home.

David saw them off with a promise that he'd be out to visit soon. Katie fought a growing sense of dread that she might not see him again. He realized how she felt, and impulsively pulled her back into his arms. His kiss left no doubt about his feelings.

"I said I'm coming to see you—and I will," he told her roughly.

His words comforted her during the long flight with Edward, who complained and whined no matter what anyone did to help him. It was a relief when the plane landed in San Francisco. They were met by Loretta, who couldn't conceal her horror that Edward was still paralyzed and that an ambulance awaited to transport him home. Katie was just glad that her own reunion with the girls would be in the morning. She'd guessed right that Edward would need her to stay with him for the first night.

Loretta drove herself to Edward's, and by the time she left a short time later, he was so distraught that Katie had to call his new doctor, who came at once.

"I'm going to kill myself!" he kept screaming. "I'm only half a man—useless!"

As the doctor administered the injection, Katie only wished she could kill the bitch responsible for his state. Loretta had broken their engagement.

Over the summer, David flew out once or twice a month, and by fall he was there almost every weekend, often flying his own plane. Katie had only grinned when she learned he was a pilot; she should have known. Somewhere she'd read that a woman fell in love with the same type of man over and over again. And she was in love with David.

He'd quickly adjusted to the girls, and that they loved him too was a bonus for Katie. "I think I'd like to have one of my own," David had confided with a grin.

Edward was Katie's one continuous problem. She had assumed command of Eastern Imports upon their return from New York and consulted daily with

Edward, by phone and by trips to his house. He had round-the-clock nurses and his housekeeper to see to his needs, and for all her efforts, he never thanked her, only complained bitterly. He never mentioned Loretta and discouraged Anna Su from visiting. All in all, it was a sad state of affairs for everyone.

Her lifeline was David. She missed him dreadfully when he was gone, although she was too busy to dwell on the idea that he'd never made love to her, or declared his intentions. There hadn't been any opportunity, she reminded herself. Often they took the girls on their outings, and they couldn't share her bedroom without the girls' knowing. That was unacceptable to her, and she suspected it was to David as well.

"I've bought a house in Pacific Heights," David announced one evening when Anna Su was on a rare overnight visit to her father's house, and Christina was spending the night with her best friend, who lived next door.

"What?" Katie glanced up from her coffee. She'd fixed a light supper and now they were side by side on the sofa, the room cozy with soft music and firelight.

He grinned, looking terribly handsome in casual jeans and a black turtleneck sweater. She also wore pants and a pullover top, as they'd been to the park earlier, where she'd taught him kite flying. "I bought a house. Remember I said I wanted to open an outlet store in the Bay Area? Well that's what I'm doing— so I'll need a house to live in when I'm here."

He moved closer and took her cup, placing it back on the table. "I'm asking you to marry me, Katie." His eyes seemed black, shaded as they were by his lashes. "Will you?"

She hesitated, her thoughts spinning now that he'd finally expressed his intentions. What would marriage to him mean? How would Christina feel about

it? And what about her obligations to Edward and
Eastern Imports? She loved her job; would he expect
her to quit?

"I love you." His whisper was edged with sudden
doubts about her feelings. He pulled her closer, still
keeping his desire, his rising need, on a short leash.
But when he kissed her, all his good intentions
vanished. He'd restrained himself too long, beyond
what he'd believed himself capable of. He knew he
couldn't stop himself; he was going to make love to
her.

She moaned against his lips, her body alive under
his touch. Her feelings for him had grown into a
gentle love, different from the all-consuming love
she'd once had for Max. But now Max was only a
passing thought. She wanted David—wanted him to
love her, wanted to know him completely. Katie felt
tenderness for him, but she wanted passion too—
she wanted to feel the ecstasy that came from the
joining of a man and woman.

"I love you too, David," she murmured.

Her words were a catalyst; he helped her out of her
sweater, and she helped him with his. In seconds
they were both naked, lying on the sofa, his eyes
devouring her, his hands exploring, and hers doing
the same.

"You're so beautiful," he kept telling her. "So
perfect."

"You're pretty special yourself," she whispered
back, her eyes wide with wonder at his size.

"It's yours, my darling, all yours."

And then he proved it.

Later, after they'd picked up their clothes and
gone naked up the steps to Katie's room, they found
time in the night to talk.

"Will you?"

He was propped on his elbow, looking down into
her face. His features were in shadow because the

room was dim, but Katie saw the seriousness in his eyes. Once his first wave of passion was satisfied, he'd become an experienced lover, bringing her to climax time after time. Katie was relieved that David's lovemaking didn't remind her of Max. There was no doubt in her mind that she loved David now, and wanted to marry him. But what about her obligations?

In a soft tone, she honestly expressed her concerns. "So maybe my situation isn't one you'd be happy with," she finished.

"I'm a modern man," he replied, equally candid. "I love the girls, and I don't object to keeping Anna Su with us. I know you must see that Edward is taken care of—and I certainly don't expect you to quit your job. After all, I'll probably be in New York half of the time." He paused to drop a kiss on her mouth. "Does that answer your worries?"

"What about your family? Will they approve? I'm not the Jewish girl they'd hoped you'd marry."

"Jesus, Katie! I'm a man past forty. I don't need their approval."

"Will they?" she insisted.

"Maybe. Maybe not. It doesn't matter."

"Then I will."

"You tease!" he cried, and as she giggled, he began to make love to her. She didn't giggle for long.

Because she wanted to include Edward in her happiness, the wedding was held in his elegant parlor right after Christmas. He gave Katie away, Anna Su was the bridesmaid, and Christina was a flowergirl. Katie wore a burgundy velvet cocktail dress with a plunging neckline, perfect to set off the diamond necklace and earrings David gave her as an engagement gift. He wore a black suit, and his pearl tie pin was her gift to him. They'd hired a justice of the peace to officiate, in deference to David's religion.

Even so, his elderly parents sent a polite but firm note of their intent to refuse to see Katie. She tried not to let it bother her.

After the ceremony, she had a moment alone with Edward, to reassure him that everything would go on as before, even though she was married.

He sat in the wheelchair, heavier than he'd ever been, and expressed his concerns, oblivious to spoiling Katie's special day.

"I think David wants to take over Eastern Imports for himself," Edward blurted out.

Instantly angry, she managed to keep it hidden. She'd be damned if she'd have an argument on her wedding day. That he was in a wheelchair didn't give him license to spoil things. She felt like telling him to not judge others by his own motive in marrying Michiko.

"You're letting your imagination run away with itself," she told him instead. "You're still in control of your company. I supply you with daily financial reports, and you make all the final business decisions." She didn't mention that everything he did was based on her facts and figures. She would never demean him by telling him he was only a figurehead.

"Just keep it in mind, Katie," he insisted. "I have a feeling this marriage will bring you nothing but heartache."

"Thanks, Edward," she snapped. "I needed that to start my honeymoon."

She left him, and a final glance told her he was as stubborn as ever. Well, let him stew in his own juice, she told herself, and went to join her new husband for their honeymoon trip by car up the coast.

But his words stayed with her until they reached their first night's lodging. After that, she concentrated on David alone.

CHAPTER 20

IT WAS INCREDIBLE TO KATIE THAT SHE LOVED DAVID AS much as she had once loved Max, although her love for each man was different. Max had been a more rugged man who loved the frontier life, whereas David was a cultured man who enjoyed the finer things a city offered. They shared a dominant aggressiveness in their separate goals of building an empire.

Their home in Pacific Heights was everything she'd ever wanted, and Katie had taken her time over the past months to decorate, blending European antiques with touches of the Orient. The total effect suggested the peace and serenity she'd known as a child, while the exterior brickwork and stucco, shutters and portico were typical of California opulence.

David had left it in her hands, approved all her choices, and gave her unlimited funds to do the job. "You have an eye for decorating. Sure you don't want to go into that business instead?" he'd said, half teasing.

Now, as Katie stood at the long windows in the living room, her eyes on San Francisco Bay in the distance, gray under the October sky, her life felt complete. David sat in an overstuffed chair reading the paper; they both waited for the girls to change out of their school clothes so that they could join Edward for dinner at his house. It was Anna Su's twelfth birthday.

"I went to the doctor today," Katie said, turning from the window.

David glanced up. "Are you sick?" His voice was instantly concerned.

She smiled and didn't realize how lovely she looked to him in her brown tweed dress, her small waist cinched by a wide leather belt. Her hair lay in soft waves over her shoulders, loosened from the more severe style she wore to the office. She looked twenty, he decided, and then realized she hadn't answered his question.

"I'm pregnant, David. Due the end of next May."

The paper flew out of his hands as he jumped up and went to her. "Oh, my darling Katie," he murmured. "You're really giving me a son?"

"Or a daughter," she childed him gently. She tilted her face as he drew her into his arms. "Happy, David?"

"You know it!" He kissed her soundly, then suddenly loosened his hold, his face stricken.

"God, I can't be so rough—not with you in such a delicate condition."

Her laugh was spontaneous. "For heaven's sake! Women have been having babies since time began. I'm not delicate, or fragile, or unwilling to have my husband make love to me." She hesitated. "I'm in excellent health." Katie didn't mention the doctor's one concern—her Type A-negative blood. It hadn't affected her first pregnancy, so she didn't expect it to affect her second. She'd decided not to even bring it up. It would only worry David.

He kissed her again. "I love you so much," he whispered. "I'll show you later."

Christina's giggle from the doorway separated them immediately. But David was so delighted with Katie's news that he couldn't contain himself.

"Guess what?" he asked both of them as they came into the room. "We're going to have a new person in the family—about next May."

Christina shrieked with joy. "We're having a new baby?"

David nodded, his dark eyes filled with as much delight as Christina's. But when Katie glanced at Anna Su, she wished they'd waited with the announcement until after her niece's birthday party. Although she smiled and looked genuinely happy for Katie, Anna Su also seemed to separate herself from them, as if she weren't a part of the little family.

All during the ride over to Edward's, Katie couldn't shake her perception about Anna Su. And when Christina blurted that "my mom is having a baby," even Edward was aghast.

"Does that mean you'll be leaving Eastern Imports?" he asked sharply.

While David and the girls went to the dining room to look over the party decorations done by Edward's housekeeper, Katie explained patiently. She had an urge to tell him to stop thinking of only himself. As it was, he ate and drank too much, and when cautioned about the state of his ballooning body, he only whined that he wasn't about to curtail the only joys of life left to him.

"I intend to stay on the job until the baby is born,

and then go back to work as soon as I can." She looked him in the eye. "I told you long ago that it's only right that Anna Su—a Kono—control the company one day. I'll run things until then."

The evening went flat for Katie, but she didn't spoil it for anyone else. When they returned home, she decided to have a talk with Anna Su, to see what was bothering her niece.

She knocked on the bedroom door and, as was her custom, went on in. Katie smiled at her niece, who was already under the covers reading a history book. She sat down on the foot of the bed.

"Is everything okay?" she asked gently.

Anna Su nodded. "Just fine, Aunt Katie. Why?"

"You seemed a little—a little preoccupied this evening," Katie replied, softening her words with a smile.

"I had a wonderful birthday."

Anna Su's gaze was candid and intelligent. But it was also very mature—too mature for her age, Katie thought. She'd worried before about her niece being too studious, too anxious to please her teachers, her father, even her aunt. *She's insecure*, Katie realized suddenly, and suspected the reason behind Anna Su's preoccupation.

"How do you feel about our having a new baby?" Katie asked, carefully casual.

"It's very nice." Anna Su lowered her lashes. "The new baby will have a wonderful home."

"Thank you. That's a nice compliment, Anna Su. Especially since the baby will be sharing your home too."

Her gaze darted to Katie's. "You mean you won't want me to go back to Father's house?"

"Why on earth would I want that?" Katie retorted, seeing that she'd guessed right. The new baby had brought Anna Su's insecurities to the surface.

"Because I'm not really your daughter." Her voice was low with suppressed fears.

"But you belong with me nevertheless," Katie told her firmly. "Of course your father loves you too," she added quickly. "But since his accident, we thought it best that you stay with us, since we love you just as much."

Anna Su lowered her head, and her silky black hair fell forward to obscure the delicate features of her face. "Father didn't want me even before the accident. He was ashamed of me. And my mother abandonded me when I was little—" Her voice broke.

"That's not true, Anna Su," Katie replied gently, inwardly shaken. "You know the story of your mother. She was my best friend, and I've told you many times how much she loved you. She would be with you if she could." As she reassured Anna Su, Katie also felt sad. *You can't fool children*, she thought. *They understand more than adults realize— until it's too late.* She vowed to take more time with her niece, a budding beauty who was destined to reclaim the Kono empire one day. Katie wanted her secure and happy for when that day came.

David left for New York a few days later, but managed to return by Christina's birthday in early December. He was gone for a week before Christmas and missed the church program when Christina sang. Katie was so proud and wished he'd been there. After the first of the year he was gone even more, but their reunions made up for his absences. Katie understood his business obligations; she had her own.

By May, she had trained her assistant to fill her place when she took maternity leave. Everything was in place for the birth, except for a few items like diapers and baby shirts. One morning shortly before her due date, Katie left the office and went downtown to shop. After she'd bought her baby things, she went to look at bathing suits for the girls. Summer was coming and they'd outgrown last year's model.

"I'll take these," she told the clerk, handing over the two suits she'd chosen. About to take out her wallet, her glance fell on the woman in the next aisle.

"Johanna!" she cried. After a moment of stunned disbelief, Katie ran to her sister.

Johanna glanced up, even more surprised than Katie. She opened her mouth and then closed it again, for the moment beyond words.

"What are you doing here?" Katie asked. "Why didn't you write? I worried about you when you didn't answer my letters."

"I—I'm glad to see you," Johanna began hesitantly. "I'm sorry about not writing, but—"

"It doesn't matter," Katie interrupted, seeing her sister's embarrassment. She'd long since resolved herself to the fact that Dion wouldn't keep his promise. Katie was too happy and contented in her own life to hold a grudge. It was enough to see Johanna again. Katie assumed that she was visiting in California and had been too ashamed to call either her or Edward.

"How are the children?" Katie asked.

"Just fine—growing." Johanna fidgeted, as though she were about to say something and couldn't find words. "And Christina?"

As Katie told her about both Christina and Anna Su, she noticed how much older Johanna looked, much more than the mid-forties Katie knew her to be. Realizing that she'd stopped writing before Edward's accident, Katie briefly explained about their brother's condition.

"Poor Edward!" Johanna grabbed the display

counter. "I'll call him—go see him. Poor, poor Edward!"

"And as you can see," Katie began, moving her armful of packages from the front of her coat, "I'm married again." She was anxious to change the subject to something more pleasant.

"And you're pregnant!" Johanna's eyes widened in shock. "Oh, dear God!"

Taken aback, Katie blurted out the first thing that came to mind. "Goodness, Johanna! Aren't you at least going to congratulate me?"

"Oh—of course," Johanna managed, then went on quickly, as though she were in a hurry. "Where do you live, Katie? Maybe we can get together and talk. Dion and I live here now."

Katie nodded absently and wondered what on earth was wrong with Johanna. To have moved from Anchorage must mean that Dion had lost the company. She resisted asking, then realized that was it; Johanna was terribly embarrassed by what Dion had done.

"Pacific Heights," she replied. "And Edward has also moved, but he's still on Russian Hill."

"Pacific Heights," Johanna repeated, looking even more uncomfortable. "You must have married a rich man, Katie."

Before Katie could answer, the clerk summoned her and she went to pay for the bathing suits. She told Johanna to wait, but when she turned back several minutes later, her sister was gone, and even though Katie looked all over the store, she didn't find her. She finally came to the conclusion that Johanna, for her own reasons, didn't want to continue the conversation, or to give Katie her address.

All the way home she was unsettled, and after a week went by and Johanna hadn't contacted either her or Edward, Katie assumed she wouldn't. Maybe she was intimidated by their good fortune, Katie thought. And maybe that only emphasized Dion's failures. It was a puzzle with no answer. Finally, Katie felt only sad.

Her labor pains wiped all other thoughts from her mind; the delivery went fast and without problems. Baby Peter David arrived on Memorial Day, and David was so excited that he bought football, basketball, and baseball equipment for his new son, and flowers and candy and a frilly black negligee for Katie. She couldn't help remembering the day Christina was born. How different her life was now!

"This is the happiest day of my life," he said as he gently kissed her, then the dark-haired baby in her arms. "Thank you, my darling, for giving me a son."

The summer was idyllic. Little Peter was a contented baby who resembled his father. By Labor Day, Katie felt she could leave him with a nursemaid, and she went back to work. The office needed her leadership and she couldn't put it off any longer. Her baby, doted on by everyone, didn't suffer. She drove home at lunchtime, called numerous times during the day, and put him to bed each night. The family was flourishing, even though she and David were rarely at home together.

"There's a man here who insists on seeing you," Katie's secretary said from the doorway of Katie's office. "I told him you were busy, but he keeps insisting that—"

She broke off as a slight man in a gray business suit came around her so that he was in Katie's line of vision.

"So sorry, Katie," he said politely. "But it is most important that I meet with you."

Katie jumped up, waved her secretary away, and came forward to greet Isami Kono. A rush of emotions surged through her as she met his black eyes—

surprise, guilt for being the one running the company that was once his, and shame for Edward's past dishonor to the Konos.

"Mr. Kono, I'm honored," she said, aware that her words reflected an earlier time, the Japanese influence.

He gave a slight bow. Then he asked after her family, commented on the fall weather, and noted the efficient way she was running Eastern Imports. She was suddenly reminded of the proprieties, and that his good manners dictated that he get them out of the way before he got down to the reason he'd sought her out after all this time.

At first, she'd assumed it had something to do with the company, perhaps a belated chastisement, but as that topic had been a part of the proprieties, she knew something else had brought him to her. Katie waited patiently, another habit from the past.

"I seek a favor, Katie," he said, abruptly direct. "I wish you to accompany me to my home. Someone wishes to see you concerning Anna Su."

"Who?" She knew Anna Su was in school.

He raised a flat hand in the gesture of silencing questions. "I must ask you to trust me—and my honor," he said, and she knew he wouldn't say more. She would either go with him, or not.

She took her coat from the rack and slipped it on. Then she followed him out of her office, telling her surprised secretary that she'd return later. Once they left the building, he helped her into his late-model Dodge and closed the door. She was committed.

It only took a few minutes to reach the Japanese section of the city. He parked the car on a steep hill in front of an apartment house with a magnificent view of the bay, and immediately led her into the building. As they climbed the steps to the top floor, Katie couldn't help remembering where the Konos had once lived in Pacific Heights, only blocks from her own house. They'd certainly gone down in the world, she thought sadly. A silent Mrs. Kono let them into the apartment, and Katie wondered what she was thinking.

"Please, Katie," Isami said, and Katie heard something in his voice—emotional pain? "Please, to enter." He indicated the next room.

Apprehension pressed down on Katie as she stepped through the doorway into a shadowy bedroom. A figure on the bed was propped up by pillows.

"Katie? Katie, is it really you?" a soft voice said.

The woman's voice was familiar. Katie's heart pounded as she moved closer, her eyes on a face no longer beautiful, a face ravished by sickness. But the eyes were still as gentle and loving as Katie remembered.

"Katie—it is Michiko!"

A cry tore free of Katie's throat, and she ran to the bed and took the frail body of her old friend into her arms. "Michiko—Michiko—oh, Michiko," she murmured, tears streaming down her face. "My dearest friend. Oh, my God! Michiko, what's happened to you? We believed you were dead."

She'd pulled back enough so that she could see Michiko's face, an anguished face that bore evidence of terrible suffering. Katie felt shuddering sobs deep within herself, and forced them back. It was a time to summon all of the *kendo* she'd once known. It was a time to be strong—for Michiko's sake.

In her soft voice, Michiko told what had happened to her, how she'd not been allowed to leave Japan, the decision by her father to move the family to Hiroshima where it was deemed safer—and then the bomb.

"It was so horrible—beyond imagining. The beautiful city of our girlhood was gone, Katie, in one blinding flash of light." Her voice shook. "I was far enough away to be spared, and when I could, I tried to get home." She took a deep breath, trying to maintain her calm. "But my home was gone. My honorable parents were gone. Nothing was left—nothing but gray ashes."

There were no words to comfort Michiko. In silence they held each other and clung to the memories of those wonderful days that were filled with golden promise.

"I will die soon, Katie-san."

Her voice was brave. Like the samurai who'd resolved his own fate, Katie thought, so shattered by the unspeakable that she couldn't speak herself.

"I have leukemia—from the radiation."

And then they both cried together, once more the two little girls who'd giggled and played and shared dreams, black hair blending with white, Japanese and American. Sisters.

Later, when they could, they talked. Katie excused herself once to call the office and say she wouldn't return that day. Then she talked for the next few hours about Anna Su and all of her accomplishments and how beautiful she was. Michiko cried again when she heard about Edward.

"I cannot see him now," she said, her lashes lowered to hide her pain. "He must not see me like this. Will you promise not to tell?"

Katie honored her wishes, understanding. There were some things that were not to be borne. And perhaps it would be as Michiko believed—that she and Edward would be together again in the next life. If nothing else, that belief would help her get through her final days, Katie thought sadly.

"I want to see Anna Su, Katie." Michiko's voice was tentative. "Do you think it would frighten her to see me now?"

"Oh, my dear friend. Your daughter is much like you." Katie's words shook with conviction. "She would want to know you more than anything else. Can I bring her?"

Michiko nodded, suddenly looking so tired that Katie feared the worst. Quickly she stood up. For a moment longer she hesitated, then stooped to kiss the scarred face.

"I love you, Michiko. I've always loved you as a sister. And I'll remember you always."

She left her then. Mr. Kono led the way to the front door, where Mrs. Kono stopped them. Wordlessly, and with great dignity, she hugged Katie.

Mr. Kono drove her home in silence until after he'd stopped the car. "Thank you, Katie. You were good for Michiko. She has suffered so much, more than she was able to bear."

Her eyes questioned, but she didn't ask questions. He would tell her what he wished.

"She was in a mental hospital after the war. Her mind blocked the horrors of her eyes. By the time she was released to Tak, she was already dying."

So Tak was alive. Somehow knowing that lifted her spirits just a little. After promising to prepare Anna Su for her meeting with Michiko, they decided on a time. Katie went into the house, and after seeing to the children, went to her room. She needed to be alone, and for once she was relieved that David was gone.

The lights had come on in the city below her bedroom window, and she stood for a long time watching the reflected light on the bay—like fairy dust sprinkled over an enchanted sea. Katie swallowed hard, but she couldn't stop the tears now. Or the gulping sobs that suddenly tore through her body.

A long time later, spent and drained, she climbed into bed. And from somewhere in her remembering

came the voice of an old Japanese man. "*Karma* is
karma."

Being reunited with her mother did wonders for
Anna Su. Katie had prepared her, and although there
was the underlying knowledge of her mother's impending death, Anna Su's own emotional scars began to heal. When Michiko died a few weeks later,
Katie went to the memorial service with Anna Su.

"Oh Aunt Katie, I loved her so," Anna Su sobbed
later. "Why did she have to die?"

"I don't know," Katie replied honestly. "But at
least you did know her, honey. And you've realized
that all I told you about her over the years was true."
Katie's voice shook. "She was the most genuinely
selfless person I've ever known. It was a privilege to
have been her friend."

Michiko's body was sent to Tak in Japan for
burial. Once Anna Su was over the worst of her grief,
she spent more time with her father. "I promised my
mother," she told Katie. "I understand him better
now."

Smiling, Katie encouraged her, because it was
good for Anna Su to feel a connection to her father.
But secretly she suspected that Michiko, who'd loved
him so desperately, had romanticized Edward, blind
to his flaws.

Life eventually reverted to its even flow, and Katie
was surrounded by her loved ones. Her baby Peter
was already walking by May and he wasn't even a
year old.

"I think we should have another child," David
suggested one night after they'd made love. "Just
think about it while I'm in New York," he added
with an endearing grin.

"I'll give it some thought." She raised her brows
suggestively. "But maybe you've already given me
one tonight."

"Or I could try again," he said, and pulled her closer.

When he slept beside her an hour later, Katie thought about having another baby. The doctor had advised against it, not because she was already in her thirties, but because of her negative blood type. He thought it might cause complications with a third pregnancy.

David brought up having another baby again at Peter's first birthday party. His hope that Katie might be pregnant had been dashed when she'd turned up with her monthly period that morning. She'd been secretly relieved, but reassured him nevertheless that it was a future possibility.

The next day she saw David off, then went to the office. When five o'clock rolled around, she realized she hadn't even stopped for lunch. As she left the building, a portfolio of papers under one arm, a man stepped from the doorway in front of her, bringing her up short.

Their eyes met. For a shattering moment, Katie was stunned, suspended in time. The portfolio dropped onto the sidewalk, spilling its contents. It couldn't be—wasn't possible!

The man was Max!

CHAPTER 21

"HELLO, KATIE."

Max stepped close; his dark eyes were filled with her, but he didn't touch her. Katie shook all over. Her body felt as if it had received an electric shock that left her as weak as a rag doll. *It was Max!* A Max whose face had an older cast, whose black hair was winged with gray, and whose body was leaner than she remembered. She shook her head, unable to find her voice, licked her lips, and tried again.

"Dear God. I thought you were dead." Her voice was hardly above a whisper. "What happened, Max? Where were you? Why didn't you come back?"

"We have to talk, Katie," he said, unable to find simple answers to her questions, but his words were even more strained than his expression. In one quick

motion, he took her arm and led her to his car.
Mutely, she slipped onto the front seat, and as he
slammed the door and then went around to the
driver's side, panic suddenly overwhelmed Katie.
Oh, my God! How can I tell him the truth—that I'm
married again, and have a son?

His door closed and they were abruptly cut off
from the traffic noise of the street. Max didn't start
the car; instead he sat gripping the steering wheel, his
gaze on the parked car in front of them. His jaw was
set, a pulse beat erratically at his temple, and Katie
knew he was gathering his thoughts.

It was like waking up from a nightmare and
finding it real, Katie thought desperately. During all
the nights she'd wept for Max—longed for him—
she'd never once thought that he'd come back to life
years later. And now, watching him, she felt all of
that longing and love surging back, so strong it was
like yesterday.

"I went looking for you that day," she began
shakily. "To apologize. And you'd already gone—
and you didn't come back—and I never got over the
guilt." Her voice trailed off when he didn't look at
her.

"Didn't you?" He was suddenly direct, the force of
his eyes pinning her to those agonizing days when
she'd thought her life was over. "Then why didn't
you wait for me?"

"I did—for two years and two freezing winters
that no one could have lived through without shelter
and food." She hesitated, defeat swelling within her.
"Max—oh Max! Can't you understand? I finally had
to face the fact that you were dead. I had to go on—I
had Christina to think of too."

"So you left Alaska." He looked away, and his
voice no longer accused. He sounded like a beaten
man.

"You don't understand Max. I—"

He turned so fast that she faltered. "I know, Katie," he said hollowly, and she saw the anguish and disbelief on his face. "*I know*. You married someone else."

She couldn't look away from the pain in his eyes, wasn't even aware that the tears streamed down her face, until suddenly she was sobbing against his chest. Finally, when she was able to speak again, Katie begged him to explain what had happened. Her own explanation could wait, but a terrible fear was knotting in the pit of her stomach. She wouldn't allow herself to think about the ramifications of being married to two men. It was beyond her fragile emotions at the moment.

"I started having engine problems when I was flying over the Brooks Mountains." He lit a cigarette, cracked his window open and then continued. "It was snowing and blowing. I was lucky enough to make it to a valley, and when I tried to land, I crashed. I must have passed out, because when I came to I was outside and the plane was in flames a hundred yards away."

"You were thrown out?"

"Pulled out. A prospector saw my plane go down, and he got me out before it exploded." He hesitated. "The old guy was only there because he'd stayed into the fall, later than he'd intended, working a gold vein until it played out. If he hadn't stayed, I'd be dead—" His gaze caught hers. "As everyone assumed."

"Oh, Max. I'm so sorry."

He looked beyond her, his eyes remote, as though they saw again those tragic days. "The area was isolated—inaccessible for most of the year—and there was no radio, nothing left of the plane."

The bustle of San Francisco went on around them as Max related, in a monotone, the circumstances that precluded his return to civilization. His legs had

been injured, and even after his cuts and burns
healed, he still wasn't able to do more than hobble.
The old man had stayed with him in the summer
shack, nursing him throughout the winter. By spring,
Max's legs weren't much better, so the old man went
for help without him—and never came back.

"I knew the old man must have died. Maybe a
grizzly got him. But by then I was committed to the
second winter." Max lit another cigarette, the first
having burned out in the ashtray. "So I prepared for
surviving until spring. And all winter long I exer-
cised, strengthened my legs."

He went on, explaining that when he finally
started walking out, it was about the time he was
being presumed dead in Anchorage. "All summer I
limped south, hoping to find a river to follow." He
hesitated. "It's one hell of a big land out there, and
no people."

"Oh Max—how awful for you," she said almost
under her breath. She couldn't bear the thought that
he'd been in the wilderness struggling for survival
when she'd been flying back to California.

"I finally came to a mining camp, one I recognized. I'd flown supplies and miners to it each
spring. And I'd flown the men out each fall." He
shook his head, and she glimpsed how hard it had
been. "I was too late. They'd already been flown out
for the winter, so I figured it must be October by
then."

"So you stayed for another winter."

Nodding, he blew smoke. "It was my only option.
I knew where I was, the cook shack was stocked with
canned goods, and I knew a plane would come in the
spring."

"That was still a couple of years ago, Max! Why
didn't you write, or call me once you were back?"

"Oh God, Katie! Don't you think I would have—

if I could? That last winter was the worst kind of hell. My food ran out, my legs were swollen up like stovepipes; it was all I could do to keep wood on the fire. In the end, I ran a fever and was out of my head. I didn't know when the plane came and the men found me. I woke up in a Fairbanks hospital and didn't even remember who I was or how I got there. I was a skeleton no one recognized, and I had no identification. They assumed I was a prospector. As the weeks passed and I regained weight and strength, I began to remember. Dion was notified around Christmas-time, and I assumed you were too."

"I was already in California for over a year by then. And had just sold our house," she added in a small voice.

"They finally told me that, and all that had happened." He ground out the cigarette and turned to her, his expression regretful. "My ordeal was nothing compared to the hell of knowing what had happened in my absence. I couldn't believe it. You gone—Dion stealing my company."

"But you still could have contacted me."

"The doctor had operated on my legs, resetting the bones, when they first brought me in. But I needed more operations, and was flown down to Seattle. Since you were already in California, I wanted to be whole when I saw you again." He spread his hands in a gesture of futility. "I still wasn't thinking right. They said I'd been in bad shape mentally as well as physically."

Katie clenched her hands in her lap; fresh tears welled and rolled down her face to drip onto her jacket. First Michiko had come back, now Max. How could she go on? The pain was endless. How could she ever make things right again? David's son waited at home for her, with Max's daughter. She needed time to think, to sort things out alone. It was a relief that David was in New York for a couple of weeks. How could she face him? How would he react to knowing she wasn't really his wife?

"I want you back, Katie." Max pulled her against him, and gently stroked her hair. "I want my family back."

A sob caught in her throat, but she forced herself to meet his eyes. "I married again, Max. I have a son."

"Sweetheart, I know," he said, and his old endearment brought even more tears. "We can work it out somehow. It'll be all right, if only you'll come back to me."

He was so much her beloved bush pilot, and yet he was different too. He'd suffered greatly, and now she was responsible for yet another kind of suffering, and there was no way to make things right for everyone. The dilemma was horrible. She still loved him. But she loved David now too—and Peter.

He read her thoughts on her face, as he'd always been able to do despite her *Kendo*. Without a word he started the car, the new Ford he was having shipped back to Anchorage.

Before he let out the clutch to ease into the traffic, he said, "So you love him—this David?"

She couldn't lie; he didn't deserve lies. "He's a fine man—I didn't expect to love him, Max. It just happened—because I thought you were gone forever."

A moment later they were in the traffic, headed toward Pacific Heights. He even knows where I live, she thought sadly. Mental images swirled in her mind—the first time she'd seen him in the park, their flight to Alaska when he'd made love to her, and their years of loving each other. As he drove up the hills, he was all of those precious memories, and yet he was a stranger, who hadn't even kissed her.

But a glance at his strong profile told Katie that he

hadn't given up. What was his belonged to him. The realization frightened her. Max could be a formidable enemy.

"Oh Max, of course I intend to tell Christina." Katie sat across from him in the coffee shop near the office, a place they'd been meeting each evening before she went home for the day. Although they'd talked over the situation in great length, they were no closer to a solution than on the first day. And now David was due home in two days. Katie was panicky.

"There's but one solution, Katie. That's getting back together. You know it's the only recourse we have. You're still married to me."

He watched her—so beautiful, so familiar, and yet so different from the old Katie. She reflected the confidence and presence that came from running a large company. In a few short years, while he was trying to get back to her, everything had changed drastically. His confidence had been shaken to the core when he'd learned of her marriage. But the fact that she had a son—who wasn't his son—had almost sent him back into the grayness of his long recovery.

Yet he understood her position too, and hated to cause such anguish in her life. But she was his wife, and he had a daughter, and he loved them and wanted them back. He meant to have them back. He was willing to take her little son, as he knew his loyal Katie could never leave her own child behind. Max wouldn't acknowledge that her strong sense of loyalty might be the one thing that would preclude her return to him.

They'd reached a stalemate, and Max knew his only hope was to break it. Since the day two weeks ago when he'd come back into her life, Katie had insisted their meetings be in a public place. He suspected she didn't trust her feelings any more than he did his. He'd seen desire for him in her eyes more than once. It was time he did something about that.

"Can we have dinner together?" he asked. "And just forget everything for one night?"

She hesitated, wanting to agree more than anything else. But she feared the intimacy of being alone with him. It had become harder and harder to be with him, remembering how his touch had once set her on fire, how he'd sent her soaring into an ecstasy she'd never known with David, even though she loved David as much as Max, in a different way.

But did she? she asked herself. If she were free, which man would she choose? Katie sipped her coffee and forced her thoughts to the issue at hand. She couldn't look at the answer to her own question; it would only complicate matters.

"Just dinner," he coaxed. "At the Mark Hopkins Hotel, where I'm staying. And then I'll send you home in a taxi."

"I'm—I'm not dressed for having dinner out," she said, but he saw her indecision and pressed his advantage.

"You're lovely," he told her, his dark eyes hooded, as though he appraised her black gabardine suit and pale green silk blouse and nothing else.

"I'll have to call Mrs. Mendoza and see if it's possible," she replied, having lowered her gaze. She couldn't stand to see the hope in his.

"Go ahead," Max urged. "There's a phone by the door. I'll wait here."

She slid out of the booth, and without glancing at him, went to call home. *Maybe there'll be a problem with the children*, she thought, *and I won't be able to stay.* But as Mrs. Mendoza assured her that all was well, her excuses were gone, unless she lied to Max.

But as she went back to him, Katie nodded. As he paid for the coffee, a surge of joy swept over her. She was suddenly looking forward to a candlelit dinner at the top of the Mark Hopkins. It might be the last one she ever had with him.

The fish dinner, and all its courses, looked delicious, but Katie hardly tasted it. The view of the city and bay from the top of the Mark was spectacular, a wonderful backdrop for a last night together, Katie thought, and was determined to enjoy it. For a few hours they talked, and it was almost like when she first met him. They laughed about the good times and reminisced about the war. The wine and soft music mellowed her, and as even more feelings were reawakened, Katie suddenly knew she was on dangerous ground. But still she felt regret when it was finally time to go.

They were alone in the elevator, and when it stopped she assumed they'd reached the lobby. They stepped out, the doors swooshed shut behind them, and it was only then that Katie realized she was in the hotel itself. Her eyes flew to Max.

For a second neither spoke. Then, slowly, he pulled her to him and claimed her mouth. She tried to resist, but his kiss deepened, was suddenly demanding, igniting their old passion. She went weak from it, and strained for more. All her nights of longing and loss were forgotten in the reality of his being alive, a flesh-and-blood Max whose very touch electrified her. And she knew she couldn't deny her need for him, or his for her, even if it was now taboo.

A minute later, they were in Max's room, the door closed and locked. There was no turning back now. She didn't resist when he took her jacket and unbuttoned her blouse. She only murmured his name, her eyes closed, as they fell across the bed, their bodies entwined. And for a long time nothing at all registered in her mind but the man beside her and the reawakened sensations of his lovemaking. She was his completely—if only for tonight.

"I love you. You know that, don't you?" Max said later.

She nodded, her head resting on his arm, her hair splayed over the pillow.

"We have to work this out, Katie," he went on gently.

"Shhh," she whispered. "But not now. Tomorrow."

She turned her face so that their eyes were only inches apart. "Thank you, my darling," she said softly. "For loving me." She didn't want to spoil the afterglow of their love by bringing up their situation.

He nuzzled her, and she saw that he would honor her wishes. When it was time for her to dress, he pulled her back, for a moment fearful to let her go. "Not yet," he said against her lips, and made love to her once more.

After that, she couldn't delay any longer. Showered and again in her suit, her hair repinned, Katie was ready. He took her down to the lobby, called a cab and saw her into it. Then he watched it out of sight.

The coffee shop was packed, and Katie was glad she'd arrived early and secured a little table in the back. But she was unsettled, and fatigued from lack of sleep. Having Max make love to her hadn't helped in the long run; it had only pointed up her loss, and hadn't changed a thing. Max wanted her and Christina, but to go with him meant leaving Peter and David, because David would never give up his son. It would also mean leaving Eastern Imports, knowing Edward couldn't manage it without her. And there was Anna Su, who wouldn't inherit the company if it went bankrupt. Her life no longer belonged to just herself. There were others to consider. She had no choice; too much had happened. She must stay.

Max read her decision on her face as he sat down a

few minutes later. In a halting voice, Katie tried to
explain, her own feelings so near the surface that
tears stung her eyes.

"But we love each other. How can you turn your
back on that?" Max asked in a low tone, and Katie
saw that she'd rocked him to the core—that he was
fighting the hopelessness within himself. "How can
you push aside our years together? Our marriage?"
He snapped his fingers. "Just like that?"

"That isn't what I've done," she cried. "I love you,
you know that. But can't you understand? There are
others to consider now."

"We were first." There was a bitterness in his
words. "And our daughter was there before your
son."

"I can't abandon Peter. And David would never
give him up. He'd fight me for Peter."

"I understand what you're saying, Katie. And I
understand how hard it would be for you." He shook
his head, his own pain obvious in his eyes. "But you
must weigh everything—how you want to live the
rest of your life—with me, or with David."

She couldn't stand seeing his desperation, hearing
the anguish in his voice. "Don't make it a choice,
Max—because it's not. I have no choice. David
married me, loves me, loves the girls. I can't destroy
him—and Peter."

"But you can destroy me instead." His voice was
hardly a whisper.

"God knows I don't want that." Katie began to
cry, great silent shudders that she tried to swallow.
There was no answer. Why did it happen—*why*? she
asked herself over and over. And yet, when she
thought of her beloved baby boy, she couldn't wish
that David had never happened. It was simply too
late for her and Max.

He stood up, resigned. Fate had dealt him a
terrible blow, and he didn't know if he'd ever recover

from it. Katie was still his wife, but she belonged to another man now. He had to accept that.

"You won't change your mind?" He asked one last time.

Slowly she shook her head.

"You think David will understand when you tell him?"

This time she nodded, even though she wasn't sure. Yet she couldn't hold out false hope for Max, play one man against the other. It was a nightmare. But at all costs, she must keep her family together.

"I can't give up my daughter either," Max said, his tone hard all at once. "I love her as much as David loves his son." He put money down on the table for their coffee. "I want equal custody of Christina, Katie. I won't lose her too."

He strode to the door, leaving her shaken. What had he meant? Surely he wouldn't take legal action —try to take Christina away, and in doing so expose Peter's illegitimacy? Katie took a mirror from her purse and dabbed at her eyes, fighting the overwhelming urge to cry. Somehow, the thought hadn't occurred to her that she might lose Christina.

Katie left the coffee shop, caught a cab, and tried to stay calm. But the fears kept coming. She could lose her son, or her daughter, or both. David loved her—but would he understand? She wouldn't lie; she had to tell him the truth. She couldn't be married to two men.

He was silent for so long that Katie's fears wouldn't allow her to wait any longer for him to say something—anything. She'd told him the whole story—except that she still loved Max and had been alone with him in his hotel room.

"I'm so sorry, David," she whispered, and willed him to understand. "I know this is terrible for you."

"It's incredible!" David turned from the window

where he'd been contemplating the city, his expression grim. "Unbelievable!"

"I know. It was an awful shock for me too." She maintained her calm, but there was a quiver in her voice.

Her distress suddenly communicated itself to him, and his face softened as he went to her. "Oh God, Katie. I'm sorry too. I was only thinking of myself. This has to be hell for you."

She leaned against him, welcomed his strength, and tried not to think of how she'd betrayed him.

"This isn't your fault," he said. "We'll work it out, darling. You'll get a divorce so we can make our marriage legal. You didn't marry me under false pretenses, Katie; you believed Max was dead."

"Thank you for understanding," she managed.

He kissed the top of her head. "I love you," he said simply, and she realized how much he trusted her. It hadn't occurred to him that she might still be in love with Max. He believed she'd buried those feelings when she fell in love with him.

"Max has a right to equal custody, Katie," he went on. "It's only fair that a man know his own child. I know how I'd feel about Peter. I'd fight to the death for him. Christina should be told at once."

His words only reminded her that she'd been right. David would never give up his son either. Max and David were alike in that way too, she thought, and concentrated on Christina.

"How will I explain? How—"

"Don't worry about it." He interrupted her, trying to head off her upset. "Children accept changes better than adults. But we do have to keep this situation within the family. It wouldn't be good for people to know we weren't married—that Peter was born out of wedlock, as they say," he added with a hint of wry humor.

They talked at great length about the situation and

agreed it should be resolved as soon as possible.
Katie contacted Max the next morning, and in a
stilted voice explained their feelings. Max's response
was equally formal, and she sensed his hurt and
anger. But he agreed at once to see Christina.

"We'd like you to come here this evening," Katie
told him.

"Agreed," he said, and hung up abruptly.

It took a few minutes for Katie to pull herself
together and explain things to Christina.

"You mean Daddy's alive!" she shrieked. "Oh
Mommy, I'm so happy. My own daddy is alive!"

Katie swallowed hard. Oh God, would the sorrow
ever end? And deep inside her, a little voice said it
was only beginning. But she wouldn't listen to imagi-
nary thoughts that grew out of her own sadness.
Somehow it would all work out.

David's assessment of Christina's reaction was
proven right. At nine, she was unaware of Katie's
predicament. The thought of marriage ramifications
didn't enter her head. She simply accepted that her
mother was married to someone else now, and she
loved David too. But when her father arrived, she
forgot all about her step-father, who'd taken her
baby brother out for a walk, and was oblivious that
he'd left on purpose to save Katie embarrassment.

By the end of the reunion, plans had been made
for Christina to fly to Anchorage on the first of
August for a visit. *Just six weeks away*, Katie
thought. It would be the first time she'd ever been
separated from her daughter, but she kept her feelings under tight control—because she had to. Although Christina heartened Max, Katie also knew he
was suffering behind his veneer of pride. Oh God,
she was sorry—so sorry. But there was no going
back. Her decision was the only way to keep both of
her children, even though Max would share in
Christina's upbringing.

That night, after David was asleep beside her, she lay awake for hours, and wondered how she could be in love with two men at the same time. In the eyes of the world, she was an adulteress until she was legally divorced and remarried.

And that all depended on Max. "I can't think about that now, Katie," he'd told her when she'd mentioned divorce. "I'll give it some thought after I'm back in Alaska."

It was hard to say good-bye to Christina when she flew north. David's being in New York made it easier for Katie, as she needed time alone. She took the day off from work and spent it with Peter. But she missed Christina and worried about her being alone on the plane, even though Max had arranged for her to take the same flight as one of his employees, so she'd have someone to look after her. Christina called from Anchorage when she arrived, her voice excited about being in such a beautiful place.

"Mommy, I miss you," she said, and before Katie could respond she rushed on. "But I love it here already! Daddy said he's going to take me flying. And I get to meet my Aunt Johanna and Uncle Dion and my cousins; they just moved back too. I'll write you, Mommy."

Katie wrote that very day, anxious to keep the communication open with her daughter. She tried not to worry. But over the next weeks, her concern grew. Christina's letters raved about her father's house that overlooked the water, and Katie wondered if it was near their old one. Her daughter bragged about her "darling bedroom," and that she was "the woman of daddy's house," all of which brought new fears to Katie. When she received the letter from Christina explaining that she wanted to stay for the school year, that her father needed her, Katie panicked. The enclosed letter addressed to both her and David added Max's hope that Christina would stay until spring.

"I want her to come home!" Katie cried.

"I don't think it would hurt for her to stay," David said. "It's obvious that Christina isn't being coerced, for God's sake!"

It was their first major disagreement, upsetting on top of her worry about Christina. "She's too young to be away that long!" Katie cried.

"Jesus, Katie! Max is her parent too. It's not as though she was being thrown to the wolves. It's the least we can do considering what the man has lost."

That took her argument completely. She turned away, feeling defeated, and for once David didn't comfort her.

"Besides," David went on, "Max hasn't done anything about the divorce, and if we cross him, he might dig his heels in and cause trouble. There's your son's legitimacy to consider," he reminded her sharply. "And the fact that we don't want anyone to find out about this whole mess."

Taken aback by his real feelings—his anger—she finally agreed to let Christina stay. Katie knew she was in good hands; it was just that she missed her daughter so much, and worried that Max would influence Christina to stay beyond spring.

Katie felt manipulated by both men, and she didn't like it. Nor did she like the rift she felt developing between her and David, or the fact that he denied there was one. Over the following days Katie felt even more depressed and decided it was time to take matters into her own hands.

"Since Max hasn't filed for divorce, I intend to do so instead," she told David.

"Are you crazy?" he cried. "You haven't a leg to stand on. In the eyes of the law you're the one in the wrong, not Max. If you instituted a divorce, and he contested it, we could end up with a scandal—and I won't have that. We must be patient."

"Are you worried about Peter—or yourself?" she asked quietly, but she was furious. For a moment he'd reminded her of Edward.

"Don't be hysterical," he said, and his eyes glinted with a coldness she'd never seen in him before. "As I've said, we have to be patient and not rock the boat."

David left the room to work in his study, leaving Katie to fume in silence. He didn't want to rock the boat—even if that meant leaving Christina in Alaska.

"Aunt Katie? Are you all right?"

Anna Su stood in the doorway, hesitant to disturb her aunt. She'd overheard their conversation and understood Katie's feelings. Even though Christina was too young to understand the situation of her parents, Anna Su did, and sympathized with her aunt.

"Of course," Katie replied smiling. "Please join me. I'd love your company. Besides, we have to make some plans for your birthday, which is right around the corner," she went on, glad of the opportunity to change the subject. "Fourteen—I can't believe it."

"It's hard for me to believe too," Anna Su replied, and sat down next to Katie on the sofa. "I'm sorry Christina won't be back to help me celebrate." She hesitated. "I'm sorry, but I overheard."

Katie patted her knee. "I think everyone in the house heard. I admit, Anna Su, that I hate the thought of Christina staying away."

Nodding, Anna Su glanced away, and something about her struck Katie as being different. She appeared upset, and not just about Christina being gone.

"Is something wrong, Anna Su?" she asked gently.

Her long lashes flew up as her gaze met Katie's. About to deny her feelings, she suddenly decided to share them. It would give her aunt something else to think about beside Christina.

"It's my father," Anna Su began hesitantly.

"Edward? Is he sick?"

"Sort of." Anna Su glanced at the oriental rug, tracing its pattern across the floor. "His housekeeper told me he gets drunk every night. Would you talk to him, Aunt Katie? He won't listen to me."

"Of course," Katie agreed. She wasn't surprised; the housekeeper had told her too. Concerned that the woman would quit, Katie had broached the subject with Edward, and he'd only retorted in anger, "There's nothing else to do other than eat and watch television. I'm entitled to some of life's pleasures, for Christ sake!" She'd dropped the subject.

"I'll talk to him tomorrow," she promised Anna Su, and didn't mention her earlier conversation with Edward.

But Edward only became angry when she brought up the subject again the next day. Katie was in no mood to argue; for the third morning in a row she'd been upset to her stomach. Her concern for Edward vanished in a second when she realized what was wrong with her.

CHAPTER 22

"I BELIEVE I'M PREGNANT," SHE TOLD DAVID, CATCHING
his eye in her dressing table mirror as she sat
brushing her hair.

"That's wonderful, darling!" he cried, and dropping his shirt on the chair, he went to her and kissed
her on the cheek.

"But I won't know for sure until I see the doctor."
She stood so that he could take her in his arms. "I
hope it's all right, David," she said softly. "You
know the doctor cautioned me about a third pregnancy with my negative blood."

"It'll be just fine," he reassured her gently, and his
eyes sparkled with excitement at the prospect of
another child. "You didn't have problems in the
past, so you probably won't this time either."

They'd just gone to their bedroom for the night,

and Katie had waited until they were alone to give him the news she'd suspected for a couple of weeks. She'd been upset at first, remembering how David had reacted over Christina's staying in Alaska. Because of the mess over still being married to Max, she'd thought another baby would only complicate matters. But as she became more certain of being pregnant, she began to feel more optimistic about the future. And David's pleasure at having another child made her feel even better. Her lingering doubts about Max diminished. Her life was in California now—with David.

"Has there been any word from Alaska?" David asked a few minutes later when they were in bed.

"We had another letter from Christina." Katie stared into the dark room, evading the real question behind David's words. "She seems to be having the time of her life up there."

For a minute, David didn't respond. "I was wondering about the divorce. Any word on that?"

He spoke with a light tone, but Katie knew he was very concerned that there'd been only silence on the subject since Max returned to Alaska. It worried Katie, too, but she reminded herself of Max's flying schedule. It had always prevented him from getting around to personal business; he'd once put off changing his will, a neglect that had ultimately influenced her move from Alaska into the life she now lived. She suspected that filing for a divorce was something that wouldn't take precedence over other pressing matters.

"Nothing yet." Katie didn't mention that she'd written a brief note to Max, and he hadn't responded to that either. "But he'll take care of it soon, I'm sure he will."

"Yeah," David agreed, and pulled her close. "Once he's past all his hurt." He hesitated, and thought about how he'd feel in Max's shoes. "It has to be tough for him. Giving him some time to adjust is the least we can do."

"Thanks, David."

He turned on his side so that he could look at her face. "For what? Giving you a new baby?"

His voice teased, and she was suddenly filled with love for him. She was so fortunate that he understood. "For being you," she whispered softly. "I love you, David. And I'm so happy that we're having another child."

He feathered her face with kisses. "I love you too," he murmured. And then he proved his declaration by making love to her.

Within the week, she kept an appointment with her doctor. After the examination he gave her the verdict.

"You're pregnant all right, Katie. Looks like little Peter will have a new brother or sister around the twelfth of next March."

"Are you sure about the date?" She tried to sound normal, as though his words hadn't given her a horrible jolt.

He raised his brows, his expression tolerant, as though he expected all his female patients to question such an important date. "About as sure as I can be for a doctor who's been delivering babies for over twenty years."

After a few instructions on diet and vitamins, and a brief caution about her negative blood situation, he left her to dress. But Katie's hands shook as she buttoned her blouse, and by the time she reached her office she was so upset she could hardly settle down to work. She went home early, frantic about her latest problem.

David had flown to New York just before Max

reappeared in her life, and she had her period after he left. He'd returned in mid-June, and because of all her upset, they hadn't made love until after the Fourth of July holiday, even though he'd been understanding and held her in his arms every night. By the time they had sex, she'd already missed her monthly period, and hadn't even realized it. If her due date was the twelfth of March, then David wasn't the baby's father. *Max was.*

Her fears intensified as the days passed and David went out of his way to see that she was pampered. "We've got to take care of this new little person," he told her. "I'm hoping for a girl this time, how about you?"

She tried to be as excited as he was, but each time he commented on "his baby" she became more upset inside—and more depressed. How would he feel if he knew the baby she carried belonged to Max? Her mind spun with possible solutions, the obvious one being to let him believe the baby was his.

"What's wrong, Katie?" David asked one night when they were alone. "Aren't you well? Don't you want this baby?"

He spoke sharply, as though he was losing patience with her. She smiled and shook her head. "It's nothing, David. I've had a touch of morning sickness. I'll be over it in a few weeks."

"Are you sure that's all? Maybe you should take a leave from work."

Contriving a smile, Katie reassured him, but as the days passed, she felt a strain between them. She knew that she hadn't convinced him that everything was all right, and she didn't know how to change things either. She was worried sick. It was awful to deceive him, but she feared telling him the truth. How could she have let Max make love to her? she asked herself endlessly, in such inner turmoil that she didn't know which way to turn. Sooner or later, she wouldn't be able to hide the fact that her due date was a month earlier than it should have been.

Even Anna Su and little Peter realized something was wrong, each in their own way. It was a Saturday afternoon when the pains began, and Katie knew something was terribly wrong. When she began to bleed, she called for Anna Su. David had flown to Los Angeles on business, and Peter was taking a nap.

"What's wrong?" Anna Su cried, seeing that Katie was doubled up on the bed.

"Call my doctor," Katie managed, the pains now so intense that she felt as if she'd gone into labor. "His home number—is in the book." She indicated her personal address book on the nightstand. "I—I can't seem to manage it."

The blood staining the spread gave wings to Anna Su's feet as she ran to find the number. Then she quickly dialed, and when the doctor answered, she blurted out the situation—that her aunt was doubled over in pain and was bleeding all over everything. He interrupted her with "I'm sending an ambulance."

She repeated the doctor's words, then hesitated, unsure of how to help. "Are you having a miscarriage?" Her words shook with fear. She'd never seen her aunt look so pale and sick.

Kattie nodded. "Get some towels," she said weakly. "I need to stop the bleeding." Now that she was losing the baby, she was stricken with remorse. Whatever the cost, she didn't want it to die. It was all her fault, because she hadn't wanted it. She'd always called Edward selfish, but she was the one who was being selfish now.

For the next few minutes, Anna Su did everything she could to help, and she was so relieved when the

ambulance arrived that she shook all over. "I'll mind
Peter," she told Katie. "You just be all right. I'll call
Uncle David."

But the words blended into a monotone to Katie.
She fought the gray that edged her vision. *Father in
Heaven*, she prayed silently. It wasn't the baby's
fault. Don't let it die.

Then the gray deepened, and as the siren shattered
the afternoon, it went black.

Katie woke up in the hospital, the doctor beside
her bed. When he saw her eyes were open, he took
her hand.

"I'm sorry, Katie," he whispered softly. "You lost
the baby."

Her lashes fluttered shut. She couldn't bear it. *I'm
responsible*, she thought. *I worried myself into a
miscarriage, too concerned about myself to even think
of the baby.* Tears welled and slid from under her
eyelids to run down her face. She'd murdered her
own child.

A needle pricked her arm, and she slipped back
into the gray mist. When she awoke, it was dark and
someone else sat beside her bed. She tried to struggle
further up onto her pillow, and David soothed her.

"Just rest," he said gently.

"It's my fault!" she cried, fresh tears sparkling on
her lashes. "I killed my baby!"

"No, Katie, no. It wasn't your fault."

"Yes it was. I only thought of myself, not my
baby."

"Darling," he crooned. "You did nothing wrong.
A miscarriage is no one's fault."

Nothing he said helped to lessen her guilt, and
David finally went to get the doctor. When he didn't
come back that night, Katie thought nothing of it,
because she'd been given another sedative and didn't
wake up until the next morning. At noon, David

came to get her, as the doctor said she could go home.

All the way back to Pacific Heights, David hardly spoke, and she decided that he felt as bad as she did. Once he'd helped her into the house and Mrs. Mendoza had assured her that Peter was fine, she went to her room for a rest.

"I understand your upset now, Katie," he told her once she was in bed. "It was more than just losing the baby, wasn't it?"

An alarm went off in her mind, and her gaze flew to his, and she knew something was really wrong. "What—what do you mean?"

"Your feelings of guilt stemmed from the fact that the baby wasn't mine. After my talk with the doctor, I realized why you'd been so upset about being pregnant. You discovered it was Max's baby, and were terrified I'd find out that you were a month further along than you should have been."

He hadn't raised his voice, and his flat tone scared her more than if he'd screamed at her in a rage. But she saw the anger glint in his dark eyes. She started to explain, and he interrupted, his hands spread in a gesture of supplication, as though he couldn't bear to hear her excuses now.

"No, Katie. Don't say anything. When the doctor told me how far along you were, I knew all I needed to know." He began to pace. "Oh, he didn't know he'd let the cat out of the bag; he was only concerned about the bleeding because you were four months along."

He jerked to a stop, his whole body so tense he looked brittle enough to snap. "And the baby couldn't be mine then, because I was in New York— and when I got home I resisted my natural urge to make love to my wife because she was so upset." He gave a harsh laugh. "Christ! What a God-damn gullible fool you must have thought me, Katie. You didn't want sex with me because you'd been sleeping with Max!"

"I love you, David—I love you. Please believe me."

Her words were little more than a whisper; she'd never felt so weak and vulnerable in her life. If only she could take back that one foolish night with Max. She had to make David understand, and she didn't know how—because the deed spoke louder than her words.

"Then how could you betray me—my trust in you—my love?" His words ran together on one long breath.

"Oh God, David! I didn't mean to. It just happened. I was so upset, and Max was so devastated." She shook her head, pleading with her eyes as well as her words. "It was a terrible time. I felt pulled in all directions. You weren't here, and I lost my perspective."

"I'm sorry, Katie, but that's no excuse. You could have called me; I would have come." He leaned toward her, his face a mask of anger all of a sudden. "I loved you so much. And I trusted you. You were the only woman I ever wanted to marry." He drew in a sharp breath. "And now I can't cope with knowing you slept with another man, that he made you pregnant."

His laugh had a ring of finality to it. "I stand corrected. You slept with your husband." He spun around and strode to the door.

"David—David! Please don't go! I love you. You're the man I want as my husband."

"But you told me that before—and *after* you slept with him," he reminded her. He glanced back, and his face was so stricken that Katie could hardly stand it.

"I need time to consider all this, Katie," he said. "I can't think about anything right now—not your divorce, or our remarriage." He hesitated, then seemed to pull himself together. "So I'll be spending more time in New York, until I sort out my feelings." His voice sounded almost normal. "Of course I still want the best for Peter; I don't want a scandal for his sake." He left her then, closing the door softly behind him.

The next morning he left early to fly himself back to the East Coast. Shattered, Katie knew her only hope of winning him back was to let him go. She'd brought it all on herself. Now she had to hope that David's emotional wounds would heal, and he'd return to her and Peter.

During the days that followed, it was hard for her to stick to her resolve. They talked on the phone; he asked after her health and wanted to hear all about Peter. He avoided making a definite date to return to California. Never once did Katie have an urge to contact Max concerning her state of affairs. Returning to him was out of the question, even though she admitted to herself that she loved him. Her reasons were still the same. She couldn't give up Peter, and she knew that David wouldn't either. And she'd never allow her little boy to be labeled a bastard. She had to be patient, so that David would realize that she'd been honest with him, even if that honesty came after the fact.

"I love you," she ended each phone conversation with David.

"I understand," was always his response.

Katie vowed not to give up. He was a proud man with a big ego when it came to women. He hadn't made his commitment of love lightly—and she'd humiliated him. But his hurt would lessen in time. *She had to believe that!*

For the first time since her birth, Christina wasn't with Katie for the holidays, although they talked on the phone. David flew out for Thanksgiving, and then again for the Christmas week, returning to New York right after the first of the year. Although they appeared the perfect family, Katie knew it was a sham. They didn't sleep together, and David included Peter in everything they did. The thought occurred to her that he wouldn't have come at all had it not been for his son. He had presents for everyone, including Katie, but the one thing she wanted above all else eluded her—a private conversation with her husband.

Right after the first of the year, Edward called her at the office, requesting that she stop by on her way home. Since Katie's business meetings with him had dwindled to twice a week, she wondered what was up. The first-of-the-year audit had shown the company in even better shape than she'd believed. New business was coming in weekly, and the profits had made Edward a very rich man.

Now, as they sat facing each other in Edward's elegant living room, she waited for him to reveal what was on his mind. He'd poured himself a whiskey and water from the tray beside him on the table, and a brandy for Katie. As she sipped, she couldn't help noticing how much heavier he was, how puffy his face had become. She suspected his health was bad, and his overeating and heavy drinking wasn't helping one bit. But she knew from past experience that he would retort in anger if she reprimanded him again.

"You're doing a great job at Eastern Imports," he told her suddenly. "I was surprised and pleased by the last financial report."

"Thanks, Edward. I'm pleased too. It takes a lot of work to cover every detail of the business, but it's paid off far better than even I expected."

He smiled wryly. "You know, Katie, from the time you were small you had guts—more than either

Johanna or me." He swirled the whiskey in his glass, and then met her eyes suddenly. "Did you know that I've always admired your courage—and wished I'd inherited some of it? Somehow it was like all the strong traits that eluded Johanna and me came out in you."

Taken aback, Katie didn't know how to respond. It was unlike Edward to be complimentary, and she wondered if he was drunk. "Why—thank you, Edward," she managed.

"Which brings me to the reason I asked you over." He downed the last of his whiskey and poured another. Then he handed her a document. "Read this."

Quickly Katie scanned it, and then looked up surprised. "You're giving me another ten percent of Eastern Imports? That'll give me thirty percent altogether."

He nodded. "It's only fair," he said. "If it hadn't been for you after the accident, I'd have lost the whole thing." He hesitated, his eyes hooded. "You earned it, Katie."

She could only incline her head. It was so unlike Edward to give anything away. Was alcohol affecting his brain?

"I'm in my right mind," he said dryly, reading her expression. "I've just had lots of time to think—and I wanted you to know how much I appreciate all you've done for me over the years."

"It's what families do," she said quietly, still trying to figure out the motive for his sudden generosity.

He shook his head. "Not everyone, Katie. You've always been there for me—because you have genuine feelings for your family. My own have been more self-serving." He gave a sharp laugh. "You've taken care of my daughter all these years, and also my business. It's far above what most would do—and I wanted to show my appreciation." He indicated the document. "What I'm giving you, you've earned a hundred times over."

"Thanks, Edward," she replied, too floored to say more.

A short time later she went home, wondering all the way about Edward's change of heart. Maybe Anna Su had been a good influence, she thought. Or maybe he was just mellowing with age. He certainly wasn't getting ready to die, she told herself firmly.

But happiness was elusive. As the days moved toward spring, Anna Su couldn't help but notice her aunt's unhappiness, even though Katie tried to hide it. She was old enough to know something was wrong between Katie and David and that he stayed away on purpose. The estrangement had occurred in the months after Max had turned up alive. Although she didn't know exactly what had happened, and she knew that she couldn't fill the hole in Katie's life since Christina had gone to Alaska, she could include Katie in her visits to the Konos. She was pleased when Katie accepted the first invitation for dinner.

The Sunday afternoon visit was such a success that it became a regular event each month. Both Anna Su and Peter enjoyed hearing about the Japan of Katie's childhood. It especially pleased Anna Su to see the bond developing between Katie and her great uncle Isami Kono.

"Would you consider coming back to the company?" Katie asked him after they'd all eaten a Japanese dinner prepared by Mrs. Kono. "As a consultant?"

They'd been talking about imports, and as Anna Su had listened enthralled while Isami explained his own approach to business, Katie had suddenly asked the question.

He looked thoughtful, considering the matter and all of its ramifications. Finally he bowed slightly, and in a formal voice gave his acceptance.

"I would be pleased."

But his pleasure at being asked was not as great as the pleasure both Anna Su and Katie felt at his acceptance. Somehow, Katie felt it was proper, a part of the circle that would be complete when Anna Su took over one day. Katie knew her own percentage of the company didn't preclude that.

By late spring, Katie and Isami were consulting on all pertinent matters; she was grateful for his business opinions, and the company flourished even more. In a strange way, he was like a substitute father to Katie, although his honor precluded his ever mentioning his awareness that her marriage was in trouble. The Konos became an extension of Katie's family.

But nothing alleviated her sadness about David being away so much, or her fears when Christina wrote that she hated the thought of leaving Alaska. Uncertain about everything, Katie hesitated to push Max about the status of their divorce. The last thing she wanted to do was create more problems to upset David. But that didn't stop her worry that Max was dragging his feet until he'd influenced Christina to stay with him permanently. Katie even wondered if David saw other women, as he no longer wanted sex with her and left no doors open for discussion of their relationship. She tried to believe it was all just his way of getting over things and that he'd do the right thing, for Peter's sake if nothing else.

But it was hard to keep her faith. Each time Katie looked at the morning sun and remembered her mother's words about hope, she vowed not to give up on David or Christina—or on Max doing the right thing.

When Christina flew home, Katie was e-

especially since David was there at the same time.
They spent days together as a family, and Katie's
hope soared. But when Christina returned to Anchorage "because of plans with my school friends"
and "they're depending on me for a Fourth of July
program—I'm the only one to sing the part," Katie
didn't lose hope. Christina promised to come home
in time for the new school year.

When David left as well, explaining that his business would keep him on the East Coast for most of
the summer but that he'd call every other day, Katie
still kept hoping for the best.

"I have faith that everything will be resolved by
fall," she confided in Anna Su. "We'll be a real
family again."

And when she heard that Max finally had a
divorce in the works, she knew she was right this
time.

PART FOUR

1956–1964

CHAPTER 23

THE BRILLIANCE OF SAN FRANCISCO SPRAWLED BEYOND her upstairs window, all the way to the bay that glowed with the city's reflection. The distant shore of Marin County glittered like a jeweled constellation, its scattered points of light sprinkled up the far hills to their peaks. As Katie stared into the night, perched on the window seat, her back against the jamb and her chin resting on her knees, she watched the circling sweep of the light from Alcatraz Island.

In a way I'm a prisoner, too, Katie thought, and couldn't help a tinge of sadness. She was a captive of responsibilities and obligations—and of circumstances beyond her control, such as her daughter's choosing to live in Alaska.

Once she'd been as free as the kites she'd flown as

a girl, her hopes soaring high with the promise of the future. Now she ran a company, no longer with the option to quit—because of Edward's health and because Anna Su wasn't old enough to take her place and because she was a single woman with two children to help support, one who lived with her, one who didn't.

Shifting on the cushion, Katie knew she was still not ready to sleep, even though a glance at her clock told her it was after two in the morning. Her mind wouldn't rest, dwelling on the news—or perhaps it was her karma—of yesterday. After three years, she was finally divorced from Max. And somehow the relief she'd expected wasn't there. It had all gone flat. David never even mentioned the issue any more when he visited. She realized that she no longer knew how he felt about anything.

It's all so ridiculous, she thought. But she also knew the time had come to resolve their situation once and for all.

Getting up, she crossed to her bed. Tomorrow would be a long day at the office and she needed her sleep. Tomorrow she'd call David and ask him when he planned his next trip west, because there was something important they needed to discuss. She threw her robe on the bed and climbed between the sheets, finally able to sleep. She was optimistic. David was a sensible man, and he loved Peter. Katie knew he'd do the right thing, now that she was finally a free woman.

But David's next visit was brief, and although he expressed relief on Katie's behalf, he was noncommittal about their marriage. "We've waited this long—there's no need to rush things now," he told her, turning away so that she couldn't see his expression. "I'm so damn busy at work I don't know which end is up—there are more orders than we can fill even on overtime, and I've got employees threatening to strike."

When he returned to New York, Peter was tearful for days afterwards. "Why can't Daddy stay with us?" he cried. "Doesn't he love me?"

Katie reassured him, explaining that his daddy worked on the East Coast and she in California. She even showed him a big map so that he'd understand the distance that kept them apart so much. By Christmas, when David came again, bringing presents, Peter was more accepting of his father's being away so much. Katie worried, though, because she sensed that David no longer had a desire to be married. During his few visits in the months after the first of the year, she realized that they no longer had much in common other than Peter. Their separation had made them virtual strangers to each other. Although she still believed they needed to marry in order to secure Peter's legitimacy, Katie no longer saw much hope for them as a happy couple. Too much had happened, too much time had passed.

The phone rang just as Katie came down the stairs, dressed in a yellow linen dress and matching high-heeled sandals, her makeup and upswept hair perfect because she wanted to look her best for Peter's birthday party—and because David would be there. Despite all of her realizations about their relationship, she still harbored a tiny hope for them, and she had found herself taking extra pains with her appearance. She ran to grab the extention in the front hall, wondering if it was David.

"Hello," she said into the receiver.

"Mom? Mom, is that you?" Christina's voice sounded far away and was accompanied by faint static.

"Christina!" Katie cried. "How good to hear your

voice. When are you leaving Anchorage? I'll meet your plane."

"I called to wish little Peter happy birthday," Christina replied. "And give you my arrival time."

Her voice sounded happy, and Katie marveled at her daughter's habitual high spirits. Christina had never let the problems between her parents color her feelings for either one. Although Katie had never reconciled herself to living apart from her daughter, she knew that Christina hadn't chosen between them. She loved them both equally and simply considered that her father needed her most—that she was his only family, while her mother had a husband and son. She spent the summers with Katie.

They chatted and Katie explained the many suprises she and Anna Su had in store for Peter's fifth birthday.

"Won't David be there too?"

"Oh yes," Katie replied at once, careful not to interject her own upset because, for the first time, David had taken a hotel room rather than stay at the house. He'd explained that he didn't want to cause more commotion on such a big day for Peter. She'd started to argue that Peter would be more upset that his daddy wasn't staying with him, but she had fallen silent when David became adamant, his tone set with resolve.

"Mom, I have some other news, and I guess I put off telling you. I don't know why—it wouldn't make any difference to you." Her nervous laugh came over the wires. "Dad got married last week."

For long seconds, Katie couldn't respond. She plopped onto the chair next to the telephone table, suddenly trembling so hard that it took both hands to hold the receiver steady against her ear.

"Mom? Are you there? Did you hear what I said?"

"Yes, I'm here, Christina," she managed. "And I heard—your father is married."

There was a hesitation on the other end. "Are you upset, Mom? I didn't mean to upset you."

"No—no, of course not. The connection isn't good, that's all."

"Oh, typical!" Christina exclaimed, accepting her mother's excuse because the lines were always bad.

While Katie listened in numb silence, Christina went on to explain that Max had married the widow of another Alaskan pilot. "They aren't madly in love or anything," Christina went on in a rush of words. "Dad said Sarah is *comfortable*. Golly, can you imagine not marrying for love?"

Despite her own shock, Katie smiled at her fourteen-year-old's romantic side. Once she'd had similar beliefs—and thought love and marriage were forever. Recently she'd even considered letting Max know how things were between her and David and that if they remarried now, it would only be to give Peter his birthright; then they'd get a divorce.

After they'd talked a while longer and confirmed Christina's arrival time in a week, Christina spoke to Peter before she hung up. And for the rest of the day, Katie kept her smile in place. David came for the party, and when Peter became upset when he left, David promised to take him flying the next day, so long as the rain that had started earlier stopped by morning. Peter went to bed happy, unaware of his mother's devastation.

Once in her room, Katie pulled the pins out of her hair, hung up the dress that David had hardly noticed, and put on her nightgown. She sat by her window in the dark, oblivious to the splendor of the night with its kaleidoscope of lights, fractured by the rain drops that beaded the pane.

She hated feeling unhappy; it had gone on too long. It was time for a change. Once she'd known golden days, and then her parents had died, and nothing had ever been completely golden again. *But that's life—and growing up*, she reminded herself. She'd been one of the lucky ones to have had such a wonderful childhood. She sat long into the night, dry-eyed, resigned, remembering. It was as though she'd been transported back to her garden in Japan, so that she could go deep into herself to find meaning for the rest of her life. Both of the men she'd loved no longer loved her. She'd hurt them both, however unintentionally, and now she was the one hurt. It was an ending, and because it was, it was also a new beginning. She had her honor, and her resolve to lead the best life she could for herself and her family. And one day maybe she'd know golden days again.

A week later, Anna Su graduated valedictorian from high school. Katie arranged for Edward to be taken to the ceremony and he sat in his wheelchair next to her aisle seat. After Anna Su, in cap and gown, her young voice inspired, gave a speech on *Soaring Into The Future*, a topic influenced by Katie, she received thunderous applause. With innate dignity, Anna Su briefly acknowledged the audience, then, as graceful as her mother had once been, she walked back to her seat, her long black hair shimmering like silk under the overhead lights.

"Michiko would have been so proud," Edward whispered to Katie, and she saw the sparkle of tears in his eyes before he looked away.

"Yes, very proud," Katie replied, and images of Michiko and her as young teenagers came to mind. Oh, how positive they'd been about love and happiness! And how naive those dreams seemed now. And yet, Katie thought as the diplomas were being handed out, her niece was the next generation, and perhaps all that had happened in the past was the foundation for all that Anna Su would accomplish in the future.

From somewhere long ago, wise words came back to Katie. *We do not know our destiny until after we have lived it, Katie-san. The course of life is not to question fate; it is a journey to understanding.*

The words stayed with Katie as they congratulated Anna Su later. She went with Edward to his house, as her brother was having a small reception for Anna Su. They didn't see the Konos at the graduation, although Katie knew they were there. She didn't mention their presence to Edward, as she respected Isami Kono's feelings and knew they'd rather not sit with the man who'd once violated the Kono honor.

Anna Su went to work at Eastern Imports for the summer, and Katie missed her when she left in the fall to attend Stanford University. The house seemed empty without her and Christina, who'd gone, too, back for another school year in Alaska with Max. When Anna Su came home for the holidays, Katie noted a new maturity in her niece, who divided her time between Edward and Katie. Anna Su also managed several visits with the Konos. *She's a combination of Michiko's gentleness and my determination*, Katie thought with a start. But Katie also felt pride—and love for the girl who was like her own daughter.

The holidays also brought David, who again checked into a hotel, his habit ever since he'd made the break that first time. But Katie managed to finally pin him down on Christmas Day, while Peter played a board game with Anna Su in the next room.

"We have to settle this situation once and for all," she told him firmly as he was about to leave. "Four years is long enough for us to be in limbo."

He stood in the doorway to the hall, a tall, dark man who was as attractive as when she'd first met him. Still dressing with impeccable taste, his lean body and sharp gaze suggested a man in his early forties, not fifties. This time he didn't evade the subject.

"You're quite right, Katie," he said. "But I haven't resolved a course of action for us." Although he spoke in a pleasant tone, and his expression denoted his appreciation of her in her velvet dress that was as brilliant a green as her eyes, there was a reserve in him as well.

It's as if I'm just another attractive woman to him, she thought suddenly. *A stranger.* The realization angered her. Did he think she was desperate to land a husband? She tilted her chin, her eyes sparkling fire.

"Not for us," she reminded him, abruptly cold. "For Peter—and his future. As you know, I've never taken money from you since—since that situation happened," she finished in a rush of words. "I'm perfectly capable of supporting myself."

"I support Peter!" he snapped. "He's my son, and I intend to do what's right by him!" He drew in his breath sharply. "Surely you can't believe otherwise."

She waited several seconds before replying, forcing herself to be calm. "Of course I don't doubt that. But Peter is my son, too. And despite whatever problems are between us, David, I want Peter to have legitimacy—the right to your name."

He busied himself with his gloves. "Peter has that; it's on his birth certificate."

"But he's not legally yours because he was born out of wedlock." Her voice had lowered and her words were heavy with emotion. "And that's what we have to fix."

He was abruptly direct, and she saw anger in his eyes. "I won't be blackmailed into marriage," he said, equally cold. "I don't even know if I want to be married now."

"I see," Katie retorted. "And I too don't know if I want to be married. But I'm willing to place Peter before my feelings. Believe me, David, I'm not trying to trap you. We can work this out to suit everyone."

He glanced away, his expression suddenly closed. "I'll think about this, Katie," he said. "For now, all I can assure you of is that I will do right by Peter."

She nodded. "Just remember one other thing, David. If we remarried, we wouldn't have to stay married. It would be a way to settle this, to give Peter the birthright he deserves. Then we could be divorced."

Something flickered in his eyes, and for a second Katie wondered if there was another reason why her proposition might not be acceptable to him. After all, she knew nothing about his life now. Did he have another woman? she wondered suddenly, and then dismissed the thought. If he did, wouldn't he want his past resolved once and for all?

"As I said, I need time to think about this," he said, evasively. "I was a bachelor most of my life, and now that things are different, I'm hesitant."

There was no time for Katie to reply, as Peter suddenly bounded into the room. She hid her anger and her frustration with David's flimsy excuses. And as she watched him promise Peter new outings, even as he withheld his son's legal standing, she realized that there were facets to his character that reminded her of Edward. She would no longer consider marriage to him either, but for Peter.

A short time later, David was gone, and Peter went back to his toys. The earlier conversation preoccupied her for the rest of the day, and in the coming weeks. She finally decided to let things ride for awhile. One thing she couldn't do was force David's hand and risk Peter's future. And she could afford to wait a little longer, give him time to "think about it," because she didn't have a compelling reason to settle things immediately—like a man in the wings who wanted to marry her. All the men she'd dated were too insipid when compared to someone like Max. And Max was gone forever. So she could wait.

The following June, Alaska became the forty-ninth state, and Anna Su came back to work at Eastern Imports for the summer. Business was booming. "Sales are far more than last summer," she told her aunt. When she said the same thing the summer after that, Katie only grinned and reminded her that she was repeating herself.

Anna Su laughed. "You're a whiz," she said. "My father is fortunate that you run things so well—probably better than he'd have done."

Katie glanced up from her desk and wondered if that was Anna Su's perception, or one she'd picked up from Isami Kono, who still consulted with her on problem issues, although the old man had retired. She let it pass, as she knew her niece loved Edward. Anna Su was a bonus to Katie; she was as intelligent as she was beautiful, and Katie looked forward to her working at Eastern Imports on a permanent basis when she graduated from college in two years.

The summer passed quickly, and Katie hardly had time for anything else but her work and spending time with Peter and Christina. She so valued those weeks when she had both her son and daughter with her. She never asked questions about Max and his marriage, and Katie was lonely when Christina left again in September.

During the fall and winter, David wasn't able to fly out but once at Christmas. "The garment industry is getting so damned competitive that I can't leave for long," he explained to Peter, who didn't really understand and was hurt. Katie knew it was another excuse and came to the end of her patience with him. It was only Peter's feelings that allowed her to hold her tongue. Peter, like everyone else, thought his parents were married. And like everyone else, he'd come to think it was a strange kind of marriage, not like the families of his school friends. Katie silently agreed. They'd created a false life, and now she wondered how it would all end.

The following May, Christina graduated from high school in Anchorage. Katie felt terrible about missing the event. She had a big transaction in the works for materials from Southeast Asia, and she couldn't leave. Besides, Peter's school wasn't out yet. But her main reason was Max. She didn't know how she could attend a graduation celebration with him and his wife. So she planned a big party for Christina when she finally arrived in San Francisco for what Katie hoped would be a permanent move.

The house was alive with activity once both Christina and Anna Su were back. Katie felt so proud when she saw the girls confiding in each other, becoming friends on an adult basis. *Like Michiko and me*, Katie thought with a pang of nostalgia. Her blond, brown-eyed daughter and Anna Su with her black hair and eyes were equally beautiful.

"You hardly look older than we do," Christina said one evening as the three of them sat talking after dinner, Peter being away for an overnight visit with a school friend.

"Well, thank you, dear," Katie said, flattered.

"It's true," Anna Su added. "You don't have an ounce of fat on you, nor do you have a wrinkle, and your hair is still as blond and bright as ever."

"And you two are good for my ego," Katie managed with a laugh.

The two young women exchanged glances, and finally Anna Su said what was on both their minds.

"We worry about you sometimes, Aunt Katie. You're so young and pretty, yet all you do is work.

We're wondering—and please don't think we're
prying—but we're wondering about you and
David."

Katie lowered her lashes. She'd known the question would come up sometime, but she found herself
unprepared to answer. Neither girl knew the whole
story—whether or not she and David were married
—but it was only normal for them to put two and
two together once they were no longer children.

Anna Su moved next to Katie and took her hand.
"Please don't be upset, Aunt Katie. We've both
guessed the situation, me a few years earlier than
Christina. But neither of us wanted to interfere, so
we've never said anything to you. But now—now we
just want you to be happy."

"Did you and David ever remarry, Mom?" Christina asked softly.

Tears stung Katie's eyes and she swallowed against
the tightening in her throat. At first, she could only
manage to shake her head. "Peter doesn't know," she
said finally, and briefly explained David's position,
knowing she owed them the truth. "I have to have
your promises that you won't mention this to Peter.
He wouldn't understand—and I intend to talk to
David again soon."

Christina hugged her. "Oh Mom, I'm so sorry
about all this. It's been hell for you."

"And it's selfish of David to have let this go on so
long," Anna Su said, her tone reflecting her dislike of
him. "What kind of a man would punish you for
something you couldn't help?"

There were no words to explain. And Katie had no
intention of confiding the whole story—about the
baby she'd lost. She couldn't do that to Christina—
or to Max who knew nothing about it either.

David *was* selfish, Katie realized suddenly. Because of her own guilt, she'd made excuses for him
too long. It was time they behaved like adults. The

next time someone guessed the truth, Peter could be hurt. She was glad that the girls had finally confronted her; it impelled her to take action herself. As soon as work allowed, she would fly to New York and settle things even if she had to embarrass David in front of his whole office staff.

The ringing of the phone brought their conversation to an end, one so complete that the subject wasn't brought up again for some time to come.

"I'll get it," Anna Su said, and went to answer in the hall.

A moment later she was back, standing before them with her face ashen, her eyes wide and brimming with tears.

"It was Father's housekeeper. He went to bed early. She checked on him—" Anna Su broke off as silent sobs shook her body. "He's dead. Oh, my God! My father's dead!"

It was a heart attack that killed Edward, brought on by his heavy drinking and overeating. His funeral brought Johanna from Anchorage, and for the first time since leaving Alaska, Katie saw Elisabetta and Ollie again. She wouldn't have known them if she'd met them on the street, although Elisabetta reminded her of someone. Since becoming adults, both had lived in California, much to Katie's surprise.

The funeral parlor was packed, and because the family sat in the mourning room, Katie only glimpsed the people who listened to the minister give the eulogy. She was surprised by the turnout, and suspected that many of those attending were business associates. Everyone had been asked to her home after the burial service, so that the family could greet the mourners. Katie hoped for a chance to visit with Johanna.

A mantle of sadness settled over Katie's thoughts.

In many ways her brother's life had been a waste. He'd always manipulated everyone else for his own benefit, and in the end all the wealth in the world hadn't made him happy. He'd died a bitter and unfulfilled man. But he'd tried in his own way, Katie reminded herself. He'd given her the percentage in the company, and he'd been so proud of Anna Su in the later years. She even remembered his warning about David on her wedding day. Poor Edward, she thought. He'd finally realized how precious Michiko had been and, too late, grieved for his loss.

But it's all over now, Katie told herself as she welcomed people to her house after the funeral. Perhaps he had finally found happiness somewhere. Maybe Michiko was right, and they were together, having fulfilled their *karma*.

Her thoughts on Edward, Katie hugged Johanna when she arrived with her two children. "I've so missed you," she told her. "I want us to have a chance to talk later, after everyone is gone."

Johanna nodded, but as she glanced around Katie's elegant Pacific Heights house, she was subdued. Both her sister and brother had grown rich over the years, while she and Dion still struggled along as they always had, Dion once again working for Max. Johanna felt inferior somehow, drab and unattractive, and it was a relief when the focus of conversation turned to Elisabetta.

"You've really grown into a lovely young woman," Katie told her warmly. "I was there when you were born."

"Everyone calls me Lisa now, Aunt Katie." She smiled, a wide smile that showed perfect teeth and transformed a beautiful face into one so absolutely radiant that for a second the conversation stopped. And then Katie remembered why Lisa looked familiar.

"You're *the* Lisa," Katie said, surprised, taking in the tall woman whose dark eyes and hair and high cheekbones all contributed to the perfection of her beauty.

"Didn't you know that, Mom?" Christina said as she joined the small group. "Lisa is a covergirl model. She lives in Los Angeles."

Lisa put up a hand to stop the compliments. "I'm just now getting some good assignments," she said, her voice low and attractive—and nice, Katie thought. "And I've only been on two national magazine covers," she added truthfully.

"And Ollie lives in California, too," Johanna added, obviously pleased by the success of her daughter.

The focus turned to the young man who resembled his father. But Dion's features in Ollie were diluted by a surly expression and a weak chin. He wasn't as tall as his father, nor did he have Dion's confident swagger. Katie suddenly saw the little boy Ollie, and knew he'd only grown into an older version of the childhood bully. When she asked him what he did, he was evasive.

"Just getting my feet under me," he said, his eyes shifting to one side.

"Ollie lives with me for now," Lisa said, and Katie had another revelation. She was still the big sister, and the little mother who'd once protected Christina from Ollie.

But the biggest surprise of the day came when Katie walked into her living room and came face to face with a man she never expected to see again.

"Tak!"

He gave a polite bow, as did Isami Kono, who stood next to him. "My condolences, Katie-san," Tak said, his expression as polite as his words. "I'm sorry for your loss."

So taken aback was she that Katie found it hard to think for a second. He was older, but still lean and fit and very handsome in his expensive black suit. His appearance, that of a successful businessman, was very different from the Tak she'd last seen that winter night in Alaska.

"I'm surprised," she managed. "But pleased that you would come."

Again he inclined his head, his dark eyes unreadable, and Katie wondered what he was thinking. That she'd changed? That she was older than he remembered? He was still the Tak who gave nothing away.

"Have you forgotten that Edward was my brother-in-law?" He gave a brief smile. "It would not be proper respect to miss Edward's funeral, not to you or Anna Su—or Michiko."

She acknowledged his tribute, unable to detect any subtlety in his manner. But Katie also remembered that he had mastered control long ago. Ever so slightly she straightened, determined to remain unruffled by his presence. Maybe he *was* only here out of respect, she told herself.

Watching her, Tak followed her thoughts and smiled to himself. She was still unaware of how very beautiful she was, still unaffected, which was surprising for a woman of her position. Over the years he'd met many women—Japanese, European and American—and none ever came close to matching Katie, the fairy child of his youth. For a moment he saw her as they were then, flying kites, listening to the teachings of his father, she and Michiko giggling together. His memories came up short when he thought of Michiko. Everything was different now. The past was gone forever, and he must never forget that, he reminded himself sternly. It was the reason he was here—to look upon Edward's dead face.

Sensing the sudden strain, Isami Kono took command of the conversation, directing it to the weather, and then the funeral itself. It was a relief when Anna Su joined them, oblivious of the old feelings between her Aunt Katie and Uncle Tak.

At once it became apparent to Katie that Tak was extremely fond of Anna Su. Even his expression softened as he watched her talk about her university classes, where she pulled down straight A's.

"You've done well by her," Tak said a few minutes later, after Anna Su had led Isami away to the refreshment table in the dining room.

"Thank you," Katie replied sincerely. She lowered her lashes, too aware of his penetrating gaze. "I love Anna Su like my own daughter."

"I, too, love her." His tone was low, bringing her gaze back to his.

"I know you do, Tak. She's very much like Michiko."

His face didn't alter by even a twitch, but Katie sensed a tightening of his whole body, suddenly reminding her of the other Tak who'd frightened her in Alaska. *Foolish,* she reprimanded herself as he smiled a second later.

"She is also very much like you, Katie-san."

The words brought a flood of memories, and she remembered the feelings she'd once had for him. Conversation swirled around them, the day beyond the windows was typically balmy, and they were suspended somewhere beyond all of it. Anna Su was the bridge between them, the child they might have had if things had been different.

"I married after the war," he said softly, bringing them back to their surroundings. "But we've never had children—and won't. You are fortunate, Katie, to have a son and daughter."

Katie understood. Anna Su was his replacement daughter, the last of his honorable family. She swal-

lowed hard, a sorrow ripping through her at the
realization of all he'd lost.

"I'm so sorry about your parents, about Michiko,"
she began and faltered. "In a certain way I loved her
more than anyone in the world."

"Yes, I know." He hesitated, as though considering whether or not to go on. "And I apologize for not
making contact after the war. I promised Michiko I
wouldn't because she planned to do that herself—
when she was well. But I watched from afar and kept
track of Anna Su. I attended her high school
graduation—did you know that, Katie?"

She shook her head. Somehow it didn't surprise
her. Anna Su was a Kono after all. "Did Anna Su
know?"

"No, but we've become reacquainted since then.
I've visited her on several occasions since she's been
in college."

"I see," Katie said, her eyes steady. "Anna Su
never mentioned it."

He held up his hand in a gesture that had once
belonged to his father. "Not intentionally, I'm sure.
Although I never said so, I'm sure she knew the
Konos never approved of her father, and perhaps she
was unsure of your reaction to her knowing me."

It was the first time she'd known Anna Su to keep
something from her, and Katie felt hurt. Surely
Anna Su wouldn't think she'd disapprove of her
knowing her uncle? She put the thought out of her
mind that Anna Su had been manipulated and
fastened on another part of his explanation.

"You still hold a grudge against Edward—even
now that he's dead?"

"That died with Edward," he said at once. "Soon
Anna Su, a Kono, will control Eastern Imports
again, and that's justice enough. Life has a way of
coming full circle, Katie-san."

What did he mean? she wondered. Did he know

that she now owned a sizable chunk of the business? She was sure he did; nothing escaped Tak.

"I've found that to be true, Tak," she said finally. "Although the circle isn't complete until we've lived our allotted years, and can look back over our lives—and understand."

"You remember your early training."

"I'll never forget," she said quietly. "Those years were the foundation of all that's happened to me since." Outwardly she smiled politely, while inwardly she reflected on the strangeness of life. Aside from his midnight visit in Alaska, this was the first time she'd spoken to Tak since that day in Japan when she'd heard him walk away forever. And now, with only years separating them, they were next to strangers. Whatever emotion stirred under his stoic face would stay buried. Was he friend or enemy? she wondered. She didn't know.

Anna Su rejoined them, and a moment later Katie excused herself to see to the other guests. For the next hour, until people began to leave, she felt Tak's eyes on her—dark unreadable eyes that unsettled her, not because he made her apprehensive, only sad.

Johanna and her son and daughter left as most of their guests were saying good-bye, and Katie didn't have a chance to coax her to stay longer. Later, she was sorry that there had been no time for them to visit, to reestablish a kinship, and Katie suspected that Johanna had planned it that way. Johanna had looked tired, and in awe of Katie's house and Edward's wealth. During the next few days, Katie's thoughts lingered with her sister. She wondered about Johanna's life with Dion. One thing was for sure—Johanna was an unhappy woman.

Edward's death brought Katie new responsibilities, and she found herself delaying a visit to New York to discuss Peter's future with David. Even

Christina worked during the summer in Katie's office, but in September she announced that she was returning to Alaska for the winter.

"I'm involved with a theater group up there," she explained. "They're all amateurs, of course, but they're depending on me for the singing role, and I feel I can't let them down."

"What about your own voice? Weren't you planning to study with a good coach down here?"

Christina grinned. "I still will, Mom. But—oh, I guess I just miss Anchorage—and Dad. Do you mind? I promise I'm moving down permanently one of these days. I'm just not ready to do it yet."

"It's your decision, dear," Katie told her, hiding her disappointment. "I suppose I'm just selfish when it comes to my daughter." She hesitated, a slow smile curving her lips. "I'll miss you, Christina."

"I know, Mom." She laughed suddenly, unable to suppress her usual good spirits. "And one of these days, when I'm living down here, bothering you all the time, you'll wish I was back in Alaska."

When she was gone, Katie worried. Alaska had a way of claiming people. And she hoped Christina hadn't gone for the old reason—because she believed her father needed her more than Katie, who had Peter. Katie's wish was for Christina to be her own person. Wherever she lived, it should be because that was what she wanted, not what either of her parents wanted.

And Katie had the same wish for Anna Su, who'd become even closer to the Konos. Her niece was so impressed with Tak, who now divided his time between Tokyo and San Francisco, that Katie feared Anna Su might be overly influenced by him.

"Uncle Tak has told me so much about Japan when you and my mother were growing up," she told Katie, "that I feel I know my mother better now."

"Those were wonderful years for all of us," Katie

replied with a nostalgic smile. "Japan was a different place then."

It was spring break from the university, and Anna Su had spent the whole week with Katie in the office, going over Katie's expansion plans. Now, as they were finishing dinner, Peter excused himself to watch his favorite television program, and Anna Su confided to Katie about Tak.

"But Uncle Tak won't discuss Hiroshima."

"I think that's understandable. It was too horrible, his loss too great."

Anna Su stared at her plate. She'd grown to love her uncle as a father, and she knew he looked upon her as a daughter. But she also sensed a reserve between him and Katie, and that grieved her, as her aunt was the only mother she'd ever known and she loved her too. She'd confided Katie's expansion plans to Tak, how Katie wanted to add goods from India, materials to be sold in boutiques and to garment factories that specialized in more exotic, trendy clothes, trying to impress her uncle with her aunt's abilities. When he'd listened without speaking, Anna Su had found herself even revealing Katie's secret project to start their own line of silk apparel to be sold at reasonable prices to the middle-income mass market. To her surprise, Tak had spoken in flattering terms about Katie and had offered advice on how to approach the new markets. She'd gone back to Katie with his advice, but had promised not to tell that the ideas had been his. It had bothered Anna Su a little when Katie was impressed, believing her to be the business genius, not Tak.

So she didn't confide other things her uncle said— that his own firm in Tokyo had changed since the war and was now manufacturing television sets, radios, and other electronic products which they were beginning to market in Europe and America.

Her uncle Tak had even told her about the first computers, saying "computers will be a huge industry in twenty years, and the Konos will be in on the ground floor." She believed him. She also saw possibilities for Eastern Imports in the future. Maybe, when she took over one day, she and her uncle would do business together.

That thought grew as Anna Su completed her final year at the university. When she graduated, she was pleased to see Katie sitting with Tak at the ceremonies. She was hopeful that the two families would be closer in the future. So, conscious of not hurting Katie, she didn't tell her that it was Tak's suggestion that she take up residence in the house she'd inherited from her father.

"I think it's appropriate, although I'll miss you," Katie reassured her. "So long as you don't mind living alone."

Anna Su shook her head. "We see each other every day now that I'm working permanently at the office."

Katie was pleased with Anna Su's sense, and she welcomed her into the business. There was another bonus for Katie as well; she had more free time. As David's visits had dwindled even more over the past year, she decided that there was no longer any reason to wait. Peter was older, at an age when he might ask too many wrong questions. It was time for the trip to New York, to settle things once and for all.

"Why can't I go, Mom?" Peter cried. "I never get to see Dad anymore!" His eyes filled with tears.

"But you'll be seeing him more soon," Katie reassured him. "I promise."

Peter turned away. He couldn't understand what was wrong with his parents. Why did they live apart? Didn't they love him? Was it his fault?

"I just wish I had parents who loved me!" he cried. "Parents like my friends have—they don't live apart!"

Katie reassured him that both she and David loved him very much, until he seemed to understand. But all the way east on the long flight, she couldn't get Peter's sad little face out of her mind. And that gave her the confidence to know she was doing the right thing. Now it was David's turn to do the same.

CHAPTER 24

"YOU KNOW I WORSHIP PETER—HE'S MY ONLY CHILD."

David stood by the marble fireplace, an elegant man in elegant surroundings. His whole Fifth Avenue apartment had been redecorated in a multicolor, multistyle Renaissance drama since Katie's last visit, which had been several years ago, she suddenly realized. Long windows gave a breathtaking view of New York City, and she was struck with how different their lives were now. Perhaps they had always been so, but love had made up the differences.

"I've never doubted that," Katie replied, then put down her glass of sherry on the sidetable next to her chair. "But, as I've said before, it's time we took care of the legalities, David. Our situation has gone on far too long, and it will affect Peter—drastically I'm afraid—if he learns his parents aren't married."

David considered her words, his eyes hooded but steady on her face—as though he were forming his response in the best way to soften his reply. In the end, he was bluntly honest.

"I no longer love you, Katie."

She wasn't surprised, or even upset. When love died, there was no power on earth to bring it back. She'd known their relationship was over for a long time now, and she told him so. "But I feel we should still marry, David, for Peter's sake. Then we can get a divorce in—say, a year?"

Pursing his lips in thought, he moved to the chair opposite her and sat down. "No Katie, marriage is no longer possible. I admit that I've been avoiding this conversation, but I'm relieved that you're here and we can settle it for good." He hesitated. "I'm marrying someone else, and I'm afraid she wouldn't understand if I suddenly married you instead, whatever the reason."

His revelation hit her like icy water. "Then what—"

He waved his hand in a gesture of impatience. "Wait! You didn't let me finish." There was an edge to his voice that annoyed her, but she subsided—for the moment.

"Go on then."

"I intend to take care of everything for Peter," David replied, his voice gaining momentum as he spoke. "Don't worry, when my lawyer finishes there will be no doubt as to my being his father. And in any case, the situation is explainable to Peter when he's old enough to understand—that we'd married in good faith, believing your first husband dead, and that we couldn't help the rest."

Katie, still taking it all in, wondered about the other woman. How many years had he been seeing her? But she didn't ask, because she didn't want to know, didn't want something else to think about in the middle of the night when she couldn't sleep.

He took her hand. "I'm sorry things didn't work out, Katie. I've thought about it, agonized over it, but in the end I just felt different. But I want you to know that I loved you in a way I've never loved any woman. You were my ideal."

"And then I had clay feet."

"Perhaps you were only human." He kissed her hand, then gently replaced it on her lap. "I've forgiven you, Katie. But right or wrong, it took me a long time."

"Until you met the current woman in your life?"

"Yes, I suppose that's true." He busied himself with his scotch. "She's about my age, Katie, much older than you, and we have everything in common —including religion." David met her eyes again. "So of course we'll never have children. Peter is the only child I'll ever have, and he'll be my sole heir when I die."

"Your future wife agrees to all this?"

"Of course. She doesn't need my wealth; she has far more of her own."

"That's it, then," Katie said, and rose. Although she would rather that they'd married, she was resigned to its being impossible now. She felt only relief, so long as David did right by Peter. And she trusted that he would; he'd always been honest— except when it came to the other woman, she reminded herself.

Refusing his offer that she spend the night in his guest bedroom, she left after final details were discussed. And the next day, as she flew west once more, her relief grew. She felt as if a weight of stones had been lifted from her back. In the end, the resolution had been so simple—because their feelings for each other were no longer involved. Peter wouldn't suffer from the decision either, as he was old enough to visit his father in New York now. *But with my restrictions,* she told herself. She wasn't about to lose a second child to the father.

"But that would mean opening a whole new division of the company," Katie protested. "And right now, our reserves are depleted."

The week after she'd returned from New York, Anna Su had come into her office with a business proposal from Tak's Tokyo company. He wanted Eastern Imports to handle his products in the United States.

"We can swing it, Aunt Katie." Anna Su, so professional in her suit and pumps and upswept hair, had the maturity of a woman in her thirties even though her prettiness precluded anyone ever believing she was older than her actual years. She placed a portfolio of papers on Katie's desk. "You'll see by the figures, and the fact that Uncle Tak already has customers in America, that we can't miss doubling our profits within the next couple of years."

Katie took her time going over the prospectus. When she finally glanced up, Anna Su still waited. "It would launch us into a new dimension of growth," Katie mused aloud. "One that may have more possibilities for profit margin—that is, if this is all accurate."

"Completely," Anna Su replied. "Uncle Tak is an astute businessman." She paused, letting her words sink in before she continued. "And don't forget, Aunt Katie. Electronic products are the way of the future. If we get in on the ground floor, we could grow far beyond our wildest dreams for Eastern Imports."

"Or we could go bankrupt if we overextend our financial capabilities," Katie reminded her, trying to keep a balance. "We've invested in my silk apparel venture, and it's not far enough along to be off the

ground. If we take on this new project, it will mean
placing all of our assets at risk should it fail."

"I know." Anna Su's gaze was candid. "But I feel
it's worth that risk—because I know the figures are
correct, and because my uncle would never allow us
to take on anything that would fail."

The street sounds below them and the office
sounds beyond her door all seemed louder in Katie's
quiet office. She went over the prospectus once more,
this time checking each detail. It was solid, but Katie
still had reservations.

"I feel we should wait, six months maybe, until
we're in the clear on the silks."

"It's now or never, Aunt Katie. Uncle Tak will
contract with someone else, if not us."

Pushing back her chair, Katie considered her
feelings. Why was she apprehensive? She couldn't
pinpoint her reluctance, which went deeper than just
the facts and figures. Was it intuition? Or just her
own emotional baggage of fears and forgotten
dreams?

"I vote to go with Uncle Tak," Anna Su said, and
Katie saw that she was determined.

"You won't change your mind?"

Anna Su shook her head.

"All right then, we'll do it." Katie didn't add that
she really had no final say anyway. Anna Su owned
the controlling interest in Eastern Imports.

"Great! This decision is going to take us into the
big leagues!"

It was apparent to Katie that the decision was very
important to Anna Su, and she suspected that her
niece might have gone over her head, had she not
agreed to the deal. The thought was disturbing to
Katie. However, by the next day she was smiling
over it; Anna Su was becoming a first-class business-
woman.

It was also obvious over the following days how

much the decision would impact the company. Along with establishing a new division of Eastern Imports, they also had to hire new personnel. Katie and Anna Su became so busy that it was hard to get away from the office. Katie was glad when school started in September, so that Peter was occupied during the day and only had to spend a few hours each afternoon with the housekeeper before Katie returned home for supper.

By October, they'd met with Tak numerous times, had gone over the agreement terms in minute detail, and had leased the neighboring building for more office space, with an option to buy. Rather than her work slacking off once the new project was in the works, Katie's responsibilities grew, as did Anna Su's. Katie picked up the phone one afternoon, expecting a call from their banker, and found herself speaking to the nurse at Peter's school.

"Peter is sick," she told Katie. "He's running a high fever and has a blinding headache. We'd like to send him home."

"I'll be right there to get him," Katie said at once.

A few minutes later, she'd left things in Anna Su's hands and was on her way to school, fearful and worried. Peter was a healthy boy and it was rare for him to be sick. Suddenly stricken with foreboding, she urged the taxi driver to go faster. She was appalled when she arrived and found her son looking ashen and trembling from the fever, too sick to do more than barely acknowledge she was there. It was obvious he needed the doctor. She'd asked the driver to wait, and once she had Peter in the taxi, they went directly to the doctor's office. The nurse took one look and led him to an examining room.

"He's a very sick boy, Mrs. Feldman," Dr. Simms told her after they were alone in his office, having left his nurse to see to Peter. "I advise immediate hospitalization," he went on, as he scanned Peter's record. "He's had his polio shots and all the rest, but—" He broke off, his bespectacled eyes serious and concerned. "I'd like to call an ambulance. He'll need more tests, and—"

"What's wrong with him?" Katie tried to maintain control, but she was scared. Nothing must happen to Peter.

"I'm not sure."

"But you suspect something, don't you?" Katie didn't care if she pushed. She had to know. It was her son. "I want to know."

"We'll want to rule out several things—like encephalitis, or meningitis." As her eyes widened in horror, he tried to calm her. "You must stay calm, Mrs. Feldman. We won't know anything for sure until the tests are done. It could just be a bad case of flu. In the meantime, I have your permission to send him to the hospital?"

She nodded mutely and he dialed, making the arrangements. Within a few minutes, Katie accompanied Peter to the hospital, and when he didn't protest—didn't even seem to register that he was in an ambulance—Katie's fear turned to absolute terror. Only twice before in her life had she seen anyone so suddenly and deathly sick. And both of her parents had died.

Once at the hospital, she was asked to stay in the waiting room while they took Peter to an examining room. Dr. Simms had followed in his own car, and he briefly reassured her before he joined the hospital staff.

It seemed forever before Dr. Simms returned. "No change, Mrs. Feldman," he said solemnly. "We've started him on penicillin, and we won't know the results of his tests for a few hours."

"Can I see him?"

He shook his head. "Not now. Perhaps later. We're trying to get his temperature down."

Dr. Simms strode away, and Katie was left with a knot of fear in the pit of her stomach. Dear God, she prayed silently. Please let Peter be all right. Don't let him have a terrible sickness. Oh God—*please*!

And then she thought of David. She had to call David. He should know how sick Peter was. A passing nurse directed her to a pay phone, and not having enough change for the long distance call, Katie reversed the charges, a thing she'd never done before.

"Katie! What's wrong?" David's voice sounded alarmed.

"It's—it's Peter," she managed, suddenly ready to cry. "He's in the hospital."

"What happened? Is he all right?" When she didn't reply at once, trying to gain control of her emotions, he went on, this time with an urgency born of fear. "Katie! What in hell has happened?"

Quickly she explained—how Peter had suddenly taken ill at school, and that the doctor still didn't know what was wrong. "It's serious, David," she said, her voice shaking with suppressed sobs. "And I knew you'd want to know."

"Of course I do!" he retorted, and she heard her fear echoed in his words. "I'm flying out, Katie. I should be able to leave almost at once. I'll call the airport to ready my plane as soon as we hang up."

She gave him the name of the doctor and hospital, and a minute later they hung up. After calling Anna Su, Katie went back to the waiting room, and hoped that the doctor would have word soon.

It was morning before Katie knew that the fever had broken, that Peter didn't have a dread disease after all.

"He's still a very sick boy," Dr. Simms told her. "And I want him to stay in the hospital for a few days, until he's well on the road to recovery." He paused, and for the first time, smiled. "It appears he's suffering from an especially virulent case of flu."

Katie slumped back against the chair she'd leaped out of when the doctor had appeared, suddenly too weak with relief to stand. "Thank God," she whispered. "Can I see him now?"

He nodded, and she followed him to Peter's room, where she took a seat by his bed. Her son was asleep, but he still looked very sick to her. Her gaze flew to the doctor.

"He'll be fine," he reassured her. Then, with a nod and a whispered, "We'll talk later," he left her. Sometime later someone else came into the room, and a glance told her it was Anna Su. Her niece had also stopped in the night before, prepared to stay, but Katie had insisted she go home—that "someone had to tend to Eastern Imports in the morning."

A second look brought Katie to her feet; Anna Su was motioning her to leave the room. A moment later, they were in the hall and headed to the waiting room where they sat down. Katie knew something was wrong.

"Aunt Katie," Anna Su began and faltered. "It's—it's about David. I had a call right after I reached the office."

"From David?" Katie was puzzled. "He told me he was flying out. Did he change his mind?"

"No—he didn't," Anna Su replied slowly, and her eyes suddenly filled with tears. "Oh, Katie! I hate to be the one to tell you."

"Tell me what?" Katie couldn't even guess what could be wrong with David. Was he bringing his fiancee? Was Anna Su upset because she didn't realize Katie knew about David's plans to marry another woman?

"His plane crashed, Katie. David, and two others, were killed."

The words dropped into a silence so heavy that

Katie thought it was squeezing the very air from her lungs. "What did you say?" she managed faintly, denying what she'd heard.

"He's dead, Katie," she repeated gently, crying silently.

Then she pulled her aunt close, and together they cried. Katie was already emotionally drained, and knowing that David, the man she'd once loved, had chosen over Max, was gone forever, was more than her system could stand. She couldn't stop crying, and finally Anna Su called the nurse. After she explained, the nurse checked with the doctor, who ordered a sedative. Katie was put to bed in the room next to Peter, and she knew no more until hours later.

When she awoke, she lay staring at the ceiling, quiet tears slipping from her eyes to soak the pillow. *Oh, David,* she agonized. *It's really my fault this time. If I hadn't allowed Max to make love to me, if I hadn't gotten pregnant, if you hadn't left, we would have still been together—and you wouldn't be dead.* Oh, dear God. When did the sorrow stop?

And then she noticed Anna Su in the chair by the window. Her niece, seeing her awake, came to her at once. She smiled sadly and kissed Katie on the cheek.

"I'm so sorry, Aunt Katie."

Swallowing hard, Katie nodded. "I know," she said, still unable to completely accept that David was gone. She blinked away more tears, trying hard to stay in control. She had to be strong now—for Peter's sake.

How would she tell Peter?

As though Anna Su read her thoughts, she expressed the very thing on Katie's mind. "Peter is better," she said. "Dr. Simms said he'll make a full recovery—and the doctor will be in to see you soon. He was waiting for you to wake up."

Even as she spoke, the door opened and the doctor came into the room; his expression was calm, but Katie saw the concern in his eyes. He expressed his condolences and went on to explain about Peter.

"I don't recommend telling him about his father's death, Mrs. Feldman. Not until he's better. The shock would be unpredictable in his present condition."

Katie nodded, but it was all so horrible, like a living nightmare. She knew Peter would be beside himself; he loved his father so much and had often said he wanted to be just like him when he grew up.

Taking a deep, ragged breath, Katie tried to pull herself together. She assured the doctor that she was better and intended to get up. He agreed, and a minute later left the room so Katie could dress. Anna Su waited until she felt her aunt was really coping, then she too left for the office, promising to return later.

After seeing Peter, Katie used a private phone to call David's parents in New York, but she was only able to leave a message with their housekeeper who told her in a crisp tone that the elderly Feldmans were "unable to come to the phone."

During the next several days, she was still unable to speak to David's parents, so she called his office and left a message to be passed on to them. She wanted them to know that she and Peter would have attended the funeral but for Peter's being in the hospital, and how very sorry she felt. She sent flowers and a long letter to the Feldmans, people she'd only seen twice, as it had always been made clear that they didn't approve of her.

When she finally took Peter home after a week in the hospital, a frail and pale little boy, Katie decided to wait until he was stronger before telling him about David. When she could delay no longer, she picked a time after they'd been playing checkers—and he'd won.

"You've sure been home a lot, Mom," he commented happily. "I like playing games with you."

She ruffled his hair. He was looking stronger every day, and he would be going back to school soon. Trying to find the right words to begin, he opened the subject unexpectedly.

"Didn't my dad care that I was sick?" he asked, his eyes round with hurt. "He never even called to see how I was."

"He cared very much," Katie began, suddenly disconcerted.

"Then why doesn't he call, or come and visit me like he used to? Doesn't he love me anymore, Mom?"

"He's always loved you, darling," she said. "And I did talk to him on the phone when you were in the hospital. He planned to fly out, but—"

"Then why didn't he?"

Katie took his hands in hers, and with a silent prayer, began what had to be said. "He did, Peter— that is, he tried to."

"What do you mean?"

His little boy's face was suddenly anxious, and Katie wished with all her heart that she could turn back time, change the events of the last couple of weeks. But she couldn't. All she could do now was be honest and temper that honesty with all the love she possessed.

"His plane crashed on the way, Peter," she said gently. "Daddy was hurt and—and he passed away."

The dead silence was unbearable. She watched him grasp the words, reject them, and then consider them again.

"Does that mean—mean that my dad—died?"

Slowly she nodded as his eyes went bright with tears. She folded him against her, her heart breaking

to feel the great shuddering sobs that shook his slight
body. For long seconds he lay in her arms, and when
he suddenly pulled back, it took her by surprise.

"He's not dead!" he cried. "You're lying! I know
you're lying!" His voice rose with a note of hysteria.
"You didn't want me to go to New York with you.
You just don't want me to see my father. He's not
dead! I know he's not!"

"Peter, Peter," she crooned, trying to calm him,
knowing he was denying the horror of his father
being dead. But when she couldn't calm him, and he
only grew more hysterical—screaming and kicking
at her—she motioned to their housekeeper, who'd
come running, to call the doctor.

It took a sedative to calm him, and once he was
finally asleep, Katie sank into a chair and tried not to
be upset that her son blamed her. She knew his life
revolved around David's visits, especially after
they'd become so infrequent in the past few years.
He was devastated by his loss, and it would be her
job to make him feel secure again and put David's
death into perspective.

He didn't return to school for another week after
all, and Katie didn't go to the office either, fearful of
leaving her distraught son alone. Gradually, he
seemed to accept that David was dead, but Katie
knew his wound had only scabbed over and was far
from healed. Once he was back with his classmates,
Peter seemed better, and Katie went back to work.
But she made sure that when he was home, she was
too.

She thought it strange that she never heard from
the Feldmans, and she wondered just what David
had told them about their marital status. In any case,
she reminded herself, Peter was David's son. But
when she was notified by the Feldman family lawyer
that Peter was not David's legal heir, Katie was
appalled. It was obvious that David hadn't com-

pleted the legalities substantiating Peter's birthright.
Her anger was instantaneous. What kind of people
were they? Their son was hardly dead before they
were claiming his estate—which should belong to
Peter. *They weren't getting away with it!* Not if Katie
could help it.

She was hiring her own lawyer. If they wanted a
fight—they'd get it!

"Oh, my God!" Anna Su said one morning a year
later. "It hit the newspaper! Can you believe it?"

Katie took the paper, scanning it quickly. "This is
terrible!" she cried. "Those Feldmans are cruel and
inconsiderate! How can they do this to their own
grandson?"

Over the months since Katie had contested
David's estate on behalf of Peter, it had been a messy
legal battle that culminated in court. The case had
been heard in San Francisco, as that was where Katie
had filed her appeal. The Feldmans had remained on
the East Coast, represented in court by their lawyer.
Somehow it had all blown out of proportion, and
Katie found herself the focus of the Feldman attack,
they claiming that she really wanted the estate for
herself, not her son. Her lawyer had explained that
they were fearful of legally recognizing Peter, because then she might have a claim on the Feldman
empire. In the end, the judge ruled in their favor,
stating that he had no choice, as Katie's background
was too clouded. Both she and her lawyer wondered
if the Feldmans had paid someone off. And only
yesterday, when they'd gotten the verdict, someone
had called the press, and now everyone would know
about the whole mess.

She glanced at Anna Su, who stood waiting for her
to finish reading. "God only knows why anyone
would think this newsy enough to print!" Katie
threw the paper down on her desk. "I'm just glad I

discouraged Christina from coming down. They'd have included her in the article as well."

"They're just bastards!" Anna Su looked more angry than Katie had ever seen her. "It was never a matter of money to the Feldmans, or they wouldn't have set up such a sizable trust for Peter when he's older. They simply didn't want Peter to inherit the empire. Who will inherit it?"

"A son of David's cousin."

"Awful!"

"I know," Katie said, spent. Her worry now was that someone would tell Peter about the lawsuit, something she hadn't wanted him to know. He still wasn't past his father's death, and she didn't know what it'd do to him to know his parents had never been married—and he'd lost his birthright. Katie had never wanted money, only recognition of Peter's legitimacy.

When her lawyer called a few days later with news that her home at Pacific Heights now belonged to the Feldmans, and they intended to sell it, she was only resigned. Nothing they did surprised her anymore. But a moment later, the anger hit her again. This was one thing they wouldn't get away with.

But her own personal funds were low, and Eastern Imports, still in a financial bind from their expansion projects, was also unable to give her a loan. Then, to her surprise, Tak came forward with his own offer of help.

"You can't lose your home, Katie-san. I'll lend you the money."

His eyes were genuinely concerned, although he was all business. "We'll sign a note to be paid back in a year's time. By then, your share of profits in Eastern Imports will allow you to pay me back."

Grateful, Katie agreed, relieved that she didn't have to move her son from the security of his home. It would have been the final humiliation for her. The lawyers drew up the loan papers, listing her interest in Eastern Imports as collateral security. She signed, and it gave her great pleasure to buy back her house from the Feldmans. But at the same time, she was more angry and frustrated than she'd ever been in her life. She didn't like knowing what they'd gotten away with—the future David had promised his son.

CHAPTER 25

THE CHRISTMAS HOLIDAY WAS HARD FOR KATIE, BUT SHE tried to make it festive and fun for Peter. Although he'd regained his good health months ago, he still missed David, especially so during his Christmas vacation. It was his second holiday without his father. "I just wish Dad was here," he told Katie many times, and Katie worried that he'd magnified his memories out of proportion to the actual time David had spent with him. She was just glad that she'd managed to keep the newspaper accounts of the lawsuit away from Peter, but Katie knew there would come a day when she'd have to explain everything. By then, he'd be able to understand, she told herself.

The first of the year brought shipping delays, back-order delays and even labor problems, all costing Eastern Imports thousands of dollars. By spring, Katie knew she wouldn't be getting her usual bonus from annual profits, money she'd counted on to repay her loan to Tak.

But her work was the least of her worries; Peter hadn't snapped out of his depression. In an attempt to spend more time with him, she hired a pilot with a four-seat Cessna to take her and Peter flying. The man was a licensed instructor, and she often took the controls, accruing hours toward her own license. Peter enjoyed those times, and gradually he became more interested in his former activities.

When the phone rang one Saturday morning shortly after she'd gotten up, Katie expected the caller to be Anna Su. To her surprise, it was Christina.

"Mom! Mom!" her daughter cried over the static of the lines, her voice hysterical. "Dad crashed in the interior. We've had no word since his plane went down. Oh, my God, Mom. What if he's out there suffering and we can't find him?"

The air went out of Katie's lungs; the floor felt as if it was tilting, and she sat down so fast on the chair next to the phone table that her whole body was jarred. She took some deep breaths and concentrated for the next couple of seconds on slowing her heartbeat. The years rolled away, and Dion stood before her with the fatal words, "Max has crashed."

Christina rushed on in a torrent of words, words Katie had once voiced. "He went down around midnight, but it was still light. We lost radio contact. They're out searching for him now." She took a ragged breath, and Katie knew she was crying. "What if we never find him? What if we never know what happened for sure?"

Horrible images flashed in Katie's mind as she remembered the treacherous, mountainous terrain —and that other time Max had crashed. Shocked and shaken herself, Katie somehow managed to block her own feelings and concentrate on Christina's. Although she knew Alaska still took its toll of pilots despite improved airplanes and technology, she pointed out all the reasons Max might be safe.

"Oh, Mom, I couldn't bear it if something happened to Dad." Although a little calmer, hysteria still edged Christina's voice.

"I know, darling," Katie replied. *I know very well,* she thought. *Oh, my sweet little girl, how well I know.* "I'll book the first available seat to Anchorage," she said instead.

"Will you? Oh, will you really come?" She hesitated. "But can you leave your work?"

Katie reassured her. "I'll be on the first plane I can get," she told her. "In the meantime, don't forget that your father is a survivor, Christina."

When they hung up, Katie called the airlines and was confirmed for the next flight. Then she phoned Anna Su, briefly told her what had happened, and asked if she'd stay with Peter while she was in Alaska.

"Of course I will," Anna Su said at once, and then hesitated. "And Aunt Katie—how are you doing? Are you all right?"

Her concern brought a sudden lump to Katie's throat. Anna Su had put two and two together long ago. "I'm fine, Anna Su. But thanks."

She sat facing the phone after she'd hung up, trying to compose herself, to stop the shaking deep inside of her.

"You're going to Alaska, Mom?"

Peter spoke from behind her and Katie faced him as she stood up. "Yes, dear," she said, her voice amazingly level. "Christina's father has—is overdue on a flight."

"He's crashed his plane?"

Nodding, Katie found it hard to say the words. "Christina is very upset. She needs me in case—"

"Her father dies?"

Again she nodded.

"Can I go Mom—please?" His eyes were suddenly bright and eager. "I want to be with Christina too! And I've always wanted to go to Alaska. Please Mom—please!"

She pulled him into her arms. "I wish you could," Katie began. "But there are only two weeks left of school, and you have your final tests, your baseball team." She shook her head. "It's not possible, Peter. There's no way to make up school once it's out for the summer—you know that."

He looked so disappointed that Katie almost decided to take him anyway. But good sense prevailed. She didn't know what she'd find in Alaska. And she didn't want Peter reliving the death of his own father.

Memories of Alaska flooded Katie's mind as the DC3 flew her north to Anchorage. It was still a long trip, with stopovers in Seattle and Juneau, but surprisingly smooth, with little turbulence. The plane came in low over the Arm, the water a brilliant blue under clear skies, and when she finally stepped down the ramp onto solid ground, it was like walking into the past. The same snowy mountains hugged the horizon, like jagged teeth about to bite the sky, indomitable and remote as ever. She felt the vastness of the land touch her with a remembered sense of isolation—and a reminder of the stoic patience the land had shown throughout the ages, awaiting the advent of men who would challenge its might.

Had Max finally become a casualty to this fickle land that took the blood of men as its due? She hesitated, and a light wind touched her with the fragrance of the sea, a fresh smell that spoke of the

pure Arctic waters of the north—another memory
from the years when she lived in Alaska. Somehow,
it was all so tragic. She'd left believing Max was
dead, and now, after all these years, she was back for
the same reason. She braced herself and walked into
the terminal.

"Mom!"

Christina ran to her, a slender young woman in
black slacks and a white cashmere pullover sweater.
Katie only caught a glimpse before she was in her
daughter's arms. "I'm so glad you're here, Mom. You
don't know how many times I've wished that you'd
visit."

"Christina," Katie murmured, stepping back so
she could look at her daughter. "You've matured
somehow since I saw you last—you're quite the
young lady and—" She broke off, remembering her
reason for being there. "Has there been any word yet
about your father?"

To Katie's surprise, Christina smiled broadly.
"They found him, crash-landed on the tundra. He's
okay, Mom. We're all so relieved—I can't tell you
how much."

It was an anticlimax for Katie. All of a sudden,
there was no reason for her to be there. But she was
relieved. Max had cheated death once more. A look
at Christina's radiant face told her how devastated
she would have been had the news been different—
like little Peter.

They collected Katie's suitcase and walked outside
to the car Christina had parked nearby. "It's a
company car," she explained, and Katie merely
smiled. It was a new Ford; Max had always bought
Fords.

"And I've reserved a room at a hotel for you,
Mom," she said once they were settled on the front
seat. "I didn't think you'd be comfortable staying
with me, as I'm still at Dad's and—"

"Heavens no!" Katie retorted. "I wouldn't even consider such a thing—and I'm sure your father's wife wouldn't like it either."

Christina started the car and they were soon on the road to town. "No, I don't think she would." She hesitated. "Sarah is a little possessive—sometimes she's even threatened by me."

There was no doubt about it, Katie thought, surprised. Christina didn't sound fond of Max's wife. But she didn't feel right discussing Sarah, so she changed the subject to Anchorage and how much it had changed.

Even more than I expected, Katie thought as they drove through the main business section. It was a small city now. Once checked into the hotel, Christina went upstairs with her, and they visited for the next couple of hours. Katie declined an invitation to dinner, pleading travel fatigue, but feeling that Christina should be with her father, who'd only been brought in shortly before her arrival. But they made plans for the next day, so Christina could show her around.

"Would you like to go out to the airfield tomorrow? See how much our business has grown?" Christina asked eagerly.

"I'd love to." Katie replied at once. "But will it be all right? I mean, I wouldn't want to upset Sarah—me being the first wife and all," she ended lamely.

"Of course it's fine." With a grin and a kiss, Christina started to go, then ran back to hug her mother. "I'm so happy you're here, Mom." Her dark eyes, so like Max's, were warm and sincere. "It's the first time in years we've had time to visit like this. I'm sorry I scared you into coming. But I'm glad you did."

Katie hugged her back. "I'm glad too, Christina. And grateful that your father wasn't hurt." She pulled back, smiling. "So we'll just have fun for the next few days—okay?" She ended on a lighter note.

When she was in bed, Katie found it hard to go to sleep. She would see Max tomorrow—for the first time in almost a decade.

"My God!" Katie cried as they drove into the business area of Stefanini Air Service. "I wouldn't recognize it at all!" Behind the two-story office building were the hangers, and beyond that she saw a number of planes, from DC3's to small Cessnas. Gone was the small operation she remembered. In its place was an airline company that had all the earmarks of success.

Suddenly unsure, she wished she'd begged off from seeing the airfield. But it was too late; Christina was already out of the car. Slowly, Katie got out too. At least she knew that she looked her best in her turquoise pant suit, her hair dressed in a traditional chignon, her makeup carefully applied. She walked with Christina to the office, her daughter chatting all the way, explaining the changes over the years, unaware of her mother's state of nerves.

It was a weekday, and as they went into the office, the sounds of typing and employees speaking in hushed tones filled Katie's ears. There were at least twenty people at work in the room. She couldn't help but remember the little shack in Fairbanks where she'd worked so many years ago—when she'd been madly in love with a bush pilot. She sighed and kept her composure. Somehow, she hadn't expected such a change—or that coming back would be so painful.

Leading the way to a door at the back of the room, Christina spoke to everyone as they went, and Katie was pleased to see how well-liked she was. Then they were in another huge office with windows facing the field. It was a functional room, not elegant. As Katie glanced around she was suddenly aware of the man standing before a bank of filing cabinets.

It was Max.

He turned at that exact moment, and their eyes caught—and held. Time fell away, and it was like yesterday, like all those years ago. He was still lean and straight, but his eyes seemed even darker in contrast to the gray in his black hair. And something else hadn't changed either. Katie's heart thumped in her chest, out of sync, just like that day in the park when she first met him.

"Hello, Katie," he said, breaking the silence, his gaze still holding hers. He made no move toward her.

"How are you, Max?" she replied, wondering how he found her. Older? No longer attractive?

"Fit," he said, and reached for a cigarette from his shirt pocket. His hand came away empty. He laughed then, and Katie thought her knees wouldn't hold her. "I guess you make me nervous, Katie. I haven't smoked for years."

She smiled back. Max thought she must have no inkling that he was equally shaken. Christina had told him, only this morning, what had happened, and that Katie was in Anchorage. The words, so casually spoken by his daughter, had jolted him with something like an electric shock. It had been Sarah's observation that had steadied him. "Christina's mother flew up to be with her, because we all thought the worst." He'd chosen to disregard the edge to her tone, as Sarah had always been jealous of Katie, who'd been well liked in Alaska despite the cloud on her integrity during the war. And now, as he gazed at Katie, so lovely, still so youthful and shining, Max knew his wife wouldn't be pleased at all to meet her.

A slow smile curved Christina's mouth as she observed her parents. She'd always been so proud of

both of them. She found herself wishing an old
wish—that they could be together. They seemed
perfect for each other. If it wasn't for Sarah—who
could walk in at any moment—she'd have made an
excuse so they could be alone. Instead, she covered
the awkward seconds with a continuation of her
commentary on the company. A moment later, her
father joined in, pointing out his airplanes through
the wide windows, and the tension in the room
lessened.

"What have we here?" a woman's voice said from
the doorway.

They turned as one from the window. The woman
was a little older than Katie, well-dressed, although
her skirt and blouse did little to flatter her spreading
figure. Her hair was teased into a bouffant style that
was all the rage, but it gave her heavy features an
even fleshier look and added years to her face. But it
was her narrowed eyes that chilled Katie. She
guessed the woman was Sarah, and was shocked to
know this was the woman Max had married.

"Katie, I'd like you to meet my wife, Sarah," Max
said, and moved beside her. "And this is Christina's
mother, Katie."

"I'm happy to know you," Katie replied as Sarah
nodded acknowledgment. She sensed the woman's
dislike, feelings that were reflected in her pale blue
eyes and in the hard set of her mouth. "Max was just
pointing out how his company has grown," Katie
added, and managed a smile.

"You might remember that my mother was in on
the conception of Dad's big dream," Christina said
coolly, and a glance told Katie that her daughter
didn't like Sarah's attitude either.

"Not quite, dear," Katie said, carefully controlled.
"Your father already had his dream when I met
him."

"Hmmph," Sarah retorted rudely. "It's only in the

last ten years that Max has become a success, and that was—"

"Enough of that," Max interrupted, his tone sharp. "I'm sure no one wants a history lesson."

An awkward silence dropped into the room, and again it was Christina who broke it. "C'mon, Mom. I've got lots to show you, so we'd better get going."

"Yes, we have to let you get back to work," Katie told them, damned if she'd let that cow Sarah scare her out. She crossed to Max and put out her hand. "I'm very relieved that you weren't hurt, Max. And I'm happy that you've made your dream into a success. It's what you always wanted, above all else."

He took her hand and held it for long seconds. "Thanks, Katie." His words were stilted—with suppressed feelings? "Have a nice visit. You'll find Anchorage has grown even more than my company."

Then Katie followed Christina outside, feeling great satisfaction at not having said a proper goodbye to Sarah. *The bitch!*

She had no way of knowing how her final words had affected Max. *There was one other thing I wanted more than my dream*, he thought, watching her go. *The reason my dream became so important—you, my darling. You.*

The visit became an unexpected pleasure for Katie, as Christina, who'd gotten her pilot license right after turning twenty-one, flew her to some of the places she used to fly herself. "Dad's company is one of the largest in Alaska now," she told Katie. "We've expanded our flights to the States."

Katie only smiled and gazed out of the cockpit window to the mountains below. When she'd last flown the Fairbanks route, she was married to Max, was a part of his dream for the future. But now he'd built his empire without her.

"Here you are, Christina," she said a few minutes

later. "Flying your own plane." Katie had been watching her daughter's skillful handling of the controls, so lovely with the sun shining on her golden hair, so confident of her ability. "Does this mean you've given up your goal to study voice in San Francisco?" She hesitated. "I've been wondering, as you've postponed moving back to California several times these last couple of years."

"No," Christina answered after a pause. "I'm still involved with the local theatrical group—but it's strictly an amateur thing. It's still my plan to go south, but—" She broke off and glanced at Katie. "I feel a terrible pull in both directions. I want to sing and live where I can be trained, but I love flying and will miss Dad."

"You can still fly in California," Katie offered softly. "And come back here often to visit your father."

There was another pause, as though Christina considered her next words carefully. She adjusted altitude and flaps, and then glanced at Katie again, her eyes now serious. "Dad doesn't approve of my going—to California, or into music as a profession."

"What?" Katie's surprise sounded in her voice. "Is that why you haven't made the move?"

Christina nodded. "Oh, I may be exaggerating a little. He would never stop me. It's just—just that I know he'll miss me so much. He won't really have anyone after I'm gone."

"But he has a wife!"

"Sarah!" Christina's word rang with disdain. "She was the biggest mistake of his life—although he'll never admit it. Sarah is a grasping, cold woman. I've always believed she's an opportunist." She grinned, a little sadly, Katie thought. "You never knew that, did you?"

Shaking her head, Katie said, "No, you've never spoken against her before."

"So it's my own dilemma," Christina said, almost under her breath. "I feel Dad has had so much unhappiness that I can't cause more."

As Christina prepared for a landing, Katie was thoughtful. A long time ago, Christina had remained with Max in Alaska for the same reason. Had she become so used to worrying about his happiness that she'd lost perspective about her own? And was Max manipulating, however subconsciously, his only daughter so that she would stay close to him? Christina was no longer a child and had a right to choose her own path without undue influence from either parent. Katie decided to have a private talk with Max after all.

With only one day left of her visit, Katie left a message for Max with his secretary to phone her that evening at her hotel, because she needed to talk to him concerning Christina. Katie and Christina had an early supper in the hotel dining room, and their conversation turned to Peter, and David's death.

"Poor little guy," Christina said, her eyes tearful. "I understand how he must feel; I know how I felt when I thought Dad might have died."

They arranged the time that Christina would pick her up in the morning for the airport, and then Katie went up to her room. After a while she realized that Max hadn't called, that perhaps he hadn't even gotten her message. Maybe Sarah got it instead, she thought, and decided to call him in the morning. About to undress, Katie was startled by the sudden ringing of the phone.

"Hello," she said, and was surprised to hear Max's voice. It was almost ten o'clock.

"I got your message," he said in a matter-of-fact tone. "So instead of talking on the phone, why don't you meet me in the lobby."

"You're here—at the hotel?"

There was a pause. "Yeah." She could almost see

his hooded eyes from hearing the tone of his voice.
"I'll buy you a nightcap."

"All right," she replied slowly, trying not to read
anything into his action. After all, she'd been the one
to request the talk. "I'll be right down." She replaced
the receiver on its cradle.

But it took her a couple of minutes longer, as she
hesitated before the mirror, checking her makeup
and brushing her hair that she'd already unpinned.
Then she went out to catch the elevator. When she
stepped into the lobby, Max was the first person she
saw.

He watched her walk toward him, her black sheath
dress molding her body, just as her hose molded her
shaply legs all the way down to her high-heeled
matching pumps. For a moment, with the ceiling
lights shimmering her hair to silver and sparkling in
her green eyes, Katie looked twenty again.

"Hi, Max," Katie said, suddenly calling all her old
kendo into play. "Thanks for coming."

Inclining his head, Max took her arm and led her
toward the bar. "We can talk better sitting down," he
told her, and she was reminded of his masterful
ways.

They sat at a corner table, across the dimly lit
room from the piano player, whose light touch on the
keys added feeling to the old favorites he played.
Max ordered scotch for himself and a brandy for
Katie, and she was suddenly stricken with another
flash of memory. He remembered too.

"Well—cheers," he said, lifting his glass. "To
happiness."

"Once you would have said success."

His eyes glinted over the glass. "That was then,
Katie. This is now."

She sipped, then put down her glass, trying not to
be disconcerted by his cool bearing, by the fact that
he looked so handsome in his casual jacket and

khaki pants. "I wanted to discuss Christina," she began. "Christina's future."

He arched a brow, and waited.

"We've had a good visit—mother and daughter conversations," she said, keeping her gaze level. "We've talked about her plans for the future." She hesitated, choosing her words so that she didn't hurt him.

"Go on," he prompted, and Katie decided to be direct.

"She tells me you don't approve of her desire to pursue her singing." He looked surprised, but before he could speak, she went on, explained Christina's feelings, although she was careful to be tactful so that he didn't feel his daughter had been talking about him behind his back—or his wife's.

"I believe she's so worried about leaving you Max—has developed such a strong belief that you need her—that she isn't getting on with her own life." Her words trailed off into a brief silence.

"It's true that I've expressed concern about a singing career," he began slowly. Gone was his earlier noncommittal demeanor; he was genuinely concerned. "But she's a grown woman; I wouldn't stand in her way. For Christ sake! I want her to be happy above all else."

"I know that," Katie replied at once. "So do I. And of course I'd love to have her in California. But regardless of what she chooses—staying in Alaska, or moving to San Francisco—I just want the decision to be hers, based on what she wants for her future." She hesitated to take a breath. "She needs to stand on her own, Max, without the influence of either of us."

He took a sip of his drink, giving himself the seconds he needed to regain his perspective. At first, he'd felt anger at what she said, then a growing sense that she wasn't being critical, only concerned for

Christina's future. But it was his awareness of Katie, so close and yet so unreachable, that diluted his concentration. He kept remembering how it felt to hold her—and to make love to her.

"I suppose I'm hanging on," he said finally, his eyes holding hers and reflecting the flame from the candle on their table. "She's important to me, and it's hard to think of her living so far away."

"I understand." Katie's lashes lowered suddenly. "It's hard to have your child leave you."

His hand covered hers. "I'm sorry, Katie. I once did that to you, didn't I?"

His touch was unexpected; Katie hadn't braced herself for it and her breath caught in her throat. She didn't remember glancing up, only knew she was suddenly caught by eyes too aware of her reaction. Her mind flashed to other times when he'd touched her—the first time he'd kissed her in San Francisco, made love to her on the remote beach so long ago, and the progression of their passion over the years they were together.

She nodded, unable to do more at that moment.

He withdrew his hand, as though he made an effort to resist her. "I'll see to Christina," he said, sounding normal, and she felt foolish all at once. "I'll have a talk with her."

"You won't tell her I—"

"No," he said, anticipating her concern. "I won't tell her we talked about this."

An awkward silence fell between them. Their reason for meeting was over, yet both resisted ending it. As they hadn't finished their drinks, they lingered.

"I wasn't able to see Johanna and Dion," she said, directing the conversation away from forbidden topics. "I understand they're in Nome for the summer."

Max inclined his head. "Dion is doing a job for me up there, and Johanna went along."

"Are they—all right? I mean, Christina said Dion drinks too much, and Johanna just goes along with it."

He shrugged but Katie saw a flash of annoyance on his face. "Dion never changes, Katie. I didn't speak to him for a couple of years because of what he did to you and Christina. But I got over it and gave him another job." He gave a harsh laugh. "Because he couldn't get one anywhere else—and there was Johanna."

"Some things never change." Katie shook her head regretfully. "I'd always hoped Johanna would develop a backbone."

"And I always hoped Dion would stop being weak—like our father was."

"What do you mean?" Katie leaned forward. He was touching on a topic he'd never discussed, even with her.

He emptied his glass, then carefully replaced it on the table. "I never told you—had too much pride I guess. My father got involved with criminals shortly after he arrived in America before the first World War. His death wasn't of natural causes; they killed him."

"My God, Max!" she cried. "You carried that around all these years? Why didn't you tell me? I wouldn't have cared what your father had done because I—"

She broke off, shocked because she'd almost said *I love you*. But he seemed too preoccupied with his own memories to notice, and went on to explain that he'd been influenced one way by the scandal, Dion another. Then the conversation moved on to reminiscences of their life together during the war and progressed to his company and her work at Eastern Imports. Somewhere in-between he ordered more drinks. Neither brought up spouses, except that Max offered condolences on David's death. Finally, Katie glanced at her watch, suddenly conscious that he had a wife waiting at home.

After dropping a bill on the table, Max escorted her to the elevator, and to Katie's surprise, he rode upstairs with her and saw her to the door, which she unlocked.

"I've enjoyed this, Katie," he said as she turned to him for a final good-bye. His tone was soft, and his eyes seemed filled with her in the subdued light. "I'm sorry we weren't friends again sooner. That was my fault, I'm sure."

"I'm sorry too, Max," she managed. "And it wasn't your fault. It was no one's fault. It just happened."

He took a step closer. "Fate? There was a chain of events beyond our control? Would you agree?"

Swallowing hard, she gave a nod. They stood without touching, the door behind her, and when he moved forward, Katie had nowhere to go.

"It's still beyond our control, sweetheart." He pulled Katie to him, roughly, possessively. "And it's still part of the chain."

He kissed her, tentative at first, but as her lips parted, and her arms crept around him, his mouth became more demanding. She knew she was lost to him—because she wanted to be, because she'd always belonged to him and always would. He had a strange power over her, one she'd never completely understood. When she was in his arms, nothing else mattered; it had always been so and the passage of time hadn't changed that fact.

Somehow he opened the door, then closed and locked it without letting go of her. Once in the privacy of her room, Max pulled her down onto the bed. "Darling—darling," he murmured, the slight movement of his mouth tickling hers. "I've never stopped loving you."

She lay under him, her body in exquisite agony because of her need for him. For one brief second, she remembered Sarah. But then, as Max undressed her and then himself, even Sarah didn't matter.

"You're so beautiful," he murmured huskily. It was hard to believe she lay naked, unashamed, waiting for him. She was different from Sarah in that way; she'd never been embarrassed about her body, never cringed or made excuses, because she gave unconditionally to the one she loved. Long ago he'd given up hope of ever possessing her again.

"I love you, Max."

Her whispered pledge gave him pause. He raised himself to look into her face; she was even more beautiful with the flush of love staining her cheeks, with desire alight in her eyes, with blond hair splayed around her. She was a flesh-and-blood Katie, not the specter of a Katie who'd haunted his dreams.

He pulled her to him and kissed her, tenderly, humbled by the very thought of her being in his arms. "Will you be mine? For only tonight?" he whispered, because he had to be honest with her.

The lowering of her lashes hid her pain from him. She realized what he was telling her. He was married to someone else—perhaps even loved his wife more than her. He was reminding her that their lives were separate now. And always would be regardless of fate.

It's *karma*, she decided. The old master was right; we can't escape our *karma*. She raised her lashes. "Yes," she whispered. "For tonight." *Forever my love, throughout eternity*, she told him silently—the words she'd once had inscribed for him.

And he did as he promised—he made her his for the night.

"I guess that means it's time to go." Katie turned to Christina, her overnight case in hand. The flight

had just been called and people were already boarding.

"Mom, are you sure you're all right?" Christina
peered at her, concerned by her mother's pale face
and overall look of sadness.

"I'm just fine," Katie reassured her, and smiled. "I
didn't get much sleep last night, and I'm just tired.
I'll sleep on the plane."

Relieved, Christina grinned back. "Don't tell me
you picked up a strange lover after I left," she joked.

For a second, Katie looked guilty, before she
realized that Christina was only teasing. But her
daughter had noted the expression and wondered
what it meant.

Then Katie hugged her, and they said their final
good-byes. "I'll expect you in California soon," she
told Christina. "I love you, darling. Take care."

Christina stood watching, a lump in her throat,
until the plane taxied away, then took off, soaring out
over the Arm to veer south. It was only as she was
driving home that she remembered that her father
hadn't been home last night, had phoned to say work
would keep him at the field. Her lump tightened, and
tears blurred her eyes. She suddenly knew they'd
been together. God! It was too sad to even think
about.

And Katie, the clouds pressing against the window, thought the weather was fitting. Unlike her
daughter, she stared dry-eyed into the gray mass,
feeling the same sense of loss she'd felt the last time
she'd flown out of Anchorage. Max was as lost to her
now as then.

CHAPTER 26

Back home, Katie concentrated on Peter, who was more upset about not being taken to Alaska than he'd thought. "I'm the one who's always left out," he told her, and she saw his anger and hurt and tears before he turned away. "My dad never put me first—and neither do you, Mom!"

"That's not true, honey," Katie said gently. "Your father loved you more than anyone, and so do I—you and Christina."

Over the next few weeks, she included him in everything she could. Katie even gave him a part-time job running inner-office errands in the building, so that he could be with her for the summer. She took extra care to make him feel secure again, realizing the loss of his father was still painful and

that he had a child's fear that she would leave him
too.

Even though she was strapped for money because
her note to Tak was due the first of December, she
managed to buy a small, single-engine plane on time
payments. She took Peter to the airport and surprised him.

"Oh, Mom! You mean it's really ours?" He danced
around it, inspecting the wings and propeller. "Can I
learn to fly it too? Please?"

Laughing together, they climbed in with the flight
instructor she'd hired to help her meet the require-
ments for her pilot's license. "Of course you can,"
she replied. "Sometime in the future when you're a
little older."

The summer flew past, with flying outings each
weekend. Katie was licensed by fall, and after that
she even let Peter take the controls when conditions
permitted. "Oh boy, oh boy!" was his usual response
on such occasions. Katie only smiled. Her son was a
natural flyer. *It shouldn't surprise me*, she thought. It
seemed to be a family trait. Gradually, Peter was
able to talk about David with fond memories, recall-
ing his flights with his father. Often Katie remembered hers with Max. But the important thing was
that she'd reestablished a good rapport with Peter.

"I can't wait to show Christina that I'm a pilot
too!" he often told Katie. But Christina again postponed moving to California. Although disappointed,
Katie realized after talking to her that her decision
was her own, not based on how her father would feel.
Max had been true to his word—as she'd known he
would.

She sat staring at the phone long after she'd hung
up, her thoughts in Alaska. Mental pictures flashed
in her mind—herself as a young women in love with
a daring bush pilot, her first house, the war, and the
progression of years.

Abruptly she shook herself and stood up. She was becoming maudlin, and she seemed to be doing that more often lately. She went to find Peter and reminded herself that she had too much going on in her life to be lonely.

Christina wrote often, and the day after Katie received a letter saying that Johanna's son Ollie was fighting in Viet Nam, President Kennedy was shot in Texas. It was such a shock that Katie found it hard to concentrate on her work for the next week. When Tak made an unexpected telephone call to her office, she blurted out her horror at the assassination. Although her note was due in only a couple of days, and she was going to have him sign an extension, the loan was not uppermost on her mind.

"I want to discuss our business transaction," he told her after she'd vented her emotions. Something about his tone brought her back to the business at hand.

"I know, Tak," she began, having regained her poise. "It's due on the first. I haven't forgotten."

There was a moment of silence before he responded. "You can make the check out to me, not my company," he said, and his manner was impersonal. "I'll come by on Monday for it, Katie. That's the second of December."

She quelled her sudden apprehension and reminded herself that he didn't know that she needed an extension until Eastern Imports was showing a profit again. But she suddenly found it hard to ask.

"Anna Su told me you arrived from Tokyo yesterday, Tak." She hesitated, forming her words carefully, suddenly reminded of the Japanese protocol of her childhood. "I was about to call you. As you know, Eastern Imports was put on the financial line when we went into the business venture with your company. And because of all the problems we've had getting it off the ground, the company has been feeding the costs and we haven't made a profit yet. Because of that, my own income is down." She hesitated again, and made the plunge. "I need a six-month extension on my note, Tak. Will that be all right?"

"I'm afraid not, Katie. I find that I, too, need the money."

"But I don't have it."

"Perhaps you can secure another loan with your bank."

Before she could say another word, he said goodbye, and there was a click, followed by the dial tone. Dumbfounded by Tak's coldness, she stared at the receiver. Then the magnitude of it all hit her. He wasn't extending the term of her note—did that mean he was calling her loan? If she didn't pay, would he take her collateral? Chilled, she got on the phone and made an appointment with her banker for that very afternoon.

The news wasn't good; her limited assets weren't enough to secure a loan for $200,000. Even her percentage in Eastern Imports wasn't enough, as it had been running at a loss for over a year. Katie ended up going to two more places and the final decision was the same—no loan.

On Monday, when Tak appeared in her office, meticulous and well groomed in his expensive silk suit, she told him she couldn't pay. He merely nodded, offered his regret, and then went on to explain that he would take her collateral instead.

"But that's my source of income—my future security!" she cried. "You can't do that. I've worked too hard. I'll sell the house and pay you."

His eyes were remote, unreadable. "If you remember Katie-san, your house is all tied up in our agreement. You aren't at liberty to do that—unless I approve."

"And you don't? Good God, Tak! I trusted you!"

Her fear was gradually being overpowered by anger. The heat of it was already staining her cheeks and sparkling in her eyes.

"I intend to take back all that the Konos have lost," he said with great dignity. "It is a matter of honor, Katie-san. I'm sure you understand. After Hiroshima, I made a vow to my honorable parents that their deaths would be—"

"Avenged?" she interrupted angrily. "By manipulating an old friend, who was like a sister to you?" Katie threw her pen down on her desk, then stood up so fast that her chair hit the wall behind her. She strode around the furniture to confront him face to face.

He was suddenly reminded of the Katie he remembered from their childhood—fearless when angry. Tak was pricked with guilt over what he was about to do. She was so beautiful—the perfect woman in all ways. But there was his honor, he reminded himself, and he hardened his resolve.

"Manipulate?" he retorted. "As Edward manipulated Michiko? As he took advantage of the war to take this very company away from my uncle?"

His veneer of control slipped, and Katie saw his anger, a fury at all that had happened to his family, an immovable force that, coupled with his honor, would never allow him to relent. But still she tried to reason with him. His raised hand in the flat, silencing gesture stopped her.

"No use, Katie-san. I have no grudge against you," he said, his mask of control back in place. "Your house will remain yours, and also your silk venture will be signed over to you by Eastern Imports as a means for you to start your own business. You will no longer own an interest in a Kono business, but you will keep those assets."

"You damn right I'll keep them!" she retorted, too upset to remain polite when he'd just stripped her of

the business she'd worked so hard to keep solvent—
given up part of her life to make into a success. She'd
always meant it to belong to Anna Su one day as her
way of righting the wrongs of the past. Tak had even
taken that away from her. "I earned them—and a lot
more! And you know it, damn you!"

He walked to the window, so that his back was to
her. For a second she thought she'd seen something
else on his face—regret? But she dismissed such a
thought. Tak's sense of honor would never allow him
regret for very long. And when he turned to her
again, he was all business—as if she were someone
off the street, not the woman he'd once wanted for
his mistress.

"I think you'll ultimately find my settlement fair."

"Fair?" she flung at him. "Anna Su is still the
owner of Eastern Imports, not you. And I think our
niece will have something to say about this."

To her amazement, he only gave her a slight bow
and moved to the door. "Our lawyer will be in touch,
Katie-san." And he left her, frustrated and upset to
the point of being physically sick.

And it was only the beginning. When she called
Anna Su into her office for a conference, it didn't
take long for Katie to see that her niece already knew
what had happened. Surely she hadn't been in on it?
Katie told herself, already beginning to understand
that she'd been set up. All the shipping delays and
other problems had probably been orchestrated by
Tak so that she wouldn't be able to meet the note.

"Uncle Tak's claim is legal and binding, Aunt
Katie," Anna Su said, feeling in the middle between
the two people she loved most in the world. Her
uncle had told her his plans if Katie didn't pay on
time, but Anna Su couldn't believe her uncle had
maneuvered the end result. She couldn't take sides;
it would be unfair to the other one.

"But I'm not being given a chance!" Katie tried to

keep the shrill note of anger from her voice. "Can't you see that?"

"I love you, Aunt Katie, but your deal was with Uncle Tak. I had nothing to do with it." Anna Su hesitated, wanting to stay impartial. "And Uncle Tak does have a point, and he was fair in giving you the silk line. That alone is probably worth far more than the note amount."

Hurt by Anna Su's reaction, Katie ended the conversation. She needed time to be alone and think. But it was a long time before she could get a handle on her feelings. She felt betrayed by both Tak and Anna Su, and she found she couldn't talk about it with her niece. Even though Katie sensed Anna Su's upset when she cleaned out her office, neither of them quite knew what to say or do about the situation. Katie couldn't explain the whole story to Anna Su without undermining Edward for what he'd done to the Konos, and Tak for seeking revenge, so she said nothing. Anna Su had been an insecure child; Katie wouldn't be a party to stripping away the security she'd found as an adult.

After the first of the year, Katie rented space to carry on her own little business, and she was soon so busy that she rarely saw Anna Su, although they sometimes spoke on the phone. There was a rift between them for the first time, and Katie didn't know how to change that without causing more pain. Katie sensed that she was now losing Anna Su to Tak as well, and many times the thought occurred to her how unnecessary it all was. Why hadn't Tak been open and honest about his feelings? They could have worked something out to the satisfaction of everyone. She was only beginning to realize how deeply Tak was affected by the war.

It was hard to explain to Peter, who asked questions. Katie decided it was best to be honest, as he was bright and perceptive and would know if she evaded the truth. Briefly, she explained, and tried to be fair. When she'd finished, he surprised her with a maturity far beyond a boy of almost twelve.

"Poor Anna Su. Mom, can't you see? She's right in the middle. You've always been her mother, but her Uncle Tak has become her father these last few years. She loves you both."

His words gave Katie perspective, and she felt a little better about her own future, especially since her new business was already flourishing.

They'd been getting ready to leave for an early movie, a thing they often did on Friday night if they were both free, when they heard about the earthquake. Peter, waiting for Katie to freshen up, was watching television and the station was interrupted by a news bulletin.

"The quake might well be the strongest ever recorded, and fragmentary reports coming out of Alaska say Anchorage has been leveled," a stern commentator said from the screen. "There is no report yet as to the number of casualties."

Katie entered the living room just in time to hear. Both she and Peter were struck dumb, their eyes glued to the television set. When the regular programming was resumed, they both talked at once.

"What about Christina?" Peter asked, his face stricken with fear. "She can't be dead—she can't!"

At the same time, Katie was thinking aloud about what she'd do. "I'll call Anchorage to find out what's happened."

With Peter beside her, she tried to phone, but all lines to that part of Alaska were down. She called the airlines and couldn't get through because of busy signals. When she did, Katie was informed that all flights were canceled to Anchorage.

Remembered earthquakes in Alaska surfaced in her mind, quakes so strong that they would have devastated populated areas had they not occurred out in the uninhabited wilderness. Now one of those had hit Anchorage. Christina could be injured—or worse. And there was Max and Johanna and Dion. Oh God! she thought. She had to know they were safe.

Quickly she called the airfield and told them to get her plane gassed up and ready for her at first light in the morning. She would fly herself to Alaska—and if the landing field in Anchorage was destroyed, then she'd land where she could. Hadn't she done just that in the past?

"Can I go too, Mom? Please! Christina is my sister too!"

She shook her head. "It might be dangerous, Peter," she began. "And there's school and—"

Instant tears welled in his eyes, and he knuckled them away, trying not to be a baby. "You never take me—never!" he cried, his voice breaking. "You always leave me out, even when someone I love might be—might be dying."

His disappointment was all mixed up with fear and his old feeling of abandonment when she'd left him in the past. Katie suddenly knew she couldn't leave him. She wanted him with her, and told him so.

Eyes shining with new confidence, his fears tempered by being included, Peter ran to his mother and hugged her close. "Christina will be safe when we get there, Mom! You'll see!"

Katie watched him take the steps two at time up to his room. "I'll get packed right away," he called back, his voice high with excitement, and despite the terrible fear clawing at her insides, Katie managed a smile. She'd done the right thing.

At the airport she wasn't stopped by words of caution. She couldn't be—her loved ones might be dead. She knew from experience that she'd be in Alaska long before communication was restored.

And Katie knew she'd make it fine. Hadn't she once flown the very route with Max in his flimsy little plane? And hers was better and much faster.

She took off at dawn, flying into the morning sun, her son beside her. Katie remembered her mother's words of long ago—and she prayed to herself. Let us realize the hope of this day, dear God.

PART FIVE

1965–Present

CHAPTER 27

THE TRIP PROVED REWARDING. CHRISTINA AND MAX were safe, although Max's house had been destroyed when the bluff gave way and it slid into the Arm. And during the long round trip, Katie and Peter reestablished a mother-and-son relationship based on mutual respect. The Stefanini Company sustained only minor damage to its buildings and planes, and was able to continue limited flying service, although the airfields were badly torn up by crevasses and fissures. She even had a short, but awkward visit with her sister Johanna, a socially backward woman who seemed intimidated by Katie's sophistication. It was sad for Katie to see how worn and old Johanna appeared, how Dion's handsome features had become bloated and flushed from years of hard drinking. She knew their meager lifestyle was the result of

Dion's weakness for liquor and gambling. Katie was glad they hadn't lost their house; so many other homes had been leveled.

Anchorage was hard hit by the quake, 4th Avenue so destroyed that it took Katie's breath away. Stores had been reduced to piles of rubble, cars smashed flat, and the street itself had sunk thirty feet, leaving the downtown area destroyed. The violence of the land never stopped, she thought. Its great beauty had been forged from volcanic eruptions, and it would continue to take its toll from those who dared to try to tame such a formidable opponent.

"Experts are saying it's the worst earthquake in recorded history," Christina told them as they surveyed the destruction. "You were fortunate to make it up here, Mom. So much has been destroyed— bridges, highways, railroads, airports, docks. It's a wonder that only a hundred or so people in Alaska died."

Katie only nodded, so relieved that her family had survived such a holocaust. It had to be seen to be believed. The quake had generated massive tidal waves in Prince William Sound, waves that had wiped out the towns of Valdez and Seward.

They stayed only four days, and despite the continued after-shocks that rumbled underfoot, Peter fell in love with Alaska, much to Katie's surprise. Even while the gigantic power of nature held him in awe, his senses were seduced by the unsurpassed beauty of the vast forests, by the endless snowy mountains with their ice-blue glaciers, and by the hundreds of virgin islands dotting the coastline and waterways. He was intrigued that Alaskans flew everywhere, as casually as people in California drove their cars. And he took an immediate liking to Max, spending most of his time at the airfield puttering around the airplanes and watching the mechanics work on the engines. Within a short time of their arrival, Peter had developed a full-blown case of hero worship for Max, the man who was a flying legend in Alaska.

"That's what everyone who works for Max told me. You should have heard the stories, Mom!" Peter told her as they'd flown south, not realizing that his own mother had once been a part of some of those stories. "One day I'm going back! Being a bush pilot is the most exciting job in the world! I love Alaska!"

The situation was ironic to Katie. She'd maintained a casualness between herself and Max, aware of Sarah's watchful eye. But Peter and Max had become great buddies, and when she watched them together, the thought occurred to her that they looked enough alike to be father and son. But then, David and Max had resembled each other. So she only smiled and listened all the way back to San Francisco. Katie realized that Peter would want to be a bush pilot only until he grew into the next stage of his life.

But Katie had little time to reflect on the trip once she was back; her new business needed constant attention if it was to survive in the competitive business of silk imports. Her catalog orders were up, and she had to make sure the garment production stayed on schedule. She poured all of her profits back into the company, and for a while times were lean, although she never revealed that fact to Peter, who continued at private school. Katie wanted her son prepared when the time came for him to attend an Eastern university.

The summer passed quickly, and in the fall Christina moved back to San Francisco. She managed, with a little behind-the-scenes manipulation by Katie, to secure the best voice coach in the city. Then she began her training for the opera.

"I don't really expect to sing at the Met," Christina confided to Katie. "I just want to be good enough to sing in local productions."

By Christmas, Christina was settled into the family unit, and into her new lifestyle. She worked for Katie part-time, and mother and daughter became close. Equally important, Peter now had a confidant.

"You're lucky, Christina," Peter said one evening as he and Christina sat watching television, waiting for the new program that starred their cousin Lisa in the leading role. "You have a father who loves you."

Startled, Christina wondered what had prompted her young brother's remark, as it seemed out of the blue. Then she remembered reading him the letter from her father earlier, the one that said he and Sarah would be down in February for a visit. The letter had been full of news of Anchorage and their business, and had ended with his love.

"Your father loved you very much, Peter," she said gently. "I remember how happy he was when you were born. Even though he's gone now, and can't tell you himself, you mustn't forget that he loved you."

Peter glanced away to the commercial on the television screen. "Mom explained the situation to me, Christina," he confided in a low tone. "But only because I found out from a kid at school whose father was one of the lawyers for my dad's family." He hesitated. "My grandparents in New York have nothing to do with me—I guess they don't believe I'm really their grandson."

Horrified, Christina moved next to him on the sofa, but resisted hugging him because she didn't want to treat him like a child. He was confiding in her because he trusted her and loved her.

"You know all about my father being assumed dead when our mom married your father?" she asked instead.

He nodded. "They weren't really married when I was born, because Max was still alive."

"It wasn't our mother's fault—you know that, don't you, Peter?" Christina asked softly, sensing that his hurt was deep, and that this was the first time he'd ever talked about his feelings.

Again he nodded.

"One day you'll understand better," Christina went on, expressing some of her own feelings. Once she hadn't understood either. Now, being a young woman herself, who'd had her share of boyfriends, she'd gained an insight on how her mother must have felt, married to two men at the same time, a child with each one. Christina suspected that her mother still loved her father. She must have realized it when he came back, and that was what had come between Katie and David. But this was a suspicion she would never voice to Peter.

"I understand that my father didn't love me enough to legally claim me as his son," Peter retorted. "Why wouldn't he have done that, Christina? I didn't want his old money—only the right to be his son."

Christina did hug him then. "Of course you didn't," she said. "And you must believe that he would have taken care of that had he not been killed." She hesitated, willing her words to make a difference. "Remember, you were his only child, and he was on his way to your sickbed when he crashed."

"I know," he said, pulling away to perch on the edge of the sofa. "I guess I'm just jealous. You have such a great dad—he's so interesting and—nice."

"He is pretty special," Christina agreed. "And when he comes down, you can get to know him better. You and he are really very much alike."

"Really?" His face brightened. "Do you mean it, Christina?"

She grinned. "Of course I do."

Peter jumped up, suddenly all little boy. "Max is great! A real bush pilot!"

"He's that all right."

"I love Alaska—and flying—and being with your dad. We'll have a great time talking about things," he cried, his eyes filled with anticipation. "You know what, Christina? I'm going back up there when I grow up."

"We'll go up together," she told him with a laugh. But she was concerned; her thirteen-year-old brother was insecure and unsure of himself because he felt abandoned by his own father. Christina wondered if her mother realized the extent of his feelings. She decided to have a talk with Katie at the first opportunity.

"But I can't go for a long time," Peter went on, deflated all at once. "Mom expects me to attend an Eastern university when I graduate from high school —and I don't want to. She'd never understand my going to Alaska when I'm eighteen to become a bush pilot."

"We'll manage to visit before then," Christina promised, and added that topic to her private discussion with their mother. Peter needed to be heard, for the sake of his future happiness.

The conversation ended when Lisa's television series came on the screen. Their cousin had made the leap from model to actress, and her performance kept Peter and Christina engrossed. Peter's insecurities were forgotten—for the time being.

Christina and her mother had their talk, and Katie agreed to let Peter accompany Christina to Alaska sometime in the future. But she was adamant about Peter going on to an Eastern university when he graduated. "It's a must if he's to succeed in business," she told Christina. "He's just romanticizing Alaska now, but he'll get over that when he's older."

Christina had her doubts, but she didn't push. Her mother could be right.

The time seemed to fly for Katie, who was so busy building up her business that she didn't have time for random worries. It was enough that Christina pursued her singing and was doing community theater, and that Peter was doing well in school and had been chosen for the baseball team. Before she knew it, several years had passed and her little silk enterprise was flourishing. It pleased her that she now competed for business with Eastern Imports, and she was once again seeing Anna Su on a regular basis, even if it was mostly professional.

Isami Kono had remained her friend and often advised her on business matters, although his suggestions were always subtle, so that he didn't give away Kono company secrets. Katie knew this was his way to maintain family honor, as she suspected he had disapproved of Tak's method for taking back Eastern Imports. But once her company was on its feet, Isami had retired again to spend his time reading and gardening.

By Peter's junior year in high school, Katie's company was having growing pains, and she didn't have the resourses to expand. On impulse, she chose to see Fenton Stone for a loan, remembering that other lenders had turned her down when she needed to save her ownership in Eastern Imports.

"Of course I know who you are," an elderly Fenton Stone said after Katie was shown into his office. "I'll never forget the girl who saved my son's life—not as long as I live."

She smiled and took the offered chair, pleased that he remembered, because she wouldn't have used the incident to get money, even if Edward had once done it to buy Kono Imports. She was there only because he'd done business with Edward, and he knew that it was Katie who'd seen to it that the loan was eventually repaid in full. So she explained her present situation, and her expansion plan that needed financial backing.

"I see no problem, Katie," he told her, and offered tea. As they drank it, he explained that he'd been aware of what had happened at Eastern Imports only after the fact. "You should have come to me, my dear," he told her. "We would have backed you against Tak Kono, even though he's a respected businessman. I always felt the deal was unfair."

"Mr. Stone," Katie began, wanting to make her position clear. "I don't want a loan based on saving your son, but because I'm a good business risk."

"Precisely so," he replied with a smile. "We have to answer to our stockholders. Times have changed. It's not like the war years when we could do your brother a favor."

They finished their tea and their negotiations, and Katie went away feeling good about her standing in the business community. That she imported only the finest quality materials and now supplied some of the top clothing designers in the nation, who in turn sold the finished product at affordable prices, had become known in financial areas important to the continued growth of her company.

But her total dedication to her work had precluded much of a social life, and there was a deep, abiding loneliness within her. So long as she didn't slow down in her goal of success, she wouldn't have to think about how very alone she was without a man in her life. And certainly not think about the one she still loved with all her being—the man who'd never belong to her again.

The invitation to Anna Su's wedding was a surprise; Katie hadn't known her niece was seriously involved with a man. But then, she no longer knew much about Anna Su's personal life, she thought as she stood in the reception line with Christina and Peter, waiting their turn to meet the groom.

"Aunt Katie," Anna Su said, looking radiant in her white satin gown. "I'd like you to meet my new husband." She turned to the slim man at her side. "Thomas Naoki."

Smiling, her tone warm with love, Katie acknowledged the introduction, and then presented Christina and Peter. She was aware of Tak, who stood with his plump Japanese wife next to Anna Su, watching with inscrutable eyes. He'd given Anna Su away in the traditional wedding, but Katie understood that there had been a private Japanese ceremony prior to that, and she was hurt that she hadn't been invited. It was just one more incident that reminded her of how completely Tak had influenced Anna Su away from Edward's family. She was sure that Tak had been the one to encourage Anna Su's alliance with a proper Japanese family.

"Congratulations," Katie told the bride and groom, and restrained herself from giving Anna Su a fond hug. Somehow, the formal setting precluded the gesture, and again Katie felt left out and sad that there was now a distance between them. As she moved on, Katie gave Tak a brief bow, in the old Japanese manner—as if to remind him of her honor, and that it had been disregarded in the handling of Anna Su's wedding.

For a brief moment their eyes met, each measuring the other, neither giving away feelings by even a flicker of a lash. But after Katie had moved on, Tak felt shaken, although no one would have known from looking at the tall, impeccably dressed man in black formal attire. He watched her move gracefully across the room to the refreshment table, her blond hair in its stylish chignon shimmering silver under the lights of the crystal chandelier. Dressed in an aqua silk suit that emphasized her slim figure and long shapely legs, Katie was still the most stunning woman in the room. Even her daughter Christina, equally beautiful in red, didn't command the same attention. His Katie-san was still the fairy child, he thought. Courageous and not entirely predictable—and forever touched by the oriental mystique of her childhood.

He sighed and put his nostalgia aside. *Karma* was *karma*, and nothing could change that. Honor had to be satisfied, old debts repaid—and that meant the Konos taking back what belonged to them. Tak was glad that Katie was doing so well. Yet, as he turned his attention to his wife, he felt a tinge of sadness for Katie, because he felt her hurt about Anna Su. *But she has two other children*, he reminded himself. And I have none but Anna Su. Somehow he felt better, and forced his thoughts away from Katie who was now greeting another niece, a dark beauty who was also a famous television star.

"Elisabetta!" Katie cried. "I would have recognized you anywhere—you so resemble your father."

"Anyone would, Mom," Peter said, straightening up to his full height of almost six feet, conscious of his cousin's glamour. "She's on television every week."

"And the most gorgeous woman on the tube, I might add," Christina said, taking in the burgundy dress and matching coat that wore the stamp of haute couture. "It's good to see you again, Lisa. It's been a long time—years since you were last in Alaska."

"I don't get up there much." Her dark brows arched as she considered her remark. "And I can't persuade my parents to come down, even if I—"

She broke off and Katie knew she'd been about to say "paid their way." Her tone was friendly, but for all her success there was a hint of shyness in her that

Katie found surprising in one as famous as Lisa. She
suddenly wondered if Lisa was insecure.

Impulsively, Katie hugged her. "I'm really so
happy to see you, dear. I regret that I never see your
mother. A family should be closer somehow."

Lisa's response was instant, her smile giving her
beautiful face an even more dazzling beauty, the
quality that had helped take her niece to the top of
two competitive fields, Katie thought, watching her.
She suddenly wondered if Lisa would ever consider
doing some media ads for her, to promote her silks.
The idea grew on Katie, and she decided to give it
more thought later. It could be just the thing for her
next phase of expansion.

They chatted for another few minutes, and when it
was time to go, Lisa left with a promise to visit Katie
soon, and an offer for Christina to stay with her when
in Los Angeles. As they drove home, Katie felt
pleased after all. Anna Su was slipping away from the
family, but perhaps Lisa would become closer. Katie
hoped so.

When Max was in town to visit Christina, Katie
was careful not to interfere or to be in his presence,
aware that Sarah disliked her and would sense the
attraction between her and Max. They were sitting in
the living room and Christina had just mentioned
that her father was arriving tomorrow. Katie had
managed to appear casual about the news.

"We'll be having dinner together after they fly in,"
Christina said. "You and Peter are welcome to join
us, Mom."

"Thanks, but no," Katie replied. "I can't. In any
case, I don't think Sarah would appreciate your
including me."

"Sarah's jealous," Christina replied. "Don't pay
any attention to her. She's gotten dumpy while you
have the figure of a sixteen-year-old."

"C'mon, Christina," Katie retorted. "She's the one married to your father, not me. Why should she be jealous of me?"

Christina gave her a long, serious look, and realized that her mother was not entirely conscious of just how attractive she was to men—especially to her father. She had been too busy creating an empire, Christina thought, and wished she could influence her mother to go out more. But she only responded, "Why indeed?"

Peter, who was doing his homework, exchanged a glance with Christina. She knew he felt the same way. Their mother worked too hard. "I can't either," he said. "I have a game. But I'll be seeing Max later."

As he went back to his studies, Christina was thoughtful. Peter, who was in his final year of high school and was already flying the family Cessna solo, looked forward to Max's visits. Although neither Peter nor Christina said much about Peter's growing friendship with Max, both realized it was better left understated, the two men spent time together each time Max was down, often flying. Christina knew that their relationship upset Sarah and that Sarah was jealous of Peter too, but she didn't mention that to her brother. It was good for Peter to have a male influence in his life, and she'd be damned if she'd allow Sarah's pettiness to ruin it.

"I'm flying to Los Angeles for a few days to meet with Lisa," Katie went on, ignoring Christina's last remark. "So if you'd like to have your father and Sarah over for dinner, I won't be in the way."

"I don't think so," Christina said, somehow not liking the thought of Sarah in her mother's house. It didn't seem right. "I'll just meet them for dinner," she added. "But thanks, Mom."

Katie only smiled and went on with the work spread out before her, a portfolio of designs she'd brought home from work so that she could go over them before the meeting tomorrow. Lisa had agreed to endorse her silks for the new campaign, had in fact been delighted that Katie asked her. But when Christina and Peter had gone upstairs, Katie's thoughts reverted to Max, and in seconds old feelings began to surface.

Giving herself a mental shake, Katie forced herself back to the designs; she needed to decide which ones Lisa would model in the ads. She'd become extremely fond of Lisa. They'd managed several visits, and it pleased Katie to see that Christina and Lisa had become close friends too. Lisa, although almost thirty, had never married, and Katie realized that her beautiful niece had an inferiority complex, one that stemmed from childhood. She hid it under a veneer of sophistication so that no one suspected, but Katie knew it was Lisa's motivation to succeed. "My father is an alcoholic," she'd confided to Katie during their last visit. "And my mother is too fearful to face the world alone." She'd hesitated before expressing her deepest worry. "And Ollie lives on the fringe of the criminal world."

Katie stared at the designs and knew they were the best ones yet. She appreciated Lisa's help; it was basically a favor to Katie because Lisa didn't need the money, even though she supported her parents now, and Ollie. Still the little mother, Katie thought, remembering how the child Lisa always took care of the other children.

We are all the product of our past, Katie reflected, and felt the sadness move closer. Again she shook herself out of the mood, and went on with her work.

When Katie returned from Los Angeles she arranged a meeting with Fenton Stone, who was again financing the project. Christina was present when he arrived at nine sharp with a younger man.

"I thought you should finally meet my son, Katie,"

he said proudly. "Jonathan will take over the Stone empire one of these days, and he needs to know his customers."

Jonathan was tall, with sandy hair, blue eyes, and broad shoulders—and he was as charming as he was attractive. Katie noted that her secretary and Christina had their eyes glued on him.

"So you're the lady who pulled me out of the bay," he told Katie, and took her hand. "Would you believe I remember? At least, that a man and a woman both helped rescue me." His tone was low and cultured. "Please accept my belated thanks."

Smiling back, Katie nodded. "I'm so pleased to meet you after all this time. Somehow it seems incredible that you're that little boy."

Christina stepped forward, smiling too. "The man who was with my mother became my father," she said. "I'm Christina Stefanini, Katie's daughter."

His eyes shifted to Christina, and something altered instantly in his gaze as he looked at her. She stood within a pool of sunshine that shone in through the windows, and it gilded her long hair with a golden sheen, reflecting its sparkle in her dark eyes and accentuating the yellow of her dress. Katie thought her daughter had never appeared more beautiful, a perception shared by Jonathan Stone.

By the time the meeting drew to a successful conclusion, it was obvious that Jon—as he'd told Christina to call him—and Christina were attracted to each other. And later it didn't surprise Katie to know they had a date on Saturday night. A week after that, she realized they were falling in love.

"Life has strange twists," she said aloud one night as she stood alone by her window looking out over the shimmering city at her feet. At that very moment, her daughter was out with Jon, and she knew their relationship was serious. Katie sighed as re-

embered words from her childhood surfaced in her
ind—wise words Michiko's father had once said.
"When people cross paths in a dramatic way, they
ill one day understand why when they meet again."

Turning from the window, Katie walked to her
d. The words spoken by a man long dead haunted
r thoughts as she lay in the darkness. Was life
eordained, as the Japanese people believed?

And then her mind shifted once more. She and
lax had met in a dramatic way too. And their lives
d come together. Was it preordained that their
me would be so short? Or did it mean that there
ight be something more for them?

A smile touched her lips, and when she slept, it
as still there in her dreams.

CHAPTER 28

"WELL, THAT'S IT," PETER SAID COMING DOWN THE STE[
with his final suitcase. "All that's left is to get to th
plane on time."

Katie watched him place his jacket and oth
things next to the larger suitcases by the front doo
He looked so grown-up, so much more mature tha
eighteen. Her throat suddenly tightened and tea
stung behind her eyes. David would have been s
proud of his son who was about to leave home for th
first time. Peter had applied at several Easter
universities and had been accepted at all of them, h
academic standing being far higher than average. B
he hadn't chosen Yale or Harvard, deciding again
an ivy league school, and had enrolled in New Yo
University. "I'm not ivy league material," he'd in
formed Katie firmly, and she hadn't argued, as he'

been against going East for several years. She knew
he was only going to please her, but she also knew he
needed the education to get anywhere in life, so
he'd insisted. She'd feared that if he stayed in
California, he'd become sidetracked by his love of
flying and the dream he'd never grown out of—
being a bush pilot in Alaska.

"Let's go then," Christina said as she joined them
in the hall. "Planes don't wait." She gave him a fond
jab to his arm. "I'm going to miss you, Peter."

Impulsively, he hugged her. "And I'll miss you,
Sis." His expression clouded, and before he could
say more, Katie rushed forward and embraced him
too.

"But you'll be home for Thanksgiving," she reminded him softly. "Once you're back there the time
will fly, and you'll be back for a visit before you
know it."

"I guess so, Mom."

Peter picked up his cases and they went out the
front door to Christina's car. But on the way to the
airport, Katie had sudden doubts. *I've done the right
thing*, she told herself. *Peter has to get on with
realistic plans for his future.* She wouldn't allow
herself to think she was influenced by her own fear of
losing him to Alaska too.

As he kissed her goodbye at the airport, Katie had
such a lump in her throat that she could hardly talk.
She would miss him dreadfully.

"Don't work too hard, Mom," he said huskily and
turned to his sister, but not before Katie saw the
sparkle of tears in his eyes. "And don't you go and
marry Jon before I get back," he told Christina,
forcing a laugh so that he could get hold of his
emotions.

"I promise," she said, her eyes overbright. "No
announcements until you're present."

And then he was gone in a last flurry of good-byes.

"C'mon, Mom," Christina said as the plane taxied away from the terminal. "I'll buy you lunch."

Katie nodded mutely and suddenly wished Peter wasn't going. Had she done the right thing? Or had she taken too much responsibility for his future at the expense of his own feelings? She knew he hated to go—and she'd forced him.

"It'll be good for Peter to be so far away," Christina told her a half hour later over lunch. "And who knows, maybe he won't stay more than a year or two. But in any case, it'll make a man out of him so that his future decisions are based on realistic goals."

"Thanks, Christina." Katie smiled. "You knew how I felt."

"Of course." Christina's smile was concerned. "You only want the best for him—and you don't want him running off to Alaska because he's romanticized bush pilots."

Glancing down at her salad, Katie nodded. "Something like that." When she looked up again, Katie changed the subject to a lighter note. "How's Jon these days? Seems like the two of you are always going somewhere together."

The topic brought an instant smile to Christina and as she went off in a description of the play they'd attended the night before, Katie saw that she'd been right—Christina and Jon were in love. She wasn't surprised.

Even though Christina still lived with Katie, her daughter was often away, involved with her voice training or a theatrical production, her work in Katie's company, or outings with Jon. For the first time since her parents died long ago, and she'd come to California, Katie was completely alone, her house empty. She found herself thinking more and more about Max, wondering if increased nostalgia came with age—after the children grew up and left home

Unless she was working, Katie felt at a loss. She wandered around the house late at night, unable to sleep. It didn't help to know that Max was unhappy too. According to Christina, Sarah manipulated Max by claiming bad health, and Max couldn't see it. His company had gained international status and he, like Katie, was able to forget personal happiness so long as he kept his mind on new expansion projects. But there should have been more for both of them, Katie thought each time her thoughts dwelled in the past.

By mid-October, Katie took herself in hand and decided that it was time to get on with her own life, perhaps find an escort to take her to the theater and opera. When the phone rang late one afternoon, interrupting her concentration on the projections for the new spring line, she expected a typical business call. Instead it was long distance—a call from Peter's roommate.

Stunned, Katie listened as the young man asked for Peter, and then informed her, when she expressed surprise, that Peter had dropped out of school the week before and that he'd assumed Peter was back in San Francisco. The roommate left a message for Peter to call him, as Peter had left his camera behind. Then he hung up, seemingly anxious to cut off the conversation once he'd learned that Katie knew nothing about Peter's leaving New York.

For a minute, Katie stared at the phone, unable to credit what she'd heard. Surely it was a joke. Peter wouldn't have just left school, not without telling her. She decided to check. His roommate was probably playing a trick on him, she told herself. Wasn't it common to perpetrate pranks on new freshmen?

But a call to the university proved futile, as the offices had already closed for the day. Calling his room number only gave her the roommate again, and he was suddenly vague, as though he realized he'd already said too much. Katie began to worry,

fighting panic. Guilt suddenly overwhelmed her. Sh
hadn't listened to Peter's wishes about his ow
future. But if he wasn't in New York, then where wa
he? Had he been hurt and she not told? She manage
to get hold of Christina, who was equally surprised
but knew nothing about Peter either. Unable t
finish her work, Katie grabbed her coat and purs
and left the office. If she didn't find him soon, sh
was calling the police.

The phone was ringing as she stepped into th
front hall of her house, and she ran to answer it.

"Hello," she said, and her voice sounded breath
less.

"Is this Katie?" a familiar male voice said abov
the static of the long-distance lines to Alaska. "Thi
is Max."

She dropped into the nearest chair. *Max*—the las
person on earth she expected to hear from at tha
moment!

"Are you there, Katie?"

"Yes," she managed. "You took me by surpris
that's all."

"Peter's here—in Anchorage, Katie." He spok
quickly, as though he didn't want her to interrup
until he was finished. "He's been here a couple o
days. I wanted him to call you to let you know, bu
after Christina phoned a few minutes ago, and
knew how worried you were, I decided to call righ
away. Peter planned to let you know, but he's in tow
at the moment, so I took matters into my ow
hands."

There was a pause. Katie tried to take it all ir
Peter had dropped out of school and flown t
Alaska—and didn't tell her?

"Don't be upset, Katie," Max went on, his ton
lower, soothing. "The boy is confused about a fev
things. He says he just didn't fit into universit
life—that it was all too juvenile for him."

"But why didn't he tell me?" Katie's words shook despite her attempt at control.

Again Max hesitated. "Now don't take this wrong, Katie, but Peter didn't feel you'd understand."

"But—but—" She broke off, realizing that would be Peter's conclusion. Hadn't she been the one who insisted he go away to school, when he hadn't wanted to? "I see," she said finally, feeling awful. She'd lost off her own son because she'd believed she knew best. The thought didn't occur to her to be angry with him. She was only relieved that Peter was safe—that she knew where he was.

"He wants to work with me for a while, Katie. Fly some of the short routes."

"But winter is coming," Katie interrupted, a new fear beginning deep inside her. "Flying in the winter isn't safe in Alaska!"

"I won't let anything happen to him. He's your son, Katie. You know I'll watch out for him." There was another pause. "But he needs time to work out his life, and this is a good place for him to do that."

"What do you mean, Max?"

"He's disturbed about some things, Katie. He has been for a few years." She heard Max take a sharp breath before plunging deeper into the conversation. "He's hurt over being illegitimate and unsure of his own father's feelings toward him, because David never legally claimed him."

"Oh, my God!" Katie cried, the old pain pressing down on her.

"Christ! I'm sorry, Katie. I don't know what happened between you and David—and I know it's none of my damned business, even though I'm interfering now." His voice lowered and she knew the conversation was hard for him. "But the past is gone, and now Peter needs to cope with his insecurities and become a man."

She swallowed against the tightening in her throat,

but the tears rolled down her cheeks uncheck
"What are you suggesting?" she managed finally.

"That he stay up here with me. He loves Alask
and flying and all the challenges that go with both.
he stays, he'll find his direction, and I guarantee he'
become the caliber of man who'll make you proud.

"Has Peter discussed all this with you?"

"Yes, he has," Max replied honestly. "I hope yo
can understand that, Katie. He and I have develope
our own closeness over the years, sort of a man-t
man relationship."

As they discussed the situation for a few mo
minutes, Katie tried not to feel left out. It wa
obvious that Peter would have called and explaine
himself, still would, so she and Max decided to kee
their conversation private. She agreed that Pete
should stay.

"I'll keep you posted," Max said before they hun
up. "And keep your chin up, Katie. Everything'
going to work out fine eventually."

For a long time after the connection was broken
Katie stared into space. Her relief was immense. Bu
she was unsettled too. In his time of crisis, David'
son had gone to Max, the man who should have bee
his father. Although Peter was in good hands now
Katie felt more lonely than ever before. Everyon
had someone. She was alone.

Every week, without fail, Katie heard from Peter
and knowing how poor her son was at writing, Kati
suspected Max's influence. She relived some of he
own experiences in Alaska through the vivid wor
pictures of Peter's letters, and she tried to keep
perspective about his admiration for Max. He wasn'
able to travel south for Christmas, so Christina an
Jon, with Katie present, called Max and Peter t
announce their engagement.

"We plan a May wedding," Christina told the

over the phone. "And I expect you both to be here—you to walk me down the aisle, Dad, and you to be one of the groomsmen, Peter."

They agreed and congratulated both Christina and Jon, and then hung up after Peter and Katie talked. The wedding plans got underway at once, and spring was so busy that Katie wondered if they'd ever manage to have everything done in time. It seemed that the Stone family knew everyone, and invitations went out to all the prominent families in the city, as well as to people as far away as England and France. The guest list read like a Who's Who, and it made Katie a little nervous to even think about it.

But Katie managed to have everything in place by the night of the wedding. The church was a fairyland of spring flowers and lighted candles and soft organ music as she held on to Peter's arm and started down the aisle to her seat. She couldn't help but feel proud. She and Christina had taken care of every detail, and the result was breathtaking.

She'd had a dress made for the occasion, a pale pink oriental brocade with a fitted waist and flared skirt. It rustled against her legs as she walked, and a silver thread in the material was accented by the diamonds she wore and by her elegantly styled blond hair. Brocade pumps and clutch purse matched the dress, and Katie was aware that many eyes watched her progress to the front of the church.

"You're lovely, Mom," Peter told her as she sat down.

"And you're pretty handsome yourself," she whispered back, feeling proud that the straight young man in the black tuxedo was her son.

She hadn't seen Max yet, but farther down the pew she saw Anna Su and her husband, and Lisa with Ollie, who didn't appear pleased. Katie figured Lisa had pressured her brother into coming with her. Neither Johanna nor Dion was there, and Peter had explained earlier that Sarah had stayed in Anchorage too, and that Max was upset that his wife was always sick when special events came up in his life. It was Christina who'd confided to Katie that Sarah was mad that Max had taken Peter in, and was punishing him by not attending his only daughter's wedding. "She's making a huge mistake to play games with Dad," Christina had said coldly. "She'll go too far one of these days and he'll finally see through her."

Now, as the bridesmaids came down the aisle in their pastel blue gowns, flower bouquets in their hands and wreaths in their hair, Katie forgot everything else but that her beloved daughter was about to be married. The music paused, and when the first notes of the wedding march sounded, a hush fell over the church. Then Christina, radiant in her gauzy white gown, its long train trailing behind, came down the aisle on her father's arm. For a second, Katie's breath stopped in her throat. She'd never seen Max look so distinguished, so handsome, and so tall and lean and fit in his black tuxedo. Seconds later, he'd seen Christina to the front and given her away, then taken the seat next to Katie.

For a long moment their eyes met, admiring black eyes and suddenly hesitant green ones. Wordlessly he took her hand, and then he held it for the whole ceremony. When Christina and Jon were pronounced man and wife, Max's pressure on her fingers increased just enough to communicate a silent message of mutual love for their daughter.

"You're very beautiful, Katie," he whispered later, as they stood next to the bride and groom in the receiving line. "As lovely as when we first met."

His words brought back the memories, and he saw them reflected in her brilliant eyes just before her lashes swept down to screen her thoughts. She was so desirable that for a moment it was hard to believe she wasn't still his, especially in the surroundings of their daughter's wedding. Life had never been fair when it came to their relationship, he thought with a flash of the old pain. He no longer even knew how she felt about him. She was so successful and sophisticated, and yet he suspected that she was still the old headlong Katie.

"You're looking well, too, Max," she replied, so carefully in control that she was suddenly unreadable to him, the perfect mother of the bride who just happened to be married to him long ago. The inscrutable Oriental, he thought with more than a touch of wryness.

But still it was a wonderfully successful day for both of them, each a little uncertain, but completely aware of the other. Neither guessed that they shared the same feelings of vulnerability, because their daughter's marriage had added a dimension to the love that lay unspoken between them. The last thing on Katie's mind was Sarah. Somehow, Christina's wedding day was a time apart, a few magic hours that belonged to only Max and her.

"I had to leave New York, Mom."

It was the day after the wedding, Christina and Jon were on their way to Hawaii for a honeymoon, and Katie and Peter had just finished lunch. Katie was glad for the chance to talk with him alone, as he was going to a party later and spending the night with old school friends, and tomorrow he and Max would return to Alaska. Max had called earlier and invited her out for dinner, "To celebrate Christina's happiness," he'd told her, and brushed aside her excuses. As if I could have refused, she thought, as she waited for Peter to continue.

"School wasn't for me—the kids were into drinking and partying and having a good time. Not that they didn't study too, but they seemed so immature somehow. I just didn't fit in."

"Why didn't you phone me—about your feelings?" Katie said quietly. "We could have talked about it."

Instead of being defensive as he might have been a year ago, Peter only smiled with a tolerance she'd never seen in him before. He covered her hand with his, and she couldn't help but notice how much larger it was than hers, and how much rougher. They were strong hands—hands that knew how to work. A boy's hands no longer, she thought, and felt a surge of pride.

"I'm sorry about that, Mom. And I apologize for scaring you. I understand you had a few bad hours until you knew I was safe." He grinned, but his dark eyes—expressive eyes that still belonged to the little boy Peter—were serious. "I love you. You're the best mother a boy could ever have, and I'll never hurt you again. Cross my heart," he added, and then laughed self-consciously, his candid words still a little unfamilar to the Peter who'd been fearful to express his innermost feelings.

"And I love you," Katie said softly. "And I'm sorry too—for being so unbending, so sure my way was right." She hesitated. "I believed I knew best for your future. I guess I was trying to make sure you were happy, and then I made you unhappy."

He leaned over and kissed her cheek. "I understand now. Max and I have talked a lot. He explained how parents can be overprotective—he said he was like that with Christina."

At the mention of Max, Katie busied herself by pouring more coffee. After a moment she went on. "So what are your plans?" she asked. "Will you be coming back to California?"

His eyes didn't waver, and when he replied, she

knew he spoke truthfully. "I don't know. I'm enjoying my life so much up there that I'll be staying on
for a while anyway."

The conversation drifted into other aspects of
Alaska, and as Katie listened to his opinion of how
the North Slope oil was about to make the state
boom, why the fishing industry was the best in the
world, and how airplanes were still the main mode of
travel, she realized again how fast he'd matured.
Max was a good influence.

She sat on at the table, sipping her coffee, as he
went upstairs to shower. After he'd gone to meet his
friends, Katie went upstairs herself, suddenly aware
of how the time was flying. If she didn't hurry, Max
would arrive before she was ready.

But the very thought gave her another pause.
Memories of other times, when she'd hurried to get
ready for a date with Max, swirled in her mind. For
all the years between, somehow she felt the same as
she had then—eager, nervous, and all fluttery inside.

"Silly—silly!" she chided herself as she stepped
into a scented tub of water.

The evening was perfect. Max, impeccably dressed
in a dark suit, picked her up in a rented Cadillac and
drove them across the Golden Gate Bridge to
Sausalito, where he'd made reservations at a bayside
restaurant. The moon rose into the sky as they ate
the catch of the day, and then had after-dinner
drinks with coffee. The lights of San Francisco
sparkled across the bay, reflecting with the moon-
light on the surface of water. Katie couldn't remember having a more pleasant dinner with a man.

She'd chosen a simple black sheath of raw silk,
sleeveless but with enough plunge to the neckline to
give it a stylish flare. She wore emerald earrings and

a bracelet, and her shoes and purse were dyed green snakeskin, giving the outfit a dramatic touch, one that hadn't gone unnoticed by Max.

They'd been talking about the early years in Alaska, and inadvertently they touched on Max's crash, when he'd been presumed dead, only to turn up several years later in San Francisco. A sudden silence dropped between them, and Katie was aware of their surroundings for the first time—soft piano music, hushed conversation, and the occasional laugh from a nearby table.

"I always wondered if my turning up like that was the reason your marriage went bad." Max spoke in a soft drawl, but an inflection in his tone suggested that his remark was one he'd pondered over the years.

Her gaze flew to his, and a faint flush stained her cheeks. "You knew? That David—"

He held up a hand, silencing her. "Not until much later. After I was married," he added dryly. "Christina said something—oh, innocently enough—that caused me to wonder. And then there was all that trouble about Peter—the legal battle—because you and David never remarried."

Her lashes fluttered as she glanced down. "It wasn't your coming back that did it," she began and hesitated. "David understood after the first shock. It was because—because of the result of your coming back into my life."

"I don't understand."

She met his eyes, and then said the thing no one other than David had ever known. "I was pregnant, and had a miscarriage. That's when David discovered I was further along than I could have been if he were the father."

Not a muscle twitched on Max's face as he took in what she'd said. He sat frozen, her words dropping another sorrow into his store of sorrows. "The baby was mine?" His question was hardly above a whisper.

She only nodded and glanced away.

"Oh, Christ! Oh my God, Katie! Why didn't you tell me? I wouldn't have let you face that alone."

"There was Peter to consider. Oh, Max, I wanted to make everything right somehow. And I was never able to—not ever."

The tragedy of it all was suddenly in her eyes, and he was jolted by the depth of what her suffering must have been. All those years—he wasn't the only one who'd suffered. Why hadn't he guessed? He wanted to hold her now and make such passionate love to her that all the sad memories would be banished forever; he wanted to kiss away the tears he saw glistening on her long lashes. If only he could turn back time. Oh, God! Their lost child—and all the wasted years without her beside him! He didn't know if he could bear it. The loss was too great.

"Max—I'm sorry." The sudden devastation Katie saw on his face scared her. She reached across the table and covered his hands with hers—the same hands that had once touched her so intimately, that had set her whole body on fire for him. "I shouldn't have told you. It's—it's all so long ago."

"No, Katie. You did right to tell me. I just wish to God you'd told me then." *Before I was married to a woman I can never divorce,* he thought suddenly. Sarah wasn't well and sometimes spent days in bed with blinding headaches. She had no relatives and few friends, and without him she'd have no one. He didn't love her, but he couldn't hurt her either, as he'd been hurt.

She shook her head sadly, resigned. "No, Max. It would only have made matters worse then. There was David and Peter, even Christina." She hesitated. "I didn't know how things would go. I've wondered many times since if I let things slide too long with

David because I felt guilty about my feelings for you." She glanced away. "I'll never know now, and in any case, I can't change the past."

The finality of her words shook him, because it was true. He couldn't change the past either, and it affected the future. She'd stayed with David, and he must stay with Sarah.

"Let's get out of here," he said, abruptly getting up. The waiter was immediately at his elbow with their check. Max dropped a hundred-dollar bill onto the tray, helped Katie into her coat, and led her out to the car.

Once they were on the road, he turned on the radio, so that soft music filled the swelling silence between them. There was nothing left to say—except things that were taboo now. He pulled into her driveway a few minutes later, then walked her to the door. The porchlight reflected a sheen onto his head, and placed tiny pinpoints of light in his eyes. He stood undecided, looking down at her. The garden surrounding the house was shadowy and quiet, but far away on the bay a ship's horn sounded, a plaintive note that pierced them both with all that might have been . . . should have been.

He kissed her then, a loving kiss, as gentle as it was sad. He lifted his head as her eyes opened to his. He would have gone, had meant to, but he couldn't bear to let the moment pass so quickly. It might be all he ever had of her. So he kissed her again, and this time her arms embraced him too, tentatively, ever so lightly.

"Goodbye, my Katie," he whispered against her lips, his voice breaking.

Then, with resolve, Max set her aside, took the key from her hand and unlocked the door. With a final salute, he turned and strode from the porch.

Katie didn't watch him go, couldn't. She stood mutely, her need for him greater than she remembered. Fragments of old memories soared free to tantalize her and remind her of the ecstasy she'd known when Max had made love to her. She listened to his footsteps recede, walk to his car, where they paused. She couldn't watch him go—and couldn't beg him to stay. He belonged to Sarah, not her.

It took several seconds more for Katie to realize that the sound of his footsteps had changed. They were returning, fast—as though he feared he'd hesitated too long, and the door would be closed on him—forever.

Wordlessly, he pulled her into his arms. Then he pushed open the door and locked it behind them.

"I'm staying the night," he whispered against her lips. "Oh, my darling Katie, I can't let you go, not yet."

"Yes—oh, dear God, yes," she managed before his mouth closed over hers.

And this time his kiss demanded, was savage in its hunger for her, ruthless to reclaim all the nights he'd been denied. As she was all the times before, Katie was lost—because she wanted to be possessed by him. He was her man; she was his woman. Nothing and no one on earth could ever change that.

CHAPTER 29

EACH TIME MAX CAME FROM ALASKA DURING THE NEXT couple of years, he came without Sarah. And during each visit he and Katie managed to spend time together, although the intimacy of their relationship was kept a secret from the family.

"I've told Sarah that I want my freedom," Max told Katie. "But she's not well. She still has those damned headaches. She's not like you, Katie, able to take care of herself. She's crippled, in a sense. If I left her, she'd have no one, and I'd be responsible if her health worsened."

That conversation always annoyed Katie, even though she realized that Max was sensitive to hurting someone who loved him—especially since he'd been hurt so badly in the past. He couldn't see that

Sarah was motivated by her own needs and position, not by love. Why was it that the strong people always had to be strong, while the weak ones got away with a tyranny that ruined lives? Katie asked herself many times. Sarah made sure that Max wouldn't leave her so she'd never have to accept responsibility for her own happiness. Katie didn't doubt that Sarah suffered from headaches; the woman was neurotic. But the headaches corresponded with getting her own way. The situation frustrated Katie completely.

But again Katie allowed the situation to drift, because she felt she had no other option anyway. Her thriving company kept her busy, and after Christina delivered her first child, a boy they named Robert Massimiliano Stone, Katie spent as much time as possible with her little grandson.

"I suppose I'm not the typical grandmother," she said one evening when she'd managed to get home from the office in time to have dinner with Christina and Jon and the baby.

"And I'm not the typical mother in some ways," Christina replied with a laugh. "I'm still involved with the opera, and I didn't even have my first child until I was thirty-two."

"And our son will benefit because his mother and grandmother aren't typical," Jon added, and Katie smiled fondly at him. She loved her son-in-law, perhaps in part because he understood that her business responsibilities didn't preclude her loving a grandchild—even if she didn't babysit.

By the time little Robert was a year old, the family was hit by another scandal. Ollie was arrested for armed robbery. His trial was held in San Francisco, and although Johanna came from Alaska to attend it, the family connection to Lisa went unnoticed by the media until right after his conviction and sentence to prison. The story was suddenly splashed on the front

pages of tabloids all over the country when it became
known that Ollie was Lisa's brother. From that point
on, there was no stopping the press.

"My God! Look what they're saying now!" Lisa
cried, glancing up from the morning newspaper. "'It
has been learned,'" she read aloud to Katie and
Johanna, who sat with her at the breakfast table in
Katie's kitchen, "'that Ollie Stefanini's grandfather,
an Italian immigrant to this country before World
War I, was also involved in criminal acts, and was
killed by gangsters shortly before the Great Depression. Sources hint that the Stefanini family could
have ties to a crime syndicate.'"

"This is terrible!" Johanna cried, her lined, thin
face sticken.

"We'll demand a retraction," Katie said, trying to
remain calm. But she knew the implications could be
far-reaching, and she wondered how the accusation
would affect Christina and Lisa and the rest of the
family.

"Damn right we will!" Lisa cried, and then she too
tried to control her anger, for the sake of her mother.
"We can't let Dad find out," she told Johanna. "He's
too sick to worry about this too."

As Johanna nodded mutely, Katie tried to think of
a way to handle the situation. Lisa was right that
Dion shouldn't know; he was suffering from the
long-term effects of alcoholism and was in bad
shape. But Max should be told, she decided, and
went to call him. As she dialed, Katie couldn't help
but reflect on the course of fate. Ollie's troubles had
brought both Johanna and Lisa to her house for the
duration of the trial, and despite the worry of it, she
and Johanna had managed to clear away some of the
old grudges and stumbling blocks to a positive
relationship between them. And now this! she
thought angrily as she waited for Max to pick up his
phone in Anchorage.

When he answered, Katie quickly told him the gist of what had happened. He listened until she'd finished. When he spoke, his voice was more angry than Katie had ever heard it. The newspaper had touched on the one thing that had bedeviled Max since he was a boy—his shame over what his father had done.

"I'm flying down at once," he told her. "The bastards'll retract the story—or prove it! It looks like I'll have to threaten them with a libel suit, and carry it out if they don't back down."

"I agree," Katie replied softly, hurting for him. "And I'm sorry, Max. Why they'd want to dredge up something like this is beyond me."

His sigh came across the wires. "To sell papers, Katie. Because Ollie is Lisa's brother, and people relish reading about a celebrity with a skeleton in the closet. I just hope to hell that the notoriety doesn't damage her career."

"Surely it wouldn't!"

"Time will tell." His voice lowered as he changed the subject. "I look forward to seeing you, Katie. I'll let you know my arrival time." He paused, as though he made sure no one heard him. "I love you, Sweetheart."

As she hung up, his last words ringing in her ear, Katie was heartened. But not enough to believe the current scandal would right itself very soon.

It took several weeks before the newspapers printed a retraction, and that came only after Max had seen a lawyer to draw up papers for a lawsuit. But by that time the damage was done. Even Dion had read about it in one of the Anchorage newspapers, and once Johanna was back in Alaska, she wrote that he'd been so upset he had a setback, which meant he'd gone on a drinking binge.

"It was irresponsible reporting," Max told Katie privately. "They couldn't back up their innuendoes

with fact, so they had no recourse but to retract—
thank God!"

A feeling of anticlimax settled over Katie after the
whole issue died down and they all went back to
their own lives. Yet, for all the worry over the
scandal and heartbreak for Johanna and Lisa, the
family had pulled together, and by the time Johanna
left San Francisco, Katie knew she'd finally gained a
sister.

She was pleased one afternoon when Lisa called
her at work to say she was in town and would like to
have dinner with Katie. They met at the Top of the
Mark, and Katie saw at once that something was
bothering Lisa. But it was after they'd ordered their
food and were sipping wine that she finally blurted
out her concern.

"My television contract isn't being renewed for
next season," she said, and the look in her large dark
eyes told Katie she was very upset.

"Good Lord! Why on earth not?" Katie retorted.
"I thought your series was extremely popular."

Lisa inclined her head, and her long hair shimmered under the subdued lighting, a black cloud that
framed her delicate face. "They say it's the ratings.
It's their excuse for letting me go." She gave a sharp
laugh. "Oh the series is to go on—but my character
is being written out."

Katie didn't know what to say. She'd heard about
the ruthlessness of show business, and she suspected
that she was seeing a first-hand example of it now.

"Can you do anything to stop it?"

"My agent says not." Her lashes lowered as she
took a sip of her wine. "He says my career has been
affected by the notoriety and that I just have to wait
it out and hope that I have another chance for a good
role."

"You mean—you'll be out of work? But you're so
popular, so—"

"The viewing public is fickle," Lisa said, interrupting. "And unexpectedly moral. They don't like the thought of criminal connections, especially if you're Italian."

"But that's ridiculous!"

Lisa's brows shot up. "I know, and perhaps it isn't so, even if that's what my agent thinks." She hesitated, and then added drily, "Time will tell, so long as I don't have to wait years and go bankrupt."

"You can always work for me," Katie said at once. "I could use you, Lisa—and I'd pay you well. Until your own career opened up again, of course," she added, not wanting Lisa to think she was taking advantage of the situation.

"Oh, Aunt Katie, I love you. You're always there for everyone." She smiled, just a little wistfully. "I wish we'd all been closer over the years."

Katie patted her hand. "But we are now, Lisa. And that's all that matters."

"Thanks." Lisa brightened suddenly. "And I may just take you up on your job offer. I'm a good worker, you know, if I do say so."

"I know, dear. And I hope you do call. You'd be a great asset to me. You'd be doing me a favor."

The conversation turned to other things then, but Katie saw relief settle over Lisa. She suddenly knew that her niece, for all of her celebrity status, was a lonely woman, with no one to fall back on in a pinch. Somehow none of Lisa's romantic attachments had lasted, and she'd once mentioned that she attracted the wrong type of man—lightweights who were drawn to her cover-girl image but were intimidated by her brain. "I think I emasculated them," she'd told Katie. "Anyway, that's what my shrink told me," she'd added with a wry, almost puzzled laugh.

Now, as Katie realized that Lisa's career was her whole life—her whole sense of worth—Katie vowed that Lisa would never be without moral support

again, not as long as she was around. Loneliness wa
hell. Katie knew how it felt.

Johanna met the plane and took them right to th
hospital. The day after Katie and Lisa had dinne
Johanna had called with the news that Dion was i
the hospital—the same one where Christina an
Lisa had been born. Lisa and Katie had flown nort
on the next plane.

Being at Providence brought back memories t
Katie, and as she walked along the quiet hall wit
her sister and niece, her thoughts went back to th
time of her daughter's birth, when Max had bee
grounded in Nome. For one reason or other, she ha
always been alone for all the major events of her lif
Was that her *karma?* she wondered.

Johanna hesitated when they reached Dion's doc
and faced them, her face pale and ravaged by he
fears for Dion. "I told you he's had a severe hear
attack—that his liver and kidneys are damaged, an
that he's all connected up to tubes and wires." Tear
welled in her eyes and she brushed them away, tryin
to get hold of herself. "I just wanted to warn you"—
Her voice broke off as she grabbed Lisa's hand—
"Don't be too shocked, or he'll know he's going—

She wasn't able to say the final words, but Kati
knew Johanna had meant *going to die.* A momer
later they entered the room, and even with Johanna'
warning, Katie was shocked. She didn't recogniz
the frail, yellowish man in the bed as the Dion of th
early years. A deep sadness pierced her as he recog
nized her and spoke her name.

"Katie," he said, so faint the word was hardl
more than a rustle of dry leaves. He indicated tha
she should come closer.

He mouthed something, but none of them unde
stood what he was trying to say. She leaned forward

uddenly concerned that he was trying so hard to alk.

"Don't talk," Johanna soothed, trying to calm iim. "It can wait until you're stronger—we'll still be iere."

Lisa bent and kissed his cheek, so sunken and ined. "Mother's right, Daddy. Just rest for now."

But Dion wouldn't be pacified. He seemed even nore determined. "So sorry, Katie," he managed, 'About—war—"

Abruptly his eyes closed; spent from his effort, he vas unable to go on with what he was trying to say. Then the doctor came in and, in a whispered tone, uggested that the visit was over. The women went iut to the hall again, and Katie wondered what Dion iad been about to say—that he was sorry for what ie'd done after the war, taking Max's company?

A few minutes later, in the hospital cafeteria, iohanna brought up the incident again, her own hame of that time reflected on her face. "Dion was rying to apologize, Katie—that's what Max and I lecided, because he keeps trying to tell Max the ame thing when he's here."

"I know," Katie replied gently. "Please reassure iim that I've forgotten—and forgiven—all of that ong since."

Johanna did something unexpected then; she got ip and came round the table to hug Katie. "You're a ietter sister than I deserve," she whispered. "I love ou, Katie. I always have." And then she went back o Dion's room, leaving both Katie and Lisa in tears.

That night Dion died, and Katie stayed in Anchor- ige for the funeral. She saw Max, but there was no :hance for them to be alone. Sarah managed to ittend the service with him, clinging to his arm.

"She's really convinced Dad that she'll die next— f he leaves her." Christina, who'd flown in for the

funeral, spoke with disgust, and the words wer'
meant only for Katie's ears. "But I predict that he'
about had it. There's no reason for him to stay witl
that ungrateful woman. He can afford to settl
enough money on her so she can hire a whole staff t
take care of her—and listen to her whining."

"I agree," Katie said firmly, much to her daugh
ter's surprise—and delight. It no longer seeme
necessary to conceal her feelings for Max from he
daughter. She suspected that Christina had guesse
anyway.

The day after the funeral, Max drove Katie an
Christina to the airport and kissed them both good
bye.

"You know something, Mom?" Christina sai
seriously as they were boarding the plane.

"What's that, dear?" Katie said absently, he
mind still on Max's whispered words in her ear. *I'
be down soon, sweetheart.*

"Dad sure kisses you differently than he kisse
me." And with a perky grin, Christina went ahead t
find her seat.

Once the legalities were taken care of, Johann
sold her house in Anchorage and moved to Sa
Francisco, into a mansion Lisa bought not far from
Katie. Still unable to get her career going, Lisa sol
her own house in Los Angeles and moved in with he
mother, then took a position working for Katie i
the advertising end of the business.

"Amazing," Johanna told Katie one evening as th
three of them had dinner. "The only thing I mis
about Anchorage is visiting Dion's grave—and m
involvement in the Historical Society."

"You can get involved in the Historical Societ'
here," Katie told her. "They're always looking fo
volunteers."

A week later, after Katie had made a few calls

ohanna went to her first meeting. Katie only smiled
and nodded as her sister talked eagerly about the
various city projects that needed people like her.
Katie felt a security she hadn't felt in years—a
family around her.

A week later, the news that Eastern Imports was
consolidating with an American conglomorate was
the topic of conversation in business circles. Even
the *Wall Street Journal* ran coverage of the deal.
Anna Su now headed one of the largest import firms
in the world. It wasn't long before Katie realized the
impact on her own business. Her prices were being
undercut by the elaborate promotion schemes of
Eastern Imports. Katie was at a loss. Accounts she'd
believed solid suddenly went to the other company.
She knew her business was in trouble unless she
came up with a creative scheme herself, one that
would allow her to continue competing in a business
world that was becoming more ruthless each year.
She agonized over the situation, and she and Lisa
discussed their possibilities for hours, coming up
with new options as the old ones proved ineffectual.
Finally Katie called Anna Su.

"Surely our company policy can't affect yours so
drastically," was Anna Su's reply when Katie suggested that prices should be fixed in some areas, and
that quality and style should be the point of competition, not price wars.

"I'd like to have a meeting with you," Katie
suggested, "and outline some of my suggestions."

"I'm afraid I'm too busy for a while," Anna Su
hedged, and Katie saw that there was no use in
pushing her.

After they'd hung up, Katie felt a sense of loss,
more for Anna Su than her lost contracts. They'd
grown so far apart because "business was business"
and nothing else seemed to count. Katie wondered
how it had really happened. But she knew. Tak.

That same day, Jon dropped in to see her, a thing
he'd never done before during work hours unless h
had an appointment associated with business. H
interrupted a meeting she was having with Lisa
concerning new advertising possibilities.

"Katie, I'll come to the point," he told her, after
she'd indicated that it was fine for him to speak in
front of Lisa. "I know what's been happening to your
contracts since the Eastern Imports merger. So that
presents me with two concerns. The first is for you
Christina's mother. The second is for our financial
investment in your business. We need to make sure
your company doesn't lose so much ground that it'
bankrupt."

"We were just discussing the possibility of more
glamour in our concept for reasonably priced prod
ucts," Katie began, wondering what Jon really had in
mind. "Lisa thinks she can induce some of her
friends—top models and television stars—to en
dorse our lines. In other words, use women who are
the epitome of American beauty and glamour t
influence potential customers to choose our clothing
because it's in vogue to do so."

Jon glanced at Lisa. "Do you think you can do it?

"I believe so. So long as we have enough financia
backing." She glanced at Katie. "I had another ide
as well, but I hesitated to mention it."

"Go ahead, Lisa. I'm up for anything at thi
point."

"Well, I've made a lot of money in the past an
have some to invest. I'd be willing to place it in thi
company—if you'd be willing to have me as
partner. However, it wouldn't be enough for th
broader base we need to compete in the market
place."

"We'll back the rest," Jon offered. "I like this ide
and I think it could work. If your sales volume goe

up, you'll be able to compete with Eastern Imports, Katie."

All of a sudden there was new energy in the room. By the time the meeting was over, Katie had agreed to the terms of Jon's financial offer and had taken Lisa on as a full partner in the company, retaining a controlling interest for herself.

And she didn't regret her decision. Lisa, with her dark beauty and cover girl image—and her surprisingly good business sense—proved a great asset to Katie in their new approach. Within a few months their ads could be found everywhere, and within a year their profits were better than ever before.

There was hardly time to think about what the future held for her concerning Max; she just enjoyed his frequent visits. But gradually she came to the place where she wanted to pin him down. He needed to decide if he really loved her.

Even Peter hinted that Max was up to something in his personal life when he came for an unexpected visit. He'd flown down on business for Max and surprised Katie. One look at him told Katie that he had something on his mind, and knowing Peter, she knew she'd hear what it was in due course.

"I'll be coming into the Feldmen trust soon," he told Katie after supper when they sat talking over coffee. "And I've made a decision on my plans for that money. I wanted to tell you, Mom, before I tell anyone else."

She gave a nod. "I appreciate that, Peter," she said, and waited, knowing it meant his staying in Alaska. But his next words took her by surprise.

"I'm buying into Max's company. He and I have already worked things out. We both think it's a great idea."

Katie's mouth dropped open. Somehow Peter and

Max being partners had never occurred to her. Bu
as she listened to him outline the proposed plan, she
saw even more maturity in Peter—and she saw the
feasibility of his decision. It would benefit Peter, and
it would benefit Max, who had no one to carry on his
empire.

"I intend to stay in Alaska," Peter said softly.

"I know," Katie replied, and smiled lovingly. She
wasn't surprised. Alaska had become his roots. And
Max had become the father he never really had.

Adding to this latest turn of events, Max arrived
the following day, and Katie realized later that Peter
had known all along that Max was flying south—and
why.

"I've filed for divorce," Max told Katie after he'd
gotten her alone. "You don't need to know the
details, but I've worked them all out."

"Sounds like it!" she cried. "You and Peter have
been busy!"

He grinned, his lean face relaxing so that he looked
years younger—like the Max she'd first seen that day
in the park, his dark eyes a little mysterious, but
definitely interested in her.

"Dion's death was the final jolt. I realized life was
too short to tolerate Sarah, who only wanted to
control me for her own selfish needs. I intend to
enjoy the rest of my own life." He laughed. "And
now I can even look forward to retirement."

"Oh Max," she whispered, hardly daring to think
what it all meant for her. He'd finally seen the light
concerning Sarah.

"Will you marry me, sweetheart? Just one more
time?"

She swallowed hard, her throat so tight she
couldn't speak for a moment.

His eyes clouded, ever so slightly, and she saw that
he misread her hesitation.

"You have to marry me, Katie," he said, his tone

edged now with a fear that she was about to refuse. "Because I love you—more than anything in the world. I always have and I always will—forever."

Her eyes brimmed. How she'd waited to hear those words! All Katie could think of was being in his arms again, Max holding her, making love to her. Somehow she was so lost in her feelings that she forgot to let him in on them.

"And if you're my wife, then Peter is my son, and that makes it even more important that he take over my company." He pulled her roughly into his arms. "I won't let you say no. *I can't!*"

"Yes!—yes!—yes!" she cried. "Oh, God! Don't say anymore. Just hold me, Max! Make love to me!"

For only a second he hesitated. Then, with a low growl, he was kissing her, again and again, until their passion consumed them. Then, as he would have done when he was the romantic bush pilot, he swooped her up in his arms and strode up the steps to her bedroom.

The door closed soundly behind them—and didn't open again until the next morning.

CHAPTER 30

THE SUMMER PASSED TOO QUICKLY. NOW THAT KATIE
had Max again, she wanted to hold back time, to
savor each hour she was with him. As Peter took
more responsibility in Anchorage, Max was able to
spend longer periods in San Francisco. It was during
one of his visits, over the Labor Day holiday, that
they discussed marriage plans.

"My divorce should be final soon," Max told her.
"And then we're getting married immediately."

A note of authority had crept into his voice, and
Katie hid an urge to grin. He looked so handsome in
his black turtleneck sweater and casual pants, so
virile and determined at that moment. They'd just
finished breakfast and were about to drive up the
coast to a favorite place on the ocean for a picnic.

The food was packed in a basket, and all she needed was her straw hat and a sweater to put over her slacks and blouse. She popped a kiss on his cheek as she went to get her things, but he grabbed her and gave her a real kiss on the mouth.

"Couldn't resist," he told her, his dark eyes hinting of sexual arousal as he lifted his face. "I can't get enough of you, sweetheart, now that I have you within reach."

Before Katie could do more than smile, the front doorbell rang, startling them both. Eyebrows raised in a question, Katie extracted herself from his arms and went through the house to the hall and opened the door.

"So sorry, Katie, to disturb your holiday," Isami Kono said, and bowed slightly. "But there is a family emergency, and I've come for your help."

For a second Katie could only gape, so surprised to see him that she didn't take in his words at first. When they registered, a ripple of alarm touched her with a chill.

"Come in, Isami," she said, and as he stepped inside, she went on quickly, "What's happened? Is Anna Su all right?"

His expression, usually so inscrutable, revealed deep concern. He shook his head. "Anna Su is in the hospital. She's had a miscarriage—her third." His voice faltered, the first time Katie had ever seen him lose his composure. "Ann Su hemorrhaged and needed blood transfusions. Now she needs more and the hospital is having difficulty finding donors. And you—"

"I understand," Katie said at once, interrupting. She knew what he'd started to say—she and Anna Su shared the same rare blood type. "Tell me where to go, Isami. I'll leave right now."

As he gave the instructions, he looked so old and

frail—and relieved—that Katie felt like huggin
him. But she resisted, remembering the propprietie

Max, who'd come into the hall behind her, wa
introduced to Isami, and then he drove Katie to th
hospital where she gave her blood. He watche
thoughtfully, and when they were out in, the ha
once more, he dropped his arm around her as the
walked to the waiting room to await word on Ann
Su.

"This is the problem that caused the miscarriag
of our child, isn't it?" he asked softly, his eyes fille
with compassion.

She nodded and glanced away. Before she coul
speak, Tak suddenly appeared in the doorway. H
hesitated when he saw them, then stepped forwar
his hand outstretched to Max.

"We've never met," he said with typical reserv
"although I've heard about you over the years—fir
from my sister Michiko, then from Anna Su."

"And I've heard about you," Max replied, his ton
equally cool. "We almost met once—in Alaska."

They sized each other up as Katie made th
introduction, then watched with interest as the tw
men shook hands. Tak was almost as tall as Max, an
although they were from different cultures, bot
were dominant men, both single-minded once they'
decided on a course of action. Katie was momentar
ly struck by a random thought. She'd always know
that David reminded her of Max, and for the fir
time, she saw the similarity between Tak and Ma
The realization startled her; she'd chosen the sam
type of man all three times.

"Thank you, Katie," Tak said, his gaze havin
shifted to her, and she saw his fear for Anna S
reflected in his eyes. "Anna Su almost died th
time." He shook his head, as if he were trying t
block the whole episode from his mind. "If she'd ha

a shot of RhoGAM before her first pregnancy, none of the miscarriages would have happened. Now she's thirty-eight, and will never have a child of her own."

"I know," Katie said softly, and didn't mention that the drug wasn't available back when she could have benefited from it. "May I see her?" she asked, unable to keep the sad note from her voice.

"So sorry," Tak replied. "She's asleep, and the doctor won't permit her being disturbed. Only her husband is allowed at her bedside."

"I understand, Tak," she replied quietly, remembering how weak she'd felt when she'd lost her baby. "I'll visit later, after she's home."

He nodded and gave a slight bow. And then he watched them all the way down the hall until they'd disappeared through the wide swinging front doors. When he finally turned away, Tak was inscrutable once more.

Outside, as Max held the door for Katie, his eyes were warm with love. He bent and kissed her gently, then held her close for several seconds.

"You've always risen to the occasion, haven't you my darling?" he murmured into her hair. "Always the fearless Katie when it comes to your loved ones."

Then he tilted her face so that their eyes met. "I love you, Katie. *I love you.*"

A moment later he helped her into the car. But as he started the engine he glanced at her once more.

"Tak's quite a guy." His tone had altered ever so slightly. "It's obvious that he's the caliber of man to command an international empire." Max didn't add that it was clear that Tak was in love with Katie, probably always had been. It wasn't necessary to say it because it was also clear that Katie wasn't in love with Tak. Whatever their feelings had been long ago, he knew they'd never been consummated.

"Yes, he is," she replied thoughtfully, then turned

to Max as he drove out into the traffic. "But he's not Max Stefanini. I love you, Max."

So she'd known his thoughts after all, Max thought. His only reply was a quirky grin. And a soft "touché."

A week later, Katie had a note from Anna Su, inviting her for tea on the following Sunday. Katie sent back her acceptance, and then went alone, as Max had flown back to Alaska for a final meeting with his lawyer.

"Please come in, Aunt Katie," Anna Su said, with an innate dignity that reminded Katie of Michiko and brought the threat of tears to her eyes.

She'd been ushered into the living room by Anna Su's husband, a somber but kindly man, and sat down on the sofa next to her niece. They still lived in Edward's house, but now the former opulence had been replaced by an understated elegance—in the Japanese tradition, Katie thought in passing. Tak and his wife were also present, although Katie doubted that the woman understood much English, as she only smiled and nodded and fluttered around them pouring the tea.

"I want to thank you for giving blood," Anna Su began, and then hesitated, her lashes blinking nervously. She seemed to be forming her words mentally before she spoke them, as though she had more on her mind than a blood transfusion.

Katie was reminded of the little girl who'd struggled to express her deepest feelings, fearing rejection. She reached to pat Anna Su on the knee, as she'd often done in the past to reassure her. Their eyes met; Katie smiled and was relieved to see her niece's delicate features relax, her lips curve into a return smile.

"I also want to apologize, Aunt Katie," she began

a rush of words. "After all you've always done for
me—been the mother I never had—I haven't been a
good daughter these last few years."

Her words took Katie aback. Although what Anna
Su said was true, and she'd felt great sadness over
their estrangement, Katie hadn't expected her to
ever say so. Before she could reply, Anna Su went on
quickly.

"Losing this last baby was an awful experience,
more awful than the others even." Anna Su hesitated. She knew Katie had once lost a baby and
understood the sense of loss that went with a miscarriage. But she wouldn't mention that now, because
Katie had never really admitted what had happened.
Anna Su had never confided to anyone her belief that
Max might have been the father, and that was the
reason David hadn't remarried Katie.

So Anna Su went on, keeping the conversation to
her need to make things right with her Aunt Katie.
"Perhaps because my hope of ever having my own
child is gone, I'm now turning that hope into adopt-
ing children. I've realized that I'm capable of loving
a child who's not mine. I can do what you did for me,
Aunt Katie."

Katie's cup tinkled against its saucer as she put it
down. But sensing the hurt and struggle behind
Anna Su's words, she kept silent and allowed her
niece to continue at her own pace.

"And I suddenly had a new realization of all that
you've done for me, Aunt Katie—all that you gave
up for me, the price you paid because you loved me
unconditionally—as much as your own children."

Her voice broke, and Katie couldn't have spoken
at that moment if her life depended on it. Her own
throat had constricted, and her eyes blurred with
tears.

"And I took it all for granted, too preoccupied

with my own feelings of never having my own re
mother and father. And then, after all this time, yc
still came to help me . . . because you love me.''

The tears rolled unchecked down Katie's cheel
then; she couldn't stop them. She'd just been give
back her beloved Michiko's little girl—the chil
she'd always loved as her own. All the sorrows of th
past fell away; Katie and Anna Su were making
new beginning.

Watching as the two women embraced, Ta
glanced away, somehow feeling an intruder to th
reunion—and guilty. He knew his influence ha
contributed to Anna Su's estrangement from Kati
And his motives hadn't all stemmed from the trag
dies that had befallen his family during the war. H
gaze returned to rest on Katie, her blond head be
to hug Anna Su. Even though she was middle-age
now, she was still the beautiful fairy child who wou
remain in his most secret heart forever.

"I, too, wish to apologize," he said when th
women had regained their composure.

Startled anew, Katie's gaze flew to Tak. His ey
caught hers; she was unable to look away from the
compelling intensity. For a moment, she was back i
Japan before the war, suspended in that pause i
time just before Tak left her, after she'd refused to k
his mistress, to be forever kept in the *floating worl*

"I was bitter after the war—and selfish in m
desire to influence Anna Su away from the Aalan
—partly because she was the last descendant of th
once great Kono family. I perceived the Aalands
the enemy, for all the reasons you already know." H
hesitated, but his eyes didn't waver. "So I disho
ored a trusted family friend—you, Katie-san."

Again she stayed silent, this time for Tak. H
words were simple and honest, and Katie respecte
him for having the courage to speak them.

"I carried a grudge against Edward for ma

ears, but it's gone now. If Edward had not married
Michiko, there would be no Anna Su to cherish
now." His voice lowered. "I too, like Michiko and
Anna Su, have always—liked you, Katie. Please
accept my humble apology."

The room was abruptly quiet; even Tak's wife no
longer fluttered, as though she sensed the drama
around her. But it was Tak who held Katie's attention. *How sad,* she thought suddenly, and knew he'd
really meant *always loved you.* What he'd said told
her a great deal, but what he'd left unspoken told her
even more. He, like her, had always known that
Anna Su could have been their child. And although
he would never speak of it, he cherished Anna Su
even more because of that.

"I accept your apology," she told him softly, with
the solemn dignity he would expect from her—
because she was the girl in those golden days of his
youth, who'd been taught, as he had, the ancient art
of honor and respect. How important it all was then,
he thought sadly, and how impossible that first love.
But Katie knew those feelings would always be a part
of her, closed away in her trunk of precious memories. And now, after all the years, Anna Su—half
Maland, half Kono—would inherit the family empire anyway.

Something flickered deep in Tak's eyes, an understanding of their unspoken thoughts. A moment
later, his formal bearing returned, and Katie knew
there would never be a need for it to slip again. The
old proprieties were too ensconced in both of them.

"There is only one thing left to clarify," Tak said,
accepting more tea from his wife. "It concerns the
suspicion of your being a spy during the war, Katie."

"I don't understand," she said, her eyes widened
by yet another surprising change of subject.

"You were suspected of being a Japanese
collaborator—oh, we knew," he added when she

started to speak. "It was Dion who gave
information—for money, of course," he adde
dryly.

"Dion?"

He nodded. "That's why our scout didn't fire
you when you rescued Dion after he'd crashed-
because it was there to meet him."

"So that was how he had the money to establis
his own company after the war?" Katie spoke almo
under her breath.

"Which he ultimately lost," Tak added. "Then
tried to steal his brother's business."

For some reason, Katie wasn't surprised by Dion
hypocrisy and treason, or by Tak's awareness of
that had happened. The pieces all fit now. Poor Ol
had come by his criminal inclinations honestly—
loser just as his father and grandfather had been. B
she felt compassion for Johanna, who hadn't know
about Dion's spying. And she'll never have to kno
either, Katie decided. A lifetime with a cheatin
dishonest husband was enough.

When Katie finally went home, she was uplifted
all she'd experienced. The road into the future w
clear now. The whole family had exorcised their ow
personal ghosts. They were fortunate, she thought
she prepared for bed that night. Some families nev
had that opportunity.

They were all present when Katie became Max
wife for the second time. But it was a small gatherir
nevertheless—Christina and Jon and little Rober
Johanna and Lisa; Anna Su and her husband; ar
Peter. After long thought, Katie hadn't invited Ta
she knew he'd find that appropriate.

"You're such an attractive couple," Christina sa
with a slow smile, right after the minister ha
pronounced them man and wife and Max had kisse
her tenderly. "Far too young-looking to have

daughter my age." Her words were filled with pride and love—and joy that her parents were finally together again.

Katie's answering smile was equally joyous. She and Christina had planned the wedding together and pondered over suitable dresses for Katie. They'd finally decided on a brilliant green silk to match her eyes and set off her hair—long sleeved, low-cut, and molded to Katie's slim figure.

"Congratulations, Mom," Peter said, dropping a kiss on her cheek. "You couldn't have married a better guy than Max."

"Thank you, Peter," Katie replied, her gaze moving between Peter, who stood before her, and Max at her side. Both men were dressed in black suits and white shirts, both were tall, with dark eyes and hair; they could have been father and son.

Anna Su and Johanna and Lisa crowded around them too, adding their best wishes, and Katie felt Max's arm around her waist as they talked. Then they went to the dining room where the housekeeper had prepared a buffet.

"For my wife," Max said, looking deep into Katie's eyes, his own filled with love for her. He raised his champagne glass in a toast.

"For my husband." Katie spoke in a low tone, heavy with emotion, and raised her glass too.

"I love you Katie," Max whispered as the others sampled the buffet.

"Oh, Max," she murmured. "I can't believe how lucky we are. I can't believe I'm Mrs. Stefanini again."

"Believe it, sweetheart. Because you're stuck with me. Forever."

Her senses reeled; for as much as she loved her family, she wished the reception was over. She wanted to be alone with her husband, and she read that very wish in his eyes too.

"And you're stuck with me too, don't forget," she teased, toning down her sudden desire for him.

His reply was to pull her closer to his side, so that they stood as one. And somehow the family tuned in on their wishes, for within half an hour everyone had congratulated them again and left with the promise to see them soon.

And even though it was still mid-afternoon, they went upstairs, leaving the clean-up to the housekeeper who would also look after the house when Katie flew with Max to Alaska for their honeymoon.

Much later, they went to the airport, and as Katie sat in the cockpit with Max, watching as he went through his check-out with the tower before takeoff, she couldn't help but reflect that her life had come full circle. She was flying off with Max again, as she'd done that first time so many years ago. And once more she was married to him, the one great love of her life. *Karma,* she thought. Max was her *karma.* Everything had happened as it was ordained. The future spread before her, a gift from all the obstacles and sorrows, hopes and dreams of the past. It would be a future of sharing their children and grandchildren, with the added gift of knowing that all they'd faced in the past was the foundation for future generations.

A smile touched her face as Max took off, soaring into a sky that blazed like a heavenly fire from the setting sun. They gained altitude over the Pacific Ocean as they veered north to begin another chapter in their lives. Katie's contented sigh was lost in the sound of the engines. Everything in her life was worth reaching this moment, she thought, and watched as the sun began to slip behind the horizon.

Her mother had been a wise woman. The sun would soon be gone, ending Katie's wedding day. But the morning sun would rise tomorrow, and bring

vith it new hope for another day—and all the
emaining days of their lives.

With the passing years, Katie was proven right.
he retired from her company and passed the reins
nto Lisa's capable hands. She and Max divided their
ime between Anchorage and San Francisco.

Christina continued to enjoy singing for the local
pera company, but her first love was her family, her
usband and son and two more daughters. She
vould make sure that her children grew up in a
oving family, prepared to take their place in the
vorld when it was time.

Peter became the president of Stefanini Air Serv-
ce, married an Alaskan girl of Native Indian decent, and gave Katie four more grandchildren. Max
laimed Peter's children as his own grandchildren,
nd his genuine gesture gave Katie even more joy.

Confident at last in her old age, Johanna surprised
veryone with her involvement in historical restora-
ion projects in Northern California. Lisa finally had
mother to be proud of, even if her brother re-
nained estranged from them once he was out of
rison. Ollie moved to a small town in Montana and
tarted over, married, and rarely visited California.
ut it was enough for Johanna and Lisa to know that
e owned a gas station, had two little boys, and
tayed on the right side of the law.

And Lisa, the uncertainty of television roles long
orgotten, enjoyed the challenges of the business
orld; she'd found her niche. She became as well
nown for her successful negotiations and financial
oups as she'd been as an actress. She continued to
ombine both. Although she had two more serious
elationships with men, she chose not to marry.

Isami Kono died with as much dignity as he lived,
nd Tak, suffering from a weak heart, retired. Anna

Su, secure in a happy marriage, took complete control of the Kono empire in the United States and Japan, and spent more time in her mother's country. She adopted two Japanese children, who shared their holidays and special events with Christina's children. The thought of the children growing up knowing each other pleased Katie. And somewhere, she knew Michiko was pleased too.

Katie was contented, proud of her whole family. All the obstacles of her life had been worth the efforts and sacrifices. Her life remained in the loving care of Max, just as his was in hers. Each morning brought new hope, and Katie knew it would always be so, even after she and Max were gone.

"A STUNNING GEM OF A BOOK THAT ESTABLISHES
PATRICIA GAFFNEY AS A STAR!"– *Romantic Times*

THIEF of HEARTS

PATRICIA GAFFNEY

Beautiful young widow Anna Jourdaine feared her dea
husband's twin brother, John Brodie. His manners wer
abominable, his language unbearably crude, and hi
heated glances made sheltered Anna burn with shame
But when Anna was forced to pretend to be Brodie'
wife, she found herself weakening to his seductiv
appeal. In her brother-in-law's embrace, she knew tha
her future happiness depended on learning whic
brother was an immoral character and which wa
merely a thief of hearts.

__2973-1 $4.5

SIZZLING CONTEMPORARY ROMANCE...

BY MAGGI BROCHER

Jericho

Behind the walls of a nunnery, a penniless Irish girl brought forth her illegitimate baby. Leaving her tiny son in the care of the sisters, she vowed that one day she would return. But married to a wealthy politician, she surrounded herself with the trappings of power and money, determined to forget the past. She had built her life on a foundation of lies — until her shocking secret was trumpeted to the world, and the walls came tumbling down.

_____2477-2 $3.95US/$4.95CAN